*And so man reached towards the universe.
Not for what he needed,
but,
for what he wanted.
The heavens responded in kind.*

-Malef's lament

KASMAH
FORMA

Table of Contents

PRIMER
THE MAHARAAN EXPANSE.................................2
LAND OF THE GADORI................................18
INTEGRUM..28

CHAPTER I
THE MAHARAAN EXPANSE...............................44
LAND OF THE GADORI................................52
INTEGRUM..60

CHAPTER II
THE MAHARAAN EXPANSE...............................78
LAND OF THE GADORI................................84
INTEGRUM..94

CHAPTER III
THE MAHARAAN EXPANSE.............................104
LAND OF THE GADORI..............................116
INTEGRUM..132

CHAPTER IV
THE MAHARAAN EXPANSE.............................148
LAND OF THE GADORI..............................160
INTEGRUM..174

CHAPTER V
THE MAHARAAN EXPANSE.............................190
LAND OF THE GADORI..............................198
INTEGRUM..204

CHAPTER VI
THE MAHARAAN EXPANSE..................218
LAND OF THE GADORI........................224
INTEGRUM..232

CHAPTER VII
THE MAHARAAN EXPANSE..................242
LAND OF THE GADORI........................252
INTEGRUM..262

CHAPTER VIII
THE MAHARAAN EXPANSE..................280
LAND OF THE GADORI........................292
INTEGRUM..304

CHAPTER IX
THE MAHARAAN EXPANSE..................326
LAND OF THE GADORI........................342
INTEGRUM..364

CHAPTER X
THE MAHARAAN EXPANSE..................390
LAND OF THE GADORI........................416
INTEGRUM..442

CHAPTER XI
THE MAHARAAN EXPANSE..................468
LAND OF THE GADORI........................480
INTEGRUM..502

FINAL CHAPTER
FINAL CHAPTER....................................524

Regional Glossary

World of Kasmah..564
The Maharaan Expanse.......................................566
Land of the Gadori..570
Integrum...574

PRIMER

Promise me Kasmah!
Promise me these three things, and I shall not fight.
Give your promises to all,
and to you...
I will give you me.

-Malef's request

THE MAHARAAN EXPANSE

*This world will breathe life into you,
and you unto it.*

-The Birth Promise of Kasmah

"Close your eyes, little one," said Kahli's father, crouching so he was eye level with her.

Young Kahli tilted her head and looked at him confused. "But if I close my eyes, how will I see my gift?"

Her father's soft but strong voice rumbled on. "You do not need your eyes for me to show you something, as this gift is for your mind, Kahli. You are soon to be a young woman, and this gift will help you become one befitting my name."

"... I don't understand."

He chuckled lightly — a sound filled with warmth and love. "You will, in time. But for now, close your eyes." Kahli reluctantly did as her father asked. She always trusted him — it was just hard when he talked about things she didn't understand. "Now I want you to picture 'your' happiness, whatever that might be."

Kahli stood still in her father's large tent and tried to imagine all the things that made her happy. She liked helping people, she liked it when her father praised her for trying her hardest, she liked watching people, she liked the color blue. Her father's voice came once more and encouraged her to keep following whatever thoughts were coming to her.

Images whirled around her head — each one shouting

joyously to be picked. She wished that she could somehow pour it all out for her father to see so he could help her figure it out, but all the swirling thoughts only made her scrunch her face up. The more she focused the less she saw, and there was a moment where she thought maybe her father was playing a trick on her.

"Don't get upset if nothing springs up right away, you have to give yourself some time. Have you summoned your thoughts at least?" With eyes closed she nodded her head. "Good, now don't try to pick them up, just let them settle," said her father as if reading her mind.

Impatient, Kahli screamed at all the thoughts to stop whirling around, and to her surprise, they obeyed. Stretched out before her were all the thoughts of happiness, but it was a big jumbled mess and she didn't know what to do. She reached out at every one that floated by, but her father's words would always gently remind her to let them go. In that routine of catch and release she found a calmness, and soon her thoughts were things she could just sail through with her father's strong voice keeping her steady. But the memory of his words faded, and when she could no longer hear them she felt her grip weaken. Not long after she became impatient and frustrated at not understanding, at not seeing the gift. She mumbled under her breath, "What am I —"

In his soft voice, tempered by years of hardship, her father said, "Don't speak Kahli. This gift can't be spoken, seen, or heard. Keep your eyes closed and merely look at what your mind has given you. Settle and be calm, soon you will see it."

"*What am I supposed to see?*" she thought angrily. In frustration she bunched up her fists and pushed through what felt like a wall, and then, suddenly, a calm washed over her.

As her father watched his little girl squirm with what no doubt was a strange request for her, he was elated at seeing her make an effort. She was strong, capable — even in the face of the uncertain. This was when his eldest daughter brought him pride — when she looked just about ready to give up, she would soldier on.

Her raging thoughts settled, and the one that seemed to cover every thought on the ground like a fine dust was, *"I... am happiest when other people tell me that I am useful."*

She opened her eyes wide and looked at her father excited. Before she could even think of the words to describe what had just happened, her father said knowingly, "And that is my gift Kahli: Knowing who you are and what you want. You are soon to become a young woman, and in those times it will be hard to remember who you truly are amidst the chaos of your growing years to come. Clarity does not last forever, and the darker the day, the harder it is to find. So, try to remember this gift, and every year I will help you make it stronger. That way, even when I am gone, you will always know how to find your way back to yourself. I pray that with my gift, you will never be lost."

Kahli had felt like she understood completely what he had just said, but when he finished talking the calmness and understanding she had felt vanished. She panicked. "What... what just happened? ... Did I do it right?"

He could see that Kahli was confused once more and he chided himself for speaking words beyond her years. She would come to understand them in her own time. "Well, let's see. Was there one thought above all that made sense to you?"

Kahli was afraid to say it out loud, but knew her father would not judge her. "But was it the right one? All I could see was that I am happy when people say that I am useful. But that sounds... weak." She feared that word more than anything.

"Is useful so weak?" Her father stood up tall and touched his chest. "Do you think 'I' am not useful?"

"Of course you are!" she cried, her mind wanting to fill her words with nothing but love and admiration for him.

"Think how unhappy I would be if 'you' thought I wasn't useful, or how you would feel if I thought you weren't useful." A small amount of terror filled Kahli's heart at that prospect. "When you are in the sort of position I am in — I have to be 'useful' to everyone, but can you think of anyone that would dare call me weak to my face?" he asked, and they both shared a light giggle.

Seeing his daughter's mind filled with distracting thoughts he reached out his hand and cupped her cheek softly. Kahli looked up at her father. "I helped you to see the core of you, Kahli. It is a skill people forget, or never learn, or rely too much on others to do for them. If you find worth in reading the book of you, remember: You wrote yourself."

He brought his face closer to his favorite daughter and said, "All I helped you do, was find the words you've already written."

"Forgive me, my desert flower...."

BREATHE...

The Maharaan Expanse spanned the entire north of Kasmah and its lands were known to range from dry-brush, sun-baked and cracked ground, to deserts strange and dangerous.

Toka-Rutaa was a remote village in the most northern part of the Maharaan, and was where the Heca clan called home. It was a place where the sun shone constantly, the air always dry, where water was scarce, and where even plants had abandoned all hope of growing. The Heca though were a tough people, and only in this most inhospitable part of the Maharaan could they ply their skills. Here they could hunt the most dangerous of creatures that roamed the Maharaan, and for hunters as hardy as the Heca only the strongest Kasmah had to offer would do.

The village was sparse in construction — built only for the harshest of desert heats and coldest of desert nights. Comfort was second to practicality as the heat sapped all desire and energy for anything other than hunting. Besides the uncommon occurrence of one of those creatures stumbling upon their village, little happened to change the day by day events, and most years for those who lived there were of no significance.

However, for those reaching the eighteenth year of their birth it was a time of uncertainty. A time when each young man or woman would be placed in their life role of either hunter, or the less desired helper. The placement ceremony took place during a portentous week, when the Night-Sparks would burn brightest in the night sky. Which week that would be was never the same, but it was always signaled by an intense display of night-sparks the day before. Throughout the week they would build, and on the seventh day, when the night-sparks were at their most lustrous, the ceremony would be held.

This year's ceremony though was not to happen like all others before it, for on the day the night-sparks signaled the start of it, an Integra Humanus arrived in Toka-Rutaa from the north. Clad in her robes of flowing white that had been damaged by the desert sand and sun, she strode into the center of Toka-Rutaa's high spirits and greeted everyone. She caught Kahli's attention, but why that was she couldn't quite put her finger on.

At first Kahli thought it looked like the woman was going to be chased out, as most who entered Toka-Rutaa did so with great caution — those from the Integra Pol in the far-off lands of the Integrum however tended to walk wherever they pleased. She thought it a blessing to have such a revered visitor but was still surprised at the frenzy the camp got whipped up into at her arrival. Then again nothing much had happened at all worth remembering before the Integra Humanus had arrived, so maybe everyone was just really, really bored. It was hard to remember them getting this excited before about anything except a hunt but at least they seemed happy.

The Integra Pol was known to send out emissaries far and wide to help many with their problems and practices. Then again she had to admit she could not recall the last time any had been sent to Toka-Rutaa. Nobody, or... anything for that matter, came close to the village. The searing heat and harsh life that came with living in a sun-baked land was not for those with a weak constitution.

What surprised her the most about their new visitor was how anyone from the Integrum could reach this far north. Toka-Rutaa was the farthest northern village in all of

Kasmah, and so close to the northern edge of Kasmah that even two day's travel north would mean being in a heat so great that most things burst into flames. Given its location Toka-Rutaa had few visitors, even from neighboring villagers or traders — yet this woman appeared to have traveled to her village from the north, unharmed.

Toka-Rutaa's leader, an elderly woman named Gola, appeared reluctant to welcome the stranger at first, but then quickly succumbed to what Kahli assumed was Integra Humanus charm. When the clan all saw Gola welcome the newcomer she declared a halt to the day's work and that there should be a celebration in honor of their new visitor.

This year would definitely be one to remember, thought Kahli, two celebrations in one year? She couldn't remember the last time such a thing had happened. Who knows? Maybe this one would be different, as the placement ceremonies themselves she recalled were rather dull affairs and in essence days like any other except with less work.

During the celebration held for the Integra Humanus, she announced that she would also stay the week to help with the placement and asked all if she could have the honor of helping on the day of the ceremony. There was little argument and the request was welcomed — even Gola seemed happy at sharing the glory that was usually hers alone on that day.

The lead up to the placement ceremony was always a stressful time for the clan, even for those sure of themselves and what they would become. There was always the risk of being hurtled down a path unknown — to be chosen as something unexpected. Hearing that so many lives were going to change made Kahli idly think about what it would be like to go from being comforted by what one has always known to being frightened by something new. It was not an experience she was in any great hurry to have.

Kahli took no particular interest in the fate of others, or her own, and soon found the excitement of the day fading from her mind — it was the best way she found to go about tending to her daily chores of caring for her home. Her life was not filled with complicated work and she was glad for that. It made her feel like the world could go on without her, but that there was a little place for her if she wanted to be in it. She enjoyed feeling useful in that small place. Being content enough with the here and now was all that mattered to her — the future was for others to worry about.

She had long ago in her mind committed herself to be one of the helpers of the clan and had always believed that was her purpose. It would not be a glamorous life, but she would always have someone to need her and her talents, however minor they may be.

A rumor reached Kahli's ears that the Integra Humanus had taken a liking to someone, and that someone might be chosen to be taken back to the Integra Pol. Kahli merely nodded her head when she was told while inside she shrugged and wished people would stop interrupting her chores with things that didn't matter to her. Pushing the interruption to one side, time marched on as she cleaned and ferried goods to and from people.

What was supposed to be an ordinary day for Kahli though held a surprise when the Integra Humanus appeared, seemingly out of nowhere, while she was alone in her family's hut. The woman reached out to touch her forehead without invitation. Paralyzed from uncertainty,

Kahli looked directly at her and panicked a little when she felt the woman's finger connect with her own forehead. It felt real, so real. Had anything felt so real before?

The woman softly said, "It is time to wake up," and quickly walked away.

BREATHE... just breathe...

Kahli's younger twin brother and sister, Jak and Jall, whom she affectionately called the Jackals, giggled like idiots as they ran around the inside of their hut — as per usual making a nuisance of themselves with their silly games. They always made her feel out of place as she looked nothing like them — they got their looks from their mother while she took after her father, or so her mother said. She had been too young when her father died in a hunting accident to remember him very well, but she did remember one time with him, and that he was a good man. Still, it was hard to feel like an outsider in your own family, but she knew that they loved her and she loved them, even if the young pair was constantly getting into trouble.

Being the eldest she was in charge of taking care of the home while their mother hunted, which was just fine with her — if only the twins wouldn't make her chores that much harder. When things felt like they were getting too hard she would always find strength in the memory of her father and what he had said to her once. She lived her life as she saw fit to honor her memory of him — strong and proud.

The twins shot out of the hut and Kahli went to picking up after them. As their childish giggles faded away the realization dawned that it would be next year when she herself would have to take part in that silly placement ceremony. She secretly hoped that she would not be subjected to all this fuss when that time came and that it would just pass her by quietly. Attention from the people in her village had never been something she craved.

Thinking about her own future made her wonder about that rumor again, of someone being taken away to the Integra Pol. The prospect was a fascinating one, even if a little scary and not at all for her. To travel to the Integrum city of Orbis and become a charge of the Integra Pol — the bastion of civilization — and to discover what truth there was in all its tales of unimaginable wonder.

Her daydreaming however was interrupted by the Integra Humanus, who once again sauntered into her hut without invitation and touched her forehead. "It is time to wake up," she said before walking away once more. That eerie sense of 'real' came over her again, but this time it was different. Her body felt heavy, filled with sand, but she forced herself to follow the woman out of her home and watched her walk to the empty center of the clan's small village — where all meetings and celebrations were held. The woman then sat down on a small blanket and put up a small umbrella to protect herself from the sun.

Kahli shook her head and walked back into her own hut. She was trying to think hard about the woman, but she couldn't even tell what her face looked like.

BREATHE... just keep breathing...

Kahli's mother was one of the Heca clan's hunter elite, and

so loved and respected within the clan for her ferocity and bravery. She wished her mother brought her more comfort, but all she could remember when she saw her was the sad news of her father's death — haunting her still all these years. The worst thing to come of that time though was not the sadness, even though it clung to her to this day, but the unexpected change in her mother.

She'd become more aggressive than before, perhaps forcing herself to be twice the parent to make up for the failure of not protecting her husband. Anything could set her mother off, and Kahli accepted whatever she would dish out. She believed that her mother had no other way to let her demons speak, and that the only way she could soothe her mother's pain was to take the blows, and love her still.

It was not all bad though for Kahli's mother had over the years shown her how to do things, in her strangely stern loving way. Learning what she had to teach was not difficult, but dealing with her temper was. Every time her mother disciplined her it conjured up a feeling of being rushed, when all she wished was that her mother would just let her do it at her own pace. Her mother was far from cruel, but while there may have been kindness in her actions it was sometimes difficult for Kahli to see the love in them.

In time Kahli began to feel that the world had decided to live her life for her, instead of her it as she was pushed every day to perform and succeed. The pressure put on her was far greater than the importance of the task, but she would never dare say that out loud.

Her days now were spent mostly outside of her family hut in the oppressive heat, but that didn't bother her as much as she had thought it would. Many kept giving her jobs to do, and more often than not she would find herself near the Integra Humanus as she carried them out. The more time she spent around that woman though the stranger she felt. Everything felt more 'real' around that woman, but why? How was that any realer than now?

"*So, she is going to take someone away? Make them a part of that... Integra Pol,*" Kahli thought as she mended the ceremonial clothes and arranged the decorations. She admitted to herself that it would be hard for the person chosen, or perhaps a great honor that many would hope to be a part of. Chore after chore was piled on top of her, and Kahli took it in her stride. It was good to be useful. It was good to be needed.

As time passed her thoughts seemed to get louder, which was strange because she had never thought of them as being soundless before. Every day that went by brought more weight and light to her life, but she could not fathom why. She rejected all of these things and believed that she was probably just getting caught up in everyone's excitement.

One thought that came to her however, loud enough to make her look around like it had been spoken aloud, made her puzzled. The thought was, "*Why am I being asked to do damn near everything for this ceremony?*"

BREATHE... fight the false memories... and breathe...

The night of the celebration arrived with the largest and most colorful display of night-sparks in memory and all were drunk either on drink or delight. The night sky flashed with its sparks of color and light while down below people tried to match the intensity in their own way. Kahli was dressed up for the occasion but was content with just sitting back a little distance from it all and watching the festivities.

Everyone was dancing or fighting, but the Integra Humanus seemed to reject all invitations and instead spent a lot of time looking at Kahli. She felt uncomfortable being watched like she was some sort of interesting show. Thankfully though it was soon time for the youths of Toka-Rutaa to line up and for the ceremony to begin, bringing that woman's gaze to an end as she then joined Gola while Kahli was left sitting and observing.

Gola began the ceremony and a heavy silence fell on all as she went from person to person, anointing each in turn, and after all had been placed there was a whooping cheer and applause. It was the shortest part of the ceremony even if it was the most important, and when it had finished the Integra Humanus made a request for all to gather in a circle.

Everyone gave her all the attention they could and Kahli watched on with interest as something erupted dimly from the Integra Humanus which quickly became a small ring of flame that danced on its own between her outstretched fingers. She then reached her hands down and beckoned all to link hands with hers. The Heca were fearful at first, but she calmly reassured them that there was no harm and soon one by one all were joining hands. When the last link was made the ring of flame coursed with alarming speed from person to person, over and through each hand held. The initial shock everyone experienced was overcome by the beauty of it all when they saw that the fire did not burn.

Shortly after a thick tendril of flame slowly extended upwards, before shooting up high with a fierceness and exploding with such brightness that night became day — hiding the night-sparks. Kahli could feel the power from the woman and found it quite pretty to watch what such a small spark could become. As the light faded and the night-sparks returned she felt like something heavy had been lifted from her shoulders.

Duly humbled by the woman's demonstration of power, the villagers looked on at the Integra Humanus in awe. Kahli however couldn't help but wonder what her name was. She'd spent enough time casually bumping into her that it seemed rude to not know her name. Maybe it was better to not ask though — if she'd wished it to be known no doubt she would have told her.

The clan celebrated and fawned over the Integra Humanus and her awesome display, and Kahli smiled — feeling in some way that she had helped all this happiness come into being. Walking back to her hut to fetch what she would need to help with the inevitable cleanup she was startled by someone grabbing her shoulder. Fearing that she was in trouble yet again for something, Kahli turned to find the Integra Humanus looking at her.

"That was... really impressive," said Kahli, hoping to appease her in some fashion.

"What I have done and what you can do is no different. It is not the scale of something that is impressive, merely that it exists at all — for scale, is just a matter of effort. *Sum ergo veritas*," said the Integra Humanus cryptically.

"... Sorry?" replied Kahli, not wanting to offend.

Strangely, the Integra Humanus' usual smile now seemed to be one of desperation and effort. "When was the last time you spoke?" Kahli opened her mouth to glibly say 'sometime today', but knowing that would have been disrespectful and vague she tried to recall a specific moment. She drew a blank. Confused, she cast her mind further back — still nothing. The woman interrupted her next attempt with, "True power doesn't need to be reminded of its scale, only that it exists."

Kahli then began feeling strange, filled with anticipation and life, more tangible than all other moments she could remember. She couldn't remember what happened next.

As she lay awake in her bed she could see nothing and hear nothing, she could only focus on the chaos her mind was experiencing. She tried to think through it, to call on the memory of her father, but she couldn't even remember going to bed or why she now felt afraid. Through the fear she could not understand why she was grinning, thin lipped with tears of joy streaming down her face.

For Kahli the celebration was a good day, a day to remember, and a day of feeling fulfilled.

For Kahli the celebration was a horrible day, a day to erase from memory, and a day of regret.

The conflicting feelings raged in her mind as they screamed at her, how could they both be true?

All she could focus on now was blood coating her face.

BREATHE... keep breathing... hold onto the truth... Ignore the taste of blood in your mouth and BREATHE

LAND OF THE GADORI

*This world will take from you,
what you took from it.*

-The Death Promise of Kasmah

"FUTUO!"

Short and sharp, the word rang out across the barren tundra with nobody to hear save for its speaker: a prone boy being jolted awake by a piercing pain in his brain. It began in his head and took the scenic route all the way to his feet — making a rude pit stop at every nerve ending along the way. While its intensity was matched only by its brevity it gave the young sufferer something to be unhappy about. That full body throb which shocked him into consciousness made him widen his eyes, and was almost blinded when he saw light. Shutting them tight his mind filled with confusion while he tried to ignore the orchestra of pain being conducted in his head.

Responding like a wounded animal he leapt to his feet, ready to fight, while carefully opening his eyes as little as possible so he could at least see without too much difficulty. He whipped his head back and forth to survey the surroundings and found nothing but an empty tundra landscape in shades of white and light blue. When his initial rush had died down the first thing he noticed was the cold, with the second thing being that he was stark naked. Trying to regain composure he tried his best to remember everything he could, and found that he could not remember anything about... anything.

"What's my name? Where's home? Why am I naked? Actually, a better question is..." his mind blanked before providing him with, *"WHERE the... the... VALDE am I?!"*

His mind tried to make a mental checklist of everything he knew and how he'd got there, but got frustrated at the rising number of questions and the dwindling number of answers. For some unknown reason a small part of him was wondering where the word *valde* had come from. He had no clue what it meant, but he felt better for saying it. He wanted to say it over and over, it seemed to both express how he felt and made him feel good — like some naughty pleasure.

Unprepared, his body was wracked again by a surge of pain, made all the worse by a brain awake and fully capable of processing all information his body would like to give him. Experiencing the surge from beginning to end his toes curled and he collapsed to the ground while making no effort to cushion his fall. He recoiled into a fetal position and whimpered softly, praying that it would pass soon.

Thankfully time moved on and he could feel the pain begin to drain away, and with it came relief. But it was short-lived as another shock ripped through him, blasting every nerve so hard that it was elevated to a new sensation entirely. The only thought that could pierce the veil was fear — fear that his mind may soon be nothing more than all consuming pain — fear that all he could do was lie still in the snow. Tortured until the cold wasteland claimed his body.

Another surge came.

His body strained every muscle to fight against the unknown threat, hoping through sheer effort he could fight it off. His wish for unconsciousness, or even death, went unheeded when it looked to be a battle unwinnable, but thankfully this surge too soon passed. In his respite he realized that his body had stopped shaking, but found that it was only because his skin was now frozen to the ground.

A far off tingling sensation crept over him, and he knew that another wave of pain was coming. He made a final effort that clawed its way through the fog of his mind and reached out to find anything to fight back with. As he felt the next shock mounting, a calm came over him and he went completely still. Some part of him told him to stretch out his right arm and place it palm down onto the ground. Upon doing so he felt the explosion of pain start in his brain, but now it traveled through his arm and as it reached his hand there was a dull flash accompanied by a muffled *fwump*. Steam shot out from underneath his hand and he felt the ground beneath him melt slightly and warmth enveloped him.

"*What just happened?!*" he thought. The shocks had subsided, but he swore he could feel them still happening, just... not inside him anymore. He wasn't about to question his good fortune and was thankful for the release. Now was the time to steel himself, now was the time for his instinct to survive to kick into full gear — which screamed at him to stand up. It was something he really wanted to do, instinct or no, but found it difficult as he was doing his best to lay *absolutely* still for fear of interfering with whatever it was that was saving him from the cold and pain.

He rummaged through his memories to find any information that might be relevant, and after several minutes in the small, warm pool of water, concluded that there was nothing to find. No name, no knowledge of where he was, what had happened to him, or why he was even here.

The most he was willing to do was move his head around in the hopes of finding something or someone nearby. All he found was that he was lying right next to what he could only describe as an ocean of slow moving slush that stretched for miles in either direction. Angling his head down and up the length of it, he saw it to be a mixture of solid ice and water, and the farther it got from him, the slushier it looked until what looked like just a floor of ice.

Everything else he spied comforted him even less as there was no grass or plants, no creatures or tracks, and certainly no people. Just features of small patches of snow, large patches of ice, and an unwelcoming landscape of hard, frozen ground. However, and he wasn't quite sure about this, there did seem to be a hint of a blurry, greenish-brown on the horizon. His neck was starting to hurt from craning around too much so he rested his head back into the warm pool.

As he looked straight up into the dusky twilight sky he saw far away sparks dancing across its surface. The sky danced and fought with a strange beauty as brightly colored sparks sprung to life and died just as quickly. He looked at them with uncertainty and thought, *"Wait... where... what are...?"* They seemed so far away yet so close, and he knew they were called night-sparks but... that was all. Watching the beautiful display brought him some peace, but he couldn't shake the nagging feeling that an important memory was slipping away from him. "At least I know what snow and ice are," he whispered to himself, finding some small comfort in knowing that he could at least talk to someone even if it was only himself.

Basking in the warm pool breathed new life into his ravaged body, but it was not to last forever and he could feel it begin to cool quickly. Not wanting to wait until he would have to leave skin behind in exchange for his freedom from the ice he quickly uncurled from his fetal position and sat up. A tentative moment was spent in fear as he tried to ignore the world, huddled in the cooling pool, before his desire to survive urged him onwards.

With his hands on the ground to help stand him up he found that one of them felt something that wasn't water or ice. Looking down he saw that it was a pile of thick furs. He jumped a little, fearing it to be a predator of some kind, but after a second look he concluded that it was too flat to be a creature and that it was, in fact, clothing. A full complement of heavy furs that seemed suited to the environs he had found himself in.

He stood and picked them up, and underneath them found a leather water pouch, which he gave a disapproving look — he had hoped for some big sign or written note telling him everything he didn't know. *"It would probably be too big to hide under some clothes,"* he thought. He looked underneath the pouch and was still disappointed even after shrinking his expectations. With a shrug of his shoulders he assumed all of these things were his so he dressed as quickly as he could — the clothes were a perfect fit. He then filled the pouch with water from the pool he had been lying in and tucked it away in his furs.

Surveying the land once more he found his strength returning and confirmed that the greenish-brown line on the horizon was the only thing that looked promising. The stronger he felt the more thankful he was for whatever it was that he had done, or had been done for him, to stop the pain. In spite of the ordeal he had suffered he felt amazingly energized.

He squinted at the horizon and thought, *"Must be... trees? Some sort of forest? Well whatever..."* He looked down at himself again. *"At least I'm wearing something warm. These have to have been mine... why was I naked anyway?"* The conclusion that the clothes must have been his brought him further comfort that he didn't just appear out of thin air.

Standing up to his full height he gathered his wits and began his trek towards the assumed forest. It looked the better part of a half day's walk, and the myriad of questions swirling in his mind had to be silenced for now in order to conserve sanity. Answers were a luxury — all that mattered now was finding shelter and food.

Despite his resolve he couldn't help himself and as he strode towards the distant trees tried to collect as much information as he could from his senses in order to gain some idea of what, where, and how. 'Why' wasn't a part of this equation, as he concluded that 'why' required some knowledge of the first three questions. And those were hard enough already.

Thinking though wasn't enough to keep him warm against the harsh, cold winds and so he buried his face deeper into his clothing for protection. In his little traveling fur palace of warmth he compiled his list of thoughts and conclusions. *"So... I have pale skin...."* Pulling a hair from his head confirmed it to be short, straight and black.

He held out his arms for a moment to inspect the clothing and he could see signs of wear and tear. This told him that they must have been worn before, and seeing as they fit him, HE must have been the one to have worn them. This only further perplexed him by bringing to light the possibility that he had walked all the way out here in these clothes and stripped naked. To do what though he had no idea. "*Am I just some sort of an idiot?*" he thought. The cold wind whipped at his chest and he brought his arms back in to hug himself.

The now self-professed idiot began to talk aloud in the hopes that it would warm him further. "So, my height and weight is... uh..." he looked around again to see if there was anything he could compare his height with, and after finding nothing he continued his journey onwards. "I can feel my ribs so I don't have a lot of fat.... I'm not that muscular, so obviously I'm not a fighter. Maybe I am a... clothier? Is that even a word? Someone that makes clothes?" The boy let out a loud sigh as he trudged through the wasteland, still intent on finding value in talking to himself. There wasn't much to talk about though. "Ice is... really boring. And why is it so damn cold?" he complained as his stomach grumbled. He could feel it starting to make demands that he felt were unreasonable, given the circumstances.

"Maybe that pain was important.... Wish I knew why it hasn't come back... *valde*, or even why it happened in the first place," said the boy, now wondering if his attempt at gripping onto his sanity was somehow making it slip away. Hearing him say the word *valde* again made him think that was important, and, despite not knowing what it meant, decided that every step he took should be accompanied by it. For hours the only thing that could be seen or heard was a boy walking against a harsh background, all the while saying, "*Valde, valde, valde, valde, VALDE VALDE VALDE!*"

Barren scenery passed him by, save for the crawling surface of that strange ocean of slush. Every time he looked over at it he noticed that it would get just that little bit faster, but he wasn't sure if that was either interesting or important.

He had tried to walk alongside it for the longest time but every time he looked at it the distance between him and it seemed to grow. It was slightly frustrating that he couldn't walk in a straight line alongside something so large and comforted himself by blaming the hunger, the cold, and the fact that he had to keep nestling into his furs lest his face freeze off.

Bored from the nothingness and not wanting to focus on his feelings of ineptitude he instead thought once more about his situation. *"How did I get here? Also, why? No signs of anything living except me. No buildings, waypoints, or signs saying 'Careful! This place is cold!' And, I was naked. But I'm sure I didn't come all the way out here and DECIDE to dance naked on ice — I don't feel like I'm THAT stupid. I don't feel sore anywhere, so it isn't like I was beaten and dragged out here."* Nothing he thought brought him any comfort, but he was determined to try.

"SO!" the young boy shouted in an effort to warm his body. "The WHERE is *obviously* cold. Seeing as I can't even recall the name of anywhere I'll just name this place 'Not-gonna-come-backsville'."

His walk in the tundra brought to him only the sight of a wasteland, with the only distraction being the rare necessity to maneuver around what looked like puddles of shiny ice. By the time he reached the next ice puddle curiosity and fatigue got the better of him so he just sat down and stared deeply into it. It struck him as quite a beautiful light blue — soft and transparent. Gazing into that pool of liquid glass, a sliver of a memory taunted him with the promise of revealing more. He tried to chase it, but found only frustration. He snorted angrily. Looking up he saw that the trees were much closer now, perhaps only a few hours walk.

The boy sighed heavily and felt despondent from his time wasted at attempting to piece some image of who, what or where he was, only to be met with so little. Eventually his despair turned to rage, and that was when he decided to start screaming. "I hate knowing what trees are but not who I am! I'm human for sure, but isn't my knowing *what* I am less important than who?!"

He directed his ire towards the trees that he had been walking towards all this time. "ALSO! Trees!" He pointed at them angrily. "What makes YOU so bloody important that my brain doesn't know who I am, but does know what a TREE is. What joy! Maybe I could combine my apparently short black hair and knowledge of trees to create some sort of flying machine. Who knows? Maybe I know how to do that, and just being around BLOODY trees will imbue me with super powers so great that *who* I am doesn't matter! Maybe I'm some sort of tree god!" His mental state of exhaustion combined with his long journey and constant self-questioning lent a surprising amount of weight to that belief. As silly as it sounded it did leave him with the suspicion that he just MIGHT be some sort of tree god.

With his outburst complete he felt some of his anger leave him, but when the cold crept back in shortly after he felt like he had just fought a pointless battle with nothing in particular. With a further sigh he softly said, "... I just want to know who I am."

Those thoughts were heavy enough on his mind to find their way down to his stomach, which grumbled now with both hunger AND his disappointment. He decided to grumble along with it and kept on walking.

INTEGRUM

*From this world,
you have not yet given, or taken,
enough.*

-The Life Promise of Kasmah

Mulat was known as the most powerful man in all known Kasmah, just like all who had held the title of Integra Divinitas before him. He resided at the very top of the Integra Pol, a shining beacon of honor and knowledge, and from there he would perform his tasks with the utmost care and consideration. Given his status and prestige though many did not understand why he commissioned a piece of so-called 'art', the *Simulacrum Umbrosus*, which adorned the hallway to his chambers.

His reasoning behind it was that he simply wanted to see what his shadow's shadow would look like, and so the artist first sculpted a statue out of marble in Mulat's likeness. Then behind that sculpture the artist created another statue from the shadow of the first, and repeated the pattern until there were two rows of five unique statues. The result was disconcerting and made most feel like they were walking towards some nightmare that was best avoided. The odd fifteen flights of stairs people had to take in order to reach him were hard enough without having to be subjected to this.

Those experiencing it for the first time gave Mulat some small pleasure when he saw their surprise in finding him by himself in a plain room, sitting at a large wooden desk, and smiling. The expectation of being confronted by something from their self-induced nightmares was a fun idea to propagate, so much so that he could never resist the temptation. Were people more willing to make the trip to visit him he may have felt differently about his games, but then again people only visited him when they needed something, so he reasoned why not make it interesting for himself.

Mulat's new apprentice still griped about the arduous number of steps, he himself having not yet earned the right to live within the Integra Pol, though his body had become accustomed to the physical toil. He readied himself outside his master's door and knocked — no doubt today was going to be difficult like all the others.

As soon as he had entered and closed the door behind him, Mulat said, "Where is Juvorya?" without looking up from his desk. The tall, slender man had a commanding presence even while sitting down.

Even though Mulat was normally abrupt, the apprentice still felt unsettled by it. It was still a hard road ahead, and it felt like everything wasn't getting any easier. "She has yet to return from her task, she is only a few days overdue... so I expect —"

"Expectations do not soften one's emotional state," Mulat quipped. Face intent on the work his desk provided him with, he continued. "Even my own anxieties could not be quelled for all the certainty the Integrum could provide me with. All the same I dislike sending people alone. Chances of success increase with numbers, not with idle wishing."

"Perhaps, if you are experiencing some difficulty —"

"Do not suggest a way to calm myself, it will merely

further irritate me. I am sure Juvorya will do fine, I simply needed to express myself." Mulat looked up at his apprentice with the familiar look of wanting to launch into lecturing him about something. "You will need to one day learn the disconnect between heart and mind, and that mere expression does not mean that I am actively feeling the emotion. There are many ways to stymie the emotional flow." Mulat could read his apprentice's face and knew that he hadn't really understood him. No matter though, there were more pressing questions. "What of the Vir?"

The apprentice collected himself quickly. "We have no genuine potentials, only... hopefuls."

"And Juvorya still has sent no further reports about the Mulier?"

"No, my Integra Divinitas."

A moment's silence passed, and it lingered long enough for the apprentice to start feeling uncomfortable. He hated how he always felt like he didn't know what he was doing or in some subtle way failing by just existing.

Mulat sighed to himself, obviously this apprentice still required prompting. As he spoke he gradually adopted the innocent monotone he used to set people on edge. "And what of the schedule? Come, you've been my apprentice for a month, and you should have learned by now that I hate prompting. Give the information that is necessary, stop waiting to be asked." His propensity to speak in a dull tone when people thought he would be emotional was his way of having fun — challenging them by erecting a minor mental obstacle for them.

"... Yes, Mulat. The schedule for the Deaspora has been further disrupted...." The apprentice shifted anxiously. "Am

I allowed a personal question on this?"

"Go ahead."

Filled with doubt, the apprentice asked, "I can't help but feel excited. Is this the wrong emotion to have?"

"You are asking me if your emotions are valid? The Integra Pol does not deny the existence or indulgence of emotions. You seek my permission for such things?"

He panicked. "No, it isn't like that but —"

"You have been initiated, yes? You have already paid the price that all who choose to become part of the Integra Pol pay. Your Conducutis has been tattooed, you have bound yourself to me, and you have chosen to give up your sex — I suspect in a somewhat misguided attempt to be like me. If you regret the price paid, then you did not think hard enough on what you wanted."

"Yes, I have been marked... but —" started the apprentice, but he could sense that Mulat was once more going to bury him under teachings he could not comprehend.

"Just because you chose castration for your initiation does not mean you should not have emotions. Do not seek from another for what you believe should be correct inside yourself. The public may view us of the Integra Pol as uncaring at times, but that is the problem borne of being the most powerful entity in Kasmah's most powerful city. Orbis, for all its grandeur, is still a city that has not had to defend itself from anyone or anything for a long time, so some complacency and entitlement is to be expected. To that end, we are the source of all that ails and cures. We have to accept that we will be loved and hated by many for whatever action we perform."

The apprentice began squirming under Mulat's unyielding gaze. "I did not mean I... I just —"

Mulat recognized the signs and sighed heavily. It was time to give his apprentice at least some small reprieve. "No, it is indeed something you should feel excited about." He stood up slowly and began pacing the room as he talked. "Something that only occurs around once every three hundred years? Even I am, and for most Integra Divinitas' the Deaspora is the last thing they experience. For yourself, be excited — both for being privilege to that knowledge and my trust in you." His apprentice's face flashed some disbelief at that statement — due to his conducutis he had no choice in the matter of what he could and couldn't divulge. Mulat ignored this. "All you need to keep in mind, is to not let emotions cloud your judgment. Emotions are to be savored and devoured, when you and your environment can allow for it."

The apprentice waited a little longer just in case Mulat wanted to keep talking, before saying, "... Thank you."

Mulat walked around his large wooden desk to stand in front of his apprentice. "Shall I consider that matter concluded?"

"... Yes."

"Excellent. I would apologize for bombarding you again, but I am irritated by my need to repeat basic precepts to you. The 'now' is a poor indicator of tomorrow, and the now is always based on the present. In understanding this we can create a better future, and your chosen future to be my apprentice means not placing what you 'knew' before what you want to 'know', yes?" said Mulat, always finding some pleasure in at least talking even if they weren't learning anything. He then gestured towards the empty center of his room.

The apprentice stiffened at understanding both the physical command and his master's unspoken desire for him to focus, so soon nodded his head and made his way into the center of his master's chambers. Drawing on what he was taught by the Integra Pol, the apprentice closed his eyes and focused on draining away his emotions. He tried to cast aside those fears and joys of the known and unknown, to try and find a state of mind where he was neither feeling nor unfeeling. After a minute of varying breathing patterns the apprentice disrobed and sat down on the floor, wearing only his loin wraps.

"Now... are you still tender?" queried Mulat, pacing around the apprentice.

"A bit. I will admit I would have preferred to be able to use my... uh... genitals, before their... removal...." The apprentice then hastily added, "Just so I could appreciate what I had lost and understand other people's struggle better. You know."

"Your attempts at pretending your interest in sex is for purely selfless reasons is duly noted. In future give me truth when you want to provide a reason for your desire, not what you think I want to hear. However, I admit to my own curiosity on that matter — I myself never had such an opportunity to even experiment. Still, you will find sympathy does not require the exact same situation that another is in, merely a semblance. For example, you can still touch things can't you? You can still feel the roughness of dirt or the moisture of a damp cloth. You may still feel pleasure at warmth and the rush that can come from going from a hot day outside to a cold room indoors. Just because they aren't sexual in nature doesn't change the fact that your brain is telling you that something is good."

"Surely there is a difference though."

"Well yes, it is a trade-off. You do not get firsthand experience, but you do not need said experience to accommodate it in your judgments of things. I cannot understand what it is like for a farmer's cow to be milked, but I can understand that if there is no calf it will seek the farmer to fill the need."

"I don't —"

"Sex is a drive, a force at times more powerful than the need to eat. I may never be able to share in the experience, but that does not preclude my understanding of the experience itself. The enormous Quadras of Orbis that surround our Integra Pol are those who delve into the four needs and drives of being human, while WE are at the center and above them all. It is we who help them feel safe and secure so they can be free to indulge and experiment with such things, and in their doing so they better the people of Orbis with their findings and spread their teachings to all in Kasmah who would hear. We are the center that does not indulge in those things — we are not here to empathize, only to sympathize." Mulat could tell by the way the apprentice shifted his shoulders that he was not following still. "The difference is perspective, and if we are to pass judgment on people's requests, if we empathize, we rob them of what they came to us for: An objective judgment." Mulat came to a stop, inadvertently towering over the apprentice, a mere foot away.

In a shaky but strong voice the apprentice asked, "How

can we be objective if we aren't a part of what they experience though?"

"People understand what we provide and what we sacrifice. We are there to BE the balance and give advice, not to rule or enforce —" Mulat paused for a moment, distracted by a thought. "Let us use this analogy: The color red, can I explain it to you? No, I cannot. If you were unable to see the color red because of some problem with your eye, how could I ever explain it to you? You could never truly understand it, but you can still understand colors and how they make you think and feel. Just because you can't experience red does not mean you cannot understand the concept of red — which is enough to help you balance judgments. To focus on one color is to deny acknowledgment of all others — which creates disharmony. All is equal, all is fair. We do not get to experience the pleasures brought about by sex, but neither are we controlled by it."

The apprentice furrowed his brow. "Why would people call us fair if we could not feel what they feel?"

Mulat leaned in closer and whispered, "Why would you trust a tailor to make your clothes if you do not know how to make them?"

"... What do you mean? ... Sorry."

Mulat stood back up and resumed his pacing. "Don't apologize for not understanding. If you stop asking questions then you effectively kill your desire to know the unknown. People trust the result, that is all that matters to the human mind, and that is what people remember. All this relates because one does not need to have full working knowledge of something to appreciate it. You help me every day, yet you don't have a full working knowledge of who

INTEGRUM - PRIMER | 35

and what I am. We still achieve things, yes?"

"Yes." What those things actually were the apprentice still wasn't quite sure of.

"People understand our commitment to understand them and our choice to sacrifice a part of ourselves. All of the Integra Pol make the sacrifice we choose to prove our devotion to it, some greater than others. It is a gesture to show that all the anger and desire to compete, mate or destroy, all those things tied to baser needs, we can give up. We trade what we are for others, and in turn they trust us."

The apprentice's responses began to take on a sad tone. "... It just makes me feel more distant."

Mulat sighed, no doubt it was time for a harsher lesson. "Do you believe that this world of ours is called Kasmah?"

"Of course, my Integra Divinitas."

Employing his emotionless monotone in an effort to spook the young man, Mulat replied with, "Stop with the pointless honorifics. Do not call me what you hear other people refer to me as, find your own words." Allowing several moments to pass for the fear to drain from the apprentice's face, he then fished out a piece of Vesma and walked closer to him.

"Do you believe that this is a piece of Veneficium Kasmah, a source of power so great that it is matched only by its instability?"

"... Yes, that's vesma you are holding," replied the apprentice, confused by the basic nature of the question.

Mulat then uttered, *"Mel thwane utzye."* A small bolt shot out from the crystal and hit the apprentice full force in the chest, slamming him hard against the ground. Bruised and confused the apprentice lay curled up, wondering what he had done wrong to offend Mulat. "Do you believe in that pain?" he asked.

The apprentice coughed up a little blood and was too scared to move from his position. "Yes," he replied, quivering.

Mulat looked on at his apprentice and had hoped for better, but he couldn't make the path any easier for him. "Do not fear me, a lesson is only a lesson. Do you see anger in my eyes? Rage in my heart? Calm yourself and look at me." The apprentice tentatively tilted his head up to see Mulat staring at him. "At the end of the day you can experience pain, more or less the same as another person. Can you see through the tears welling up in your eyes? Can you think clearly and analyze the situation for what it truly was? Can I trust your judgment on that pain to be fair and objective, when that is your only focus?"

Fearing for his life the apprentice blurted out, "I believe I understand better now, it will... take me time...." Mulat helped the apprentice up and aided him until he could tend to himself.

While he nursed his superficial wound, the apprentice desperately needed to fill the silence and stop Mulat's gaze so he asked, "Were those words of power?"

"Hm?" replied Mulat distantly, already bored of the situation and thinking of other things.

"That chant."

"Words of power? All words have power don't they? In the communicative sense anyway. Or are you asking if my utterances caused the vesma to react?"

"Yes."

Mulat narrowed his eyes at him in an almost caring fashion. "No, you should know better."

"I am not well versed in using... any."

"I am surprised this has not come up sooner — why aren't you?"

The apprentice shrugged. "It kills even the most skilled people who either harvest, mine, or refine it for a purpose. I didn't see much of a point to risk myself out of curiosity."

"It would appear I have made an error in prejudging you on that front. I simply assumed that all who would be interested in the Integra Pol would have found some interest in vesma prior."

"Well, I do. I just had nowhere safe to learn from."

"You could have learned from a book, they are for all intents and purposes quite safe. What one does with the information garnered however is a different matter altogether."

"It has killed more people by accident than brought any benefit in my mind, and as I said: I wasn't curious enough."

"Idle curiosity can be a wondrous thing, but still," Mulat noticed that his apprentice was not responding well to his attempt to push a new topic, "Well, anyway, when utilizing vesma from any source, all experience a form of mental and physical discord. During this time it can be hard to tell what is happening to your own body because your mind is elsewhere. If you do not control the vesma discharge well enough it can damage your body, and if your body is not strong enough to handle the vesma exertion it can tax your mind. This is what leads to all manner of accidents to either yourself, or others as you try to keep the world, yourself, and what you are trying to achieve with the vesma aligned. Many find their own method to retain their focus on mind and body while using vesma — I find it pleasing to let my mind provide an aesthetic phonetic, but it is not a required component."

A question hidden far in the back of his mind slipped out before he could stop himself. "But what about... the... blood... thing.".

"Ah, that popular 'myth' about me again. No, my blood had nothing to do with it either. Would you like to see my blood and verify it for yourself?"

The apprentice looked around. Mulat normally had a softer hand, but today he seemed impatient and more intense than he had been before. He had to get out of there. "May I leave, so I can process?"

"It would please me if you would do so — I will take this as our session concluded. Please take your time. I have no immediate need of you so you are free to do as you wish."

"Thank you, Integra Divinitas Mulat." The apprentice grabbed his discarded robe and, while trying his best to hide his fear, scampered out of Mulat's chambers.

Mulat sighed once more as he saw another apprentice flee him. He suspected it kept happening due to the barrage of information he tried to give everyone, ignorant to the fact that not everyone thought as fast as he did or could hold as much. But it was hard to know where the walls in other people were or what they could hold when his own seemed limitless. For most people he was too much at once and he often found he overflowed what small cups they had so quickly.

The way his apprentice had just left told him that he had no doubt lost yet another to fear, and would most likely not see him again. It was only when people used his full title which identified him as the most powerful and wisest man in all of the Integrum that he knew they were frightened. They thought it would appease him, show respect, but all it did was infuriate him because he knew it was a precursor to them excusing themselves from him, usually permanently.

But no doubt another apprentice would be sourced quickly as there were many who would gladly throw themselves before him. He had been cautioned by some of the Quadra Erus' that he was too casual with whom he accepted as a new apprentice, regardless of their conducutis that bound them to secrecy.

"The truth is easy to see, but hard to look at when you are blinded by the demands that your body and soul make of you," was Mulat's passing thought before trying to recall how many apprentices he had gone through since he'd dispatched Juvorya, who in private he simply called Juvo. She had told him he needed a better way to pass his time, and preferably one that wasn't as dangerous as his usual past-time. His attempt at apprentices so far had not been as successful as he had hoped. Thus far he had found a string of people eager to be one, but even so the longest any had lasted was merely a month before running away.

Mulat feared that the calm Juvo brought him would not be found in these apprentices and that he would once again seek a more thrilling fare to quell his easily bored mind. When one has learned to silence the body's demands, the brain becomes remarkably free to make intellectual demands of its own.

Juvo was the only person that could help him with the pressure that came with such mental demands, but she was also the only one he trusted to find suitable candidates for the much overdue Deaspora. If only his predecessor, Stagnos, had not fallen to his emotions and done his duty.

The Vir and Mulier had to be found or else his city, and all of Kasmah, would slowly kill itself.

"At least it wouldn't be boring," Mulat said to himself.

CHAPTER I

"I'm sorry!"

"What for, my little desert flower?"

"Everyone is sad because of me!"

"... Maybe. But, I am happy because of you, and so long as I am happy, I will always find a way to make everyone else happy.
Don't ever forget that."

-Kahli, age 13, talking with her father

THE MAHARAAN EXPANSE

Kahli's eyes creaked open, and for a while they watched light slowly flood the room from the rising sun. Wanting to make sense of last night her mind asked the question of 'what happened?' The answer her brain returned was, at best, fuzzy. The more she probed for comfort the more a sense of dread crept in, stifling any desire to think or act.

A memory flooded back to her — she could remember waking up on her stomach in the middle of the night, and when she had tried to turn over she'd found that she couldn't. Some great weight had been pressing down on her back that she could not feel, only sense. She struggled hard, so hard against that unknown, but she stopped when she began to hear the screams... so many screams... along with the sounds of flesh being ripped like paper, and laughter... so much laughter. The sounds seemed to be coming from inside her head, loud and booming, making her feel that all the noises were trying to escape her head instead of banging on her ears to be let in. Unable to move under the immense weight, her fear grew while all she could do was listen to the gruesome sounds.

Then, an eerie heart-stopping calm came when she felt warm blood splatter on her body. It might as well have glued her to the bed it frightened her so, and for hours she felt like she was doing little more than waiting for her death blow to come — anything to end her mind's fear-filled concoctions. As she waited, she prayed at least to be free of the screams inside her head and the sickening feeling of blood slowly congealing on her face and hair.

Paralyzed and helpless she could do little to stop her tears and the blood pooling, as her mouth lay open in shock — locked in a mute scream. What seemed like hours passed with her heart slamming against ribs that felt too small for her body, her heart fighting to break free.

Then, when her body could no longer find the fuel for her fear, she passed out.

BREATHE...

The weight from last night was now only a memory and she tried to get up, only to have her hands slip from weakness and her face land in a pool of congealed blood. She fought the suffocating smell, and dredged the pit of her being for the strength to try again. All she could focus on from last night was the warmth, fear, and smells... the smell of death, and something burning. Struggling to raise herself up on her arms she coughed and tried to wipe the mucus and blood from her face.

After what she felt was a herculean effort she rolled herself onto her back, and kept her eyes closed for fear that her heart was not ready for what she would see. Whatever threat from last night, real or imagined, now took second place to believing that the feeling in her chest would kill her instead. Several minutes passed while she tried to gather both the physical and emotional strength to rise up and put a picture to the sounds and smells that had pervaded her senses for far too long. Cursing herself for being weak she willed herself to sit up, and looked around her room. A silent gasp of air was the only expression her body could manage when she saw the source of the blood that now caked her body.

In shock she stood up and took a few steps, taking in only the morbid scene — chunks of torn flesh and skin adorned the walls and floors. In a trance she walked outside of the hut, when as she was about to pass through the entrance something fell onto her head. She fell backwards onto the ground and looked up to see Jak's smiling face nailed to the wall above, dripping bits of flesh. Stifling a scream she scampered as far back into the hut as possible and looked around, and now came to realize that her family was what was strewn everywhere.

Faces and names were put to what was once human and the screams echoed in her head as she saw her mother... her little sister and brother... plastered all over the hut. Everything was plastered with what was once what she called her family. Sobs began welling up, but she stifled them as best she could so as to not attract the attention of whatever it was that had done this.

No longer able to cope with the sight she scrambled outside, and walked into a nightmare that burned the echoing screams and smells directly into her memory forever. Her entire village, everyone she had known her entire life, was impaled on bits of wood and bone — some their own. She walked past many but recognized none as she made her way to the center of the village, anywhere to be not surrounded by this.

What she found there took the last of what sanity she had left, for in the center was a large pile of bodies. The people collected had been melted in such a way that the skin from each person flowed and mixed seamlessly, turning it into a large mound of still-cooling fat and muscle. The crackling sounds and stench would have made Kahli vomit had anything made sense so far. She could only see it as a pile of melted flesh, not her friends, and not her village.... She could not recognize anybody as she walked around the grotesque pyramid of death, hoping to find a survivor, or some reason as to why she herself was one.

Dazed by despair and uncertainty she circled the pile for an hour, her stupor fueled by the smell of burnt flesh and vision of human bodies unrecognizable. Her ghoulish trek only stopped when she tripped on the groove she had worked into the dirt by circling the mound. She could not even find the will or instinct to cushion her fall.

Many hours had passed since the massacre ended, and with daylight underway it brought to light all the death and destruction that had occurred. No respite had come for Kahli. None would. Through the mental chaos she tried to demand answers from her brain.

All manner of thoughts raced through her. *"Should... I get up...? Tired from trying for so long. Is there even a point, now?"* The tall woman came to mind and how she'd always approached her. *"What of the Integra Humanus? Did she bring this with her? Did she attract something evil? I don't even know what is capable of this... Where is she now? Didn't she help fight? Was there even any fighting to begin with? ... It looked like a slaughter."* Her mind was not seeking answers, it was seeking what questions to even ask.

Ultimately, all she could do was lie there, and let the fear and loneliness take its hold, dragging her into the blissful dark as her mind transported her to a more pleasant reality. A memory of her mother and the Jackals, living and breathing.

Ж Ж Ж Ж Ж Ж Ж Ж Ж Ж Ж Ж Ж Ж Ж

"Jackals!"

"WHAT?!" yelled back Jak and Jall in unison, mid-dash out of their hut's entrance.

"Stay and help me with dinner! You can wreak havoc later, or you can have havoc wreaked on you when mom gets home. Tormenting the Ladak is not worth the wrath of mom now is it?" said Kahli sternly.

Jak and Jall, contemplating with cunning beyond their years the immediate pleasure versus future punishment, scampered back inside and stood while giving Kahli their best innocent expressions. Kahli gave them both a light rap on the head and said, "Enough of that, your tricks don't work on me."

Looking hurt as best they could, both Jak and Jall slinked off to the small open space in the middle of the hut used for eating and sat down with an overly dramatic expression of submission.

"Mom will be home soon. It would be nice, for once, for us all to honor her return properly with the food prepared to accompany her kill. So, come on, wash and scrub everything properly while I make sure everything is in good shape," she ordered. She didn't even have to look over her shoulder to know that they were making a face at her. Thankfully the next fifteen minutes passed without much further complaint from the Jackals, and she couldn't help but feel a small amount of pride in being able to control the mischievous pair.

When the accompaniment sides and sauces were made for their mother's return, Kahli felt that she had earned some rest. That, however, was something she couldn't enjoy until she dealt with the twins. No matter how nice she was to them they just did not seem to behave, so she found the next best alternative. She always made a few food bribes a week, small enough and infrequent enough for them to still hold potency, and this time she had made figs, basted in caramel, and then baked long enough to make them lightly crispy.

Presenting the bribe went down well as the Jackals eyes lit up. Kahli again felt a sense of joy at being able to give someone, even borderline malevolent ones like the Jackals, pleasure through her actions. She began to tell them the conditions for receiving such a treat but their attention didn't last and they darted out of the hut and into the dusky evening before she had finished talking. She then said after them in a caring voice, "You should really think before you act. You keep getting caught and punished by Gola then sent home crying anyway." Her afterthought was that she wished they at least took their time to enjoy the treats she made for them.

Kahli looked at the mess they'd left behind and sighed softly to herself, only slightly annoyed at once again being left to clean up after everything and everyone. She expected Gola to drag the two in by their ears in a little while anyway, no doubt after punishing them — she didn't look forward to Gola punishing her as well for not looking after them. But at least she would be saved the effort of having to hunt them down to get them ready for mother's talk of the day. She always loved listening to her mother's exploits, with the thrill of the chase and the triumph of the kill — even the stories where the hunted was too cunning for them and evaded their grasp. For Kahli it was the journey that she loved to hear about.

Her favorite was the epic tale of the ladak, now a long-held captive in Toka-Rutaa. The tale also held a special place in her heart because it was the one that told of her father's death, and how her mother had tracked down and trapped the ladak herself. She was in awe that her mother could quieten the blind fury inside herself to overcome killing it and capture it, a true moment of victory over self and a vicious creature — a creature that Kahli could only feel white hot rage and anger for. Even when her mother had paraded it into the open center of Toka-Rutaa the first time, Kahli was filled with the desire to just leap on it and rip it apart for depriving her of her father's guiding strength.

Soon after her display of triumph Kahli's mother, face rigid with purpose, hauled the wounded beast into the cage she'd made for it. After locking the ladak in she walked over to Kahli and spoke as though she had taken a long time to think about what to say. "This creature took something from you.... It took something from this village as well — a great man and our best hunter. The law of nature permits me to do what I like to this creature. And what I have chosen is for it to serve our village. Killing it would bring a satisfaction that would be fleeting. I aim to see it suffer."

It was at this point that her mother's normally strong face cracked slightly and she could notice a great internal struggle between teaching Kahli something, as she always tried to, and some strong emotion. "Every day I want it to wake up and see us behind its bars or from its toil when we put it to work, knowing that it killed my man, and that at any moment I could kill it. It took the life I chose from me, so I will take the life it chose from it." Through tears Kahli could hear the words her mother spoke, but because of her own sorrow she was deaf to their meaning.

She still wondered to this day why it was allowed to live, even after her mother had explained the reason behind enslaving the creature. But that memory had stayed fresh in her mind, and it always felt like it had happened only yesterday. For some reason she would always come back to it and play it over and over in her mind, just like it did almost every other time she was waiting for her mother to return.

Kahli's reverie was interrupted by the sound of a struggle just outside her home's entrance. She expected to see Gola, filled with fire and brimstone, hauling the Jackals in tow. As she turned she was surprised, and secretly filled with joy, that it was not Gola this time, but her mother and the twins with a look of pained submission. Tossing the day's kill onto the floor with one hand and marching the twins over to their bed with the other, she commanded them to sit.

"Now listen," she instructed to the pair with a firmness that stiffened their spines with fear. "This ladak teasing stops right now, okay? It can't pay us back if it's damaged!" With the twins near tears from their mother's stern tone, Kahli ran in between the two parties. Her mother looked directly at her and Kahli tried to calm herself by breathing in and out slowly.

Eventually her mother's face softened and she instructed everyone to sit down around the center of the hut. After getting comfortable she said, "Jak and Jall, what you need is a lesson. I will teach you about the ladak so you know what it is and what it isn't. If at the end of this lesson you see no value to the creature then you will vote, if you both want it dead then you can have my permission to kill it. But before that vote can be made you must listen to what I have to say. Then you can pass judgment." Kahli's mother shooed her away, and so Kahli collected up her mother's prize and went back to preparing everything.

She felt that it was all a little unfair but found some comfort in knowing the Jackals were going to eventually be punished. They'd played enough pranks and tricks on her to deserve worse, but she could settle for what she knew was to come.

Focused on her task, Kahli did not hear any of the conversation between them, but she could not help but think, "*Why do only those two get to vote if the ladak lives or dies?*"

LAND OF THE GADORI

Finally reaching the copse of trees, the self-professed idiot boy entertained the idea of trying to communicate with them to test his theory, for a brief moment. He pushed the thought to one side and was merely grateful that he was no longer surrounded by the cold and harsh biting winds. The trees before him weren't the pinnacles of health as they were spindly and sparse, but they were at least something. Tired and hating feeling like a brain walking around in an alien body he sat himself up against a tree and began trying to build who he was in his head.

Looking out to where he had walked from he settled in and fidgeted. "So, I like talking to myself — I could be crazy." He looked around at the trees. "Would be nice if I could test my talking abilities on other people...." As he talked a very scary thought slowly came to him. "... Is there anybody else?" he said in a voice filled with worry, and the more he thought about it, the more his face lost animation and color.

Now wasn't the time for despair though, so his mind rallied and life returned to his body. "Well there has to be. I exist don't I? But... even if there were people, would they understand me? I know what I'M saying, but would they? I'm using words, and these aren't just thoughts in my head. I can HEAR my voice so... no, I'm... I must have come from somewhere, otherwise how would I know how to say anything at all? There must be other people somewhere. I know that there are things like boys and girls and there are things like... I can remember animals...." He felt like something was playing tricks on his mind the more he focused on himself so he returned his attentions to more 'real' things, like his clothes.

With the harsh winds no longer whipping at him he felt it time to inspect his belongings with greater scrutiny, maybe they could help him find some clues to the questions he still had no answer for of what, why, how, where and who. Rummaging through his heavy furs he began inspecting any available pockets to find anything — literally anything would've been welcome at this point. His hands got lost several times and he realized that he appeared to be inspecting the same pocket over and over, something that just made his frustration grow.

Feeling a little desperate he decided to strip his outer layers and gave the garments an angry shake to see if anything would come of it. What fell out was a small strange stone and a heavy pair of metal gloves that looked like they were willing to go to war, regardless of if they were worn or not.

Wide-eyed he stared at them, and then inspected the clothes with a look of surprise — wondering just a little if he had beaten them so hard that they'd coughed up something just to appease him. *"What the valde? Why didn't I notice these earlier? No clanking? No bulge?"* He gave them one more hard shake, and, seeing that they weren't going to give up anything else, quickly got dressed.

He picked up the gloves and gave them a close inspection — they looked immaculate in their construction, but scuffed up. The underside of them was a soft mesh material he could not identify, but the topside was covered in some hard plate-link metal. They had miniature spikes running along the finger bones, while each knuckle was encircled by a band of metal. The tips of the fingertips were forged in the shape of razor sharp talons, which he found slightly odd. "I'm surprised I didn't gut myself walking around with these."

Turning them over in his hands he eventually found something etched onto the wrists amidst the marks and scratches. Looking hard at the markings he mouthed out the word 'Toyo' and felt a sense of accomplishment. "Well... so I'm not some sort of moron. I know what reading is, and I can do it. Nice to learn things you didn't know you knew about yourself... I suppose," he said.

He turned his attention to the stone and, after giving it a cursory look, found that it was well-polished and had a very organized pattern on its surface. Compared to the gloves it was amazingly ordinary, and after a few attempts to break it open he confirmed that it was pretty much just a stone. "It's... pretty, I suppose. Must have slipped into my pocket somehow, there are plenty of stones around here," he thought, and promptly tossed it.

Looking back at the gloves he could not help but think, *"Are these really mine? I don't know if I'm the sort of person that needs such... dangerous looking stuff. Then again if I walked all the way out here and went skinny-dipping in the freezing cold, maybe I'm tougher than I think."* Arguing that seeing as they came out of clothes that fit him, these gloves should fit also. Sliding them on with ease he felt a little excited as they looked pretty dangerous, and by extension felt that HE must be. It was not long before confidence melted under reality as the cold metal started to numb his hands, and there was also this strange tingling sensation. Re-thinking his decision to don the gloves, he began to remove them.

It wasn't until one was partway off that he inadvertently discovered they were lined with small hooked metallic spikes that had now plunged into his hands. Feeling the tug of resistance he panicked and tried to yank the glove off, causing the hooks to tear his hand's flesh and dig in deeper, which made his blood begin to trickle down and fill the gloves. Trying to breathe calmly he felt his blood's warmth begin to coat his hands, and a sinking feeling came to him as the sensation that came before those surges of pain that had awoken him resurfaced.

He could do nothing but succumb as it slammed into him, making him fall to the ground like a soggy pile of leaves. The saving grace of the pain was that when he reactively clenched his fists, further embedding the little hooks into his flesh, his brain was already too preoccupied to pay it much attention. He screamed out in agony, and when the surge passed he swore at both the gloves and the pain — when mid-curse he was again assaulted by another surge, making him clench his fists once more.

After another surge he tried to use the reprieves in between them to find a way to think through the pain. When the fifth surge came, his body tired and ragged from the exposure, the memory of how it stopped last time finally came to him. He had his solution, but his problem now was that the gloves made that impossible. His hands felt as if they were on fire, he was dripping blood everywhere, and was unable to unclench his hands for fear of tearing out the hooks that now felt embedded in bone. With the option of his body being cooperative no longer available to him he fell back on the one thing he knew he had left, his mind.

He started to picture his arms no longer being a part of him, detached and floating just a little distance from his body. He forced this image to become more intense, kicking and screaming at his brain to play along as the next surge mounted. Trying to use the intensity of the pain to imprint on his mind that image, it became so vivid that a blankness enveloped him as he rode the unwilling journey. The pain eventually passed, and moments of fearing the next surge soon became unfounded. He waited a while more before concluding that his experiment had worked, and afterward he felt joy at his mind's surprising success — and at finally being able to unclench his fists.

The pain that came was so intense that it almost rewired his brain, to the point that after the jolt passed he was secretly surprised to find that he still had arms. After his brain reminded him that yes, he still did have arms, he was relieved that he'd found a way to stop his hands from their uncontrolled clenching and the surges. For now. Laying on his back in fear of the next wave of pain, he was thinking only of his survival and hoped that his hands would still be working if he got through all this.

The blue sky through the spindly tree branches gave him some comfort with their tranquility and he looked around at the barren trunks. Spaced far apart and with little signs of life other than the odd patch of green and blue he was hit by the realization that if there were plants, there must be other living things nearby.

Placing his hands on the ground he began to stand up, scouring his mind for anything that would help him understand his waking moment to now — anything to help him survive. His thoughts were interrupted by a familiar sense of dread. The next surge was rising. On all fours he braced for the impact, but was surprised to find that all that came was a dull throb. Simultaneously thankful and fearful he stayed in his position as several more waves crashed down on him, but found that each subsequent one was more his fear than actual pain, until eventually they stopped coming altogether.

With each throb a dying ember of pain, he noticed that the pain the surges brought were far different from the pain his hands were feeling right now. The surges' aches pierced his very being and permeated everything he could understand — his hands by contrast were so much more mundane and physical by comparison. The surges commandeered his soul, his hands however were just telling him what was going on.

In an effort to stand himself up he found his arms unresponsive and panicked again with the fear that he had willed his appendages useless. His brain had to remind him once again that, yes, he did have arms, and he pushed past his feeling stupid and lifted himself up. He winced as he left bloody hand prints on the cold hard ground beneath.

Upon standing the pain from his hands came flowing back. Sweating and quivering from the recent ordeal he shut his eyes tight so he could argue with his brain and body — trying to force them to conclude that passing out was not the smartest option and to ignore whatever his hands had to say. A few moments later after winning that battle he looked to his hands and found blood had now entirely coated the gloves.

His best efforts to not whimper were summoned while he spent the next few minutes attempting to remove the gloves as carefully as he could. He soon found that they had little desire to be anywhere else but on his hands — the hooks had dug in too deep. That was now somewhat a secondary concern compared to the amount of blood he'd lost. Being a problem that he knew he couldn't fix he decided to ignore that fact so he could focus on more important things, like the ever present battle of his brain's desire to survive and his body's demands of *'fix me now!'*

Peering into the foliage he saw that the forest only got denser for as far as he could see, which was not very far compared to the barren tundra of nothingness he had just trekked through with little to look at for miles around. He decided that this forest was probably the best place for these trees to be, what with there being so many of them.

Realizing trying to make observations wasn't going to make the pain go away, he looked for a way to dull the burning in his hands. Fishing into his discarded clothing he retrieved the pouch he had filled and tried to douse his gloves with the ice cold water in order to numb the pain. Something in the back of his mind thought that this was probably a stupid idea, and the word frostbite was softly screamed by another part of his brain. His brain however wasn't interested in all that nonsense. Dousing both gloves with water he found some relief and put his pouch away.

He looked at the gloves angrily and tried to communicate with all his heart that if they kept acting up he would happily chop his hands off just to be rid of them at this point. As if in response, a bright flash where wrist and glove met came, along with a searing burn. It was over in a second and he found it more surprising than painful. Actually, all pain his hands had once felt was now just a memory. It was infuriating to think that he may now have to be grateful to them when before he had just wanted them gone. He collected his wits in order to decide how to best express his feelings. "Bloody... GAH! Fine! You want to stay on? FINE! STAY! Enjoy the ride! I'm sure we'll be BEST of friends!" He had a little temper tantrum and shook his hands hard to see if they would come off. They resolutely didn't. "AAAAAAAAARGH!" he screamed in frustration.

Admitting defeat did not sit well with him but he didn't know how he was going to fight his hands, let alone a pair of gloves — they were staying for better or worse. At least the pain was gone and he could use his hands, so there was some comfort there. He tried to look on the bright side of things. They fit, for one. Also, he wasn't bleeding anymore, so there was that. However when he tenderly touched the scar where glove and wrist had fused just to see what it felt like he accidentally stabbed himself with one of the finger talons. "*Futuo!*" he cursed.

His so-called 'bright side' was now darkened by the thought that if the past was any indicator then the future was going to be suspiciously lacking in bright sides.

All the heat his body had generated from its thrashing and clenchings was now beginning to leave him and the cold crept back in so he slumped against the nearby tree. As he tried to let his body rest he wondered what the gloves were actually for, and if his name was what was inscribed on them. He rather liked the sound of what he'd read, so decided he may as well call himself that.

"Toyo... Sure, why not," said Toyo. "Toyo! The god of gloves!" He laughed to himself out of exhaustion from everything. Oddly enough he felt that now he had a name that things just might be okay. It was a start.

"*I'm hungry...*" thought Toyo as he started to slump sideways.

He was unconscious before he hit the ground.

INTEGRUM

"I have yet to do anything interesting, yet another apprentice's cup is already filled with fear fit to flee," said Mulat to himself idly as another candidate was presented to him. He paced around, inspecting them like a pack horse, all the while taking note of their nervous state. After a dismissive wave he walked back to his desk and the candidate sighed in relief. The frustration at the brevity of his previous apprentice's time with him, and each apprentice's limited tenacity for the pursuit of understanding, was making him feel that he had yet to find the balance necessary to keep any.

Mulat was a figure forced to be alone by situation and circumstance. He overwhelmed most people with his overly direct approach to everything, but he knew his position and title were partly to blame for how they reacted. It did not help that his intelligence distanced him, and his power forced people to be close to him. It was these two forces that caused people to flock and flee, and that strange push and pull in his life caused discord inside his heart.

Most of the Integra Pol governed itself well enough, which left Mulat having to do jobs that were performed more out of his need to do something than anything else. The only real time people sought his council was when things had truly gotten out of control, for apparently bothering him with anything less than a disaster was somehow disrespectful in their minds. So with little to do, and no apprentice at hand, he could not help but feel like he was about to reach the point of becoming 'dangerously bored'. In the hopes to not reach that he concluded that what he needed to ease his mind was some music and so summoned for a musician.

It was not long before a harpist was ushered into the room where without command or guidance he made his way to the corner farthest from Mulat and made himself comfortable. Some light tuning strums filled the air before the harpist began playing, bringing forth melodies that gave much needed comfort.

As the plucked melody flowed over Mulat he thought back to

the hesitant outrage that the Quadra Erus' expressed over his opening the Integra Pol's doors to all charges of the Quadras. An unfounded outrage to share, Mulat felt, as the few charges that did approach were from the Quadra Musicum anyway. Mulat knew the offer would only attract the intense and extreme, but he had not thought there would be so few to take up the offer.

To ascend beyond what their Quadras could teach them, the charges came forth, and like all of the Integra Pol the task set before them was to sacrifice something in order to perfect their craft. By design this was to prove to the individual that they were ready to be guided rather than a mandate of the Integra Pol itself. Ritual and tradition however had made people feel that this was more a rule followed without question, rather than a choice they could refuse if they felt the need. All who joined believed that in order for one to rise higher, one needs to strip the chaff from self.

The harpist now playing had chosen to dull his ability to speak as his way of being true to the plucked strings — so he'd had his tongue cut out. Mulat felt his choice a bit overly dramatic, but knew most members of the Quadra Musicum had within them a desire to outperform others, and those wanting to join the Integra Pol would hardly be considered normal by the public of the city of Orbis. Being the largest city in the Integrum, it allowed the weird and the wonderful to thrive, where in smaller cities and towns being different was frowned upon — making Orbis a popular place for those peculiar.

Of all who joined there was only ever one singer who'd come to the Integra Pol. The Musicum had told her that she could never exceed her range of two octaves, but her own ambitions and desires drove her to seek perfection. Musicum charges believed that all one ever needed was their instrument if they truly wished to communicate something worthwhile. Without what they called their 'second heart' they were nothing, and to stay true to their chosen 'second heart' they sacrificed all other form of expression.

As one would grow in proficiency, it is said that to listen to a master play is one of the most wondrous things an ear could experience. Transporting all listeners with fluttering high flying notes that would almost dance in the air before landing on the ear, melting like warm butter on the mind before coursing through your soul and filling you whole from the toes up. They ignited the listener with feeling — starting with the mundane act of 'hearing' the music, right before boring its way straight to emotion. The singer could not bear to think that she could never give that feeling to another.

Taking a personal interest in her desire to improve Mulat took her under his wing to ensure success, and to his satisfaction she was one of the few he had ever invested in that kept their resolve throughout. Working tirelessly on his own Mulat had taken the teachings from the Quadra Logicum and his own knowledge to create a process that helped transcend the limits of her birth and body.

The procedure devised was to fuse vesma with her vocal chords, achieved by a grueling and horrendously painful procedure which altered her very flesh. It involved attaching a smooth, wide, flat piece of stone that had been coated in liquefied vesma to a piece of string, then allowing it to slide slowly down the throat with nothing to ease the process. There had to be little obstacle between vesma and her. For the singer, fighting her gag reflex was the hardest part, made harder by the unpredictable danger of fusing vesma with anything organic — a practice forbidden by the Integra Pol.

When the stone had traveled enough to reach her vocal chords, Mulat placed a pure solid piece of vesma on her neck, and then slowly moved it up and down in a massaging motion. As the vesma from within her and outside reacted, the liquid vesma clung tightly to the inside of her throat and began fusing with flesh. Vesma vapor crawled up into her sinuses and mouth, burning every inch, and her mind reeled at the desecration of her sacred instrument. The woman's desire to scream was unbearable, and her body convulsed violently in attempts to reject everything that was happening. But she remained strong, and not long after she had healed her memories of the event were not of pain, but of fear that she may be losing the only thing she held dear: her voice.

But like all who chose to be a part of the Integra Pol, a price had to be paid — hers was her speaking voice. It took months before she could talk without experiencing immense pain as the crystalline nature of vesma intertwined with her flesh demanded it to resonate with a consistent frequency. To speak in normal speech tones caused discordance between the flesh and vesma, which would make her feel as if her throat was being ripped apart. Through the fear and uncertainty she learned to always speak with a slight melodic tone, and found now that even the act of talking filled her soul with music.

No sooner than she found comfort with her alteration she demanded to become more and began training under Mulat to expand her range. She soon found herself not only exceeding the most renowned singers of the Musicum, but that she could even sing in harmony with herself giving all who heard the impression that two people were singing. She gained such control over her throat that it felt as easy to manipulate as her own arm, and now sang with a purity that seemed uncanny. Her true comfort came from the fact that when she sang she could hear nothing else. Her singing would consume her mind and no sound could distract her when she did, going to a world of her own while she poured her heart into the real world through song.

One day Mulat was walking by the small room set aside for her and an idea occurred to him. Wishing to truly test her range he invited her up to his chambers and asked her to sing with as much force as she could. The singer obliged, always happy to be asked to perform, and began a powerful aria. From start to finish Mulat was entranced and felt proud of what he had accomplished.

When she finished her final note she opened her eyes to look at the man that had given her such a gift and gawped at the sight that lay before her. The room had been completely destroyed save for Mulat, now sitting on a broken seat at a splintered desk. All other furniture had been rended asunder, along with the doors themselves blown off their hinges, and the windows smashed through. Pleading to be forgiven Mulat simply smiled and asked why she needed such a thing.

"You wanted to become a singer like no other, I gave you exactly that," he said. It took a long time for him to get her to understand that she was not dangerous, just something so beautiful that it was also powerful.

Bolstered by Mulat's words of comfort she began to entertain the requests of the wealthy for her performances. From what she could see, the awe she inspired seemed to her only comparable to the damage she could cause, but with Mulat's guidance she had long abandoned any fear from either she created. While her voice did touch the hearts of others, the vesma alteration sadly made prolonged exposure to it fatal. Even armed with this knowledge it did little to stop the requests for her voice, even though some would be found dead with a smile on their face. Pity is what people gave her, but she felt no need for pity. She was what she loved and in entirety was what she wanted to be, and in time she grew less concerned with the destruction she could bring and focused only on the beauty of the music itself.

Mulat would never forget the look on her face when he finally named her — an honor given only to those who have become true charges of the Integra Pol, or an Erus of one of the four Quadras. New names to reflect that they chose to live a life different from before, and something seen more as an expression of passion and purpose than of sacrifice. Seeing purpose in his charges is what gave Mulat true pleasure — he wished he could see that drive in the other denizens of the city of Orbis. Regrettably though over his life he had seen that most forgot that purpose is a wonderful thing to have.

The harpist changed melody drastically, dragging Mulat out of his memory maze, and Mulat felt calmer now that his mind's refreshments were complete. He could not help but compare the harpist before him to others, and concluded that this harpist's inspiration was lacking. *"The brain can only process so much sensory information, and few dedicate themselves to less than all. No doubt if more people did, they would find their purpose."* He knew that to remove focus of a sense was to redistribute the mind's focus to all the others, but Mulat focused on everything all the time. It had always led him to wonder if he could ever really experience the passion the musicians did from such singular dedication.

Noticing his own procrastination Mulat returned to his work, for there were more than mere administrative troubles ahead. His efforts to quash the few recent reports of strange birth defects in the Integrum had been swift. With their increasing frequency however he knew that the Deaspora could only be held off for several more years at best before Kasmah experienced true chaos. In all truthfulness the report should never have even had to reach the Integrum. His predecessor, Stagnos, had wasted too much time indulging in his own fancies and apathy and had ignored the first true signs that the Deaspora was necessary: reports of mutations from the Calu-Jedde Mountain range of Kasmah.

The knowledge of the Deaspora none were privy to outside of the Integra Pol's higher echelons, and like all Integra Divinitas' before him he was entrusted with enacting it. Unlike all the others though, it was an event that he had been bred for. To that end Mulat's predecessor raised him in such a fashion that, both physically and emotionally, made his childhood an ordeal like no other. The weight of the Deaspora had been in his life for as long as he could remember, but even when he had completed his task it would still be needed to be performed again in several hundred years.

North of the Integrum lay the region known as the Maharaan Expanse, while to the south was the Land of the Gadori. Both these regions were where the Deaspora would need the Mulier and Vir to perform their sacrifice, but these places were also where the concentration of vesma was greatest — perverting geography and creatures alike the farther you went.

If any could survive the trip and carry out the task to find the Vir and Mulier, it was Juvo. He disliked having to risk his source of solace but his responsibility was to the Integrum, as was hers. Every time he saw her reports of violence and distress his heart sank, though it would be hard to tell on a face as static as Mulat's. The world held such wonders for him, yet at the same time he could not help but get bored.

Even in conversations he would amuse his mind in parallel with alternatives that could have been said before the other person finished their sentence, and when he got bored he became what Juvo affectionately referred to as *'dangerous'*. An odd concept, to be saved from boredom so others could be saved from him, but that is what Juvo did.

Mulat leaned back in his chair to focus again on the harpist's efforts. His prediction of all apprentices' future failings weighed heavily on his mind as he always put so much effort into the love and care and education of them, yet time and time again they got overwhelmed so easily. He needed something stronger for sure, but after the fifteenth one within two years he found it difficult to keep his expectations high.

In an effort to feel less bored he had taken up a 'hobby', which for him meant dressing and accentuating himself as more masculine and less neuter so that he could walk freely in public — the attention drawn by a tall masculine figure was far less than a feminine one. Juvo had asked him to stop such flights of fancy time and time again while she was away, but he found it hard to stop himself. He needed to feel useful, to feel like he actually served a purpose beyond sitting in an ivory tower. It was just who he was.

The musician suddenly stopped playing, sensing that he had reached the limitation of his instrument and his audience. Awaiting further instruction the musician laid his instrument at his side and closed his eyes.

Mulat stood up and walked over to him, sat down opposite him cross-legged, and focused his intense yet expressionless gaze onto the musician's face. After a few moments the musician picked up his harp and played a short and low strum out of uncertainty, the note carried with it the connotation of *"Would you like me to keep playing?"*

Mulat sighed and wondered why fear was always so present in people. His slender build, baldness, and height, while impressive, were hardly unique and should have made no impact on people in the face of his being the Integra Divinitas — someone sworn to serve Orbis, the Integrum, and all of Kasmah. His edict was to care for, not to harm. Outside of his title he merely wanted to share some time with another human, but people had trouble viewing him as normal.

After a further minute of gazing and the nervous plucking of strings Mulat stood up, thanked the harpist, and dismissed him. The musician stood with his harp and played a chord of appreciation before leaving. "I need another... project," mumbled Mulat to himself as he watched him go.

Turning to his desk he took stock of the workload and, without any apparent effort, appraised the amount of work and future implications of its not being dealt with instantly. Juvo had been gone too long and he needed to feel his value again — work would not sate him, and the most interesting task that he could do without upsetting anyone was literally nothing until she returned. Juvo was one of the few things that provided to him what he believed so many readily found in others, comfort. Without Juvo, or anything to focus himself on, Mulat found himself wanting.

He tried to fill his mind with thoughts of how citizens would think of his home in the hopes to feel like others. The Integra Pol! A place of wonder and amazement which was home to the Integra Humanus, Natura, and... himself. The Integra Pol! A giant tower the shade of bone-white and shaped like an animal's tooth.... It was hard to think of his own place as foreboding and awe-inspiring, but it was just as necessary to don the thoughts of the public as it was their clothing. He then tried on some outfits and found in it a thrill, but he could only distract himself for a short while before depression once more set in.

Looking into the mirror he sighed at the conclusion he had come to and went to inform the charges stationed outside his chambers that they would no longer be needed. While they found the order confusing and his clothing odd, they obeyed regardless.

Mulat then walked to the large window that took up more than half the walls' height behind his desk, and stepped onto the large sill. Standing on the edge he looked out at the city below and marveled at it all. His chambers at the top of the Integra Pol, the tallest point in Orbis, gave him an unprecedented view of the beautifully constructed radial pattern of the city below. The bone-white grounds that stretched out from the Integra Pol, housing the minor servants and those wishing to became an Integra Pol charge within a variety of oddly shaped buildings, were beautiful to look at in their own way. And then encircling the grounds were the Quadras, each unique in their construction and colors, giving a contrast to the pristine Integra Pol grounds that made him smile. Beyond the Quadras was the First Ring of Orbis, the main road that encircled the Quadras, and far off in the distance were the mighty walls of Orbis that surrounded the city.

With a light smile he softly said, "Orbis... you are beautiful."

He parted his fingers slightly and a soft glow began to emanate from his chest. A gust of air unsettled some dust as it flowed out from under his clothes to gently caress the floor around him. That dust began to dance around his legs as the glow brightened, and then he said, "I am sorry, everyone." The dust and glow fell heavily to the ground and Mulat's shoulders slumped. "I am sorry Juvo," he whispered.

Mulat stepped out into the open air, and plummeted like a stone.

Ж Ж Ж Ж Ж Ж Ж Ж Ж Ж Ж Ж Ж Ж Ж Ж

Except for the Deaspora, the only other finding of the first Integra Divinitas, Malef, that had never been shared with the people of Kasmah was what humans experience upon death — the Cadare. This knowledge was guarded well out of fear of abuse or panic, but that did not stop several over the centuries from trying to take the easy way out.

A Cadare, the passage of death, was something tied inexorably with the vesma that flowed through all living things. While alive, blood flow keeps the vesma swirling around the body while the living brain stimulates the vesma — both work in unison to prevent vesma from its natural desire to merge. Throughout one's life the most persistent thoughts and feelings would attract motes of vesma to those areas of the brain, and would act as markers come the time brain and blood can no longer prevent more from merging.

All one's fears, loves, hates, beliefs, and follies would be snatched up by their vesma, and that vesma would replay them over and over — their life, as they saw it. Every possible event, every scenario. With the fine lattice-work of vesma throughout connecting everything, a person's mind would create permutation upon permutation of each memory, stretching out further and further as the gap between mortality and eternity thinned.

Some believe that the cadare never truly ends, that the memories go on for so long that they never truly stop. A timeless, unceasing portrayal of who you had been and every possibility therein. Saint or sinner, paradise or damnation — one's cadare was dictated more by life's intent rather than action.

When a young Mulat was first told of this fact, his response was merely a softly spoken, "So… we get what we choose, even if we don't truly want it."

※※※※※※※※※※※※※※※※

In her younger years Clarus Prae would always frequent the Cave — a large hall in the Quadra Musicum dedicated to the more experimental type of performer that proved popular with the younger crowd for social gatherings. Originally it was constructed to be a grand theater, lined with a special stone mined from the Calu-Jedde Mountain range. A stone chosen by the Erus of the Quadra Musicum, Erus Ictus, in order to give greater harmonics to the hall, but all that resulted was that it sparkled in dim lighting and gave odd echoes. It was Erus Ictus' most expensive blunder, so much so that even paying to have it removed was exorbitant.

Finding the hall to be too distracting for those who truly appreciated music, Erus Ictus repurposed it from grand orchestrations to a 'free performance' area. The younger crowd discovered it to be the perfect place to go to *feel* music and help one's emotions be lifted. To young Clarus however it was a hunting ground, she had spent too much time being a musical prodigy that she had neglected her heart.

The male, and some female, suitors had been plenty, her skill and beauty saw to that, but the ease at which people threw themselves at her made her unhappy. All praise and admiration was directed at her music or body — never her. So she eventually turned it into a game — more as a way of punishing those that ignored her soul and never saw past her skill or body. Music filled her heart, but she yearned for that part of it that lay empty.

In the several months of her frequenting the Cave, only one person had caught her notice, a tall slender man that seemed to flit from woman to woman. She watched him, essentially recording his every movement — this was her hunt, and she had finally found interesting prey.

Clarus could never get an idea of what it was he said to them, the echoes in the Cave carried strange harmonics that drowned out the words, but he was only ever there for a few minutes before gliding away to the next person. Whatever it was must have been good because he always left the ladies with a smile on their face and a look of longing. *"Must be quite a smooth talker,"* she thought to herself.

What always surprised her about him was that every woman he left seemed eager to leave with him, yet he always arrived alone and left the same. With the puppy dog eyes he was earning from all the women she was sure that he could have lured them in groups of five into his bed. He wooed practically everyone there, more than once, but stopped when he got the women wanting.

"But never me! I'm just as good as anybody else! Why shouldn't I be wooed, and cooed at?" she thought bitterly, feeling oddly aggravated at being ignored in a fashion where she normally would be fawned over. Her frustration reached a feverish pitch as she watched, increasingly obsessively, for three more nights. Always the same — she would come and merely watch the process while feeling strangely rejected.

"He truly seems to be enjoying himself. So why is he never with anybody, friends OR lovers? He must have plenty! Look at those silly cows turning into cream from his smile and whatever MAGICAL thing he says." Her inexperience and inability to read herself however meant that she had yet to understand the difference between seeking love and seeking power.

Clarus had finally had enough and decided to confront this mystery man. Strolling right up to him in the middle of what she had come to call 'his routine', she tapped him on the shoulder. He turned around with his ever present smile, and after the briefest of moments of feeling like she was being inspected, he said, "Yes, little one?" His tone was soft yet deep. She shivered silently — she didn't know if it was the anticipation, anxiety, or 'him' that had actually made her.

Momentarily stunned by the result of her actions she regained her composure. "What gives? You know I'm a woman too! I've seen you talk to everyone else but me, why?"

"Hm, 'What gives?' Strange way to word something, I must be missing something." The man looked like he was doing some complicated thinking before returning to the conversation, slightly puzzled. "Nothing '*gives*', my little one, are you asking me a riddle?"

"No, of course not! I want to know why you haven't talked to me yet! What is wrong with me?" she demanded.

"Nothing. You would just not be interested in what I have to offer, little one."

"Why do you keep calling me little one? Just because you are taller than me doesn't mean that I'm LITTLE! And why wouldn't I be interested in what you have to offer? I'm talking to YOU aren't I?"

With his smile growing ever wider the man responded, "Ah, 'little one' is a term of endearment — it is not designed to offend. As to what I have to offer, you are here with a purpose in mind, no? I have seen that you yourself leave each night with someone different." His hands made a sweeping motion over the hall. "You watched me, I watched you in kind — as I watch everyone here."

At this point the female he was seducing decided that being ignored was worse than the benefit of letting this man continue his efforts, as appealing as he may be, and stormed off in the hopes to make him feel jilted. She looked over her shoulder to see if it'd had the desired effect, and was infuriated by the complete lack of acknowledgment at her departure.

"Then why not talk to me?" Clarus demanded.

To which the man replied, "You want what I can't give."

"What is that supposed to mean?"

"Exactly what it means, little one."

Irritated, she asked, "How do you know what I want?"

All gentle humor left the man's voice, and with a serious voice he asked, "If you thought me so blind, why would you think me worthy to pursue?"

The man's question caught her off-guard, which she really didn't like. "You can't SEE my thoughts."

"No, but I can see your actions."

Nothing she was saying was getting to him, what was happening? "Those aren't the same things! Is this some sort of game to you?! Don't talk down to me!"

"You would be surprised how a precursor to one can predict the other. The two can also be interchangeable," said the man, more to himself than anyone else.

"... wait, what?"

The man chuckled, and then his soft tone returned to his voice. "My apologies. What can I do for you, little one?"

"What did you say before?"

"Before what?"

"Just then, now!"

"Just then? I didn't say anything 'just then'."

Clarus was now feeling a little lost, she was however quite determined and had already decided to not let him get to her, or let him go. She calmed herself and asked, "Is this how things go?"

"What do you mean, little one?"

She kept the course, trying to match his previously stern tone. "With the others."

He appeared happy. "Ah, a direct question. No. And for the sake of clarity I should perhaps point out that it is 'I' who approach the others. However, you are only the second person to approach me. So, I thank you on that account."

"I didn't talk to you to win prizes." Inside she thought, "*I talked to you to win!*"

"No, you talked to me because I'm tall, socially accepted as being attractive, and obviously desirable as you have noticed I'm good with members of the opposite sex. When I want to be."

He'd spoken so directly that Clarus inadvertently lost her composure. "That's not it at all!"

The man nodded his head low. "If you say so. As it stands there is little else I can divinate from pure observation of a person that frequents this type of place. I will, however, admit you do not respond like the others...." His mind appeared to trail off to somewhere else.

"Well, what if that is all of it? How is it any different from what you are doing with the others?"

"So you are saying that I am pursuing, 'the others', out of a sexual need?"

"Of course."

The man said softly to himself, "I suppose it is sexual in a sense, however it would be a stretch to identify it as such."

"What?" He seemed to enjoy conversations with himself as much as with others. It was annoying, but somehow interesting.

"Nothing, sorry." The man shook his head. "Still, I thank you for the approach, as I am always a fan of new experiences. However, as it stands, there is nothing I can offer you that you would want. For that I am truly sorry." Those were his final words before he bowed and made his way out of the Cave.

Clarus stood, slightly confused, but deeply interested in what had just happened. She was filled with the excitement of finally pursuing something she found interesting other than music. Even the fact that she felt somewhat stupid after talking to him was refreshing, like she had finally experienced what it was like to be normal. However, she could see that she wasn't being treated BY a normal person, the conversation just now proved that fact.

She enjoyed her confusion — to feel unbalanced by the directness of the man made her feel alive, and as if there was more she needed to understand. Clarus was many things. A musical prodigy raised by the Quadra Musicum. A woman beautiful and talented, sociable yet isolated. The kind of person that would cry over a limping dog, but not bat an eye to a burning house full of people. Most of all, she was stubborn.

It was then and there, all those years ago, that the young Clarus Prae had made the determination within herself to pursue the man further.

CHAPTER II

"A leader's greatest fear is mute followers."

-Mulat, Integra Divinitas of Kasmah

THE MAHARAAN EXPANSE

Kahli awoke to a sharp pain in her foot. She shifted her head to look down and found a scavenging bird pecking at her toes, trying to see if she was dead enough to eat yet. She scrambled to her feet and in a mad rage ran after the bird, silently flailing after it as if possessed. It quickly took off, along with the rest of its nearby flock. A smell caught her attention, and when she turned around, once again saw the pile of people that was once her clan.

The smell burrowed into Kahli's nose and sat like an ugly lump while large heavy sobs heaved up from deep within. She fell to her knees as her body fought between despair, exhaustion and trauma. She was tired and angry — the last week that took all her efforts and assistance, given freely, had left her weak in body and spirit. All her hard work, the pushing from everyone and the persistent expectations, had been subtly eating away at her core. Awakening now to this living nightmare caused her to lose what was left of her grip on reality.

Her face, caked in drying mud and blood, was now moistened by tears and the mixture of the two disgusted her. She tried to scrape it all off but achieved little more than smearing the moist red and brown around her face. The sobs soon turned to loud wails, which unknowingly attracted the attention of something else. Slow, heavy, plodding footsteps could be heard from the other side of the pile, and when she heard the *hrrunk* of the once imprisoned ladak she tried her best to bite her tongue. *"Why is THAT thing still alive?!"* she panicked in her head, unsure of why it still lived.

Sniffing and snorting the air wildly the ladak searched for what was making those sounds, and Kahli tensed as she heard its gruff intakes of air. As the ladak strode into view she tried forcing her body to move once more — instinct however had abandoned her in the wake of all the insanity. Kahli's body argued with itself, wanting both to stand completely still while running as fast as possible, while her mind, unable to find the compromise between the two, responded by focusing on the fear and screams inside her head.

The ladak that she was looking at now she knew was the one from the cage, however it seemed different than she remembered. This one was scarred, thin — a far cry from the boisterous and muscular creature that would rattle its bars and make all sorts of noises until someone thumped it. Instead it looked like it had been starved and tortured repeatedly over a very, very long time — its gait was weak and its ears were missing. If she had not had any hatred towards the creature before she certainly would have pitied it now.

As the ladak took a step towards her, Kahli's body jerked with an intense shock of pain. Her stomach pulsated and throbbed, piercing her with such intensity that she began to convulse on the ground, and then vomit. The wounded ladak, momentarily confused, kept its distance as it watched its prey twitch and jerk wildly.

Her spasms began to subside but her body was still not under her control. While nursing the pain and fear her mind dredged up any information it had on the ladak. What came was a memory of someone long ago trying to teach her about creatures of the Maharaan. Was it her mother? An old lesson from her father? She didn't know whose voice she was remembering.

"A ladak would never attack dying prey — it prefers to wait until you are dead first. As powerful as a ladak is, it is ALSO powerfully lazy — unless you give it a reason to be otherwise. Even though it is quite long, muscular and capable of outrunning most things, one should always keep in mind that a ladak is, in truth, a scavenger. They aren't good for eating, and going out of your way to take one down isn't really worth the effort. Even though they are of medium build, their powerful short legs and slender body can...."

Kahli was too tired, and let the memory fade. She had no wish to fight anymore, and with everyone now dead she felt that she had no more reason to live. Her father had died at the mercy of a ladak, to suffer the same death made her feel in some morbid way more worthy to die.

There was however a tiny spark within her, and that spark tried its best to scream at her about all the things that life could provide. *"You still have not grown,"* said a strange voice in her head. Kahli was unsure of how to respond to this other voice, which could only have been herself.

The strange voice spoke again, *"You still have not journeyed to other lands and places, you still have yet to be loved."*

Accepting the strange event she replied in thought, *"I will never see my family again...."*

"You will, if you want to."

"I want to... hear my mother's stories again."

"Is that all you want? Stories?"

"... I have lost everything," said Kahli dismissively.

The strange voice came with a confidence that put Kahli off-balance, and it said with her own mouth, "You have lost nothing." The ladak was no longer willing to wait for its thrashing prey and charged towards her at the fastest pace it could manage, ready to deliver a killing blow.

Spurred on by the daunting weight of her imminent death a part of her screamed out that she wanted to survive, even though her heart and mind were both torn and fraying at the edges. The flurry of demands and objections coming from every corner of her reached an eerie calm as her mind went blank. From her face-down position Kahli raised herself up on all fours, all the while tears flowed from an expressionless face. There was no fear here, there was no hatred. There was only simple certainty.

As the ladak closed the distance Kahli reached out and grabbed onto that tiny spark that had spoken to her. Stretched her hand out with palm flat she made no further motion, and her eyes focused on nothing while the vision of jaw wide and muscles rippling bore down on her. The ladak lunged into her hand, and was stopped in its tracks by what may as well have been a wall of iron. There was no sign that Kahli felt the impact on any level, while the beast itself was now dazed and weak. When the creature recovered enough of its senses it began to kick and struggle against the immovable hand, trying to bite and claw its way past. Time played out the scene of a ferocious animal fighting with all its might and gaining no ground and drawing no blood against a single hand, until from Kahli's fingers a faint spark bloomed and grew.

Kahli moved her hand forward while raising herself upwards, pushing back the ladak with ease. As she watched the ladak fight with such ferocity against her hand it felt so distant to her, and the harder it fought the more she decided it deserved pain. That everything deserved this pain that she felt in her stomach, her feet, her heart, her mind. The pain of having everything torn out of her life — of herself, stripped of all value. What she'd had was not much, but it was hers, and to have what little she'd had ripped away was unforgivable.

The voice in her mind sang out, "*This beast shall know true death.*"

As Kahli contracted her hand around the ladak's face its movements began to stiffen, and the spark between her fingers grew into white-hot tendrils that began to slither across the beast's face. As the tendrils met flesh they slowly cooked everything, leaving a trail of worming black scars along the face of a whimpering beast. Its skin charcoaled and blistered, and every inch of scar made, sapped the strength from its struggle. When it was almost too weak to move the burning ropes stopped, before quickly drilling through the front of its skull all the way through its body.

Kahli, with a voice much younger than her own, said, "I will be reborn."

"*Wh... what did I just say?*" thought Kahli, before the memory of her loss of family and world came back with a righteous fury.

Her screams drowned out all further questions and thought. Her scream deafened the ladak, and became the last thing it would ever hear. After the flash of a moment all that was left on the end of Kahli's hand was a long burnt piece of what once was something living — but her emotions and power did not stop after seeing the ladak dead.

From her fingers more fire flowed, a vortex snaked out around her and began consuming everything in its path. She looked to be an avatar of living flame as her emotional and physical pain fueled the chaos. Standing in the eye of her own storm she cried and screamed as she dropped to her knees, thinking only of her father as the flames expanded higher and wider. In time it came to consume the pyramid of flesh, then the huts, and kept spreading until all of Toka-Rutaa was consumed in a fiery inferno. Every inch of land that she could remember walking on her whole life, never once leaving even the outskirts of Toka-Rutaa for fear of failing her family, was now consumed by flame.

Kahli inhaled, and with that breath all the flames vacuumed into her lungs.

Moments passed with her face in a grimace of pain indescribable, yet nothing in her showed that she understood or was aware of what was happening.

Kahli exhaled, and an explosion ripped through the surrounding land, turning everything in its wake to blackened ash.

LAND OF THE GADORI

A persistent dull throbbing pain had been bothering Toyo for a while now — then again every part of him hurt as well, so it took him a while to give it any special attention. He decided that he'd been laying down long enough waiting for it to pass and a groan escaped his sleep and food-deprived mouth as he sat himself up against the tree. Upon righting himself, he felt like his back had been dragged across a thousand cobblestones and then whipped raw with thin branches. Wincing and wondering what he had slept on to make such a bastard pain present — he congratulated himself on his intelligence when he realized that he'd passed out on a bed of sharp rocks and roots.

He grumbled and looked back out at the land to see the sun rising — the beauty of it over the barren wasteland was not lost on him, and decided to just sit still for a while and take it all in. When the sun rose high enough to cover him with its light he enjoyed the warmth on his skin. Casting an idle gaze over the nearby trees he would have sworn that when the light hit them also they seemed to be... happy.

After a few more minutes of basking and gathering his wits, his body reminded him that food was actually a thing. Reaching into his furs he pulled out his water pouch and after a swig noted that there wasn't much left in it. He shrugged and reasoned that he might as well enjoy it and, surprised at how delicious water could be, finished the rest of it off. A few extra shakes got the last few drops out before he put the pouch away again.

Standing up, he took in his environment and felt strange at the stark contrast between the featureless land of ice and snow and the thick wall of trees and plants. He clapped his hands together like someone who had a hard job ahead of them and it was time to start, and was startled by the resounding clang made by the gloves connecting. Looking down at the blood staining his forearms his being startled was replaced with a sense of panic, that was until his brain provided him with memories of yesterday. Curious, he inspected his arm closer and noticed that the scar on his wrists where the gloves had fused to his skin was no longer there. Had he imagined it?

After finally remembering the reason as to why he'd passed out yesterday he flexed his hands again, and was relieved to see that they didn't hurt. Still not convinced, and still in fear from his body's past expeditions to pain, he made a few tentative further tests. After several tries he then realized that not only did he not feel any pain, his hands didn't feel anything at all — he knew that they were there, but everything he touched registered nothing to him but pressure. Even the sensation of pressure was as flimsy as paper to him, that it was somehow optional and that his hands did not have to register that either if they did not want to. It was as if his hands were cut off from the world.

Sighing quietly to himself with some despair about the fact that he could find no comfort in the memories of his waking life so far, he tried to stay positive. He looked back towards the harsh cold tundra where he'd walked from, and then inwards where the trees grew thicker. "Well... if trees are growing, I'm sure that there is something in there to eat... maybe."

Setting his face into the expression of a person determined, he collected himself, and with a staggered attempt at walking made his way into the forest. As he traveled farther the sparse greenery went from sickly and spindly to healthy and thick, and it soon became quiet with a cool breeze that blew between the now enormous trunks — the silence was almost eerie without the sound of the violent winds. Daylight here was broken down into mere twilight as the branches fought for sunlight, an effect that added menace to what could only be innocent plants.

Wandering through the dense foliage, Toyo worried that there was going to be little else of anything other than trees — there weren't even any tracks or sounds of distant animals to be found. After a half hour of directionless meandering, and feeling like a fool for not knowing what to do, he stumbled across a marshy lake. He took a few steps from the thick greenery out onto the banks of the marsh. It was harsh on Toyo's eyes to go from the dimly lit underbrush of huddled trees to the light that pierced through the sparse canopy surrounding the lake, but when he had accustomed he marveled at the sight.

He felt his mind reach for words to describe what lay before him. "A large... marshy-swampy, mossy... type... marsh... lake." To adequately express how stupid he felt for not finding enough words, he grumbled — his stomach decided to join in. His quickly rising self-loathing was stopped short by a flash of genius, and he decided to lay in wait — hoping to trap the next thing that would stop to drink. It all made sense. A place this big must have some creatures come to it, eventually, and if none turned up then maybe he could try to look for something that lived in the lake. Patience was key.

He lost his patience quickly though.

Growing bored with waiting for his ingenious plan to bear fruit, he spied some lightly frosted lichen growing over nearby logs that stretched far up onto the banks. The massive green carpet seemed to have crept out of the lake itself and had a death grip on everything in its path. Toyo couldn't help but reach out to see if his hands would register touching something slimy. After playing with it for a bit, and with his stomach upgrading from grumbling to yelling, he wondered if it was edible. Noting the muddy colored icy sludge it became when he clenched his hands, a small part of him, after some deep thought, decided that it would be best to not sample the delicious mossy feast, lest he deprive some hungry... thing of it. After playing with the moss for a while he noted that he could easily make shapes with it and on it.

"*Footprints!*" he thought excitedly, and thanked his brain for the brilliant idea. He washed his hands off and began walking along the banks of the lake to check for signs of animals. As he made his way around the swamp he found no signs of creatures, but while he kept walking he did find himself a little in awe of how far the swamp stretched deep into the forest. He didn't really want to have to fight the forest anymore or feel lost in it, at least on a lake there are only TWO directions — unless you count the sides, or drowning. Who knows? Maybe it was a way out of here, don't people live near lakes and stuff? "Might need a boat of some kind," he said to himself.

Not looking where he was going he tripped over one of the large uprooted tree trunks that was near the water's edge. He fell onto some of the icy lichen and slid down the bank as fast as only ice, lichen and water could allow, until he went head over heels right into the swamp waters, all the while screaming, "*FUTUO!*"

Thrashing about in the icy waters showed, to his surprise, that he knew how to swim — a realization that did little to quell his irritation and decreasing body temperature. As he paddled over to the bank he idly thought about the word that he had just screamed, and mentally put it in the same category as that other word, *valde*.

Upon reaching land he hoisted himself out of the water, and was on one knee about to stand up, when he heard something in the water accelerate with terrific speed towards him. Turning around to see what was making the commotion he saw a reptile as large as three fully grown men shoot out of the water with mouth open, ready to bite whatever it found.

Toyo then experienced a rather impractical set of mixed feelings — both being glad at realizing he wasn't the only thing alive in this world, and his body's response to the prospect of immediate death. In the few moments he had to think those two feelings fought, and what won was his loneliness and need to see something other than himself. Which temporarily shut down his fight or flight response, forcing it instead to perform the mental equivalent of taking in the scenery. He saw that the light red, thick-skinned, short-faced lizard-creature had a strange skin-hood over its nose, and as it charged at him, he simply thought, "*Fascinating.*" Had he been less in awe on seeing his first creature he would have been able to get out of its way.

Instead, his brain chose a course of action for him and raised his open hands to block the creature's charge. His mind tried to desperately pick something smarter to do, the result of which was Toyo saying, "*Oh valde oh valde oh valde,*" while flailing his arms in front of him in a panic. What happened next was not wholly unexpected, and the huge creature ran into him mouth first. What was unexpected, was that after the impact, Toyo realized that he had not been crushed to death.

His hands had stopped the creature somehow, but it had bitten down hard on them and wasn't about to let go anytime soon — he decided to do the same and clamped onto one of its teeth. A single loud heart beat rang out over its already excited pulsations, and some minor relief came when seconds later a part of him realized that his hands had not been bitten off. The sensation of feeling that he wasn't living entirely in the now made him wish that his brain would keep up with everything that was happening.

In their struggle the creature galloped up and down the banks of the swamp with its stubby legs, thrashing its head from side to side, trying to break its prey's hold on its tooth. From his position Toyo got to look down the length of the reptile and watched its muscular body flex and bend. All the while Toyo could only sarcastically think, "Well this is irritating — my first friend and it wants to eat me. I mean, this could be a courting ritual, but I doubt it." Its mouth was short for its body, but filled with many large sharp teeth — leading Toyo to wonder if it ever had a problem swallowing food. Its stubby legs moved quicker than he would have ever thought they could, giving the creature surprising dexterity — in fact, most of the creature was surprising. It looked like it shouldn't be able to do what it did, but decided to do it anyway, and what it lacked in visual horror it made up for in ferocious behavior. Ignoring the situation he was in, Toyo concluded that it was truly beautiful — even if it was doing its best to mate and/or murder him.

After seven seconds of his brain operating his body on instinctive fear, Toyo, trying his best to assess this new situation, realized that his hands felt no danger from being in the creature's mouth. At least, for a given value of 'danger'. He was however feeling quite queasy from all the thrashing around. Something that was thankfully stopped, but only because it had decided on a change of tactics. The creature tried rubbing his prey off on some trees, an act that drove Toyo to finally do something.

Flexing his hands in the creature's mouth, he found himself

88 | CHAPTER II - LAND OF THE GADORI

surprised when he began to fall — his descent was accompanied by a significant amount of blood, along with some handfuls of off-white matter that smelled horrendous.

Upon hitting the ground, he felt a sharp shock of pain across his back from shoulder to shoulder. *"FUTUO!"* Toyo screamed, revisiting this morning's back pain with a force he could have done without. Lying there for a short moment he started screaming at his body to get up, or to at least start secreting some sort of tasty juice so that his being eaten alive would at least be swift.

Struggling with the agony between his shoulders he saw that the creature was squirming around, whimpering in pain and trying to deal with a newly broken tooth and now exposed nerve. With its long, flat tail flailing in panic, the creature gradually recovered and redirected its attention towards him. As its heavy footsteps fell ever faster on its approach Toyo could only react as he did before, and grabbed onto the first thing presented to him — which this time happened to be one exposed tooth nerve, and another tooth.

Pain exquisite stabbed into the reptile's brain and the beast thrashed its head wildly, repeatedly slamming Toyo into the ground. With each thud his back flared bright with pain, followed swiftly by profanity with each breath he was able to muster. Spurred on by the fact that he could fight back he decided to stop just hanging on and began pulling with the hand that had grabbed the exposed nerve. Expecting some resistance he put everything he had into it, instead what happened was he uprooted the entire nerve out of its jaw with little difficulty. This caused him some panic as he now had what must be a half ton of enraged reptile, screaming in his face out of pain, whilst breathing frantically and bleeding on him while his other hand was still inside it.

The lizard-beast howled, its brain slowly registered everything that was happening in its mouth — a new experience that sat alongside it being the first time in its life it had such difficulty in eating something so small. A few more violent shakes was all it could manage though before it was blinded by pain and went limp as it slumped to the ground.

Toyo let go of the tooth in his other hand out of confusion and watched the creature try to make itself smaller in front of him through sheer willpower. He felt blood warm him as it stained his garments and the ground. Both predator and prey watched each other from their positions, unsure now of which was which. The beast reached a conclusion and made a scramble for the water to escape its failed meal — leaving behind a Toyo who was thankful for not being smothered to death by an enraged swamp creature.

Thinking to himself that these gloves were 'finally helpful' he came to accept that wearing them wasn't so bad after all, at least for now. He felt like beating his chest after besting a creature thrice his size — powerful... invincible. He then decided, with a grin, that this was the first time where he could actually take control of a situation. "I am Toyo! THE GOD OF GLOVES!" he screamed, and chased in after the monster.

Scrambling on the mossy banks, Toyo slipped into the water again and was propelled by sheer giddiness at the prospect of releasing his frustration out on something for once — his stomach was excited too at the thought of finally being filled. As he flailed in the water after his prey, the creature regained its resolve to fight when it saw that the battle had moved from land to its domain. Turning around it charged towards Toyo with its own personal fervor of wanting to tear this tiny, long, pink stick apart.

The creature made lots of noise rushing forward with all its speed to meet an equally enraged Toyo trying his best to scream as loud as he could. But an even louder crash could be heard off in the distance as trees split apart. Another great creature came into view, and as it broke through the tree line Toyo turned his head to look. At first he saw its tiny eyes and that it had a magnificent crest atop its head, a long, hooked beak, and sleek, slender body, and then he saw how much it looked like it wanted to kill. He was struck by the impression that it was like a beautiful black bird, if you baked a demon with all its desire to kill into a bird's soul. He was then struck by the fact that it did not seem to want to slow down.

Too intent on the annoying little pink stick the lizard-beast was oblivious to the feathered beast, who unfurled its wings and pressed them firmly alongside its body. Moments later, it began to emit a dark blue cloud of light from in front of its face which cascaded down its body as it picked up speed. The creature jumped from the bank, and the cloud surrounding it froze, covering its body in a light film of ice — it appeared to be locked in mid-air. Soon after, a slick tube of ice extended out of its front like a cannon, and the winged marvel was shot out of the ice bubble at an unbelievable speed. It hit the water with its claws outstretched, and snapped up Toyo's opponent with such an impact that a shock wave knocked him back hard onto the shore.

While it hurtled itself into the woods to consume its catch, Toyo quickly got to his feet and screamed, "Hey! HEY! BRING THAT BACK HERE! I WASN'T DONE WITH IT!" at the retreating figures. When it looked like they weren't going to return, he flailed his arms and kicked and screamed for some time out of anger and frustration.

Throughout all this, he'd failed to notice the pair of people that had been watching him from the nearby treeline.

All he heard was a dull *wop wop wop* before turning around and being hit full force in the chest with an oddly shaped piece of wood. As he dropped to the ground, a pair of humans emerged from a nearby tree and walked towards him, shaking their heads.

"<Well… that was certainly different, >" said the tall, svelte man.

The short, fat man whined, "<Why did we just waste all our efforts and lure our Hachu over just to save him?! All that time wasted, and now we have ventured into Zobukiri territory, for what? Why did we have to help? >"

The tall man calmly replied, "<Would you have preferred to handle his opponent for him? >"

"<I would have PREFERRED to have done nothing at all. >" The short man huffed his displeasure.

The tall man smiled warmly at him. "<I did not offer that as an option. Now hurry up and prepare him. >"

The short one took a step back from the boy and said, "<Is he… safe to approach? >"

Toyo was gasping and wheezing, trying hard to will air back into his lungs so he could scream some more profanities.

The tall one sighed. "<After all these years together and still no confidence in yourself. I'll deal with this then. >" He took the bag that the short one was holding, and from it he fished out a handful of paste covered leaves and then clamped them over the boy's mouth and nose.

Toyo took several deep breaths of the herbal mixture while his body fought tooth and nail. A few moments later, he stopped struggling and just started to smile as he began to enjoy the passing parade of naked fairy folk.

Helping the boy to his feet, the tall one stood back up and said, "<There, see? All better now, no more threat. >"

"<I'm still not sure if bringing him back is a great idea. >"

"<Whether it is a good idea or not is for Ani to decide. >" The tall one looked into Toyo's face and asked, "<Well now boy, would you like to come back home with us? >"

Toyo was wondering where the musical chirruping was coming from as his head lolled from side to side. Concluding that these magical new fairies had prepared a great feast in his honor as thanks for wearing pants, he let himself be led by the hand by the tallest one to the banquet.

INTEGRUM

As Mulat's body gathered momentum he took a moment, one of the few he had left, to admire the view of Orbis from one of its unique viewpoints. The rigid planning that went into the building of Orbis, the radial pattern of distinct city regions and its surrounding high walls that strictly controlled the flow of trade and people, were all things to be proud of. Colors and materials beautiful and plentiful made up his home city, and every time he saw it a small part of him could forget the fact that he had never ventured outside Orbis. Maybe if he had things would have turned out differently.

Trailing behind him was a gossamer strand that was connected to the large marble slab window sill in his chambers. When his body could not travel any faster he vanished, and there was a muffled clap from the air rushing to fill the now vacant spot. Mulat re-appeared moments later just a few feet from the ground and struck it with all the force of a gust of wind, while high above in his chambers the marble slab buckled and cracked like it had been hit with a great force.

Raising himself up from his prone position, without apparent effort or injury, he coughed up a small ball of blood inconspicuously onto the ground and then began walking like nothing had happened. He mumbled to himself, "I really should learn to add some grace to that process," as he looked towards the entrance gate of his walled-off garden.

Mulat's personal garden had been specially built on the ground just outside his chamber window to hide his comings and goings. The plants that grew there were of astonishing color and size, and were frequently commented on by any who got a glimpse inside the gated area. Mulat was the only one who knew that his blood was the reason they grew to such health, and merely took people's compliments about him having a green thumb with a quiet smile. Mentally rechecking that his outfit was presentable, and internally checking that his disheartened demeanor had diminished, he set out to sate his boredom and indulge in his 'hobby'. There never were very many people on the grounds save for the servants themselves, a scant few of the public who sought Integra Pol answers, and the odd convoy.

Making his way through the gate he walked out onto the pristine white grounds of the Integra Pol, which were featureless save for the bland structures that housed the servants of the Integra Pol. Just like those who inhabited the Integra Pol itself, its servants were also subject to much public thought. Those who chose to become servants of the Integra Pol were usually those who were lost, without purpose, or to whom life had become so weighed down with responsibility and debt that they needed an escape.

Any could be accepted, so long as they undertook the pledge to care for the Integra Pol and submitted themselves to a procedure where their minds were quietened so as to not be distracted by anything beyond the needs of their body and the need to serve. All servants acted the same, dreary but efficient, and if they were not serving the great minds of the Integra Pol then they were in their dull, bare home, asleep. At the end of their long contracts their minds were returned to them, along with a hefty sum, and sent on their way — many reported that the time was like a long sleep and had passed by almost as if overnight.

The entire area from the tip of the Integra Pol tower to the very edge of the Quadras was an eerie bone white. It was a famous rumor of rational citizens that upon its creation long ago, the architects had demanded only the whitest of marble to create the center of Orbis, while the public legend was that it was the worn down tooth of a giant animal. Admittedly the tower did look like an animal's tooth, especially at a distance, and the large observatory near the tip made it look like it was somehow chipped, but it was simply a legend. Both of these notions Mulat found ridiculous, but as always fact would always be stranger than fiction. Orbis, the largest city of the Integrum, had in truth sprung up around the Integra Pol, as would any source of power gather those seeking its comfort. The origins of the tower itself however were known only to the Divinitas'.

Making his way through the grounds of the Integra Pol, Mulat kept trying to not let his emotions get the better of him — knowing full well that once again they most likely would. Patient as a mountain, or impatient as a child — Mulat had never learned the in-between. In everything else he could not be faulted, but when it came to this he knew it was a weakness that only Juvo saved him from.

Mulat soon reached the edge of the outer yard, easily distinguished by the meeting point of the Integra Pol's pristine white grounds and the comparatively grubby brownish-grey of the Quadras'. He looked at the stark difference in color and construction, and then up at the Quadra that stood before him, the Quadra Lustrum. He then looked around at the other Quadras that encircled the Integra Pol, each one a paragon of their craft: Logicum, for reasoning and objective thought — Musicum, for the creation, playing, and appreciation of music — Culinum, for all stages of food from field to toilet — Lustrum, for pleasure and procreation. The Quadras were the second oldest buildings in all of the Integrum, save for the Integra Pol itself.

Even though no walls were erected to keep people from sauntering through one of the Quadras to the Integra Pol, and despite his own attempts at informing them, public superstition still largely dictated that to be there uninvited or uninitiated was akin to suicide.

Several feet in from the edge were dirt track marks on an otherwise pristine surface, made from what some would consider a rite of passage by those who wished to test their courage and strength. Usually though it was mostly those who had just overindulged in whatever Quadra they had just visited and were feeling an excess of high spirits.

The most direct path from Mulat's garden to the city was through the Quadra Lustrum, home of Erus Criso and her charges, which suited Mulat's purposes just fine as there was far more interesting fare than him to notice so he could walk without much concern. Taking stock of himself, he prepared to walk through the Lustrum grounds, and briefly wondered if it really was a good time to go out and explore — the reports of the mutations and a dangerous new drug called Cremo Faba, or Creba by the people of Orbis, were rising and needed his attention.

Frustration and loneliness were difficult enemies for Mulat, and this time they had won — he could not focus on work when he felt empty inside. He knew that people saw his stature and position, not the man. Perhaps if they saw him differently he would not need to go to such extremes, but that was life for him. Pushing aside his thoughts and worries, he performed his personal little ritual to acknowledge the crossing of the invisible divide and stepped over the threshold, bringing with him an excited emotional surge that he had hoped to quell. Even though self-control was of paramount importance to him, he always quietly thanked Kasmah for the gift to uncontrollably feel like a child on occasion.

Mulat quickly cleared the Quadras' territory and made his way to the First Ring of Orbis, the large main thoroughfare that circled all the Quadras. He had to pause for a moment, realizing he had let his emotional state cloud the practical necessities, such as where to start.... A moment's thought later helped him decide to actively seek someone out from the lesser districts. He felt most at ease when he felt useful, and so it made sense to seek those who needed it most. To be fully bare and to face the brunt of the emotional turmoil that his approach brought was not an experience many could endure.

Musing while walking through the crowds and streets, he ran through his thoughts with a focus that would put even the most obsessive on edge.

"Perhaps a beggar? No, I do not have the time required to get past their immediate need of comfort. Could incorporate my need to raise something and this project together, perhaps someone young? No, not really something that inherently needs fixing as it is not yet broken, and I do not have the time to bore through youthful skepticism — damage either happens before or after an event, 'during' is the transitory stage. Seeking a failed Quadra apprentice may be a better bet, at least then they have the understanding of attaining value and most likely a need to obtain it. Need

to trawl the —"

Mulat didn't get to finish his train of thought as he had to take one very short, quick and deliberate step backwards with a slight inclination to the left in order to dodge a blade from behind. It missed by mere, calculated, inches. With the attack dodged, he struck out behind him to wind his would-be assailant with an effortless elbow to the chest. He then proceeded to render the attacker unconscious by falling backwards onto him as he slid his elbow up the chest and across the man's neck, forcing his head into the ground with a satisfying crunch. Mulat's brain tried its best to re-acquire his focus to the physical reality of his being attacked, but was still musing over far more interesting thoughts.

What eventually caught his attention was silence, why had the noises of the city become muffled? "Ah," he said, his mind focusing to the *now* of the moment. This helped him notice for the first time that he was lying on somebody, and the well-kept walls of the large houses that enclosed the area indicated to him that he had not gone far beyond the Quadras. The clean paved streets beneath him also told him that this was most likely an area for the wealthy. "I suspect I am being mugged."

He contemplated something briefly, but decided against making this a quick event, opting instead for the more convoluted path of using far less of him than usual — more entertaining for him, and less risk of unwanted attention. "*Would appear that they've surrounded me and blocked off the alley. Going on footsteps makes a total of five, two pairs are left. Given width of alley and lack of breeze they must be fairly heavyset, male... What district am I in again?*" He shifted his body a little. "*This one feels rather well dressed, so not common thugs, but couldn't surprise me to any significant degree so not that experienced.*"

Sighing heavily, Mulat raised himself up to a full standing position to get a proper survey of the alley and saw the two pairs of men bearing down on him. "*No real scars or wounds so not simple brawlers. Paid assassins, high-brow muggers? Could just be guards, I might have wandered onto some protected property. Would damaging and then healing one of them be an acceptable project?*"

Mulat looked at both encroaching parties and said in a loud voice, "Now, how interesting can I make this, OR, more appropriately, how interesting will you make this for me? Fair warning though, not that I expect you to understand this: If you excite my body into an intense situation, and you can't make my emotional state match, I will get bored, which may make things complicated for all involved. Make me use my brain too so I can satisfy both parts of me." He paused for an afterthought. "Please."

The remaining four, unsure of this calm response to an obviously threatening situation, hesitated only momentarily before attempting to close the remaining distance.

Mulat smiled. "Ah, I see we are people with purpose. Well, I sense no real vesma within you all so I shall assume you to be hired mercenaries — making what is about to happen to you something to be classified as a profession related injury." His speech effectively and calculatingly angered the group — relying on the fact that most tough men, true or self-deluded, become riled up after failing to frighten their prey. One broke away and charged him, lunging with a surprising amount of passion.

Mulat simply shifted quickly sideways, dodging the strike, and then sharply brought his shoulder to connect with the attacker's face. Those remaining were startled at the deftness and skill displayed by a man whose face radiated unadulterated boredom.

Addressing the uninjured, Mulat began droning in innocent monotone. "There is danger in boredom, both mentally and emotionally for me — usually the danger is greater for others. So, bring some passion, otherwise I have to MAKE it interesting for me." He watched the men try to absorb his words whilst coming to terms with how he had dealt with their comrades so easily.

The one to the south of him, now alone due to his partner's prior impetuousness, balked and stood still, waiting for some sign from the other two. The remaining pair decided to attack in unison, while the lone man felt less than confident about joining in.

Both reached out to grab Mulat by the neck. "Please," began Mulat, snaking his hand out to grab one of their outstretched hands, and tugged on it sharply — making both men collide with minimal effort. "Less," continued Mulat. Maintaining his grip he continued the man's cranial journey into the nearby wall, and then brought his elbow sharply under the other's chin. "Predictable," completed Mulat.

The last of the attackers had finally readied his nerve and his weapon but kept checking his mind for reasons to run away. He then looked into the eyes of a man that was more upset at being bored than being attacked, and he saw them change.

Mulat's blood was now getting worked up and he could feel the heat travel around him. He knew what that signaled, and it made him sad. "I am sorry, really I am...." He breathed in deeply before shouting, "ATTACK me! Bring some passion, FIGHT for your life! DO NOT LET ME GET BORED, PLEASE!" Fear crept into his voice, this was now turning into something he hadn't wanted it to. Juvo had been away for far too long this time. All the attacker could do was turn and flee in terror.

Mulat sighed and placed his palms over his chest, mumbled softly under his breath, then stretched his arms out with hands down. A light green and ethereal heavy smoke fell from his hands, and as it hit the ground it raced forward to coalesce around the coward's feet, where it hardened, trapping him in place. As the man fell, a line of the smoke raced from his feet to his head, and made his descent stop short of smashing his nose into the pavement, locking him in a strange angle of stasis.

Fear gripped the man's chest as he struggled to hear footsteps for the longest time, only to discover a pair of feet appearing into his view without sound. He felt hands grab his back and he was pulled upwards, then turned around to face the man he had been paid to attack.

"I would admit to my desire of my wanting it to be something more, but life is as it is. No more, no less. Still, what need have you of fear in this moment? I have only asked you to be interesting." Mulat's voice then started to wobble as he continued, "Be interesting! What are you? Bored rich folk? A sickly family member needed money for medicine? Perhaps you are in a cult and this is some sort of ritual? Please don't tell me you are just hired assassins, because this has been one of the weaker attempts on my life in many a year — lame, like a hobbled horse. Do you understand the word lame? Do you understand the word 'bored'? Well?" Mulat's voice then started to swell with uncharacteristic emotion, "Well, I AM BORED! My equilibrium has not been re-established, so OUT WITH IT."

As Mulat spoke, the man became increasingly frightened by the lunatic in front of him. Trembling more and more, the man's brain finally reached the consensus to answer this crazed person and his words stumbled out in a panic. "I just wanted some money, and you seemed dressed fancy enough to have some! Please, let me be!"

"So now you lie to me? You think me so stupid as to not be able to read you? Why should I let you be? You attacked me didn't you? Are you not a man of conviction? Can you not see or plan for future eventualities? One must always make contingencies, mustn't one? In the end if it goes wrong you should always account for —"

The man blurted out, "Stop talking, please just stop talking. I'm scared alright? You wanted me scared and you got it, Sir. I promise I won't do this again, just please... please."

"NO! Do not promise what you cannot keep, I would deny no man the right to choose what he wants! I AM NOT THAT KIND OF MAN!" said Mulat angrily.

"Please! PLEASE! I DON'T WANNA DIE! I'M SCARED!" The man started gurgling and his breath became heavier out of fear of an impending demise.

In a flash the green mist dissipated. Mulat reached into the man's coat, pulled out one of his concealed daggers in a flash and thrust the handle into the man's open hand. Crushing the man's hand around the handle, Mulat then thrust himself onto the blade.

Mulat never relaxed his gaze on the man, and there was only a cursory acknowledgment in his expression that he had just been stabbed.

"Which are you more scared of now? Dying? Or Living?"

CHAPTER III

*"Mundus vult decipi,
ergo decipiatur."*

-Parting words of Malef, first Integra Divinitas of Kasmah

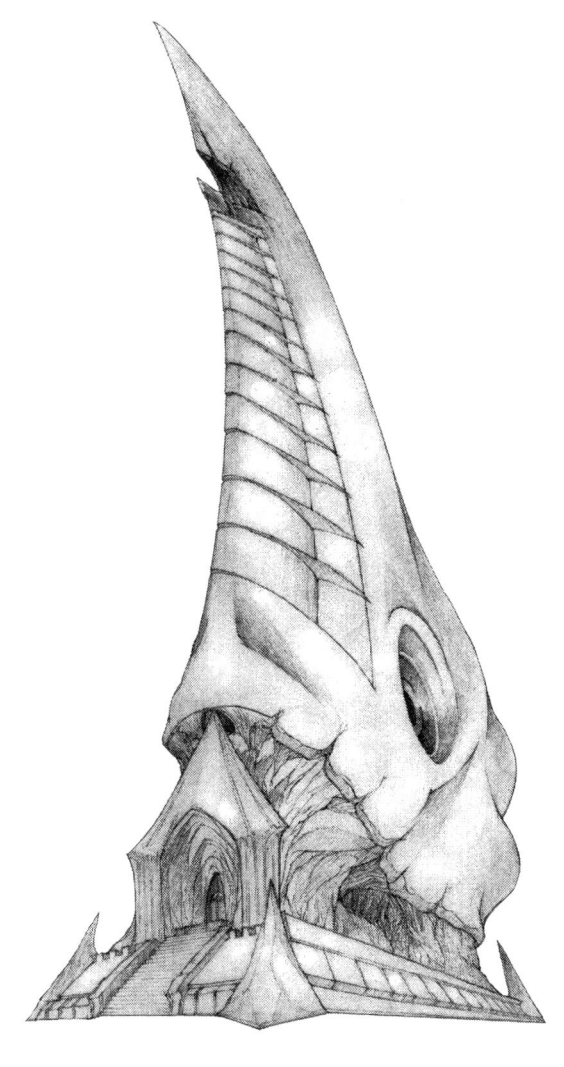

THE MAHARAAN EXPANSE

The great Vios Ocean, which split Kasmah into East and West, was a place where all would pay reverence to its waters. For those in the Maharaan it was a sacred place that held the true waters of life from which every living thing was born, and where the water of all living things returned when death came for them.

Nujah, keeper of the sky-river, and Vios' emissary to the land, was the being that all in the Maharaan praised, for allowing life to live on the land. When the sky-river overflowed with an abundance of life he would let its waters fall from the sky to share — a beautiful cycle of ever-changing life, not death.

The Vios Ocean was too turbulent, and infested with enormous and strange creatures, to cross, however there were some who knew how to traverse it in safety. The main enablers of ferrying goods and people were the Nauta family, whose family secret allowed them to control virtually all cross-trade throughout the Vios. For the farthest parts the Nauta did not cater to: The Gadori had special times in the year where sections would freeze over and allow safe travel, but in the Maharaan there was no safe passage — unless one was willing to expose themselves to the extreme heat and go north to the dry-beds, where virtually all met their end.

Because of this rift there was a separation of people in the Maharaan like nowhere else, two clans — the Harat in the west, and Jara in the east. The Harat were a loose collection of nomadic clans who wandered the desert and lived in harmony with themselves. They adhered to guiding rules that were agreed upon through discourse of the heads of the clans for they saw that they needed a code of conduct, but saw no need for a ruler.

The Jara in the east however were a ruling clan who held dominion through force, for the people in those lands had a far harsher life to live. Fighting was a necessity — they had to battle not only each other but also the land for resources, as creatures great and powerful roamed the east. For them battle was honorable and noble, and in most cases the best way to test the character of man and woman alike. Through birth and bond the Jara clan had ruled for as long as any could remember, but at all times they sought peace in a harsh land.

Those who lived alongside the Vios in the Maharaan were, like most who lived anywhere along the Vios, traders and fishermen. They had little dealings with the Harat or the Jara, they viewed themselves as people of the ocean.

It was here on the eastern side of the Vios Ocean in the Maharaan where a curious young boy stood in a hut that was strewn with strange plants and tiny insects of all kinds. He leaned over a curio and said, "Ooh, that's pretty, I've never seen one like that before. When did you fish for that?"

"Fish?" replied the youngest of the three Integra Natura that had taken up residence within the hut on the beach. All three were huddled around something the boy couldn't quite tell what they were so interested in, but they seemed very insistent on looking at it.

"For that starfish." The boy pointed at the thing splayed out on the table. "It's kinda hairy, why's that? All the ones I know are all slimy and stuff."

The two older Natura looked at the youngest one and gave a simple nod. The youngest one then stood up and walked over to what the boy was looking at. "Oh, that. That's not a starfish."

"Yes it is! I've seen LOADS of them: Big ones, small ones, spiky ones, smooth ones — just never hairy ones. Things in the ocean don't need hair." The boy then laughed as only a child could laugh. "That'd be silly! A whale with a haircut."

The young Natura smiled. "I'm sure it would be, but that, young Lik, is actually a plant."

The boy peered closer. "Really?" He had heard the rumors about the people from the Integra Pol being weird and having lots of weird things, and these three women definitely proved that. But Lik liked weird.

"Yes, here let me show you." She fetched a small blade and cut off a small segment and held it up for him. "See? It's hard and sticky inside, no squishy bits."

The boy inspected it closely and was amazed, "Shaaaa...." He looked it over and under. "Where's it from?"

"From a place in the western Maharaan, across the Vios Ocean. It's from the desert of the red sands, and there are many more like it. It belongs to a class —"

"Gah! It stinks!" The boy scrunched up his nose and tried to wave the plant away.

The young Natura chuckled. "Yes, this plant eats insects. Its smell is how it attracts them."

"There are plants that can eat things?!" The boy went wide-eyed.

"Correct."

The boy thought about this for a moment. "Why's it look like a starfish if it's a plant?"

"That is a very smart question Lik. Well, why does —" The oldest Natura coughed loudly, interrupting her and prompting the young Natura to hurry up. She put on her best smile and said to the boy, "Lik, we are very grateful to your father and the hospitality he has extended, but right now there is something important that we need to tend to. If it is not too much of an imposition, could you please ask him if we could have provisions for a long journey?"

The boy beamed. "Sure! I'll go ask him." With that the boy ran out, intent on making a pit-stop at his friend's place to tell him about what he'd just seen and how the young pretty lady with the short blonde hair and blue eyes had called him smart!

"Be quicker next time Fetu, or do you think this isn't an emergency," said the oldest Natura. In her years she had grown wise, but her face was one that had frowned far too much in life.

Fetu walked back to what they were all crowded around before. "Well none of us know what it is yet, and until then it doesn't hurt to be kind, Pala."

Pala huffed the disapproving huff of someone who had lost the necessity for tact and kindness long ago. "If you wanted to be like that you should have chosen to join the Humanus instead of the Natura."

Sercu, the last Natura to speak, was the sternest of the three and jumped in to play her part as mediator. "That's enough you two, we have a damn job to do."

They all returned their focus to the thing on the table. It was a rather simple device that suspended three vesma crystals of a specific alignment on a string, and was used to detect mass vesma disturbances. In practice the crystal on the left would point to indicate direction, the one on the right would vibrate to indicate distance, and the center one would change color to indicate intensity. Both the left and right one were acting as if something had happened at two different places simultaneously, while the center crystal kept a bright yellow color — indicating something unknown to the Natura. Seeing that made Pala think some very unhappy thoughts, worried Sercu, and excited Fetu.

Sercu peered at the direction and distance crystals and said, "One of the places must be..." she waved her hand at Fetu, "Get me a map!" Fetu fetched the map and they placed the instrument on top of their general location and began to calculate where exactly the places might be.

Before they could finish pinpointing the first one Pala said, "Toka-Rutaa." Sercu and Fetu looked at her, unsure of what that place was. "It's where the Heca clan lives."

"How do you know that?" asked Fetu.

Pala replied, "I've been there exactly once, a LONG time ago. That is my entire life's quota for going to that place. I will NOT go there again, and neither will any of you."

Pala's voice was both strong and scared, but that didn't stop Sercu from arguing. "You lead this cadre and you won't even do your duty?"

"My duty is YOUR survival first."

Sercu firmly said, "You don't even know for sure if the event happened at Toka-Rutaa, there is a lot of distance between here and there."

"There is NOTHING between here and there, and I can assure you that if anything was going to happen, it would definitely be there. We are not going to investigate Toka-Rutaa, if the Integra Pol wants to punish me later for it then I'll gladly take it in exchange for not going."

Fetu knew better than to argue with Pala when she was like this, and Sercu always respected the chain of command, but they knew that they couldn't ignore the call in entirety. Sercu and Fetu looked once more at the map and saw that the second place was in the 'sea on the sands'. All three shared a look of concern.

Pala eventually broke the silence. "That's fine. The Chamu spawning grounds we can deal with."

Sercu was content with the conclusion, Fetu however was not. "HOW is dealing with one of the Maharaan's greatest dangers somehow better than visiting some small remote village?"

Pala looked at her. She wasn't in the mood for an argument, especially not about this. "Experienced or not, you are Integra Natura, not Humanus! Handling creatures great and small, powerful and weak, is your CALLING and DUTY. The chamu are creatures like anything else, and we know how to deal with them."

Seeing the old and the young clash once more, Sercu put her hand on Fetu's shoulder in the hopes to bring some comfort and clarity. "We are Natura, and in handling the animal and plants of Kasmah there is both beauty and danger. If you shun either one, then you will forget what true beauty or danger is."

Pala was right, and Fetu knew that, but this was one of those times she had to just accept that she wouldn't understand why. "I'm sorry Pala. I did not mean to question your judgment. I just did not expect my first excursion beyond the Integra Pol to include…" she looked at the device on the table, "This." Fetu looked around the hut crestfallen. She didn't want to go, it had been so peaceful and wonderful here. "But what are we going to do with all our samples here? We can't take them with us. How are we supposed to just leave them here to die?"

Sercu replied, "I am sure Lik's father will extend his hospitality a little further given the healing we've provided. So long as they follow our instructions, everything should be fine."

"But some of these took me ages to find and maintain!"

Pala interrupted. "That's enough Fetu, Sercu. You wanted to answer the call, so let's answer it. Pack and get prepared, we need to leave by dawn."

ӜӜӜӜӜӜӜӜӜӜӜӜӜӜӜӜ

Whuffle. This particular noise was accompanied by some nuzzling, and a further whuffle.

Kahli was confused, what sort of a thing goes whuffle? Half-awake in her dream-like state she opened her eyes and looked up, and found that she was being stared at by a large shaggy beast. It looked... happy, oddly enough. Casually she raised herself up into a sitting position and kept looking at it while trying her best to wish her brain back into functioning.

After a few moments of staring at each other the creature decided to once again go, *whuffle*. Her brain decided to stop the staring contest and she looked around to see where she was. She discovered herself to be on a flat, barren and blackened landscape — as if the world itself had burned to a cinder. She ran her hand over the ground and played with what she thought was dirt but turned out to be fine black sand for a while, before another *whuffle* got her attention.

She brought the beast's large head back into view and saw that it was giving her an intense stare of interest. Some sliver of memory danced in her mind, and from it she plucked the word 'Wija' and she decided to see if she could unpack more out of it.

They had large heads and shoulders, stood just a head taller than an average person, had bulbous noses, and tiny dark eyes nestled in a bushy layer of fine off-color fuzz on their face. Their bodies were essentially barrels on legs like small tree trunks, each with large stubby toes, and a thick hide of what started from birth as pure white but became marred over time. Attached to their neck was a taut skin sack that they would fill with water and fat that they could use to slowly and steadily walk for days without tiring in the oppressive heat. They could be found roaming the Maharaan freely, as they had no natural predators, and were known to never attack anything or anyone.

Unpacking the memory confirmed that a wija was indeed what was standing in front of her. While this information was welcome to Kahli, she still wondered why she wasn't frightened of this strange creature appearing out of nowhere for no reason. Then again, beyond just looking at her, it wasn't really doing much to be scared of.

Seeing as the wija wasn't about to start doing anything else, and since she felt it safe enough, she briefly contemplating the dreamlike qualities of her surroundings. It felt like she might be close to another dream, if she wasn't in one already. Or again? It was hard to tell the difference or even think while feeling so tired. While she could remember being unconscious, she could not actually remember sleeping or resting. Everything had been filled with such a strange miasma of broken memories and feelings.

She stood up and looked around. *"Where am I?"* she thought. There was nothing recognizable as far as she could see and her last memory was of... somewhere. Home?

She blinked and tried to fight to regain her thoughts, during which she had to ignore the wija that had now decided to nuzzle her. It was quite persistent. It kept trying to gently put Kahli into the warm nook between its neck and shoulders, but she kept pushing it away. *"Hold on, wija avoid people... don't they? Why is this one here?"*

Then the wija rubbed its large face up against hers, and out of nowhere Kahli felt rage and anger — the hatred and bitterness she felt towards... something! She couldn't remember what it was, but she remembered that the world itself deserved to descend upon it and swallow it whole. It filled her with an anger so pure that she wanted to strike the ground in an effort to burn her hatred into the landscape itself. She wanted to hunt it down and destroy it, to erase it from existence! Exactly what that thing was though she couldn't recall, all she knew was that it felt good to hate.

The hate filled her, and what sense she had regained was lost in the purity of the emotion. It felt alive in her, fueling her. She looked around with eyes of hate at the world, searching for that something she couldn't remember. The hate felt real, so real, as if some part of her was on fire. Wisps of flame crept out from her eyes as she tried to wrestle with what was happening inside her. The wija, sensing her distress, tried with renewed effort to comfort her with a tenderness belying its great size.

Her eyes fell on the innocent wija — Kahli's hatred had found its outlet, and she struck it as hard as she could. After the loud crack of fist and skull she uncaringly watched it fall to the ground with a heavy whimper and a soft thud. It was a display of cruelty unexpected, but in her hate-addled mind Kahli felt all was right. Her rage felt sated, and she felt the fire inside her dwindle.

As the burning inside her died away it was replaced with the sounds of the wija, wheezing and trying to stand. The sounds of the wounded creature almost broke Kahli's heart, and where the hatred once was, was now filled with feelings of wrong-doing so powerful that she fell to her knees. "I... I'm sorry, so sorry... please..." she stammered as she reached out to it. The wija looked at her, its eyes filled with confusion.

But there was no fear, no hatred — only love, somehow.

Kahli's own eyes and heart filled with sorrow.

STOP!

Kahli was surprised to find she was crying. *"Why am I sad?"* she wondered, and tried to think about what could have happened to make her feel that way. Burrowing through her recent memories revealed nothing as everything slipped away, and she felt like she kept remembering and forgetting everything in an instant. She blinked, and was surprised to find herself looking down at a wija. She wondered what it was doing there and where it had come from.

Noticing that it was wounded she checked to see where the injury had come from, wanting only to help it. She saw that it had suffered a great blow to its head, but beyond mopping up a little of the blood with her clothes there wasn't much else she could do and felt a deep sadness that she couldn't do more. She found herself being rewarded with a tentative lick on her hand and was surprised that she felt great relief from it, and then confused as to why that made her start crying tears of relief.

Wiping her nose and face on her spare sleeve she looked around, and saw a barren and black landscape — simply black sand as far as she could see. *"Where am I?"* she thought to herself. *"Am... hm... Does it...?"* her chaotic thoughts and fractured memory stopped her from completing any sentence, even to herself. Trying to get a grip on her mind she forced it to make sense by sheer will, steeled herself, and then stood up. She was a little woozy on her feet, but she wasn't about to be deterred NOW, so she randomly picked a direction and started walking. All the fight she had left was put into that one decisive act, and so she ambled across the desert while the line between memory, thought and feeling became muddied.

A distant onlooker would have only seen a taller than average brown-skinned young woman of medium build with brown eyes and long black hair dragging her feet, adorned in tattered desert robes, while being followed by a large wija in symbiotic synchronicity. It stopped when she stopped, started when she started, and even gave her an encouraging nudge every now and then. Mile after mile went by under Kahli's heavy footfall, each step leaving a perfect imprint in the pristine black sand, and each soon covered over by one of the wija's own.

Feelings of regret and rage rose and fell as she walked, but nobody could have witnessed the battle within. Her mind kept trying to fight itself to piece together everything but it could only remember emotions, fierce and powerful. Each time an emotion came, it would come with such strength as to feel like it would tear Kahli's heart out of her chest from sheer intensity — but just as quickly she would feel it drain away from her, step after step.

Time had abandoned her long ago and she felt like every step was the first she had ever taken, but at least she was moving.

Somehow. Her body however could not be fooled or fueled by feelings alone and soon her body began to sag and her head drooped low, changing the scenery from a horizon of pristine blackness to simply a dark background. It didn't change again until she came to the edge of the black sand and a different color entered her view. She didn't know how far she had walked, where she had walked from, or even where to. All she had was her last memory of it being dusk, and now it was night.

Curious, she looked along the edge where the two colors met and noticed that the black sand curved around in both directions against the new shore of tan. She looked back, oblivious to the wija that had followed, to see huge footsteps trailing off far into the horizon — it made her feel like she was a giant striding the land that had just walked out of a sea of black sand.

The darkness that followed the dipping sun made the black sand even more inviting — like an ocean of black you could swim in and be washed clean. She turned to look at the new shore of tan and forced her body forwards, stopping several steps from where the two sands met. Confronted with the beauty of both she could not help but notice that the colors had mixed and blurred at some points. It made her think that what she was looking at now was some painter's mistake, made when the lands were first formed. She wanted to cross that beautiful blunder and explore something new.

Moving to close the distance between her and it felt hard, but invigorating. She reached the edge and braced herself, and when her foot landed on the opposite side her face contorted into a howling beast's and she screamed. A rush of anger gripped her as she fell to her knees and she began punching the ground with all the fury of a wild animal. With each strike against the yellow sand, loud piercing sounds sang out as grains of sand screeched in friction against grains of sand, leaving small craters that quickly filled back in.

A small part of her hoped that the world was strong enough to handle it, while another hoped it would forgive her if it wasn't. The wija though was not afraid, it could never be afraid of her, and simply sat and watched as Kahli's screams grew louder and louder and her strikes more furious.

Steam soon began rising off her body, and the more she struck the tanned sand, the more steam came. More and more it rose, until finally a large burst of flame erupted from her back and lit up the night sky.

As she fell once more to the ground, again the inky black of unconsciousness claimed her, but not before she noticed the wija making its way towards her.

With her desire to let the black sand and night bring her a comfort she desperately needed, she whispered softly to the wija.

"Please kill me...."

Ж Ж Ж Ж Ж Ж Ж Ж Ж Ж Ж Ж Ж Ж Ж

"Kahli... Kahli!" shouted her mother.

Kahli was so engrossed in watching the flame in the middle of their hut that she had completely tuned out her mother trying to get her attention. She looked up and saw all of her family sitting close by and felt relief, but she wasn't really sure why that was.

"Sorry mom, got distracted."

"Yes, I can see that. So do you want to hear about today's hunt or not?"

She blurted out, "Yes!" excitedly. Her mother was strong, capable, and always willing to let Kahli bask in the glory that she'd felt that day. It was always the highlight of seeing her mother. Well, that and the Jackals always behaved a little better when she was around.

Cleanse yourself; hear the truth...

Kahli felt time skip, and then the whole world felt like it had shifted slightly.

Her mother screamed, "Stupid cow! Why I ever thought taking

care of you for Gola was a smart idea I'll never bloody know."

"Wait... what?" she mumbled.

Kahli's mother chuckled to herself. "No wonder you were so cheap, you're slower than a wounded chig-chag! I don't know what that stupid bitch Gola sees in you."

"I'll be better!" Kahli had meant to say she wanted to hear her mother's story and was confused by what came out instead.

"Good, because I DON'T have to put up with you."

Kahli looked sideways and saw that, as always, the Jackals were riveted to the floor and giving mother their most attentive expression. She looked at them to make sure that she had done a good enough job taking care of them as she felt the need to, but what filled her mind when she saw them was how she hated them. Always thrusting her face into the ground, beating her just because she couldn't fight back — such vicious little bastards filled with malice and spite, just like their mother.

"Why don't we just kill her? She's so BORING," said Jak.

Kahli's mother harped back, "Shut up you little shit! Don't think I don't know you play with her behind my back."

"But you said she's ours!"

Both of the Jackals got a slap. "Yeah! But if you leave any bloody marks on her then Gola would kill us you morons! Now quit it!"

"Wait... this... isn't —"

BREATHE...

LAND OF THE GADORI

Toyo was still feeling the effects of the hallucinogenics and marveled at all the wonderful food he was stuffing into his face — which turned out to be everything that he could find in front of him, edible or otherwise. His frenzy resulted in the occasional necessity for the short, fat hunter to pull Toyo's hands away from certain things, lest he attempt to eat spoon, bowl, and at one time his own hand — along with several other items that onlookers felt had questionable nutritional content. Given the speed and force at which Toyo was shoving food into himself, the short hunter felt if he wasn't there to stop him that he'd have succeeded in his extracurricular consumption expedition.

Being made caretaker of a boy who was trying to replace all his organs with food made the short hunter grumpy, and he was more than willing to voice his dissatisfaction to anybody in ear-shot. Luckily those ears were plenty in supply — attracted purely by the loud arrival of some pale boy who seemed to be having trouble discerning the meaning of pants.

The short hunter happily complained, droning on and on about how helpful he was even to strangers, while also trying to ignore the fact that nobody was paying attention to him. They'd all come to gawk at the boy with the hands of iron, eating as if his mouth was holding a party for everything that was within arm's reach and attendance wasn't optional.

As the spectacle continued on for some time, it eventually reached a crescendo when Toyo suddenly went stiff. After a few moments a look of confusion passed over his face, followed quickly by extreme panic. Flailing around on his seat he tried to stand up, got confused as to the exact number of legs he actually had, and fell over sideways onto the grass. Hoisting himself up onto all fours he started to feel scared as his body reacted violently to nothing in particular, while at the same time everything in existence.

In this state all Toyo's brain could provide him with was the thought of "*Oh no... not again!*" as he tried to brace for his old friend, pain. The laughter he could hear started to really worry him, and for a brief moment he feared that the trees had come to disapprove of their false god and were punishing him for his lofty aspirations. A final look of confusion passed his face, before he vomited for the first time in recorded memory. He couldn't stop himself trying to look down at his mouth in disbelief as what he once ate came out in a semi-liquid form and with uncontrollable force.

The resulting distress of his body, along with his muddled mental state, created a myriad of strange facial expressions which made quite the spectacle for those gathered. Unsure of what to do he kept trying to stand up, while still vomiting, with little success. As the laughter grew, it increased his confusion and fear while his stomach continued to try and empty its contents, even though it had several heaves ago emptied itself of everything save its lining.

In the midst of his throes, the crowd went abruptly silent as a collective guilt silenced the laughter — the tall, svelte hunter had returned. The short hunter pushed his way through the crowd from his seated position and quickly said, "<Thank the night-sparks you are here Tagai. I was trying my best to stop him, but he wouldn't listen! >"

Tagai gave him a disapproving look. "<Be quiet Hoba, I saw what you were doing. And now, if you are done with your guilt, perhaps we could help the boy? Or do you prefer him pasted with his own filth? >" He sat down across the table from Hoba.

A chastised Hoba ran to Toyo's aid and tried to lift him back up onto his chair, and after a few false starts he had to settle with laying him out on the table. As Hoba wiped away the crust from Toyo with the edge of his clothing, he barked, "<Someone bring me some Monma juice. >" The quickest thinking youth of the crowd ran to find some, while the others who knew what was most likely going to happen next ran off to get their friends.

Toyo's vomiting spree had the unexpected side-effect of returning the rest of his faculties, allowing him to finally take in his surroundings... with questionable clarity. Groggily surveying the area, he finally noticed, with a slack jaw, that he was sitting on what could only be an enormous tree stump. He assumed it to be a makeshift table as food was strewn about everywhere, which upon seeing made his stomach want to punch him for reasons unknown to him.

As his brain fired up and gave him more focus he noticed that he was surrounded by a group of smiling people with slightly dark, milky colored skin, black hair of varying lengths, faces with sharp features, and all wearing odd outfits made from animal hides. Nervous, he pretended that he hadn't noticed them, and was awestruck when his eyes fell on an enormous bulging tree with branches that spread up for what seemed to be forever. The sense of scale was so out of proportion to what he had experienced so far that he took some time to take it all in.

Looking around he saw that he was in the middle of an enormous clearing that had a lovely cool breeze, and that there were some flowering and fruiting plants surrounding the enormous tree. The only foliage that could be seen until the edge of the clearing where the empty space was stopped by a wall of dense forest. The more he took in of his surroundings, the more he felt out of place with his heavy fur outfit and iron hands.

Toyo reasoned that he must have amazing survival instincts, given everything so far, and that he must have found these people in his sleep... somehow. He still found it hard to reconcile any facts or possible links from his being attacked by that lizard creature and the now. But firstly, he was worried as to how he got where he was. *"I think these people fed me, so... can't be all bad."* Casting his gaze to one side, his brain immediately went 'friend' as he looked at the short, fat hunter, but felt confused by the conclusion. Why was he 'friend'?

A young man carrying a large, wide and white rigid flower burst through the crowd of people and ran up to the supposed 'friend' and passed it to him. Making his way over to Toyo he placed the interesting flower-cup in front of him and gestured that he should drink — Toyo could see that it was filled with some frothy white liquid. Toyo looked at the cup and regretted doing so instantly

118 | CHAPTER III - LAND OF THE GADORI

when he felt his stomach decide to renew its efforts to void itself of even its empty space.

"<Now now, that's enough of that, >" Hoba said to Toyo, grabbing the back of his head and yanking hard. With his jaw now forced open the hunter poured the monma juice down Toyo's throat, and in his weakened state all Toyo could do was splutter a little at first. Panic filled him again as the juice accelerated towards his gullet, and he awaited the inevitable objection his stomach would have to the new liquid guest. When Hoba had finished emptying the contents and released the boy, Toyo scrambled off the tree table and away from it, feeling like his stomach had been filled with liquid wood. Bracing himself once more he was surprised when nothing else came up, and that after a while his mouth and throat began to relax until they eventually went numb. He wasn't sure how he felt about that.

Wiping the white crust from his mouth he looked up at the short man and asked, "What did you just give me?" Hoba and Tagai both looked at each other over the tree stump table and shared a hurried conversation.

After appearing to reach some sort of conclusion, Tagai then looked at Toyo, and after a protracted silence, said, "<Um... what? >"

"Wait... what?" asked Toyo.

"<Shit, >" Tagai said to himself.

"What are you saying?" replied Toyo. It had been a difficult time and his mind was trying to cope with the events of strange hallucinations, ensuing vomiting, actually meeting PEOPLE, and now not being able to communicate. That last fact made him wonder if his mouth was ever going to do anything useful.

Tagai stood up and said, "<Hoba, keep an eye on him so he doesn't do anything stupid while I go get Ani. >" He then made his way through the crowd.

Sighing at being left with baby-sitting again, Hoba plopped down next to Toyo and tried to help calm the boy down with smiles and touching him gently as he helped the boy to a seat next to him. He attempted to hold his hand to reassure him, but ended up yelping and cursing when he touched the iron hands. Toyo jumped back and listened to him fire off some syllables that made some people in the crowd look at the short hunter disapprovingly.

"<What was that?>" Hoba asked, now sucking his burning fingers.

Toyo looked down at his gloves and saw a faint outline of white frost where the man's hand had touched. The crowd stopped chuckling and their expression turned from mirth to inquiry now that things had taken a different turn. Toyo waved his gloves back and forth in the air, trying to see if there was anything more to them, but all that happened with each wave was that Hoba and the crowd backed away a little bit more each time as if he were holding some sort of weapon. He kept inspecting them with deep interest, when suddenly he was pulled hard backwards onto the ground. His forearms were quickly pinned to the ground by two staffs with hooked ends wielded by two serious-faced men. Men to whom jokes were nothing more than mere words without orders, and therefor valueless.

He tried to struggle against the sudden capture but discovered that he was as weak as a newborn, he also tried to voice his objection, but couldn't as the wind was knocked out of him. He stopped struggling when he was surprised to see a person with pale skin like his own come into view.

"<See Ani? Told you that you'd find this interesting,>" said Tagai, to a rather small, elderly and wizened female with a face that could only be described as distinguished and determined.

The old woman merely uttered, "Humph."

"<He was attacking a swamp hachu!>" cried Hoba, nursing a sore hand.

Tagai said, "<Well, to be accurate, he was attacked first, then it ran away, and then he attacked it.>"

"<Did he now?>" replied Ani, bringing herself down to inspect Toyo from head to toe with deep interest — she held his chin and turned his head left and right, evaluating his body like one would livestock. While tracing her fingers down his arm she paused when she found the strange fusion of flesh and metal on his wrist. Cautiously she touched it, and the glove rippled gently with a small wave of what looked like a thousand miniscule blades.

Ani did not flinch or show any sign of pain as her fingers kept moving up to the tip of his middle finger. When her hand left the glove, it went back to its usual smooth surface. She noticed that there was no blood on his gloves or on her fingers, but she definitely felt like some had been drained from her. "<Hm...>" she said, bent over a now puzzled Toyo.

Hoba pointed at the gloves and shouted, "<That! What was that?! >"

Tagai, worried, knelt next to Ani and inspected her hand for any sign of injury. Ani was deep in thought and completely oblivious to the attention. "<Strip him, >" she commanded.

The two hunters swiftly went to work on the pinned boy. They opened up Toyo's coat, removed his pants and soon had him laying on his back, essentially naked for all to see. Ani continued examining the boy in great detail and her fingers dutifully traversed up and down his chest, sides and inner thighs.

Toyo was far from happy at not being able to fight back, while the looks of shock on people's faces as they looked on only deepened his humiliation. "<He's nothing but skin and bone! How is he even alive? >" Hoba commented. Ani ignored his outburst and continued uninterrupted.

Toyo began to shiver as he felt the cold breeze caress his body and he wondered how the *valde* these people kept so warm with such little clothing. Tired of the indignation he struggled with renewed vigor, only to be forced back down hard onto the ground by what he had come to think of as the anti-jesters. Ani ignored this outburst as well, as she didn't recognize Toyo at this point to be anything more than a slab of meat to be poked and prodded.

Toyo tried his best to endure but he was now beginning questioning whether or not being alive was a worthwhile venture. It had only been perhaps a day or two since he first woke up, and with everything he had experienced so far, life had shown him very little to look forward to. Even the immediate past, what with the time taken from feasting to vomiting, and then to this quite invasive fondling, did not paint a pretty picture. Past and present were none too bright, and the future still looked like the only thing that it would bring was more of an old, prodding, wrinkly woman.

Under the 'oohs and aahs' of nosy onlookers, Toyo began to question his original thought that the short, fat man was somehow his 'friend', but it was simply another contradiction and complaint he could add to an already ever-increasing pile. None of this made sense. *"Didn't they feed me? Why are they doing this? Am I supposed to be a guest? Prisoner?"* he thought. He began wishing for the simple and happy time of chasing after some lizard beast to rip it apart. That was at least fun, for a little while anyway.

He played that short battle over and over in his mind in an attempt to not think of what was happening, that was until another event reared its ugly head — one he wanted to never remember or experience ever again, resurfaced. A surge was building, and he could feel his soul preparing itself for a familiar journey. He tried to look on the bright side of things. *"Well, at least now I know what's going to happen next."* That was his last thought as the surge ripped through him, generating forceful spasms that startled everyone and almost knocked the anti-jesters off him. After several quick-fire surges, the poles holding Toyo down started to groan under the strain, and everyone started to look worried.

Ani had seen enough. She gripped Toyo firmly by the chin, looked him straight in the eye, and said, "Be quiet," before slapping him very hard. Toyo, shocked by both the reaction and being talked to in his own language, felt his mind begin to calm and the surges subside. Looking straight at her he wasn't sure what was more surprising — the fact that she had stopped the surges by simply slapping him, or that she spoke his language.

"You can talk?" said Toyo.

Ani replied, "Of course I can talk. What a stupid question."

"I mean… you can talk the way I do."

"Are we talking any differently than Hoba or Tagai here?" she said, gesturing to the two men that had brought him here. At the mention of their name the two hunters took up positions next to Ani and looked ready to strike. A hurried exchange between the three took place as Ani told them to restrain themselves, that he was no real threat, to stop worrying and to let the boy dress himself. All information that would have been great comfort to Toyo, had he been able to understand anything they were saying.

Ani signaled to the two large men holding Toyo down and they released him. Now free, he sprung to his feet in an effort to show them he was not a weakling and gave them all his best battle face. It lasted for as long as it took him to remember that he was naked.

After his attempts to regain his dignity via putting on pants, Toyo pointed at the two men and said, "Why can't I understand them?!"

"Are you going to keep asking stupid questions that aren't the actual ones you want to ask?" replied Ani.

"What?"

Ani harrumphed. "So much for expecting intelligent conversation. Perhaps, you would like some help?"

Toyo wished the old lady would make sense. "What, help to ask questions?"

A curt, "Yes," was the reply he got.

"... I'm not stupid you know."

"I've yet to see evidence to the contrary."

He looked around. "Um...." The silent gaze of the crowd did little to help him feel confident, but it had been nothing but bad so far so he sat back down at the tree table and decided that not fighting any further was the best option. "Sure?"

"Why did you phrase that like a question? Dear boy, you aren't doing very well. Here's a tip, what you want to know is how, and why, you and I can understand each other, but nobody else. Correct?" He nodded. "I'm just talking in your tongue, that's all."

Her pointing out a specific organ to him made him squeak. "My tongue?"

The old woman looked at him like he was stupid and then shook her head. "Ah, sorry. I haven't had anyone to speak it with for so long that I forget some mannerisms. I meant your language."

"Language?"

"Do you not know what a language is?" Ani was now worried that the boy had suffered some sort of head trauma.

Toyo however was not happy at being spoken to like an idiot. "Of course I know what a language is!"

"Given the questions you are asking, you don't seem to know much of anything."

Toyo reached for all his knowledge on 'language' to shove down the old woman's throat, and found only a blank. Frustrated, he dived back into his brain to dig up something, anything, all the while unaware that he had already started speaking in a soft far away voice. "A way of referencing concepts, actions, and objects within a communicative medium to help organize others towards a unified goal. Broadly viewed as an attempt to provide structure and rules to what is in essence a process dependent on osmotic learning. Emotional checkpoints and expressions of —"

Ani had noticed the lack of expression in the boy's face while he spouted all this knowledge from nowhere and walked over to stand in front of where he was seated. She flicked him lightly on the forehead and asked, "Are you still with us?"

Toyo took a few moments before his face returned to normal. "... what did you want again?" He began to feel a discomfort in his gut and clutched at his stomach, which slowly blossomed into mute pain.

Noticing the expression on Toyo's face, Ani grabbed him stoutly by the shoulders and told Tagai to hold the boy's hips still. With both points held tightly Ani twisted his upper body clockwise, and from Toyo's confused face came a burp that could only be described as both sonorous and protracted.

"What... was that?" he asked.

"The monma juice." Nothing on his face indicated he understood what she had just said. "Sorry, the drink from the flower they gave you to stop you throwing up. It can lead to a lot of air getting trapped in the stomach, sometimes it needs to be squeezed out."

"Oh.... Um, thanks?" replied Toyo hesitantly. His eyes glazed over all of a sudden and Ani tried to get his attention again. But all her efforts were for naught — the boy had gone catatonic.

Ani addressed Tagai. "<Hm, you've definitely found an odd one. You found him in Iro'Kamun you said? >"

"<Yes, >" Tagai replied.

"<That is Zobukiri territory, but he is obviously from the Integrum. Could he be an escaped prisoner of theirs? >" Tagai and Hoba looked at her like she was mad to even consider such a thing. The Gozuri had not heard anything from the Zobukiri in decades, but even then there would be no reason for them, strange as they were, to kidnap anyone, let alone go all the way to the Integrum to do it.

The way the two looked at her got on Ani's nerves. "<Fine, then what were you doing so close to the edge of the Gadori? >" she asked in a tone where no answer could satisfy her.

Hoba jumped in, hoping to deflect Ani's wrath to himself. "<Our prey had gotten away from us and we got a little over zealous in tracking it. We had to use it to save the boy in the end. >"

"<And this boy is your excuse for coming back empty-handed? >"

Tagai was a proud, honorable man and knew what Hoba was trying to do, but he was not one to deny responsibility for choices he made. "<It looked like he came from the Gadori edge and was just aimlessly wandering. He was making so much noise that I was surprised he hadn't been killed yet. So I got Hoba to tail him, and I shadowed our hunt. The boy reached Iro'Kamun and was attacked by a swamp hachu, I flushed our prey out to save the boy and it took off with the swamp hachu. >"

While Ani was digesting all of this Hoba impatiently asked,

"<How can you understand him? >"

She replied, "<He speaks Integrum Vox. >"

"<Quite far from the Integrum, isn't he? >"

"<Yes, a bit too far... and a bit too young to have any good reason to be here. >" Ani came to a conclusion, and looked at the crowd with a stern expression. She then said, with complete authority, "<Leave. >" The crowd couldn't have dispersed any faster than it did — leaving Ani, Tagai, and Hoba standing around a sitting, catatonic Toyo.

"<So, what do we do? >" asked Tagai.

Ani grasped Toyo's chin and began pinching certain parts of his face, trying to elicit a reaction from someone who had checked out mentally. "<He's still... elsewhere. Take him to the Medishi. Hoba, show me your hand. >"

He held out his wounded hand for her inspection, and she quickly spat in his open palm and clasped both her hands over his before looking deep into his eyes.

"<Does it still hurt? >" asked Ani.

"<Yes, >" Hoba winced at the pressure exerted on his fresh burns. "<It hurts more now. >"

"<Pain is a funny thing. >" Ani released one of her hands and thrust a wrinkly fist as hard as oak into his stomach, doubling him over in pain.

"<There, now your hand doesn't hurt so much anymore. >"

Hoba spluttered out, "<W... hy? >"

"<Letting a child you doped eat himself stupid until he vomits is no different than the pain you feel now. Try a little harder next time you are given responsibility, there are not enough of us left for you to keep making mistakes, Hoba. If you can't be at least a little more like Tagai then at least learn how to pretend to be. >" Ani felt some pleasure at having a justified reason for hitting him. "<Tagai, carry him. Wrap those hands of his in his clothes and try your best to not touch them. >" Giving Ani his sign of respect, Tagai set to work. "<Hoba, you can come with me, >" she looked at him hunched over, "<When you are ready, I need some help. >" Ani stood with her thoughts, waiting for Hoba to be finished with his pain and for Tagai to get the boy bundled up to be moved.

Her deep thinking was interrupted by Toyo, who decided to barrage the world with a litany of words in a voice now much older and confident. "Land of the Gadori, most southern region of Kasmah. Home to the Gozuri tribe, self-professed caretakers of the region and maintainers of the Ogagis. Regional wildlife adaptation to the proliferation of vesma is equitable to that of the Maharaan, grossly —" he was interrupted by another heavy slap from Ani, returning his face to its prior stupor.

"<What is he saying, and how is he doing that? >" asked Hoba, visibly worried at how an old man's voice had came out from such a youth.

Ani dismissively replied, "<I don't know Hoba, and with his mouth Hoba. >"

"<You know what I mean! >"

"<Yes, I know what you mean. Shut up, I'm thinking now. >" Ani tried to control herself and her thoughts before continuing. "<Tagai, take him up to the medishi NOW. If he starts that again, send for me and keep note of how long he goes for. >"

Tagai was glad for the instructions as everything had been getting beyond his comfort level, so much so that he was starting to regret bringing the boy back at all. Lifting the young bag of bones onto his shoulders he made the short journey over to the 'Mother-Tree', one of the Ogagis of the Gadori forest — trees of such greatness and wonder that for the Gozuri they were sacred.

ЖЖЖЖЖЖЖ

The medishi were the tribe's healers, pale of skin like Ani, but, unlike her, they were silent, seemingly content to simply grant healing to everything and anything. To that end they had fashioned hammocks for the sick and wounded, hung from knots of wood on the side of the Mother-Tree. Each hammock was filled with a strange mixture of herbs and tinctures concocted to bring restfulness and peace of mind.

Slipping in and out of consciousness Toyo spouted half sentences and mumbled nonsense. He regained enough of his senses to start fighting the medishi tending to him, who were now trying to put him into a hammock. Tired of dealing with the boy, Tagai said, "<You are just determined to be difficult, aren't you?>" He unsheathed a long stick with a large knob of hard wood on the end and gave him a thump on the back of his head. The medishi said nothing, but gave Tagai a glare of utmost irritation that he would hit anyone under their care.

The fight drained out of Toyo and he went very still indeed. The medishi's, and Tagai's, medicine had taken its hold of him and he was finally ready to submit to sleep for the first time since he'd awoken in an icy cold wasteland.

A snore of peace arose from the hammock and Tagai waited until the medishi fastened the cloth over him used to prevent anyone feverish from falling out. Tagai muttered to himself. "<How something so young can be so skinny is beyond me. How he could almost kill a hachu is also, really… beyond me.>"

Honor dictated Tagai, and so, regardless of how unsettled he was about the strange new boy, he waited long enough to ensure that he was well taken care of. After he felt satisfied, he went to find Ani.

Ж Ж Ж Ж Ж Ж Ж

Ani had been raised with homes and walls, a life of familiarity and comforts. The roaming Gozuri held little stock in any of those things and so it was, for her, a difficult transition. Even though she had been a part of the tribe for many years now she was still not used to having to travel long distances every few months, but she could hardly complain. She knew what would happen to the rest of Kasmah if these Gozuri did not perform their sacred cleansing ritual of Sabana at each Ogagi at the necessary times.

Speaking vox after so long however made her sigh loudly as old memories surfaced, and she began to look for something. Constantly moving all the time made it difficult to keep anything organized so it was always a small chore to find anything.

She never thought she would begin to miss home like she did now, but the arrival of the pale boy made her think of it in ways she would've preferred remained buried. More painfully, it reminded her of when her expedition to investigate the Gadori region from the Integrum became stranded here long ago. Of the original sortie all that remained was herself, and the six Integra Natura that the Gozuri had taken to calling 'medishi' — after their own word for healer.

Circumstances had led to Ani being chosen as the tribe's elder, what the Gozuri refer to as a 'Yohju'. It still struck the old woman as strange that the people would be so willing to raise her to such a position, but then again she was one of very few learned people left, and who'd cared to learn the Gozuri tongue. The Natura would have been better suited for the task, if they were not so obsessed with the local flora and fauna — more intent on compiling note after note rather than fitting in. They didn't even bother speaking with her unless under the most dire of circumstances, that however was for reasons more understandable given their shared past.

Ani's reminiscing was interrupted by Tagai entering her tent. "<We should talk about him. >"

"<Yes, we should, >" replied Ani without much enthusiasm, rummaging around the myriad of oddities that littered her tent.

"<What do you want me to do about him? He's young... he doesn't seem to know where he is, and is obviously very far from home. >"

"<You propose we send him back to the Integrum escorted? >"

"<You know I do not have anyone I could spare for such a thing. >"

"<Then he may as well stay. He doesn't seem to be a threat and those gloves are fascinating, did you see how they reacted? It has been quite a while since I've seen anything half as interesting —>"

Tagai interrupted with his objections. "<But he's just a child, and not even a girl! He won't be of any use, and we can't afford luxuries so close to the time of the Mother-Tree's sabana! >"

Ani turned from her searching through piles and replied in tones that brooked no argument. "<He is of no threat to the Ogagi's ritual cleansing, and I will not turn him out into the wilderness without knowing more about him. >"

Tagai's resistance drained from his face out of honor for his tribe's Yohju. "<I am glad you are excited Ani, but I need to know what to do with him. >"

"<I need some time to think. >" She dismissed Tagai with a speed that showed that there was more on her mind than she was letting on, and returned to her search.

Seeing that she was finally alone, she allowed herself to unload internally and get a hold of her trembling stomach, something it had been doing ever since the boy started talking in those other voices. *"Futuo! I have NO idea what is going on! Why did that boy sound so familiar with that voice?!"*

She then found what she was looking for, a small trinket box she had hidden wrapped in a small piece of silk. Lifting it up to her face she gave it a most intense look, as if trying to engage in a battle of wits with the inanimate object. Running things over and over in her mind, she reached a conclusion.

Ani muttered bitterly, "You WILL not make me open you."

INTEGRUM

The man stood stunned at the turn of events and felt the warmth that only blood could give caress his hands, and even though his mind was racing at a million miles a minute, it wasn't getting anywhere.

"Wha... Bu..." he stammered.

Mulat could feel the blood trickling from his gut down onto his feet, but showed no signs of discomfort in his face or speech. "You just stabbed a man, and all you can do is stutter?" Mulat cocked an eyebrow. "Isn't this what you wanted?"

"Why...? Why di —"

"Really? You are going to waste this opportunity with asking why?"

A man uncertain held a blade, and tried to say, "But —"

"BUT!?" exploded Mulat, "You have a knife in my gut and you want to start your sentence with a mere BUT!? I give you power, and you choose to waste it?! This situation is hardly complicated, you wanted me weak yes? Will you now rob me like you said you wanted to? Isn't it easier now?"

The man, visibly trembling, lost his grip on the knife and fell backwards onto the alley street. Mulat gave him a look of disappointment. "And now you choose to give up your position of power? A shame...." Mulat's expression changed to one of a man deep in thought.

Looking at a man contemplative did not comfort the attacker and made him fear for the inventive death that was no doubt being devised.

Mulat directed the smoke to bind the man once more and lowered his face to meet the trembling man. He then quietly said, "... given the district I am in mugging is not so commonplace, especially ones coordinated like this. I would say I distracted myself more than you did me. But at least you did a good job, yes? The figure on the overlooking roof is far more interesting than I originally surmised." Mulat huddled himself on the ground and winked. "So, do you think this is enough for that person to believe I am sufficiently distracted?"

Shifting his weight sideways, the deft aerial strike stabbed where Mulat once was, and stopped short of the cobbled street. As the new attacker withdrew the blade in preparation to strike again Mulat grabbed it, slicing his hand open. Mulat then smiled and lunged towards his new enemy, allowing the assassin no time to recover. Caught off-guard, the assassin made a quick feint which Mulat stopped by slamming his open palm down on the blade, while forcing his other hand's open palm right into the assassin's nose with a satisfying crunch.

The assassin used the force and momentum of the blow to its face as an opportunity to roll back and create some distance. Upon recovering from its acrobatics it looked back at its target, and found it to be smiling.

Mulat stood nonplussed as blood dripped from the blades protruding both from his hands and gut. "Well? Aren't you going to strike again?" he said. The assassin remained silent. "Well done on the attempted obfuscation and attack, I do think you have some skill — I just believe I am a poor target. By the way, are you sure you want me to just stand here bleeding?" Again silence. "Ha ha, excellent! Let's see if YOU can stop the boredom! Don't create an expectation you can't live up to now, I enjoyed the distraction you created. So, let's keep that standard up." Still silence. "Are you waiting for me to bleed out? Your employer must be very poorly informed indeed."

A thousand possibilities ran through Mulat's mind of how different things could be, and realized that he was doing his usual of fantasizing about the situation being more interesting than it actually was. It could be tricky to keep a focus on reality when it could be so dull. With a sigh he pulled out the blade lodged in his palm. "Very well then, I'll finish this a bit quicker than I wanted." He placed both hands over his gut wound, and pulled them away, leaving a glistening string of sticky blood that bonded the three points.

The assassin fished out a second blade hidden about its person and sprinted with blade in striking pose, intent on stopping whatever was about to happen. Mulat finished his hand gesture as the assassin got within a finger's-breadth of him — a spider lattice of blood formed in a flash and latched on to the assassin. In shock the assassin stepped back and felt the blood crawling along skin, and silently panicked as it made its way inside via all openings. Moments later the assassin went into a limp, doll-like state.

Mulat pulled out the blade in his gut, walked over to one of the fallen men and made an incision in the man's thigh, letting the blood pool onto the ground. The unconscious man groaned slightly and his body shuddered at the wound being made. After a small puddle had collected, Mulat pressed his hand into it and the blood slowly started to shift and collect around his hand before sticking to and coating his palm. He then placed the bloody hand over his wounds, and when he moved his hands away large scabs were in their stead. Satisfied with himself he looked down at the man he had just cut and performed the same healing ritual for him.

The other man that was still stuck to the floor redoubled his efforts to shake with fear. "Please don't kill me," he said.

Mulat paced slowly to him and leaned over. "… Do you think I find value in your death?"

"… What?"

Mulat then lowered himself till his breath could be felt on the man's face. In a calm and caring voice he said, "I am sure I enunciated my words properly, so I'll assume you are having difficulty grasping who I am or what I do. To put your mind at ease, I am Integra Divinitas Mulat, and my judgment here and now is that there is no value to be gained in your death, nor the death of your partners in crime." All signs of the man's shivering had gone and had been replaced with a stiffness and paleness that would in most men indicate death.

Mulat lifted a finger on his wounded hand to his lips with a slight grin, and started going, "Sssshhhhh…." A second later his hand wound re-opened and began trickling blood, which traveled up to touch his lips. The sounds he was making now picked up a different timbre and began to occupy more space than mere speech could ever hope to achieve. Growing in strength it began to transform into an absorption of sound, blanketing everything in eerie silence.

The man went into a stupor, staring entranced at Mulat's lips and finger. Eventually the mute sound and feeling of pressure stopped and the once-trembling man fell asleep. Mulat stood up and looked down. "Memory is such a precious thing, my apologies for taking yours from you." He then looked at his hand and stared at it until it stopped bleeding. Turning to his new assassin toy, he was curious as to how this person could obfuscate so many pieces of information that Mulat could usually identify in an instant. Age, gender, intent — all of these things about the assassin were not easily read.

Placing his hands on the assassin's face blood started to flow from the ears. The assassin's eyes came back to life and began to look around in a deep panic. "Now now, calm down. I just wanted you *compos mentis* for our little discussion, I have no real intention of harming you in truth." A parting of fingers from Mulat made more blood trickle out of the assassin's mouth. "You can speak now." The assassin remained silent.

Mulat sighed. "I can just make you speak, you know — I'd rather not. Not for any other reason than things obtained by force have to be maintained by force, which is somewhat a poor exchange."

The assassin conveyed an air of deep consideration before saying, "Yes, I can speak," in Mulat's own voice.

Mulat's own face broke into a grin. "Oh, very good, well done! Thank you for the distraction, but really it seems poor form for you to be using drones — it forces me to end this rather abruptly. Next time, I would appreciate something more serious, you know I prefer our games when they are a bit more energetic." He then placed his hands over the would-be assassin's ears and said, "Forget." As the blood again drained back from the assassin into Mulat, the assassin fell limp to the ground.

Juvo stepped out from a dark patch of wall. "Perhaps next time you shouldn't be so distracted pursuing your hobby? Or am I not enough?"

Mulat walked towards Juvo and wrapped her up in an embrace. "Welcome back, little one."

"You tend to create problems for other people while I am away, so I thought you would enjoy me making some minor mischief for you — makes my return a bit more interesting for you at least," said Juvo, now reaching up and caressing the back of Mulat's head.

"I cannot help myself sometimes," Mulat's voice dropped to a more sullen tone, "... It has been too long. I do not fare well on my own." The relief of her return filled him.

Juvo took Mulat's head in her hands and brought it down, and placed a kiss on his forehead. "I know." This was not one of Juvo's regular mannerisms.

"Oh, I made a mistake... maybe this won't be so boring after all. Let's see." He looked up to see one of the tools of his Integra Pol, a *Deprimo Os*, mere inches from his face bearing down on him. He was surprised at seeing one outside of the Integra Pol, for the few that were in existence were kept under strict watch and were reserved for only the most vesma-infused of enemies.

Upon contact it clung to his face and he felt himself become weaker, but not so weak that he couldn't defend himself by exerting minimal effort. As the mask began to spread from forehead to chin he thought that if he broke free, that all this would end here and now. He wasn't quite ready to go home just yet — besides, if death was their goal they wouldn't have wasted such effort on simply capturing him.

Allowing himself to succumb to the effects of the *deprimo os* he was able to say, "What fun!" before control of his body was taken from him.

"Yes... this is fun. It is time to go to your new home, Mulat," were the only words his ears registered before they too were taken.

The *deprimo os* had transformed from its amorphous gelatinous substance into a solid mask that covered Mulat's own face. On the surface of the mask a blank face formed, indicating that the *deprimo os* had finished its capture.

Tari Scor's childhood was spent in the Quadra Lustrum under the strict tutelage of her mother, Criso Scor — herself the favorite of the then Erus of the Lustrum, Erus Ardeo. They were a mother and daughter that were near identical with their pale skin, deep green eyes, and long red curly locks.

Criso held no love for Erus Ardeo, despite the offspring they shared, but she was an ambitious woman and always ready to do what was necessary. The only thing she did with difficulty was following Ardeo's command to begin Tari's training, years before her cycles had even started — which was against both Lustrum guidelines and common sense. Quadra guidelines existed for a reason, and Criso knew them better than anyone. However, what was she to do? Ardeo was not the sort of Erus one could say 'no' to, so she did as told even though she knew instilling in someone so young knowledge and skill they couldn't fully understand to be a mistake. In Tari's case, the problem was magnified by having the Erus' protection, along with an education from its most experienced charge.

From that, Tari became a seductress unmatched at the young age of fourteen, but she was ignorant to the heartbreak that others could experience. She also grew a penchant for playing cruel tricks as an outlet for her frustration or boredom, but every time she was caught she would always be presented to her mother for punishment. Just like she was now.

Standing before her mother in what Ardeo called his 'favorite' clothes, which was simply a knee length skirt and light blouse, and pouting, she could tell that her mother was really annoyed this time. Tari however had more pressing things on her mind than to pay attention to the same conversation for the hundredth time, it was only ever going to end the same way anyway. Stupid old bag.

"What a bastard! He was here on an official visit of goodwill!" she whined. *"And he kept snubbing me! What kind of man doesn't want ME?!"* She had been furious at the lack of attention from Potentiate Mulat, the one who was in line to replace Integra Divinitas Stagnos.

Her mother quipped, "Are you even paying attention to me, Tari?"

"Yes yes yes," she replied indignantly.

"How often do I have to keep telling you! Just because I have taught you these skills does not give you free reign to manipulate and poke everything you can. You haven't even started your cycles yet!"

Tari sneered. "So? What does bleeding have to do with sex anyway? I don't see why I have to wait because some stupid old law says that I can't start until my cycle does!"

"Do you even understand the problem here?! I did not raise you to be so disrespectful, and yet here you are!" Criso sighed out loud, and then softly said, "Yet again."

"Well Mulat shouldn't have kept ignoring me!"

Criso took a moment to catch up with what she had just been told. "Mulat? The Integra Divinitas Potentiate? I thought you were here because you were just messing with the Integra Pol delegate's guards, but you were messing with MULAT too?!"

Tari ignored her mother's concern and focused on her own. "Why doesn't he look at me!?"

"He doesn't look at anyone! He's a NEUTER you stupid girl." Criso had no idea her daughter could be THIS ignorant. Was she trying to get herself killed?

Tari now chose the wrong time to be a smart-ass. "Well, if he's a neuter and I'm not supposed to have an interest in sex because I haven't started my cycles, then by YOUR logic it shouldn't matter."

Criso fought the desire to slap that smart mouth but decided against it, mostly because Ardeo would no doubt slap her far harder in turn. "You are becoming a handful, child — I have half a mind to lock you in your room for a VERY long time."

Tari fumed. "Why? Just because I made a few stupid men act stupid because they thought they would get to have sex with me?" Tari enjoyed the power she had over men and women, and played with that power constantly.

"Those MEN were guards of the Integra Pol! How do you think Erus Ardeo is going to react when he finds out that you meddled with his guests?"

Tari fell silent as she contemplated the cruelty that Ardeo was capable of, and even though her mother was Ardeo's personal attendant and concubine, Tari could not always count on a safe harbor from the storms she brought upon herself. "How would he find out?" she asked, as always trying to find a way out of her predicament.

"I SUSPECT the same way I did, with Mulat informing me personally. Why he left your games with 'him' out I do not know."

Not being able to get any direct reaction out of Mulat and now being caught out on her games sent her frustration into overdrive. "He did WHAT?!"

Criso always tried to be a good mother, given the circumstances, but it was never easy. "I will talk to Erus Ardeo, maybe I can ask for some lenience."

Tari looked at her mother through a face of scorn and ran out of the room with her mother's screams echoing after her. "*That... thing! I will MAKE him notice me!*" Given Tari's reputation, little barred her path and her questions as to where to find who she was looking for were quickly answered.

She soon found the Integra Pol delegate just a short distance beyond the Lustrum and walking on the Integra Pol grounds headed for home. When the guards spotted her, they moved in to block her path but were ordered to stand down by Mulat. She stamped right up to him, her face flushed red with blood, and she gave him her sternest look.

He looked back at her with a quizzical expression. "Yes little one?" he asked.

"Why did you ignore me!?" she screamed.

Mulat's face radiated innocence. "Did I? Was I incorrect in informing your mother as to your behavior?"

"You know exactly what I mean!"

INTEGRUM - CHAPTER III | 139

"No. I am so sorry about that, but there are many things you could be referring to." Mulat became confused, and he then asked with genuine curiosity, "Are you referring to why I didn't respond to your charms during my visit?"

"YES!"

"But... I did respond, didn't I? I told your mother," he said, believing that an acceptable answer to the question spoken, rather than the true question Tari did not ask.

"That's NOT what was supposed to happen!"

"Oh, I'm sorry, I feel like I've made another mistake. What was I supposed to do, little one?"

"React like everyone else!" She got a blank face as her response which made her bunch her fists.

Fearing that he had done something wrong, he asked, "How should I react then, young Tari Scor?"

"Like you want me, need me! Your blood should boil and you should be mad with desire!"

Mulat gave this due consideration but was having trouble reconciling her words with what he knew. "I always thought that was supposed to be a two-way experience. At least, that is what your mother and everyone at the Quadra Lustrum has told me."

"So?! Who says I have to do all the work? Aren't you a MAN?"

Mulat said, "Oh... I see," and contemplated something deeply in a moment of awkward silence before returning his attention to the young girl. "I do apologize. I was unaware of protocol as this was my first visit to your Quadra. But I am, if nothing else, one who honors protocol." Mulat stalked towards her.

Tari was scared stiff and had no idea what was going to happen, a small part of her feared that she may have finally gone too far — he moved like a predator, and she the prey. He reached out and held her head gently in his large hands, looked deeply into her eyes, and whispered softly, "I want you... I need you..." and kissed her lightly on the lips.

The mixture of fear and arousal was powerful, but a small part of her nearly leapt for joy at being able to manipulate the soon-to-be most powerful man in the Integrum, and laughed hard inside at his foolishness. But her feelings of superiority were soon replaced by the faint taste of blood in Mulat's kiss, and her body began to throb and ache. Her lips began to burn and she became weak at the knees — the core of everything she thought was shaken and her soul felt full to the point of bursting.

Mulat began to pull his head away from the kiss, but without thinking she grabbed his head and passionately began kissing him back in a desire to keep feeling the same. Full of hunger for this strange man and the need to be his, she began to misguidedly feel that maybe she could understand what true love was from this lust. Her body felt uncontrollable with her mind racing and heart pounding — she couldn't conceive of a life without this man.

The kiss was broken when someone promptly pulled her off him, but she once again lunged at him. As Tari fought to stay attached to him she froze in fear at hearing her mother screaming, "TARI SCOR CONTROL YOURSELF!" Tari's breathing was rapid, and her face flushed red as she tried to cope with the sudden rush of yearning and need for the first time in her life. She could feel with every beat of her heart, almost burning with the heat she felt, her blood rushing around her body as her mother held her tight.

Criso pleaded, "I am... SO sorry Potentiate Mulat! Please forgive my child, she is young and stupid. I am sure that Erus Ardeo will punish her thoroughly after this and what you told him... please, there will be no need to punish her further."

Confused, Mulat replied, "Why would Erus Ardeo punish her from my introducing myself as the Integra Pol Potentiate?"

Criso had yet to come to terms with Mulat's almost child-like innocence and, in some cases, intelligence of the same. "I mean for... telling him of her... um... misconduct." At this point she really wished fluttering her green eyes at him would work like it did on others.

"I told him no such thing, I merely told you because you are her mother." Mulat felt worried that he had yet again made some blunder. In earnest he inquired, "Should I have told Erus Ardeo?"

She bowed her head low. "I... it is your discretion of course, Potentiate Mulat, to inform whoever you see fit."

"As it is everyone's. Have I made some sort of mistake?" he asked, still confused.

"Of course not, Potentiate Mulat! I am sorry to have intruded on your time."

"There is no need for apologies, Criso. I only hope I followed protocol and performed as everyone asked of me." Criso was unsure of what he meant but merely gave a submissive nod, hoping that would convey understanding in some respect. "Is it improper of me to question you further?"

"Of course not, Potentiate Mulat."

"Is Erus Ardeo really as much a 'bastard' as he appears to be?" Mulat said bastard as if he was speaking a different language.

"I... the man is...." Criso's usual skill with tact failed her as she fumbled for the right way to answer him.

Seeing her struggle he asked, "Is there some difficulty in you telling me the truth of things? I only ask because you would know him best, and I believe that third party confirmation is a good way to prove observations."

Criso did her best to improvise on the spot. "No of course... he... can be difficult, and is not always the kindest of people."

"Is that not what a bastard is? Do I have the understanding of the word wrong?"

"... No, you do not."

Mulat beamed like a child praised for getting a particularly difficult question right. "Ah, good. So Erus Ardeo is, in fact, a bastard. I had always assumed it to mean an illegitimate child born out of wedlock, but I was told recently it had an alternative meaning. Thank you for confirming two facts for me. If there is anything I can do in turn, please do not hesitate to ask."

"Thank you Potentiate Mulat." She thought that their business was concluded, but he remained expectantly standing there. "Um, at this moment, no, there is nothing. I must tend to my daughter," said Criso, gesturing towards Tari.

Mulat smiled. "Of course, I will bother you no further. Good day Criso." He turned his attention to young Tari — she felt her face flush again with passion and her heart begin to race. "And a good day to you, young Tari Scor. I hope that I provided what you asked for," he said it all with nothing but the desire to be of service.

As mother and daughter watched the delegation continue their journey back to the Integra Pol, Tari felt a great longing — as if her chest had been ripped from her and a part of her soul was walking away. Her mother held her tight out of fear and protectiveness. That was, until she felt the delegation was far enough for it to be safe to reprimand her.

Criso turned her daughter around to face her, her outrage palpable, and was surprised to find that her daughter was crying. Her anger softened, diffused greatly by the fact that she could not remember the last time her daughter had shed true tears. Tari spent so much time playing games and being independent that the connection between them had dwindled, and this was the first time that realization hit Criso full force.

Uncertain of what to do, she looked at her child and felt the need to comfort her but didn't know how. Producing a handkerchief from her person, Criso began to mop up the child's tears and hush away the sobs. As she tended to her she got a shock when she noticed some blood spattered on the ground beneath Tari.

She knew that Tari had not been beaten, Mulat appeared harmless as a fly, but she checked for injuries anyway — her daughter could have likely done it to herself as part of some game. After a cursory check she found the source of the blood and a panic rushed through her. "*What?! How is her cycle starting?! The Lustrum medicine should halt it! It works for the other girls! WHY NOT MINE!?*" She looked at her child and saw her looking forlornly at the distant Mulat.

Criso's face twisted to fear and panic as she watched the Potentiate make his way to the Integra Pol, and then looked back at her little girl. "*No! No, Ardeo can't know about this. She's not ready! I'll never let him have her!*" The pair stood locked in a familial embrace while Criso's heart filled with sadness, and young Tari's with the sensation of a love lost.

When Criso found the strength to part she almost had to pull Tari off her, but she had to so she could help with the bleeding. As she watched blood speckle the ground she tried to come up with all sorts of ways to hide it from Ardeo's attentions — she had known for quite some time that he was merely grooming the child for his personal interests.

With renewed affection Criso said softly to her daughter, "Oh... my dear Tari... It is okay, my beautiful child. Everything is okay."

Tari cried heartbroken tears and hung her head low to hide from her mother's gaze, only to be shocked to see blood splattered on the pavement beneath her. Tari had not noticed what had happened and could only look up at her mother with pleading in her eyes to please tell her what was happening to her.

Criso spoke softly as she tried to comfort her daughter. "Shhhhhh... it's okay, it's okay. You are just finally becoming a woman."

CHAPTER IV

"May your life be born from want, and your death arise from need."

-*Traditional Harat blessing*

THE MAHARAAN EXPANSE

Kahli's fever dreaming was tempered with the smell of a great beast and a sense of traveling a great distance. As her mind fought with her body, she kept experiencing a waking paralysis where all she could do was watch helplessly as the scorching scenery passed her by — never knowing if it was real or not. Body, mind and soul battled each other, while the only victim of that war, was her.

BREATHE...

A field of green filled Kahli's vision.

Wary of whether this would turn out to be another passing dream or nightmare, she was surprised to find herself looking at the same image several minutes later. The longer it stayed the more her grasp on reality returned, until she eventually found the confidence to sit up, and then broke down in tears in gratitude for the passing of her delirium. As the images and memories she could not account for broke down and faded away, she felt a small part of herself carried away with them as if she were so much sand and the wind was carrying it off.

She tried to focus on the scene in front of her and the feeling of cool grass under her fingers. It was comforting. Reveling in the cold and springy touch of the ground she found a great relief in its texture — she couldn't remember when she'd touched grass so lively. After ruffling her hands through the fresh blades she heard, for the second time in living memory, *whuffle*.

Twisting her body around in a panic she once again saw a wija staring at her. "*What was it that mother said? Useless nuisances? Or is... that another... broken memory?*" Unsure of what to make of it she tried to quickly rise to her feet, only to fall down just as fast. Her body was weak with hunger and lethargic from inaction, and her spirit was faring little better.

On bended knee Kahli did her best to recover as she looked at the wija. It hadn't made any movement during her panic and was merely staring intently at her. Still frayed from her fever dreams, she felt no security in the world and maintained eye contact with it while she tentatively checked her clothes for any sort of defensive items. The only thing her fingers came across she recognized to be her task pouch — filled with pins, cloth, and other odds and ends for the menial chores she had been asked to do for the ceremony. The certainty of a memory attached to something physical brought her much needed comfort.

Raising herself steadily to full height she wondered why the creature was so motionless, a question that led her to a fresh bevy of questions: Where was she? Where was home? Where was her family? The answers that came to her were fuzzy at first, and as she focused on them they did nothing but bring uncertainty. Too much had happened too fast for Kahli to come to terms with, and so she chose not to. She fought off the memories of her family being dead, of what had happened to her home village.

A feeling of being helpless filled her, and with it the thought that if the world was going to force its will upon her, then she would do so in kind. Refusing to feel threatened for even a moment longer she charged towards the wija with snarling face, clawing fingers and teeth bared. Unknowingly she struck it hard where she had once done before, and a small *crack* could be heard from its heavy bones as it fell on its side to the ground. Keeping on the offensive she scratched and bit whatever was at hand, gouging large chunks of flesh and throwing the entire weight of her feeling that the world had done wrong by her into the assault. With each strike, a small amount of anger would be replaced by a great rush of satisfaction, as if she were trying to beat it out of herself. She kept at it, until eventually all that was left was the feeling that she was attacking a stuffed animal.

Stepping back she stared through a haze of rage at the creature, daring it to strike back. Defiance made her want the creature to retaliate, but what soon replaced her anger was crippling self-loathing when she realized that the creature at no point had made an effort to defend itself. It had merely lain there and taken all the hatred Kahli had to give, and still looked at her with its innocent face without sign of hatred or fear.

"What... what have I done?" she thought, looking at the gruesome wounds on the wija, and was startled at the gash she had torn open on its chest. "I... couldn't have done all that." A feeling of shame overwhelmed her when she finally registered that her mouth was full of blood and fur. Trying to remove all traces of both from her mouth, she began retching in disgust.

The beast was wheezing, but it never looked away from her. It just kept its gaze locked on her, attentive and patient, with only love in its eyes.

"I... didn't —" her thoughts were interrupted by a strange voice in her head.

"You did."

Guilt clawed at her. "It's not my fault!"

"Fault? Which do you care more about, the why or the what? A knife doesn't ask why it is used for cutting, it simply cuts."

"I am not a knife!"

"You can argue with your mind, but not with what your eyes and ears would tell you if you paid attention to them in this moment." This intrusive specter of a voice sounded like it had just issued a challenge rather than stated a fact, so Kahli set out to prove it wrong.

Unsure of where to begin she tried soothing the wija by caressing its head and humming, but as the blood kept seeping she began to feel useless, and her spirit waned further when all she could see were its eyes watching her with what she felt was quiet patience and hope. In desperation she fished in her pouch for anything that would help — the few things she found did not bring her much confidence. Regardless, she had a job to do! Determined, she soon found that she was able to start stitching up the beast's wounds with what little needle and thread she'd discovered.

"Thread needle... pierce skin... pull through..." was the mantra she settled on as she worked.

She tried her best to keep it neat as if she was mending sheets, but the thick hide, blood and fur made getting any sort of hold tricky. The needle would at times get caught, and several other times she had to fish it out of the wound when the wija's breathing chest, causing the thread to tighten and snatching the needle out of her fingers. These were obstacles she could easily overcome, she knew she could, but she couldn't overcome the now dwindling amount of thread.

The wound looked better and the bleeding had slowed, but the wija was still wheezing softly and winced with every bump and nudge. Every whimper stabbed Kahli's heart, and with every breath the beast took her work came undone a little more. The swelling of blood from several stitches coming loose drove her back into her pouch with vigor in an attempt to find something else to use. She tossed out its entire contents onto the grass and tried to force her brain to make further use of what was in front of her. Another whimper followed another stitch popping free, and she turned to see another gush of blood come forward.

Kahli began to cry, all the while vowing that she wouldn't let the creature perish because she could not do the most important thing for another living being — give it the care it deserves and needs.

Turning her attention back to the contents on the ground, she surprised herself with a flash of ingenuity, and grabbed a tiny blade that was used for cutting cloth and went to work on her hair. Slicing long strands from the ends she collected it into a pile in a determined but frantic fashion. Once there was enough, she twisted several strands of hair together to make them thicker and stronger in the hopes that she might use it in lieu of thread. Her idea fell short when the hair stubbornly refused to stick together, and just when she was about to give up hope she thought to rub her hair in blood so that it could. Excited at resuming her work, she huddled in close and tied together enough strands of hair to finish the job.

Returning to the creature, her feet slipped on some of the bloody fur that was on the ground and she instinctively reached out to break her fall. What she grabbed to save her was the wija's chest, and gravity did its job. The gash from before was now larger ever. Her tears grew larger as apologies streamed from her mouth in an attempt to find some magic word to undo what she'd done. Fighting her trembling hands, she found her spirit being dragged down further as the creature groaned and shivered from pain.

Kahli was frightened, frightened that the wija wouldn't allow her to tend to it anymore, that this beautiful creature that had only shown kindness in the wake of her cruelty would have finally had enough of her uselessness. She couldn't let that be the truth, so she moved in front of its head and tried to face whatever the creature was feeling without fear. Seeing only pain on its face hurt her, but she did the only thing left she could think of. She took a step towards it as submissively as she could, stretched out her hand and placed it in its mouth as she looked at the ground, all the while shaking like a leaf.

"Please... please forgive me! I will make this better, I promise... just let me try again... please... I am sorry," said Kahli, in the voice of a woman desperate to convey her feelings. When she felt the creature's large tongue flex under her fingers and its teeth gnaw gently on her hand, a wave of relief came over her. She waited a small moment before removing her hand, then caressed its head with both hands and lowered her forehead onto the creature's and whispered, "Thank you."

Turning her attention to the wound again, she set to work with a steadier hand and focus. *"Thread needle... pierce skin... pull through... Thread needle... pierce skin... pull through...."*

Through her renewed efforts her job was done in a short time. By the end of it all she was covered in blood, staining her clothes and matting her hair, but she felt a little bit better. She knew that stitching up this creature was not enough and she would be failing herself if she left it at this. What it needed now was tending to and food.

But what was she to do? How was she to care for something like this? Her mind put these thoughts to the back to simmer and stir as she cradled the now noble beast in her arms, humming as she caressed its large head and neck.

ЖЖЖЖЖЖЖЖЖЖЖЖЖЖЖ

The young Integra Natura, Fetu, looked left as far as she could see, then right, then straight ahead. "This... isn't the sea on the sands. Where's all the ocean-blue sand I heard so much about? Where's ANY sand? Where is this?!" It had been a long time since she had seen so much green, but the sight was far from comforting.

Wrinkled Pala was taking everything in, while stern Sercu walked up to where dry ground and lush field of green met. She bent down low and stroked the plush grass. "*Cenchrus ciliaris*? This occurs only in patches, and FAR, far from here. Why is there a massive field of it here?" She pulled up some blades and saw that they were healthy — they must be getting moisture from somewhere. Curious, she collected some samples of dirt to compare for later.

Pala however asked aloud a more pertinent question. "Why is it cool? The humidity seems average and the sun should be boiling us. So, why is it temperate?" The old woman took a few steps back into the baked, dry land and felt the heat once more, then walked back to just a step beyond the grass line. Her face the whole time locked in a puzzled expression.

All had questions, none had answers.

Sercu looked at Pala, and asked, "Could this be a part of the chamu life cycle we don't know about?"

Pala shook her head. "This is the largest chamu nest in the Maharaan. They would've extracted all the moisture out of every blade of grass here — they aren't things designed for a complicated life."

"Then where the *valde* are they?" Sercu said to herself.

Fetu was comforted by their exchange — she hated always feeling like the ignorant one in the group. With perhaps more glee than she intended, she said, "So long as they aren't here, I'm fine with that."

Sercu tersely replied, "If they aren't here now, they will be soon."

"Enough gawking you two," quipped Pala. "Let's push on. If this is anything to go by then….." She trailed off, but her mind finished the sentence with, *"We may have to go to Toka-Rutaa to see what the other event is."*

"Then what?" asked Fetu.

Pala shook her head. "Nothing, move." She took a step onto the grass and heard Fetu gasp. She rolled her eyes and looked back at the young Natura. "What?"

"Ah, nothing. Sorry, I thought… nevermind."

"Enough messing around, come on."

The cadre of three Natura walked into the field of green with minor hesitation, and when the desert was far off in the horizon behind them they found it difficult to remember they were even in the Maharaan. The flowers were plentiful and varied, but to the trained eye were completely wrong for the region they were in. Some of these plants may have occurred in rare patches in the Maharaan here and there, transferred far from their home by an errant band of traders or birds, but they were thriving in droves here. It was almost like a garden on a scale none had ever seen before, and for the Natura it was wondrous.

Sercu soon ran out of things to keep samples in and began filling up Pala and Fetu's bags. Fetu meanwhile was listening to Pala drone on about the 'what' and 'where' of the plants they walked past.

"That one is *psychotria elata*, you may have seen it before. It's popular in the Quadra Lustrum for decoration and some of their games — they call them hooker's lips. They can be commonly found along the northern Gadori and southern Integrum line, but down south they are mainly used for their psychoactive properties." As the elder Natura talked an edge of piqued interest crept in, which went unnoticed by the others.

Fetu hadn't actually seen them before but she could tell right away why they were called hooker's lips — they looked like big thick red lips puckering up for a kiss. Her surprise at its shape reminded her of Lik's wonderment at how a plant could look like a starfish, and here she was, experiencing the same thing like he had.

Except the last time she'd felt that way was long ago in the Integra Pol when she was training to become a Natura.

"Oh, *euphorbia obesa*, a rare native to this region. See how it is just basically a big ball with ridged edges all around? A common mistake is to think it's a fruit, it's actually a succulent, because you can hack them open and find juicy fleshy bits, which is actually poisonous sap."

"*Wow, this is actually kind of fun!*" thought Fetu as she listened to Pala talk about these stranger plants she had only read about in books. She had always thought Pala was just a crotchety old bag, but she definitely had a change of heart when she saw that wrinkly old face light up as they walked through the amazing garden.

Pala then exclaimed, "Even basic Integrum plants are here! This is *ricinus communis*." She turned to Fetu and smiled. "You'd know this as where castor oil comes from."

Fetu knew that, but was grateful that Pala was showing an interest in trying to teach her something. Usually she'd just get a derisive snort from her and told to go fetch Sercu to explain.

Sercu had been watching them both ever since they had begun talking. "You two are acting strange."

Pala and Fetu both smiled and said, "What are you talking about Sercu? Everything is perfectly fine."

"*She's right, there's nothing wrong!*" thought one part of Sercu, but another part said, "*Wait, what? There's always something wrong!*" She searched her mind for any idea of what was going on. And then, deep down, she felt something that shouldn't be there. She felt love. Not at anything or for anything, just an overwhelming sense of 'love'. That didn't make sense to her. She pointed at her senior Natura and said, "Pala, you're a batty old bitch who shouldn't have been allowed to lead our cadre let alone be out in the field. You should be back in the Integra Pol researching samples rather than risking mine and young Fetu's life out here with your feeble body."

Pala sweetly replied, "Don't be so silly Sercu, I know you care for me deep down. Why don't you come over here and look at this amazing *hydnellum peckii*." The old woman chuckled. "Fungi sure are strange aren't they? What else do they call this again? Bleeding tooth fungus?" Fetu joined in Pala's joviality and poked the white fungus. They both smiled and giggled a little when its red liquid seeped out through its pores.

Sercu looked around and shook her head. Everything felt foggy. "Pala! You take EVERY opportunity to bite other people's heads off!"

Pala and Fetu were both inspecting the odd assortment of flora, but Pala did not look up and simply waved her hand dismissively. "How could I bite your head off Sercu? You're one of my best friends."

"This isn't working!" She tried to think and found it harder and harder. *"Futuo!"* Sercu looked in her bag at the samples she had collected and inspected them as closely as possible, hoping to see past the fog and identify what was causing all this. Nothing. She ignored the pair who were off in their own little world and tried to perform some basic tests to confirm her samples were real, and they all returned positive. "This can't be right!" she screamed.

"What can't be right dear?" asked Pala, turning her head to look at her.

"All of this!" She ran over to them and picked up a bit of the fungus they were playing with. "Look! You're PLAYING with plants, why?! You never do that Pala! And why is *hydnellum peckii* growing out in the OPEN?! It's a symbiotic fungus, and it's thriving all on its own! Think about that!"

Fetu said, "We can't tell plants how and where to grow."

Appealing to the old woman's sense of logic worked. Pala scrunched up her face and looked around, then slapped herself hard. Shaking her head, she finally came to the same realization that Sercu had. She wasn't too fond of being bested by someone younger. She looked over at Sercu and asked, "... Is it psychoactive pollen?"

"No, I just checked for that. This is all real."

Pala looked around and poked and prodded a few nearby flowers. "You're right. This... doesn't make sense, more than I originally thought."

"How so?" asked Fetu, wondering why the fun had stopped.

"There is nothing here to pollinate anything. No insects, no birds. There's not even a water source. It's like a Natura research garden on a mass scale. And this weird feeling...."

"What? I feel really good," replied Fetu.

Sercu said, "Yes, you feel love."

"Well... now that you mention it, yeah. That's not so strange is it? This place is pretty magical."

Pala looked around at all the plants and noticed something odd. "Fetu, could you please make some distance between us? Take," she looked at the average distance between plant outcrops, "About five steps." Fetu did as she was told, and with each step Pala felt the feeling inside her grow dim. "Hm, strange."

Fetu felt it too. "What was that?" she asked, confused.

"I don't know. It's not really strong if you pay attention, but it was able to sneak up on us. This place... I don't get how or why, but it seems 'like-attraction' is playing a large part. All the plants are bunched by themselves in large groups, but they aren't fighting for resources. Everything here is living with itself in harmony, and THAT isn't natural."

Fetu asked, "What should we do?"

"Just keep a few steps apart and pay attention. Not that hard." Pala then narrowed her eyes at Sercu. "I still remember what you said."

Sercu innocently replied, "Can't punish me for a bad deed done for a good cause."

Pala harrumphed and signaled for them to continue on their way.

The field of green that Fetu had come to name the 'love garden' stretched farther still after the day's journey. It made their having to constantly check for signs of chamu feel almost silly, but they couldn't afford to not be careful.

When they were finally nearing the destination indicated by their instrument, they saw a young Maharaan girl and a wija lying out in the open. They circled her from afar to check that it was the correct place, and all signs pointed to them.

Even though they still didn't know WHAT the instrument was indicating, they were at least certain that either the girl or the wija was at the center of it.

LAND OF THE GADORI

While not many would choose the 'boring life' of a Quadra Logicum charge, Ani had always found comfort in the days of recording and analysis — whereas the Gadori forest she'd been stuck in never allowed her any peace. She missed her Logicum and Erus Adsum on occasion, but none so more than now. She really, really missed just being able to sit down and think the hours away on numbers, hypotheses and thought experiments. A part of her regretted ever agreeing to be a part of the Integrum sortie sent to investigate the source of the incursion that had destroyed much of the southern Integrum lands, both east and west.

At least under her supervision they had found the source, something the Gozuri called a Kusabana, but by then they were too few and the threat too large to handle. That day was when Ani had learned despair, and the passing of time made her bear witness to creatures and plants that could infest countless numbers and do gruesome things in ways both intelligent and cruel. Even the Integra Divinitas would have little hope faring against the forest, for the last time an Integra Divinitas had fought could only be found in books, while everything in the forest had been fighting for its life since its beginning. Despair killed every attempt to return home, and grew the belief that there wouldn't even be a home to return to.

The medishi had long ago stopped complaining about being stranded, knowing that they could never hope to pass through the forests on their own, and as the years passed an acceptance of their situation was inevitable. But, unlike Ani, they were happy, for everywhere they went were flora and fauna to marvel over, and language was no barrier to their craft of healing.

Ani had tried very hard to forget about her past all these years, but something about the boy, both what he said and the voices he'd used, commanded her memories back into focus. Here was a young boy that had walked in from the harsh ice fields beyond the forests wearing iron gloves that were fused to his skin, all alone. It was something that required some serious thinking. But, like always, thinking would have to wait for another time, as there was another, more pressing, task she had to perform as the Gozuri tribe's Yohju.

All Gozuri identified themselves as one tribe, even though there were once nine large groups to tend to the six great Ogagis. Even individually they did not understand the concept of last or family names — they felt bonded to each other as each tree in a forest would. From nine groups, each with their own Yohju, to one, and Ani was the last of them. Like all Yohju, Ani's most important task was to ensure that each Ogagi was visited at a specific time in its flowering cycle and was tended to accordingly.

Gozuri life was dictated by the flowering cycles of the Ogagis, the great trees of the forest that brought forth life, and they were bound to the duty of forever journeying from one to another to ensure that each Ogagi would stay in harmony with the forest. It took quite some time for Ani to decipher the words the Gozuri used for these things, as Integrum vox had no direct one-word translation, but from what she could deduce their word Hanraza meant 'harmony'. If an Ogagi had not been tended to by its own specific ritual, called a sabana, then the hanraza between Ogagi and forest would become unbalanced. When that happened, the Ogagi would undergo what is called a kusabana, the closest translation being 'a flowering chaos'.

The Ogagis were always growing and giving life, only stopping when they had become so bloated with their own sap that a kusabana would occur, where they would explode like an overripe fruit. They would then shower the local plants and wildlife with sap, which in turn perverted the nature of what it touched and from that came unimaginable horrors and oddities. Weird combinations of carnivorous mushrooms and cacti-like plants would become sentient and roam, killing or infecting. Creatures deformed and twisted would go out and kill or destroy indiscriminately. The sap also exuded a powerful smell that drove creatures wild with desire to consume it, creating a feeding frenzy of ever mutating proportions.

There had only ever been two kusabanas in the tribe's living memory, and, to her regret, Ani had been there when the last one started. It happened at the Ogagi the Gozuri called 'Of Color and Shape', and it was so violent and sudden, that all that remained of the most battle-worthy Gozuri were two initiated hunters: Tagai and Hoba. Over months, more and more of the Gozuri descended upon the kusabana in order to suppress it, and eventually they succeeded, but not without considerable loss. The Gozuri became a shadow of their former self, decimated to such low numbers, and along with them much knowledge and wisdom was lost.

Ani was chosen as the new Yohju out of respect for her age and intelligence, and the belief that wisdom from outside would somehow help patch the holes made by the death of others. She never had the heart to tell them that was foolish — they were only half her withered age! How was she to tell ones so young that she could not save them?

The Ogagis were a great fascination to Ani's party when they first learned of them. Tests performed on the sap showed an infusion of vesma so great that she was sure that was the source of the sap's transmutative powers. It was unlike the mineral vesma she had always known, which would react to everything almost explosively. At first samples were collected and sent back with one brave scout through the Gadori forest to the Integra Pol and Quadra Logicum, but the desire to continue research and experimentation soon faded in the face of no rescue party, the kusabana, and the need to survive each day.

Ж Ж Ж Ж Ж Ж Ж Ж Ж Ж Ж Ж Ж Ж Ж

Tagai had chosen to relieve the night-duty lookout as a form of self-punishment for his choices at Iro'Kamun. As he scouted to find a good point to keep a watch over his people his mind mulled over the recent events. He had conceded the point that at least one of the hachu had met its end, but to let the more dangerous one to escape him may have been a mistake. They had such limited time and resources to dedicate to eradicating the chaos-spawn, so to have the time to find any was a rare opportunity. What was rarer still however was finding anyone living, Integrum or otherwise — but strangest of all was finding a boy who looked so weak fighting a hachu at Iro'Kamun, that neither he nor Hoba would dare tackle without preparation, and winning.

Tagai did not enjoy being in the unknown and unprepared — he was responsible for too many people to let uncertainty destroy those that trusted him. The boy was undoubtedly powerful though. *"Perhaps he could be taught to help us hunt?"* He shook the thought from his mind.

He had climbed the Mother-Tree, the Ogagi they were currently tending to, and with his boot's hooks planted himself firmly on the highest branch he could reach. *"That boy... he is either missed and just somehow ended up where he did, or he was put there far away for a good reason."*

He put his thoughts on hold as his mind settled into an ever-vigilant guard.

Ж Ж Ж Ж Ж Ж Ж

Hoba was nursing a bruised stomach whilst resting in his tent, and complaining to nobody in particular about how it wasn't his fault the kid was stupid enough to do what he did. To him it was just another series of events in a long history of Ani enjoying doling out punishment to him for, essentially, just being Hoba. His whining was interrupted by his swearing when he remembered the task that he had been entrusted with that he had yet to do. Though pain dulled his desire for responsibility, the task was too important for Hoba to ignore.

Cursing his stomach he hurried over to the base of the Mother-Tree and, after slowing down and catching his breath, reverently approached the Ogaden, home of the Ogahigi. The Ogaden was a home crafted for the Ogahigi from an Ogagi sapling, each structure unique to the Ogagi it was born from — but all serving the same purpose: to act as a conduit between forest and people. This Ogaden was born of the Mother-Tree, largest of all the Ogagis, and so looked like a large tree stump with four roots coming out at both the top and bottom.

Upon reaching the Ogahigi's home, Hoba placed his hands against a section of it to let it know he was there, and after a single ebb of the roots atop its crown, that section soon opened. He sighed to himself out of relief and peered inside — their Ogahigi looked healthy still. He checked the umbilical cords that tethered the young woman to the inside of it, and that the large roots on the bottom of the Ogaden had a healthy hold in the ground next to the Ogagi. This was not something that could be rushed for an Ogahigi was sacred, and to dishonor them would mean to dishonor the great sacrifice that person made long ago to become an Ogahigi.

To become an Ogahigi one had to volunteer to be sealed away in a large sapling cultivated from an Ogagi, with vine-like umbilical cords planted alongside one that would grow to bond both Ogagi and Ogahigi. From that bond both the sapling and human would find sustenance and knowledge — forevermore it was a life of great sacrifice, of life-long imprisonment, of living the line between plant and person.

How the Ogahigis came to be, how to talk with them, how to craft new ones, all was knowledge lost in the last kusabana along with the older members of the Gozuri. The tribe had lost the days when their Ogahigi would talk and advise, prophesize and guide. The only importance an Ogahigi held anymore was their role in the sabana.

Hoba's ritual checks and cleaning now completed he kissed the Ogahigi lightly on the forehead before sealing the trunk again, hoping in some small way she appreciated the affection. He always liked to think that there was the slightest hint of a smile when she was cared for, but a part of him doubted she registered anything anymore. In all the years since the last kusabana she had not moved, or spoken, or expressed anything beyond living and breathing.

Before he left the Ogaden he placed his head and hands against it and said, "<I am one of the last hunters of the Gozuri. For my brother-in-love Tagai, and the memory of our wife lost, I will not fail you.... >" He repeated it over and over until he felt better about himself before heading home for the night.

164 | CHAPTER IV - LAND OF THE GADORI

Ж Ж Ж Ж Ж Ж Ж Ж Ж Ж Ж Ж Ж Ж Ж Ж

As dawn's light broke through the trees, Tagai was the first awake to witness the waking of the Mother-Tree to greet Father-Sun. With the first rays of light piercing the canopy and striking the Ogagi, its bark sprung to life. Slowly the light bathed the Mother-Tree, making her surface ripple softly, and the branches to unfurl and sprout forth its leaves, revealing colors so bright and pure they had to be seen to be believed. This was one of the most magical parts of the day — the waking and sleeping of the Mother-Tree to the kisses of Father-Sun's rise and fall.

Tagai watched the hammocks the medishi used for the injured sway softly as the Mother-Tree ebbed, and in his wistfulness his heart wanted to recite a story from his childhood: The tale of how Mother-Tree fell in love with the power, might and tenderness of Father-Sun.

"<And from Mother-Tree nothing grew — she was cold, alone and unloved. Unable to grow strong in the cold, unable to strive forward out of despair, even other plants avoided the small, barren trunk. Then along came Father-Sun and told her to worry no more — that she was to take some of his might. In turn he asked that she love all that came to her, no matter the how, what or why. 'So grow strong for me, Ogagi. Let my light bathe you, and be mother to all things so I can shine down on our children and make them strong....' >"

"<And so Father-Sun poured his golden light onto the roots of Mother-Tree, and with pure joy she stretched out towards him and grew, and grew, and grew. The love formed that day was so strong, that it was why they both died at night. For they were too far apart. >"

Ж Ж Ж Ж Ж Ж Ж Ж Ж Ж Ж Ж Ж Ж Ж Ж

There was a great fawning interest from the medishi overseeing Toyo's hammock — why had the bark of the Mother-Tree 'woken up', except for near the boy? The medishi treating him exchanged panicked looks of confusion but, after a light rubbing and stroking of the Ogagi, could not see anything wrong with neither tree nor child. A mixture of awe and confusion made them nervous, so a runner was sent to inform Ani of the strangeness. Not wishing to waste time, the medishi moved on to their next patient.

As the runner nimbly descended the tree, they felt a soft *whoosh* and an accompanying sound of "Ahhhhh!" as the boy with the iron hands plummeted past them.

Toyo was unsure of what was happening, he was also unsure of where he was, yet again. However that was not half as scary as finding himself sleeping peacefully, only to turn over, accidentally grab the side of a hammock, tear it with his gloves, and go from sleep to a waking fall in mere moments. This series of events was, much to Toyo's irritation, punctuated by the ground.

Toyo, being more than a little rattled by his morning's waking, stood up and saw he was once again subjected to intense scrutiny by a group of people. Shakily he said, "Hello." This made a few of the nearer people jump back slightly. The medishi, looking down from above, decided that they weren't needed seeing as there was no real need to inspect someone that was uninjured and awake — demonstrably exemplified by his walking and talking.

Ani rushed over as soon as the runner informed her of what had happened. Waving everyone aside, she walked through the crowd to see the boy standing there, waving idiotically, and standing in what looked like an imprint of him on the ground. She was only slightly surprised by this as the grass and ground around the Mother-Tree was very soft, but she still had to think, "*He must have been too skinny for gravity to care to kill him.*"

Toyo watched as the old woman with a face of sheer determination made her way towards him.

"Good morning, boy," said Ani, stopping in front of him.

Toyo replied, "Um... good morning?"

Hearing her greeting repeated back like it was a question confused her, so she tried to get more information. "It is what your people say to greet the day and each other, isn't it?"

"I don't know, do they?" Toyo felt helpless, how was he failing at conversing so quickly?

Ani tried a different tactic. "Aren't you happy that you are experiencing today? I would be, given everything."

Toyo desperately wanted to feel like he was on the same page as someone else, but wasn't sure if trying to catch up with them was a good tactic. "Uh... I'm not sure yet. So far today hasn't been very... good." He decided that maybe it would be better if he helped them catch up with him. "Then again given that I can only remember a few days so far I would have to say not being immediately threatened with death, freezing or starvation is a nice change. Not counting the immediate fear of death thing I experienced just now."

Ani again felt lost with the boy. "Hm... Maybe my vox is a little rusty." She spoke slowly and deliberately. "Are you okay?" Patting himself down, scarcely able to believe that he wasn't hurt, he reported that he seemed to be perfectly okay. "You don't find that odd, boy?"

"Well... yes, but it wouldn't be the first time so far. I'd prefer it though if you didn't call me boy."

"Why?"

"Well... I don't know, that's not my name for one."

"Do you have a name?"

"Toyo."

"That doesn't sound like a name from any region I know."

"Well, it's mine."

"Is it now."

"Yes. Even if it is just something I read off my gloves," said Toyo, offering his wrists for Ani's inspection. She was not foolish enough to touch the gloves again, but sure enough there was 'Toyo' etched on the wrist portion of the gloves. "And what's your name?"

"My full name is Anicula Amo, but it has been a long time since anybody has called me that. I am known to everyone as Ani." All she could see in front of her was a child, but he couldn't be 'just' a child. "Would you like some food?"

Toyo nodded fervently. "Yes." A memory popped up in his head and it told him to add, "Please."

Shooing the crowd away Ani led the boy to her tent, to the stares of many. Hoba decided to stand guard outside to make sure the crowd got no funny ideas, but mostly was hoping to overhear anything interesting. Several came and went to prepare the breakfast for the Yohju and her guest, but all he could hear as he strained his ears was that damned vox being spoken.

Ani gestured for Toyo to sit and said, "I would recommend you take your time with your food. Last time I saw you I was surprised you weren't throwing up bones." With his memory fogged by the drugs of yesterday he wasn't quite sure what she was talking about, but decided it was best to heed the old woman's warning. Picking some spherical and hard looking food from a bowl, he was surprised when he bit into it that it was sweet and juicy. Enjoying his chewing, he watched the old lady fill her plate and let his eyes wander — he noticed that it was quite an odd tent.

His inspecting was interrupted by, "Enjoying being nosy? You know it is quite rude to ignore the host of the meal."

"Sorry," said Toyo sheepishly.

She waved her hand dismissively. "Don't apologize, that custom implies shame. There is no onus on you to be nice to me, or even polite, unless you want to stay with us. The only thing I ask in return for the food and shelter is answers."

Toyo panicked, what the *valde* did he know that he could give her? "Answers to what?"

"Who are you?"

"I told you that, my name is Toyo."

"... Let's try a different question, where did you come from?"

"Um, I don't know. I don't even know where I am right now," he said matter-of-factly.

"Really? You don't even want to hazard a guess as to where you are? Forest of strangeness and wonders, the only forest large enough to cover the entire width of Kasmah?"

"So you're saying I'm in a forest. I knew that already."

"You really don't know the name of the place?"

"Should I?"

"Gozuri? Ogagi? None of these things conjure up any memories?"

"Nope."

"... What about the Land of the Gadori? Does that mean anything to you?"

Toyo was too excited at getting information to notice Ani's frustration. "Gadori? Is that where I am? It's a nice name. Does it mean anything?"

Ani was momentarily distracted by his exuberance. "It... is their word for forest. Sort of, that is a grossly simplified translation though."

Toyo thought about this. "So, land of the forest? Why don't they just call it a forest?"

Ani ignored him and thought to herself, "*You talked plenty about these things before. Why do you look and talk like someone that has lived under a rock for years now? You weren't this way before!*" Everything that had happened before this conversation made her feel like she was trying to fight her own brain in getting a straight answer out of the boy. "What DO you know then?"

"Uh... I'm not sure what I know," he paused for a moment, "I suppose I know stuff like don't stick your hand in a fire and don't poop in public, that kind of stuff. Is that what you meant?"

"Not really." Ani pinched the bridge of her nose and rubbed her eyes. "This conversation is a little frustrating."

Toyo gave her a look of irritation. "I don't recall being asked to be hit with some strange wooden stick just as I was about to kill something, then drugged, and then waking up in a tree and saying 'Hello' to Mr. Ground this morning either — so I suppose we can just both be frustrated. *Plaga*, I didn't even know other people existed until this morning! So far my goal in life is to have a day where I wake up without it having to be a struggle to survive the next five seconds." Toyo didn't know where the new word *plaga* had come from, but he enjoyed saying it.

Holding back her surprise at hearing a profanity, she asked, "Do you know what that word means?"

"What? *Plaga*?"

"Yes."

He thought for a moment before saying, "Not really. Is it like *valde*?"

"… Sort of. Those are Integrum profanities."

"Really? Even *futuo*?"

"Unless you are referring to Erus Futuo, the first recorded Erus of the Quadra Lustrum, then yes."

"His name is a profanity?"

"He was… not a very nice man." She omitted the fact that he was renowned in his time for being such a maligned bastard that his name became common to use when someone was really unhappy with something, or when they wanted to fornicate, or when they wanted to upset someone. It was one of the Integrum's oldest, and more colorful, profanities.

She narrowed her eyes and tried to bring focus back to more pressing concerns. "Wait, you don't remember ANYTHING from yesterday?"

"I definitely remember the big tree. But other than that, some… fairies… something about pants, I think?"

"… Pants?"

Not wanting to go into that he asked, "Why was I sleeping on the side of a huge tree?"

"It's called an Ogagi. We put you in one of the medishi's healing hammocks."

"Was I sick?"

"In a way."

"I don't remember anything…."

Ani sighed to herself. "Yes, that might be because the herbs they used on you are more designed to subdue large beasts rather than small children."

"I am not a child, thank you," said Toyo, in a polite attempt to remind her.

Ani replied, "Your physique is contrary to that statement."

"… what?" asked Toyo, unsure of all the words she had just used.

"You look like you are fifteen."

All traces of politeness vanished as Toyo said, "Well you look like you are ninety and then some, but I'm not referring to you as old withered crone am I?"

Ani smirked. "Quite a mouth on you isn't there."

"I also have ears and a nose. I don't talk up to you, so don't talk down to me," said Toyo defiantly.

"Proud too I see. Odd for someone without memory. Have anything to be proud about?"

"Well I survived walking in that bloody cold and took on a huge swamp creature, and that whole ordeal with these stupid gloves," Toyo put his hands palms up to demonstrate his point. "So yeah, I think I'm doing okay."

Ani's curiosity was piqued. "Ordeal with the gloves?"

"Yeah, when I put them on it really hurt, and now they seem to not be going anywhere else — I mean, I CAN'T get them off, and I don't know if they can be removed without taking my hands with them."

"… This may be a lot easier if you just started from the beginning. Unless you think I'm some sort of threat."

Toyo snorted in defiance at the notion this old lady could ever be considered a threat to him. "Sure, happy to tell you what I can remember from scratch," and with that Toyo launched into every detail he could provide, from waking with the surges of pain to the now.

Ani sat there absorbing everything he had to say, but was silently getting more and more apprehensive with each piece of information that passed his lips. "You were fighting a hachu, and winning? Then came another hachu, and you still survived?" she asked.

"No, one was this lizard type thing, and another was some sort of bird. They weren't the same thing at ALL."

"They are. At least, to this forest they are."

"Well that's stupid, different things should have different names. Otherwise it would just be confusing."

"It's complicated."

"Well I'm giving you answers, can't I have some? I don't want to sit here and be confused forever."

Ani sighed. "All creatures born of a kusabana are called hachu, because to name all the different ones would take far too much effort. The chances that there is another creature alive that is the same as those you saw are effectively zero. They are all hachu, dangerous things to either be killed for food, killed to save us, or killed to maintain the balance of the Gadori."

"If they all have to be killed then why haven't they done so already? They don't seem that tough."

His childish approach to a problem the Gozuri had been fighting for lifetimes may have earned him a smack from Tagai, but Ani was too curious about him to care about the indifference of youth. "It usually takes a lot of time and effort to wipe any out — days of stalking and identifying their particular weaknesses and strengths and knowing when to strike. Some hachu do not live long as they fall prey to stronger predators or simply starve, but those who survive and posses the ability to spawn are the ones to worry about. The Gozuri do not disrespect the hanraza and the forest by naming the hachu."

There were a lot of words Toyo didn't know and it showed on his face. "Hanraza?"

Her irritation at his questions grew alongside her need to be alone to think. "It is the Gozuri term for 'balance', but again that is quite a rough translation."

"How is that —" Ani didn't have time to waste with a boy who couldn't tell her anything, so quickly thanked him for joining her for breakfast and hurried him out of the tent.

It was a confused Toyo that was shoved out into a nosy Hoba, knocking them both onto the ground. Ani poked her head out after she heard Hoba's swearing and found an angry Hoba on the ground alongside a slightly stunned Toyo, who was wondering what was being screamed at him.

Hoba quickly stood up and put his boot on the boy's chest. "<Apologize! >"

"What?!" Toyo struggled under Hoba's heavy foot.

Ani translated. "He's asking you to apologize."

"For what?!" Toyo swung at Hoba's foot with his iron hands, spooking Hoba and making him step back.

"He thinks you ran into him on purpose."

Standing himself up, Toyo said, "You pushed me!" He was already irate from Ani ending their conversation without giving him the answers he wanted — to be accused of something on top of that just made him think that everyone was being unfair to him.

Ani told Hoba what had happened and to leave the boy alone, but that didn't stop Hoba from expressing displeasure via his face.

"Why is he looking at me like that!?" asked Toyo loudly.

Ani replied, "He doesn't like you."

Toyo was furious now. All he had done was his very best given everything that had happened and still people were trying to make things difficult. In a huff he began to walk.

"Where are you going?" Ani asked him.

Toyo didn't respond and just kept his course.

"Hmph, youth…" said Ani to herself.

While Toyo was walking all he could think of was that now he had found people, what he really wanted was to be left alone.

INTEGRUM

The *deprimo os* began to dissolve, gradually returning to Mulat the senses that had been taken from him. "Wakey wakey, *little one*," said a muffled, familiar voice.

Mulat was roused further by his shoulder being pierced by a short metallic spike, which was accompanied by a woman's giggling. Grunting in response, he decided that he had made the right choice and that this was indeed far more interesting than the day he'd planned on. He wondered briefly how his captor had gotten their hands on a *deprimo os*, but was more surprised by the fact that they had tweaked it to be effective against someone like him. He had not expected to be under the *deprimo os'* effects so completely.

Shortly after the mask had fully dissolved, the first thing he noticed was a rather large set of breasts. "*Breasts,*" thought Mulat. "*I wonder what purpose they are to serve in this situation.*" He noted that the clothing covering them had no ulterior motive than to bring attention to them.

"Like what you see?" said the mystery woman, before slapping him hard.

"*Ah, they want my attention. Let's see what happens if I don't give it to them.*" He recalled Juvo once saying that he was like a boy with an almost pathological inability to not make things worse, he however felt that if a situation was thrust upon him he had every right to make it as interesting as he liked. "*I wonder how long she will last.*"

"DON'T PLAY GAMES WITH ME!" screamed the woman, making a huge leap from attempted seduction to full blown screaming banshee.

Unfazed by her quick psychotic swing he replied, "That depends." She came into focus and he saw that she was quite young and had short blonde hair. The outfit she had chosen to wear said to Mulat that for her sex was the highest power.

"On what?" she asked, curious.

Mulat replied, "I am merely trying to qualify the response I give to your question, and to do so I require more information."

"You DO know you are my prisoner don't you?" asked the woman, wondering if the *deprimo os* had done unintentional damage.

"Am I? That would be a nice change of pace, and subsequently satisfy the needs of my day's goals."

"I captured you! I have you tied up, and you have a SPIKE through you!"

"And you have accentuated your cleavage," replied Mulat, visibly irritating his captor and waiting a moment before continuing. "Why are we making a series of declarative statements?"

The woman's face returned to one crazed and she began laughing. "HAHAHA! Yes! You are everything I remember you to be, and... so much MORE." She reached out to touch him with hesitation akin to touching a deity, and was transported to a world of her own as she sniffed him deeply and probed his body tenderly.

"I'm strapped to a wooden slab, shoulder still bleeding. Only available smells are my blood... something odd about my blood. Motive for capture seems to be one of passion, not purpose. She appears to be around twenty-five, highly aware of her sexuality, not at all bashful." Mulat was excited by this turn of events, finally something different!

The woman had already begun to consume her passion through touching him, and not wanting to interrupt what was making her happy he decided to at least stop his bleeding. Something wasn't right though, he was having trouble exerting his usual control over his body and began to grow concerned.

After ten seconds of being cuddled, he felt her shiver and start giggling. Expecting another manic change, he was surprised when she pulled her face up to his and looked deeply into his eyes. "Having trouble are we?" she said, grinning wide and fondling the spike protruding from his shoulder. She softly said, "Yes... yes I know all about you," before beginning to speak in dramatic tones, "Integra Divinitas Mulat!"

Another wild swing in tone, this time to one of pleading. "I know all about you! I know how you were made! Stagnos' plan to birth rather than train one! How they experimented with women who could tolerate birthing an Integra Divinitas! So many births! Over thirteen failed attempts at creating someone like you, some of those births even ended in killing many! But you... you were success! Kept growing inside your mother for nearly eighteen months, they had to cut her open constantly so they could experiment and 'improve' your developing body... I know everything." Her words came out in a hurried rush like an eager child. She hopped off and ran to a nightstand to rifle through some papers. "I have Erus Adsum's notes right here!"

She returned quickly, flourishing a piece of paper that she began to read aloud, "Human behavioral response to alpha figures are most potent when they can provoke the fight or flight response via visual intimidation — forcing the brain to consciously, or otherwise, respond. Directed fear experiments show that this is not dissimilar to when a subject is presented with a clear and immediate danger, proven by placing test subjects in a locked burning room. Postmortem analysis indicates similar blood contents as to when one is presented with a human of height over 6 feet — after accounting for being burned alive." Physically shaking from being unable to contain herself she blurted out, "And I love you!"

Quickly fingering through the sheathes of paper, she picked another at random to read aloud. "All Integra Divinitas' in recent history have demonstrated increasingly diluted concentrations of vesma, subsequently their unique 'blood powers' have waned. Stagnos' belief of starting the infusion process *in utero* has resulted in many failures, but I suspect he is on to something..." she droned on in an attempt to impress her captive.

Mulat now felt an unfamiliar twinge of uncertainty and decided that the charade had been overplayed. He prepared himself to break the slab and bring this woman to her senses, only to find that he could do nothing. He began to struggle and call on his reserves of power and unleashed what he could to free himself — the room rattled, and a strong high pitched noise sang in response, and the more he tried to exert, the more sound emitted from the walls.

"My! Such POWER!" squealed his captor as she watched the walls vibrate, resonating with Mulat's attempts. Touching the walls gently and shuddering, she drifted away again into her fantasy land.

His thoughts were interrupted by a memory, an old request he had fulfilled many years ago, and the remorse he felt from honoring it flowed through him fresh once more. At the time he'd merely thought he was being kind in granting a child's request when he was Potentiate, but by the time he had learned the damage he'd caused it was too late. He did not know how long he had been out for, but now that he knew the person who had captured him he knew that he was somewhere near, if not somewhere inside, the Lustrum.

"Tari, I am indeed impressed," said Mulat.

A grinning Tari said, with burgeoning tears in her deep green eyes, "I knew you would be, I tried so hard to make this interesting for you!"

"I see you dyed your hair — a shame, I was always a fan of your red locks. As beautiful as your mother's it was."

"I did it for you!"

"Did you? Why?"

"You like blondes! I'm growing it out for you right now!"

"*Ah,*" thought Mulat. "*She is trying to emulate Juvo.*"

The first time he met Tari was during a visit to the Quadra Lustrum when Ardeo was its Erus. Mulat was making his first trips to the Quadras to inspect that which he would work with so closely for the rest of his life and see more of the world beyond the Integra Pol.

It was a time of his life that he treasured as through them he learned over the years what made many people happy. In time though sadness sank in, for the more powerful he grew the harder it became for him to affect people in smaller and smaller amounts — like a giant's hand trying to do fine needlework. It made him distant in a way he wasn't ready for, and there were some tapestries he had left torn because of it. Tari was one of them.

There were distressing times for her after his unknowing mistake, but he could do little to help as he kept pushing her away at her mother's request, which only made her want him even more. Her constant environment of sex and lack of restrictions merely fueled her hormonal desires, and Mulat's power drove them to heights the young Tari found hard to control. Years then passed, and after so much rejection and avoidance eventually she disappeared. Until now.

"I am rather surprised that you chose to keep me clothed, Tari."

Tari smiled. "And ruin all the fun?" She began caressing Mulat's head softly. "As my mother always says, there is fun in the anticipation of things."

"While anticipation may be fun, do you really want me to bleed out?"

"Of course not!" She began fondling the spike once more. "I love you Mulat, I've always loved you… I've spent years watching you. I know everything about you, I know you better than anyone! I know you better than Juvorya! I've always loved you…." With eyes both crazed and sane she said, "… and you WILL love me."

"How can you know me better than someone you've never met? Have you even seen her before?"

"I've seen her! In… the distance. She can't know you better than me though! I knew you before she did!"

"Yes, you did. If you knew me better than her then you would know that this is a far from ideal form of seduction Tari. Talking to me directly would have yielded far better results." He mentally added, *"Then again, maybe not."*

"You abandoned me! Ignored me! And why? Every time you sneak out of your tower I always see you bored. I know what you need and I can give it to you!" She pointed at the walls. "Look! I saved up the blood you leave behind in your garden, and over so many years I've finally collected enough to coat the walls of this room in it. Storing and preserving it was difficult, but I persevered, and I had some friends help me find out how to turn it against you. That's why you can't do much. That's why the walls sing! They are singing YOUR song!" Her words started to come out in short bursts, starting and stopping like she couldn't control her mouth or emotions. "I've done good haven't I? You don't know how to get out of this, you're not bored, see? I just want to make you happy...."

Mulat had wondered as to how his power was being dampened, it was something that he had never encountered in all his years but something he had always assumed must be possible. "*A plan in the making for a few years then. Quite a determined little thing,*" he thought. It had been too long since someone got the better of him in any sense, or even expressed a direct interest in him beyond being the Integra Divinitas. Everyone saw the markings of his office and the power he wielded, rarely the man behind those things.

Tari however was a mistake — he had riled up a young thing with her hormonal stirrings, and placed within her a falsehood he did not then understand. He knew all the motions of how to woo and excite, incite fear and loathing, make people laugh — he just never understood *why* those feelings existed. The young Mulat never wondered about things beyond wanting to be useful to someone for he had never undergone any hormonal changes, never had he experienced puberty. The only pleasure he knew was from another human's emotions, so inciting lust and love to him was just his way of making people happy.

Mulat sighed slowly as Tari loomed over him, her eyes wide with anticipation. Looking her directly in the face he said, "What am I to say Tari? Would you even trust my response at this point? I am staked to a..." he shifted his body slightly, "Altar of some sort, and bleeding. You have stripped me of action and taken advantage of me at my emotionally weakest. As an opponent you have been cunning, so on that part yes you have 'done good', but killing me is obviously not the victory. Now, I've spoken truth about this situation, can you speak truth in turn?"

Tari's face sharply turned to panic and she rushed over to a nearby shelf, snatched a small pot, and hurried back to Mulat. She hastily smeared the mixture contained within over his wound that stopped the bleeding, which was surprising — he'd expected a reaction more unstable as his blood reacted unpredictably to reagents and tinctures. Knowing his blood to be dangerous, she had wrapped her hands in a special cloth to collect the spilled blood, and he remarked to himself that Tari had come very well prepared for this.

She wanted this to be hard for him, she wanted to shine for him. While she collected she said, "See? I don't want you to die, this is a challenge! Not a death sentence, no more pain for you... I'm sorry!"

"If death is not what I am threatened with, what challenge is there really?"

"I've learned your secret too," Tari said as she finished collecting up the blood. "And I still accept you, I still love you, and I will still be with you."

He was curious. "What is it you have learned then?"

"A secret that you have only shared with Juvorya, and no-one else. The secret of the Integra Divinitas' blood."

Mulat face went to one of mild surprise. "Again, impressed."

Tari broke into a manic grin, "And I still love you! Your secret is not evil in my eyes! That's why I've collected your blood for so many years! To make this room and try everything I could to find what your blood would respond to. You always thought your little fall trick would go unnoticed, but I found out, I found everything out! It took me so long and I tried so hard but I finally did it! I know what your heart wants and I can give it to you Mulat, I promise with all my heart."

The situation had crossed from simple into something far more to his liking — difficult and complicated. "If it is any consolation to you Tari, I am rather enjoying this. For once in a good long while I have to actually think." Tari almost did a little jig at this high praise. "I was sad to hear that after me you instead consoled yourself with creating quite the reputation for yourself. To be called the ruiner of men and women alike whilst still being the most sought after is no easy feat, not to mention your famed sexual escapades. But, I do not have time to enjoy this situation, nor to repair the damage I did long ago."

Mulat's face became serious and determined. "I would recommend letting me go, or I will have to leave by my own force." As his face grew ever more serious with each word, the gaze and attention that pierced most people's souls had little effect on Tari, who had been transported to a little world of her own at being praised by the man she worshiped.

Sighing to himself, he tensed the muscles around the wound to hold the spike in place, and in one swift move tore himself free of the straps, got off the table, and grabbed Tari by the throat with his good hand and slammed her against the ground. She squirmed under his grip both out of fear and excitement, never taking her eyes off him.

"It would appear you still don't know all of my power, Tari," said Mulat in a calming tone. Tari went into a panic and her eyes darted around the room while her face went from joy to abject terror, mixed with lust. "Thank you for the distraction Tari, I will let you keep the memory of what has happened. I have been impressed, and I feel the passion you have for me. I hope one day it will rise again and I will be able to taste it the way it deserves, but right now there are more important things." He leaned in closely to her. "Memories are important, but that one secret you have is not one you can keep," and with that Mulat bit his bottom lip, drawing blood, and kissed Tari deeply like he did long ago.

As his lips parted from hers, he whispered, "Today made me feel vulnerable... thank you."

Ж Ж Ж Ж Ж Ж Ж Ж Ж Ж Ж Ж Ж Ж Ж

The earliest recorded years of Kasmah were filled with many who were rich in vesma, and all the violent wars they waged. In the face of such raw chaos many perished, some to themselves, but most from each other's fears and prejudices when the ignorant and cowardly found themselves with power unearned. With the devaluation of knowledge and wisdom in the face of strength and cruelty, more was lost in the warring years than mere bodies.

Peace then was a strange concept to all, which may have been why a man stranger still was the one to bring it. He was a man unknown, a man unrivaled in strength, spouting what everyone thought to be insanities. There was no want to fight in him, only to talk, but in those days people had far more important things to do: survive.

This madman however made claims that made little to no sense, and some so wild that many began to band together in the fear that he would one day snap and lay waste to everything. The man only yearned to be heard but in time he came to understand that was a lost cause, causing him to weep with grief and lock himself away in a strange tower.

Fearing the madman's return many kept their alliances, allowing some years of prosperity to follow his departure, as the threat of a common enemy dulled the emotional blade of hatred. When fear of the madman faded, war returned. There were those however that had in peacetime grown tired of the death and destruction and decided to flock to the madman's tower. It was a strange, tall, bone-white animal tooth shaped tower, and it acted as a beacon to all.

Many wars found their way there, only for them to dissipate just as quickly. The tower was impervious to all attempts to destroy it, and retaliated with equal power any and all force exerted on or near it. Its reputation of stability in the face of an ever changing landscape of destruction helped people find comfort there. Tranquility bred community and soon a small town was flourishing around it, but none dared to approach the tower lest they somehow draw the attention of the madman and destroy their sanctuary.

Years passed, and the people in the small town were content, until, suddenly, the doors to the tower were flung wide open. From inside walked out the fabled madman from long ago, his age-old reputation once withered by time was now deified by the peace he had brought to everyone. Many ran, many offered themselves up as tribute to protect their families, but ultimately all were in awe of the man who stood before them.

With a sad face the madman spoke. "I am of no threat to you, nor of you to me. I know you are used to either conquer or rule, but I can provide neither. You may all stay. I wish for no greed or hate to destroy those who desire to live happy lives. I will bring us close together, but I can only protect you from those that desire you harm, not from yourselves."

After so long sequestered away in his tower, the madman came to finally involve himself in those who had come to him. In time the small town was prosperous and soon it became the now mighty city of Orbis, with his tower the centerpiece and its pure white grounds, and stable yet sterile visage, saying to all that we can achieve greater things together than apart. That message spread far and wide, and people of all languages and colors that had yet to find their place flocked to it.

The madman named the world, Kasmah, and the three regions within it, the northern Maharaan Expanse, the southern Land of the Gadori, and the central Integrum. Then he came to name the power that permeated the world — Veneficium Kasmah, which people in turn came to call vesma. Vesma naturally formed as crystals, ranging in color and size, transparency, and even texture, but it was also present in varying quantities in every living thing. It was a dangerous substance in truth, but that still did not stop people from trying to dilute, forge, mine, and embroider their clothes with the substance. The volatility of it and its propensity for destruction all had known for some time — many a great wielder had been seen on the battlefield immolated by expending more than he could handle.

Names however were not enough — his people needed laws, no matter how little he wanted to write them. So he searched for people of great intellect and passion to inhabit his tower to aid him, and as their knowledge grew so did their power, but being ruled by a collective led to bickering and the people were unhappy.

All cried out for the madman to rule them and even though he had spent years fighting the call he eventually succumbed, and he took on the title of first Integra Divinitas and finally gave his tower a name. The Integra Pol.

Years passed, and peace stretched out from Orbis to all parts of the Integrum, giving rise to more cities and industry — trade and knowledge became of value once more. Seeing the people's renewed affection for what he felt were the basic precepts of humanity, the first Integra Divinitas demanded the construction of public houses dedicated to the betterment of human need which he called the Quadras.

Through the Quadras he experimented with what he called his base desires, but his great power corrupted them to such extremes that it led him to cause many problems for the people he had come to care for. It reached a peak that he could not live with and culminated in his decision to castrate himself, and so dictated that all future Integra Divinitas' should be so as to not upset the pure balance the Integra Pol strived for. The tenet of sacrifice came to be an unspoken rule of the Integra Pol, the price one should pay if they truly wish to live and learn within its walls.

Decades passed, and worrying reports cropped up describing horrific births and deaths. After personal investigation by the first Integra Divinitas he concluded that the proximity of so many people and their vesma could mutate and pervert reality. The vesma seemed to call out to itself and the blood of others. At first the solution seemed simple — build cities in other regions and provide incentive for migration, but people preferred their life within the major cities of the Integrum. Those who took up the offer to live in the harsh hot lands to the north or the cool southern forest lands were only the hardiest of people.

To solve this problem the first Integra Divinitas went on a journey and reappeared years later with an answer. A ritual called the Deaspora could be performed with the aid of two special people, whom he called the Vir and Mulier, which could disperse the vesma by force and leave everyone none the wiser. For the citizens of Kasmah all that happened once every few hundred years was a beautiful display in the sky of formless color, and for a while the night-sparks would no longer be.

After the first Deaspora, population management became a key function of the Integra Pol, which led to the first important collaboration between Integra Pol and a Quadra — the Quadra Lustrum. Some years after the second Deaspora, the first Integra Divinitas abandoned his post and disappeared.

ЖЖЖЖЖЖЖ

Kasmah's beginnings had long been forgotten, as the great wars of old did what all wars do: consume history, cultures, and language alike. All knowledge of Kasmah's origins was reduced to an assortment of tales and fables of great giants or powerful beings who long ago created Kasmah from some great celestial conflict.

In time, the Integra Pol scholars isolated a central theme amongst them, which was that the world they knew as Kasmah was not the shape it had always been. That a great catastrophe had somehow thinned the world — warping it from a sphere being as wide as it was tall, to something where the distance between north and south was greater than that between east and west. In truth there was no accurate measurement of Kasmah as nobody could cross the Calu-Jedde Mountain range, or measure the chaotic waves of the Vios Ocean.

The Integrum was positively idyllic, filled with majestic fields, hills, and an abundance of fertile lands that had few native dangers. Whereas the Maharaan Expanse and Land of the Gadori were places suited only for those who enjoyed a life of constant trial. The Maharaan Expanse, with its harsh expansive deserts, dry-beds and glaring sun, provided strong materials for industry. While the Gadori, with its dense forests, ice-fields, and biting cold, offered up a myriad of plants and animals.

The only things that pierced the landscape and connected all were the great Vios Ocean, whose child rivers snaked out to traverse the land, and the Calu-Jedde Mountain range. These were called the spines of Kasmah, and each spanned through the Maharaan and Gadori with no known beginning or end, and each split the world into east and west.

Though Kasmah and its beginnings were difficult, the Integra Pol and its Divinitas' brought an end to the troubling times.

And so long as the Integra Pol stood it would always be a beacon of cooperation and hope.

CHAPTER V

*I see you Mother-Tree,
and how you come alive.
When Father-Sun bathes you in light,
and both of you beg all living things to thrive.*

-Gozuri ballad of Mother-Tree and Father-Sun

THE MAHARAAN EXPANSE

Kahli had been doing her best for the wounded wija, but all her best intentions and efforts did little to help and more often than not she felt like she was just prolonging its suffering. Every day that it struggled to stand stabbed at her heart, and each time she would run off into the field of green to see if any of the plants would heal it. She had fed it a wide variety of them to no effect, even feeding it the ample morning dew that collected on all the grass and plants around her seemed hopeless. All this had become a daily routine, and every time she would go to fetch sustenance for the wija, she would leave her pouch in front of its nose in the hopes it would keep her smell in its memory. In a way to show it that she would return soon.

While she walked through the field in search for the next miracle plant she was struck once more by the thought that it was almost as if a sea had decided to bloom and invite the world's flowers as one to come swim in its bounty. There was nothing that made where she was make any sense, unless the wija had somehow carried her all the way to the Integrum without her noticing — but was the Integrum actually this full of life?

Fear stayed her from venturing too far from the wija, its failing health did not give her much time for exploration, but from her daily walks all she had seen was nothing more than strange plants and flowers, stretching out onto the horizon. It was quite a beautiful place, tranquil and peaceful. The last few days here had brought her some peace and if she had not something to care for she would have allowed herself longer daydreams. For some reason this place made her prone to such things, and just as before she found herself having to shake her head free of fanciful thoughts, quickly gather what she could, and returned to the wija — hastened by guilt.

When she caught sight of her wounded friend, her heart stopped. It was surrounded by dead ground. Where once was fresh grass and flowers was now stripped of all its green and had become gray and dusty.

From far away the other voice in her head softly said, "*Death comes....*"

She broke into a sprint as soon as she heard the chittering noise of a thousand tiny gnashing mouths, and the feeling in the pit of her stomach got worse when she could hear the *ching ching* of a thousand tiny claws and teeth eating away at something.

"*Underground,*" said the other voice. "*They are first eating the roots of the plants the wija is on. Then they will eat the plants, and then they will eat the wija.*"

Kahli had only ever known the protection of being inside Toka-Rutaa before, a truth she now regretted as she raced towards a problem she knew nothing of how to deal with. If only she had her mother's cunning or her father's strength, if only she knew what to do.

She could see the wija struggle to do something to get away from the danger it sensed, but it could do little more than stagger to its feet before its stitches burst. Kahli's tears flowed forth as freely as the wija's blood did onto the lifeless ground. Where its blood fell came a frenzied response as small pockets of strange creatures, which seemed to be both in and under the soil, reacted violently to the veritable feast.

Small numbers of little black worm-like creatures sprung from the ground where its blood had spilled and tried to burrow into its skin. The wija's breathing became rapid and heavy as its body shook — it knew what was coming, and the only thing it could find in its time of need was fear and weakness. It rolled side to side with as much effort it could muster, crushing the black worms against the ground, grunting with effort. All it was doing now, was delaying the inevitable. Soon it would be consumed from the ground up.

Seeing its plight spurred Kahli onwards ever faster. It couldn't die, not now. Not here. It didn't deserve this. The tendrils of the black swarm that were making their way up the wija might as well have been crushing her spirit. When she was mere steps from her wounded friend, chest burning and heaving with strain, she had only a glimmer of hope that she could somehow save it.

The wija though was pushed to action when it saw Kahli in danger, and let out a mighty roar before shifting its huge bulk and knocking her away with ease. Bruised and confused, she watched the wija stand up, shuffle its front legs in a strange manner, and rear up on its hind legs, before bringing them down with a thunderous crash, bringing with them a sound and force greater than she thought anything its size could make. A shockwave went through the ground beneath the wija, pulverizing the soil and everything within. The ground became a soiled grayish-blue, and all noises of teeth and claws stopped.

Standing there majestic and strong the wija stoically endured its broken form, as if by sheer will it would be able to keep its stature. Kahli stood in rapture, before watching it collapse once more broken to the ground. She ran to its side and tried to block out the sound of its pained gasps and wheezing. *"How did it do that?!"* she thought. *"You didn't need to save me! You didn't need to...."*

She knew that wija were... important for some reason. Was this the reason? No, this one was special! Why... Why did it.... Pushing her mind's racing thoughts aside, she proceeded to tend once again to the beast's wounds and grabbed her pouch, having to tug hard to pull it out of the ground. She was worried that its strain may have sealed its own fate to die here, fueling her to be much swifter and determined this time around.

Wiping fresh blood once again over the old stains on her skirt, she tried to control her emotions and think only of what needed to be done. *"Thread needle... pierce skin... pull through. Thread needle... pierce skin... pull through."* Her brain now focused entirely on caring for the beast that she had attacked, a beast who had done nothing but show her humility and submission. A wija that saved her.

"You are no healer," said the other voice.

After patching up what little she could, she cried. "I don't have to be here you know!"

She breathed in heavily and wanted something to happen,

something to let her know that it had heard her. She yelled at the sky as tears streamed down her face. "I said I was sorry! I did my best! I'm sorry that I'm not any better at this, BUT NOBODY SAID I HAD TO BE!" She didn't hear the rumble above her and barely noticed the rain beginning to fall as she slumped alongside the wija, part of her hoping to die alongside it. Rain spattered on her face and hit the lifeless ground, bringing up puffs of loose soil mixed with smashed up bits of whatever it was that had been moving in the soil.

For her it had been too long without respite and she had done her best, but she was only so young, and the world had thrown too much at her. How could anyone expect her to win. "*You cannot save it,*" said the other voice.

"No!" Kahli stood up. "NO! That's ENOUGH!" she screamed. It was time to fight herself, so she could fight for something else. Steeling herself, she returned her attention to the wija and her labored breathing began to match the rain as it began to fall heavier and harder.

Without thinking she removed her shirt to cover the creature's face to stop it from getting wet, after which she knelt and stretched her arms out into the rain. Cupping her hands in front of her, the sliver of a memory crept into her mind, and she unthinkingly said, "Praise Nujah for this bounty, life water from the Vios Ocean. May you return in time with the knowledge that you gave me your gift of life."

Every time her hands filled up she alternated between taking a long drink and trying to pour some down the beast's great mouth, then massaging its throat in an attempt to get it to understand that it should swallow. What little success she had did nothing to raise her spirits, as she knew it needed far more than mere water to save it. It needed more than what greenery could provide it with. It needed more than whatever she was capable of.

She looked around wildly for anything that could be done and she saw that the ground had now become slippery from the rain as the loose soil and water had mixed. Curious, she ran her hand over the surface and found that it was smeared with lots of broken bits of the tiny creatures that the wija had saved her from.

A thought struck her. *"Are they poisonous? I... don't think so, they just eat everything, don't they? So why would they need venom? So, if... they can eat anything, then maybe anything can eat them?"* She collected a thin layer of sludge to test with her tongue, and the only unpleasantness she could find from its texture was that it was a little bitter tasting. She swallowed her fear and took a larger lick. Scooping some up with her tongue she found that, whilst not the tastiest thing in the world, her stomach did not tell her it was an unwanted guest.

Living off of the same diet as the wija had not sat well with Kahli's stomach, so when faced with potential 'meat' she instinctively began scooping it up, but stopped short of eating it. There was someone far more in need of nutrition than her. The top layer was thin but she gathered what she could and helped it down the wija's gullet. When it had run out she could see that there was still more of the creature swarm locked in the soil, but it was still too dry to collect. *"Maybe I should just wait for the rain to soften it further?"* she thought, and sat with strained patience next to the petrified swarm.

Testing the ground every few minutes as the rain poured on, she found that it wasn't softening. A few more minutes went by, and every second brought to the forefront of the mind a feeling she didn't want to face. "No, no! NO! It needs more! It hasn't had enough! IT NEEDS FOOD!" she cried. Her voice became tinged with harmonics not her own as she screamed, "No! **NO!**" She punched the ground out of despair and self-loathing — for being so useless to a creature that had no doubt saved her.

Emotions overtook her as she began to scratch and claw at the swarm to try and scrape something, anything, together to feed her friend. Her fingernails cracked under the strain and the more she clawed the more her hands bled, but as she bled, fire began to pour out. Her hands began to spark and burn, and soon each strike to the ground began to light up the whole frozen swarm. Flashing in response, it looked like night-sparks were happening underground as her face went blank.

Strike after strike began to soften the ground and soon she was able to scoop up more and more of the creatures into a small pile next to her. Her power did not last long and she felt so tired afterwards, but at least she had gathered what she needed. Just when she was about ready to resume feeding the wija, she was interrupted by a surreptitious cough.

Kahli stood up and turned around, but her mind was not entirely with her and she was having trouble making things out. What she could see though were three women just standing there: one old, one young, and another middle-aged, but all looking the same in their strange white garments.

"You shouldn't do that," said the oldest woman as she placed her hand on Kahli's shoulder.

With her blank face, Kahli said, "Then what am I to do?"

"That all depends on how much you want to learn," replied the woman.

Kahli, still lifeless, said, "I do not know anything... I just want to fix what I did wrong. I want to know how to do right."

"That is a good a reason as any to want to learn. Do you want us to teach you? There is a warning though: Not all lessons are easy," said the woman in earnest.

With an honesty only the desolate could attain Kahli said, "... Nothing has been so far."

"Good, that means you are trying," replied the woman approvingly.

Looking at the newcomers she asked, "Who are you?"

"Those you asked to teach you. The first lesson being: If you feed the beast what is in your hands, you will not be able to handle the consequences. We can help you fix this, but only if you truly want to learn — or you can choose your own path and deal with the consequences yourself. Do you want to learn?"

Kahli felt too weak to hold on to memories and thoughts. "... Who are you?" she repeated.

"We are Integra Natura, answering the call of an anomaly we sought to investigate."

"... What anomaly?" she asked distantly.

"You are standing in it." Kahli looked down and wondered why it was so hard to think, why did the 'now' have so much trouble keeping its shape? "We answered your question, what is your answer to ours?"

Kahli felt like she was being asked to surrender, but didn't care.

"... Yes."

"Move then." Kahli stepped to one side and allowed the three women to crowd around the beast where they began applying strange ointments and bandaging the wija in ways that she would never have known. It felt more like she was watching a tapestry in motion, with her the audience detached from the reality in front of her.

Kahli received a short sharp slap that she didn't see coming from the woman who had spoken before. "You said you wanted to learn! Do NOT ignore this opportunity! I will only say this once: Do not disrespect our offer of teaching. We do not grant it lightly. Pay attention."

Kahli stared at the woman with subdued anger and fear but could feel some understanding as to what she meant. This was not time to let her mind slip away into that welcoming oblivion, it was time to pay attention.

"You aren't paying attention at all!" screamed the strange voice in her head.

Kahli raged inside her mind, "SHUT UP! I DON'T KNOW WHO YOU ARE OR WHY YOU ARE IN MY HEAD, BUT JUST SHUT UP AND STOP TALKING TO ME! WHAT DO I HAVE TO DO TO GET YOU TO LEAVE ME ALONE?!"

BREATHE!

LAND OF THE GADORI

Toyo's attempts to storm off into the jungle had been dissuaded by strange noises and the uncertain future they painted, so he made his way back to the Ogagi. Pouting and pacing until he found a suitable spot to sulk in he finally settled down and cried out, "Stupid old woman!" Clutching his knees to his chest he tried to get comfortable, while his seething, demonstrated by his heavy breathing and red face, was hard to misinterpret in any culture.

He searched his mind for a time where he actually felt in control of something and could only come up with when he was fighting that lizard, hachu, whatever, in the swamp. It felt... good, fighting for his life was at least ONE thing he could easily come to grips with. He tried to revel in that memory so he could off-set his current unhappiness, that primal feeling of being alive and fighting to stay that way, and to his surprise he found it made him feel better. With new-found comfort his breathing returned to normal, and he'd just started to enjoy the warmth generated by his knee-hugging when he heard a soft giggle from above.

Crouching and shifting his eyes up towards its source he scanned the huge side of the tree, determined to give it his angriest look. He spied long black hair draped over the side of a hammock that was hanging off the large tree. Ready to beat anyone up that would give him an excuse, his mind got confused when a pretty girl popped her head out to look down. The giggler gave a little yelp of surprise and retreated back into her hammock after seeing his expression, and Toyo himself fell onto his back.

"<He... hello? >" said the voice from the hammock, peering over the rim.

Toyo lay still for a moment looking up from on his back before scrambling to his feet as fast he could and stammering out, "Uh... yeah... um... hello!" After a moment he realized she probably didn't understand what he had said, so gave a nervous hand wave in the hopes of opening a line of communication. She tentatively waved back.

Then a minute passed with nothing more than both parties staring at each other.

Toyo's brain thought of fairies once more as he gazed upon the most beautiful person he had ever seen. A part of his brain tried to chime in with, "*That's not very many people,*" but he chose to ignore that bit. The girl eventually got bored with staring and adopted a more comfortable position, propping her elbow over the side of the hammock.

"<Are you going to say anything, boy? >" she asked as she rested her chin on the back of her hand. Toyo got the distinct feeling that he should say something back. His brain compromised with another hand wave.

The girl wondered if he was an idiot. "<Sure, you could do that again. Does that mean something where you come from? You could just say hello back, like a normal person. >" Toyo reached the conclusion that if this beautiful person was still talking to him that he must be doing the right thing and waved even harder. This made the girl giggle again, which gave him a stupid grin.

"<Well maybe you need me to start you off. My name is Nume, I'm eighteen, >" said Nume, thinking that this boy with his black hair was rather strange and a little stupid.

"Um... you have... eh," said Toyo sheepishly, "Really beautiful hair..." He felt stupid for saying what he thought inside out loud and rubbed his hands together as if he could wash off the embarrassment. "So! I like your... tree." She really did have the most amazing long black hair.

Nume looked at him now like he was dumber than before. She pointed to herself and said, "<Nume, >" then pointed at him. She had to repeat this a few times before they were able to exchange names.

A derisive chuckle came from behind. Toyo turned around to see Hoba standing there with a mischievous smile. "<Hello to you too, Nume. I hope you are feeling better today. >" Nume just rolled her eyes and slipped back under her hammock covers, muttering something under her breath. Hoba was not someone many people wanted to have much to do with.

Irritated by this interruption Toyo clumsily parroted Hoba's words back at him in what he hoped was a mocking tone. Nume peeked out from under her covers, excited that she had finally gotten a response from the stranger, only to discover Toyo repeating the words again in an angrier voice. She shrugged and concluded that whatever was happening now was far more interesting than being sick, so she contented herself with watching the events unfold.

Hoba felt harangued at the odd assault from this child and decided to discipline him, figuring it would come with the added bonus of letting off some steam. He had been sent to start preparations around the Ogagi for the sabana but that didn't mean this lucky happenstance couldn't be a nice detour. He went to slap Toyo's head, expecting the language of physical contact to convey the message of respecting one's elders.

What Hoba didn't expect was for Toyo to dodge the slap and swing an angry fist at him. He narrowly dodged it by shuffling his feet back and watched as the metal fist went full circle and buried itself in the Ogagi, sending sticky splinters flying with a mighty thud. The Ogagi shook from the force, and as Toyo pulled his fist free he fell backwards from not knowing his own strength and took a portion of the Ogagi with him.

Nume's hammock shook from the impact, and when Toyo pulled his hand free one of her supporting hooks was knocked loose. She panicked and soon fell, wrapped up in her hammock, straight to the ground. Nothing more than a small yelp and a light thud came from the fall, but a great shock went through Nume's mind — why would anyone strike an Ogagi?!

Toyo was furious. "*Try to slap ME will he?!*" As he got to his feet to throw another punch the short, fat man's way he saw Nume on the ground with Hoba speeding towards her. Taking this opportunity he hurled the chunk of tree that was still in his hand as hard as he could, hitting Hoba squarely on the head with a satisfying wet squelch. "Squelch?" said Toyo, surprised. Looking back at the tree he noticed a bright reddish-amber sap leaking from where his fist had landed, he then looked at his hands and saw them coated in the same strange color. He quickly checked with his brain again, trying to remember if trees were supposed to bleed.

Hoba stood frozen in place when he felt the piece of Ogagi hit him. Slowly moving a hand to his head he ran his fingers through the sticky mixture of hair and sap, and a look of muted panic came over him when his fears were confirmed. With a gaunt expression he began striding towards the tree when came a *Splotch!* A fresh volley hit him in the face, but Hoba continued undeterred.

The look on the fat hunter's face and the way he was walking spooked Toyo, an effect redoubled when he saw that he was heading straight for him. Shrinking back a little but not retreating Toyo stood his ground for whatever was about to come, and became confused when Hoba passed right by him and began packing the tree's seeping wound with mud and any excess sap he could find. Toyo relaxed slightly, but was wondering why he was being ignored for a tree.

Seeing that the fat man was busy he wanted to apologize to Nume, the girl that made his heart jump. When he got her unwrapped from her hammock and after she saw what he'd done, she gave him a look of hatred. He didn't know what he'd done to deserve it, but his heart couldn't handle having disappointed this beautiful woman.

Spurred on by the expression of scorn on Nume's face he went to help Hoba in a bid to curry some favor with the beautiful girl and so gathered up some bracken and mud like the short man had done, unsure of what to do with either. Sheepishly, Toyo moved forward to help with as much of the material he could hold and was chastised by a swift smack from the man, fueled by a fury Toyo hadn't seen in anyone before. Nume cowered, shuffled her back up against the tree and started to visibly shake.

In a stern voice Hoba said, "<You don't understand me, but you WILL understand this, >" and he pointed away from the tree. Toyo started to panic at being sent away like some sort of animal, not fully realizing the damage he had done.

Unsure of what to do he looked at Nume and stammered, "I...

I'm so sorry, I didn't mean to —" he was interrupted again by another swift slap across the cheek from Hoba.

Hoba jabbed his finger in a direction away from the Ogagi and barked, "<LEAVE! >" Distraught and upset, Toyo dropped everything in his arms and proceeded to walk away with head downcast and spirits dampened.

When he saw the boy had gone far enough Hoba returned to patching up the damage done, never once showing the fear on his face that anyone, let alone a boy, could have the strength to rip out the Ogagi's flesh. Twice. He looked towards Nume and saw that she needed to be tended to and whistled out for the medishi. Quickly fixing up what he could, he watched as Nume was taken and placed again in a healing hammock. Seeing that the two mistakes had been tended to as best could be, he allowed himself to panic.

"*It is.... It might... be safe,*" he thought to himself. He walked briskly for a moment, then broke into a run as he made his way back to Ani's abode.

Panting and red in the face, Hoba was greeted with Ani sitting at a small table in her tent. She shouted at him, "<What are you doing here?! I told you to —>"

There was no time for manners. "<That BOY tore out a part of the Ogagi! We haven't even started the sabana yet! We can't be here! >"

A few moments silence.

"<He did WHAT? >"

"<He tore it out! Two great fist-sized chunks! >" Hoba said, almost not believing the truth of his own words.

"<How?! >" she asked, and waited a moment before adding, "<More importantly, why?! >"

Hoba wasn't quite prepared to tell Ani that he may have provoked him. "<He... uh... >"

"<... we will talk about that later... >" said Ani, her knowing eyes narrowed on Hoba as she drummed her fingers on the table.

"<It is still several weeks until the flowering, the hachu will... >" she tried to quickly recall the timeline of everything to see if things might be saved. "<Might be.... No, I can't risk it. Signal the evacuation Hoba, then get Tagai and ensure that we get away safe! >"

Hoba ran out of the tent and started the piercing whistle pattern that would tell all that it was no longer safe, and the time to leave was NOW. Panic gripped the camp, but no questions were asked. Life for the Gozuri was too precious to waste with asking 'why' when told to run.

INTEGRUM

Erus Cogitans, current Erus of the Quadra Logicum, walked through the doors to Mulat's chambers with little fanfare or warning and with an expediency that made it difficult for those accompanying to keep up. "Mulat, you can't keep putting us off." The rest of the Quadra Erus' were not as confident at entering the Integra Divinitas' chambers in such a fashion, and one was still trying to recover from the long ascent.

Mulat was staring out of his window with an expression of fond recollection while gently touching his shoulder. He allowed the Erus' some time to squirm uncomfortably in the silence following Cogitans' demands before turning to them and giving them a warm smile. "My apologies, you will have to excuse my being indisposed the last few days, important matters." He directed his attention to the Erus of the Lustrum. "You know how it is, Criso."

Erus Criso was a lady refined, who could easily be viewed as Queen of her domain or most salacious of seductresses with her long neck, green eyes, and flame-red hair. She was always found in well-tailored ankle-length skirts with a variety of shirts that could either inflame the imagination or abandon all need for one. She replied, "All very well and good, but we DO have a city to cater to. You cannot keep being 'indisposed' for days on end."

Mulat raised an eyebrow. "How peculiar of you to dictate what I can and cannot do, given whose domain you are standing in. Then again some of your patrons do pay good sums to be able to tell others what to do."

"And how we long to serve you, Mulat," said Criso with a sincere smile on her face, ever on the lookout to charm those in power. With Mulat though that approach was always a fruitless effort — but just because sex was not on the table did not preclude equitable emotional and mental pleasures. Yet for all her skill and talent nothing Criso had tried in the past seemed to affect him, and how she had tried over the years to find such leverage. Her efforts had gone on for so long without fruition that she had forgotten her original reasons for charming him and now continued the game more for the desire to win than to gain.

"Can we dispense with the idle chit chat please? We have urgent business to attend to," said Erus Cogitans, in what his charges had come to call his angry accountant voice. He was a dull man who wore only the most perfunctory of clothing, and his brown hair was always cut in the fashion of someone who knew nothing of style. He was, contradictorily, as boring as he was feared, and lacked a facial feature distinct beyond its complete lack of distinction.

Mulat replied, "As you wish, Erus Cogitans." Then moved to his large desk and sat down, giving a brief smile to all assembled that now stood before him.

With Mulat's blessing, Cogitans launched into the agenda. "This new drug flowing into the city — we have countless reports of people going missing, sporadic berserkers, and other acts of lunacy. Productivity is down and certain sections of the city have had to be bolstered with extra guards in order to keep the peace. If we stand by and still adopt a policy of non-interference we will not have much of a city left to organize."

"My stance will not change."

"Mulat, the —"

"Orbis and its citizens will always be free to choose for themselves — if that means the downfall of us, so be it. It is their body and they are welcome to do as they wish with it. Would you rather I prohibit what is essentially free will? It would not work, for the rather simple fact that base human needs and wants are 'basic'. Anyone, anywhere, can figure out that touching themselves feels good — or that you can get intoxicated from almost anything that grows out of the ground, if you ferment it — or that some things you eat makes your head feel fuzzy — or that you can get a tune out of anything if you hit it the right way. Trying to stop human nature is stupid, all you can do is try to make the stupid parts of human nature non-fatal."

"My predecessor's research showed that punishment and torture is a highly effective form of behavioral change and information retrieval, Mulat," replied Cogitans.

"Punishment and torture is extracting and imposing information, not imparting it. A distinction that should not be that hard to identify."

"I was merely stating the fact that —"

Eager to stop a pointless thread of conversation that, Mulat felt, missed the point entirely, he interrupted with, "Learn the difference between the practical and the theoretical — Adsum never learned to appreciate the difference, hence his being your predecessor. However, I am not a fool, and in the spirit of ensuring that the stupid parts of human nature remain non-fatal I will overlook the fact that you have rounded up some people in order to run tests regarding this new drug. So, when your tests have yielded sufficient results, dispatch the heralds to the First Ring of Orbis to explain what you have found — more specifically what the drug is and what it isn't."

Mulat saw that Cogitans was still eager to talk, and so added, "The only allowance I will further sanction is in the areas most affected, you can publicly expose a test subject to the drug for all to see and come to their own conclusions. Furthermore, you will provide one of your researchers alongside to explain and oversee this demonstration, as education is the key — not, as your predecessor would believe, a beating." The veiled threat at being exiled like Erus Adsum brought a hush to Cogitans' usual desire to spew out facts.

Erus Ictus, Erus of the Quadra Musicum, a funny little man possessing a mind obsessed beyond reason with music, was the first to break the uneasy silence. "Mulat, something MUST be done about this situation. My musicians cannot earn or practice on the streets anymore for fear of either being raped or beaten to death." With his short white curly hair, and his peculiar and diminutive stature, many looked upon him and got the impression of a very thin cello. He was also the odd-ball of the current Erus', which was saying something for an Erus, and was sometimes found wandering in his pajamas on the grounds of his Quadra.

Sometimes completely naked. With his blue eyes, hunched back, bony fingers and faraway expression he was the most noticeable of the group — and the Erus least capable of recognizing people noticing him.

"Then attach one of your guards to the more skilled and move the less skilled to protected venues," Mulat replied.

"That would just scare off anyone willing to appreciate! Who would hear my charges play with armed guards around? Swords and strings don't go together!" Ictus' face froze as he wondered to himself, "... or do they?"

"Perhaps, but you will have to weather this storm like everyone else until the people of Orbis decide to forgo this drug altogether. Do you not think that Erus Criso is not suffering too? I suspect that the only one that is not experiencing such hard times would be Erus Epula, judging from his general silence." Mulat's words brought the whole group's attention to the Erus of the Quadra Culinum — the portly man was slightly ruffled by the sudden shift in focus.

Erus Epula had found the delights of baked goods and sweets late in life, and what they had done was add fat to an already stocky figure, resulting in a very solid looking man with strong jowls. The only things that people would count against his physique would be his black, wavy, greasy hair, and propensity to profusely sweat after even the slightest of efforts. "What? No! This drug affects us all! I am with the others, and you SHOULD do something about this situation. Sitting idly by is not the act of a smart ruler," said Epula, flustered.

Trying to bring some clarity to his reasoning, Mulat said, "And what would be the act of a smart ruler? I am to respond to this incident as a citizen first and a ruler second. As an individual I tell myself what I can and cannot do, whether or not that results in my demise is the price I pay for that. A ruler cannot punish choices and decisions, only the consequences of those — with said punishment being mediated by proven intentions. People take the drug if they so wish, we punish them if they cause harm to others after the fact. The Integra Pol's stance is that people need to understand that affecting others negatively is what we can, and will, punish." He looked into the gathered faces standing in front of his desk and saw that they found no great confidence in his words.

An irritated Epula quipped, "We won't have anyone left to punish if we are to stand by so idly! What can be learned by letting our people destroy themselves?"

Mulat replied, "Whatever you like. As I recall, Adsum was one for learning anything from the strangest of situations. However, I would prefer that you all understood that excessive reward or punishment does not make for a happy city. They are both on the same scale, tipping the balance too far one way or another will lead to discord. Regardless we are a city, a great city, and we stand as something other cities aspire to be. Controlling our people with reward or punishment will lead to our downfall."

Aggravated by feeling like Mulat wasn't paying attention, Ictus cried out, "If we leave this unchecked it WILL go out of control!"

Mulat spoke calmly. "It isn't unchecked, we are educating. It is a slower process I will admit, but it is a more permanent solution. Would you prefer faster and temporary?" Ictus was irritated further by Mulat's innocent tone.

Criso gently touched Ictus' forearm, which had a rather striking and calming effect on the man. "My Erus Ictus, I have to side with Mulat on this. He has never failed us, and while I may not see what he can, I can see what he has achieved. Is that not enough for you?" She smiled at him sweetly, far sweeter than she would for any of the other Erus'.

With a small sigh Ictus continued. "How am I to reassure MY charges? What use is my Quadra if it is only to house performers too scared to perform? Musicians need to breathe too, music is everywhere."

Mulat replied, "Train them to take care of themselves then, is music and fighting that different? I am sure most operas involve fighting at some point."

"Bah! Theatrics!" replied Ictus with venom in his voice.

Epula was appalled and his jowls wobbled as if in agreement

with him. "You expect us to arm our charges?"

"Is that a problem? Both you and our people are allowed to arm themselves, why can't your charges do the same?" replied Mulat.

Ictus blurted out, "It is the aesthetics! Making music and war are two different things!"

Mulat turned his head towards Ictus. "And one cannot always make war, and one cannot always make music — there has to be a mixture of many to weather the storms. And this is a storm. But, like all storms, it will pass."

Cogitans stepped forward towards Mulat's desk and confidently said, "If you believe this is a passing storm, then provide us with the Integra Pol guards. You are under no threat of invasion and public Quadra attendance is dwindling. Give our city what it needs."

"You can't seriously suggest —" Criso was interrupted by Mulat.

"As you wish, I will dispatch the entirety of my guard equally amongst the Quadras."

Cogitans stepped back with only scant surprise showing on his face, while the shocked looks on everyone else's conveyed everything Mulat needed to know. He opened his mouth to speak further but was interrupted by an insistent Criso. "Mulat, that is going much too far, and I am sure that we all have no wish for the Integra Pol to be left unguarded."

"Unguarded? But Erus Cogitans has said that he does not believe us to be under any danger, and my duty is to the city and its people. If I am making a decision with nothing but the best information, then what am I to be guarded from?"

Criso stammered, "But... but —"

"Yes, but indeed," said Mulat dismissively and the room fell silent. "Shall I take it that the matter is concluded?" No response. "Very well. The guards will be distributed accordingly within due time, they will need some training and education as to what they are protecting, yes? I trust that you will all grant me that time, and in the meantime I trust that you can keep your charges happy."

There was a mute agreement of nods from the assembled. "Excellent, my only condition is that none of my guards will follow any orders to kill anyone, unless it is to save life. Even then, be cautious. If such an order is even inferred I WILL hear of it. Make no error in your future planning though, they will return when the threat is no more, or I will retrieve them personally." Mulat allowed a moment for this blunt threat to sink in.

"You have asked a great thing of me, so I believe it only fair to ask something of you." The gathered visibly tensed, sensing a trap had just been sprung. "Erus Criso," Mulat said, noting that the others had relaxed, "I require use of your Quadra."

All the Erus' leaned slightly forward out of deep interest, Criso however began smiling like a lazy cat that had found a mouse drowned in its morning milk.

"I will specifically need —" Mulat stopped mid-sentence and turned to the others still standing in front of his desk. "Excuse my failing social manners, was there anything further any of you wished to discuss?" The group quickly scoured their minds for anything else important to justify overhearing what Mulat could possibly want with the Lustrum. "I will take the silence as a no. Well I am no tyrant, you are all free to leave, save Erus Criso, as we do have some business." The meeting concluded with a mixture of confusion and shock as the other Erus' filed out of Mulat's chambers.

"Erus Ictus still has yet to learn how to control his temper, hasn't he?" said Mulat once the doors had closed.

Criso replied, "I don't see you doing much to help the poor man with that."

"Should I?"

She smile wryly. "I don't know, I would not question or dictate what the most powerful person in Kasmah does."

"I am hardly the most powerful person."

"I do not see how that is true."

"My title says I hold the most power, but that is not what I am, just as you are not merely a woman called Criso. If I am attacked, people are attacking my position and my reputation, my responsibilities and my...." Mulat stopped himself. "Ah, I am sorry."

"... Why?" Criso worried that she had done something wrong and tried to mask her concern.

"People do tire of my rants, I really should learn to curb them. Let us continue. How are your charges? Their health specifically."

"They are all healthy and well my Mulat, why do you ask?"

"Your Quadra out of all others has the highest flow of traffic, and if reports regarding this new drug are accurate I suspect your charges would be amongst the first to be affected or hear of it. I merely wish to avoid damage to you and yours. So if you could keep me informed as to any changes I would welcome the co-operation."

"Of course, Mulat," said Criso with as much humility and submission she could gather.

"Also... How is Tari doing?"

Criso had known that talk of her daughter would come and was prepared for it. "My Erus... if you wish her brought here for punishment I will have her summoned immediately. It would —"

"Be a waste of time," Mulat interrupted.

"Sorry?"

"I am sure you are aware of what has happened and why I've been indisposed the last week."

Criso began to apologize. "Integra Divi —"

"Stop, please — honorifics are like candy, and at some point they get sickeningly sweet. I have told you plenty of times that simply my name will suffice."

"I'm sorry... Mulat. Yes I know, and I punished her on your behalf —"

"Why?" asked Mulat in his innocent tone.

Talking with Mulat was always a difficult maze to traverse and Criso hated it when something unpredictable cropped up. "I... uh, a sign of respect, and to —"

"Did someone I know tell you I wanted her punished?"

"No, but I just assumed —"

"Do. Not," said Mulat staccato. Criso started to panic slightly. "Tari is not the reason why we are talking, and there is no need for me to punish her. If you still feel like she should be or you wish to teach her something then please do so, she is your child after all. My punishing her however would be a waste of time, and I'm sure she would do nothing but enjoy anything I do to her. I simply wish to be kept informed of the upcoming Ardeo Trial. It is always an interesting event and I enjoy seeing how you tweak it every year."

"Mulat, I would never deny a request of yours. But surely you have better things to spend your time on? Watching two young lovers take the Ardeo Trial.... If it is an education in the ways of love I am sure I can —"

"Yes, I am sure you could — this is still my request. Will you honor it?"

"... Of course, Mulat, but may I ask why?"

"I suspect the Ardeo Trial this year will be something that will help Orbis return to its senses."

Criso thought, *"Ah, that's what he's hoping for."* She smiled. "Thank you Mulat, I will of course keep you as well informed as I can."

Mulat replied with complete honesty, "Excellent, I thank you. I do hope my guards will be of some use to you. Also, if you could see to it that Tari returns to her original hair color I would appreciate it. I feel that her reason for changing it was... misplaced."

Sensing that their business had concluded Erus Criso bowed slightly and made her way to the door. A lady like herself was never 'dismissed'.

Ж Ж Ж Ж Ж Ж Ж Ж Ж Ж Ж Ж Ж Ж Ж

The Integra Pol's edict was that all Quadras were to research and provide to the public both the services and knowledge of everything they learned. For the Quadra Lustrum this was the range of everything sexual from birthing, health, and the mental and physical practice of the carnal arts.

The Lustrum had at best a turbulent past, and over the centuries public opinion and favor had risen and fallen depending on the Erus' at the time. It had been regarded as something of a much needed education, a place only for the rich, a lowly den that only the poor would visit, and a myriad of other things both good and bad. Just as public opinion about it would wax and wane, the building itself had also gone through many changes — in fact it was the most updated and modified building in Orbis. For the Lustrum, with each change of Erus came a change in its decor, and the funds it could generate allowed it such extravagance.

One of the more recent offerings to the public was the Ardeo Trial, crafted by Erus Ardeo himself out of his first heartbreak. From that was born a desire to punish and test young love, and to that end he crafted the now famous annual Ardeo Trial. Every year there was a magnificent presentation of two charges, one of each sex, from the Lustrum through a procession around the First Ring called the Taker's Procession. These two charges would be called the Takers and were selected by the current Lustrum Erus, and each were tasked with seducing one of the young lovers who had entered the Ardeo Trial.

The Ardeo Trial itself was open to any young couple who could claim to be of their first love and wished to test the strength of their commitment. All they had to do was approach the Lustrum, express their desire to partake, and await the Erus' judgment on whether or not they were suitable. Upon their acceptance they would hold the title of Lovers of the Ardeo Trial, and each member of the couple would then be escorted by their respective Taker to the Taker's rooms in the Lustrum where they would be locked inside.

Over the course of a month they would be plied with delights both sexual and emotional, and at the end of that month either the Lovers would emerge as strong as they had entered, or break upon seeing each other. Should the Lovers win they would receive a very healthy financial start to their future together and free access to, and tuition from, all Quadras for life.

The only dirty secret of the Ardeo Trial was the Androcium, a hidden room constructed directly between the Taker's rooms that was furiously bid on by the wealthy and perverse to watch the young couples of the Ardeo Trial undergo their emotional torment. Criso had wanted to rid herself of the room, but knew that the Lustrum could not survive without the massive injection of funds the bidding provided.

So she compromised and provided a condition for the room: For any reason she felt necessary, she could evacuate them from the room without warning and without refund. She thought it would reduce the interest amongst Orbis' wealthy elite to bid on the room.

She was wrong.

CHAPTER VI

"Why should I care about cattle easily replaced
Everyone needs to fuck;
so much so that no matter how hard I beat a girl,
how often I make her bleed, or break her spirit,
she will still feel the itch."

-Erus Futuo, first Erus of the Quadra Lustrum

THE MAHARAAN EXPANSE

The Integra Natura looked on at the strange desert tribe girl who refused to leave the wija's side and were conflicted. Pala said, "That is not a pet." Kahli did not hear as she tended to the creature with an approach that would rival its own birth mother. Noting the lack of reaction, Pala simply shrugged and turned to her fellow Natura. "She seems harmless enough, but her mind seems to be in two places at once. I'm not even sure if she understands that we are really here."

Fetu meanwhile was looking at the destroyed ground and dead chamu around the girl and wija. "How did it do this? Aren't these supposed to be docile, peaceful creatures?"

Pala said, "She, or that wija somehow, is the cause of all this — and power doesn't care for peace or war, it is just power." She rubbed her foot on the soil to get a feel for it and uncover some smashed up chamu. She idly said to herself, "Why didn't we see any other signs of chamu destruction along the way?"

Sercu however was far more focused on Kahli. "That girl's attachment is commendable, but she is going to do some serious damage if she thinks blind willpower will get her anywhere."

"What should we do?" asked Fetu.

Pala replied, "The best we can do at this moment is do what we offered: Teach."

The Integra Natura's exchange had gone entirely unnoticed by Kahli, who only had eyes for the wija in her care. She had watched the Natura care for it and learned how to massage the beast, make neater stitches, and the proper way to cradle its head — tasks she now held confidence and value in. She was empty, save for the wija's care, and her face rose and fell with each breath it took while it struggled to maintain consciousness.

Every time it stopped breathing for a long time she would be freshly gripped by genuine horror at the thought of this creature dying. It was important. She didn't know why, but a part of her felt like it might be lost if she were to lose the wija, and ever since she saw it rear up and defend her the feeling may now as well have been screaming in her face.

The feeling was familiar and strange all at once. A thought came uninvited. "*She is important.*" Kahli shook her head. This wija was female, of course it was. She had known that all along... how?

Kneeling beside it she watched its large chest for signs of life, and took comfort as the hair on its face rustled softly in rhythm with its breath. Every time the wija found some relief from her attentions she felt fulfilled, making her ever stronger from the sense of purpose given by something not even human. Eventually the wija found calm and fell asleep, and with the wija's finding of peace in slumber Kahli allowed herself to relax.

Confident and strong Kahli approached the ongoing debate between the Natura. "Teach me," she said loudly, interrupting the discussion. As one they turned to her and gave her a piercing stare. Kahli however felt no need to back down from these three women — there were more important things at stake.

"And what do you want to be taught?" asked Pala.

Kahli's confidence felt confused by the question. "I don't know... you offered to teach me."

"This is true. But how are we going to teach you anything if you don't know what you want to learn?"

"Why are you making this harder?!" Had they lied to her? Were they playing games? A moment of desperation filled her. "I want to learn everything!"

"So you think we know everything?" asked Sercu.

Kahli turned her head to the middle-aged Natura. "What? No, of course not!"

Pala responded with, "Then why ask for everything?"

The three made her feel like she was stupid, and she hated that. She hated feeling like she had to talk to all three at once like they were one big human. "Look, I just want to know what to do!"

"So do we... all the time. We can't teach you that."

Kahli wanted to pull her hair out screaming at this point and started to feel her body get heated and agitated. "WHY WON'T YOU HELP ME CARE FOR MY WIJA?!"

The Natura saw her reaction and turned to each other to have a quick conversation of silence — when they were done they adopted a more relaxed stance before turning back to face her. Pala said, "We could teach you how to think, unburdened by the trappings of human emotion." Sercu coughed, and Pala added, "If that is something you feel you need."

"I already know how to think! Don't PATRONIZE me," growled Kahli. The air surrounding her started to waver.

Sercu asked plainly, "Do you know how to think, clearly?"

The young girl responded by taking a violent step forward with a bunched fist — only to find herself laying on her back a moment later. The Natura had not expected her to respond so violently so fast — this girl was still an anomaly to decipher and they needed her to stay calm, and remain on relatively good terms.

They had hoped their demonstration of superior strength would cool her head.

Kahli's aggravation however was now fueled by humiliation and she rose to confront the three with her face contorted in rage. How dare they insult her! Take away the chance to help her friend, and now they laugh at her like a child! Tell her that she couldn't think! SHE WASN'T A CHILD! SHE WASN'T WEAK! SHE WASN'T STUPID! WHY DID THEY WANT HER FRIEND TO DIE?! Flames spouted from her feet, licking her legs and torching the bottom of her desert gown.

Signs of genuine fear and confusion crossed the Natura's faces as Kahli approached them. Sercu stepped forward and threw both of her hands up, and asked, "Are you thinking right now?" but those words went unheard.

A great anger gripped Kahli and she swiftly reached out and grabbed the woman before anyone could react. She began to scream and thrash, unable to free herself from Kahli's grasp.

"YOU DON'T EVEN KNOW MY NAME!" Kahli screamed, and

her mouth opened wide as a torrent of flame shot out and forced itself into Sercu's mouth, and then Kahli let go. The woman fell to the ground, clawing at her mouth as the flames consumed her from the inside out. Kahli advanced on the oldest one who had taken a defensive stance, whilst Fetu's resolve crumbled at the horrific sight of her fellow Natura slowly turning to cinders from the inside out.

Pala struck out straight with dagger in hand, only for the blade to be met by Kahli's own grip — swift, and possessing only the intent to kill. Without slowing Kahli thrust the weapon toward the woman's throat, and as the blade traveled it achieved a heat so great that by the time it reached bare skin all that penetrated was a small sliver of white-hot metal. Following the blade was a splash of fiery liquid metal that clung to the woman's flesh, cutting her off mid-scream and fusing the blade to her throat. Pala thrashed around on the ground clawing at her throat, terror filling her last moments as the metal poured into her neck and molten steel dripped down into her lungs.

Kahli turned to Fetu, the youngest and last of the Natura left, and walked slowly towards her.

Fetu trembled at the knees, and her gut felt like it was punching her with violent spasms of fear. *"HOW IS SHE SURVIVING USING THIS MUCH VESMA!? WHERE IS SHE GETTING IT FROM?!"*

Attempting to muster the courage to face her death, she held her head high towards the slow-walking Kahli and stood her ground. When Kahli got within three steps, Fetu faltered and fell to her knees with eyes clenched tight. Not wishing to see the face of her own demise she tried to wish away everything that was happening, and was surprised to find that several minutes later she was still thinking those same thoughts.

Sneaking a peek to find the reason why, her body felt a rush of relief when she saw Kahli lying face down on the ground just inches away from her. Her eyes shot open wide as she gulped in large breaths of air in relief, and as soon as she felt able she got to her feet and looked at everything that had happened so quickly. Comfort was nowhere to be found — her fellow Natura were dead, but they were Natura and death was simply the next step in the cycle of Kasmah to them. So, she did what any good charge of the Integra Pol would do: Their duty.

Granting herself a few moments for composure, she rallied and investigated Kahli's body. She still needed to know what it was about this young girl that would have made such a strange garden. Breathing in and out slowly, Fetu said to herself, "She could never have kept up such a high level of vesma consumption for so long without killing herself...."

Knowing she would not have much time before Kahli's cadare began, the young woman fished around in her pouch for her Cadacus — a tool devised by the Integra Pol to measure the quantity and type of vesma in a person's blood. The cadacus itself was a collection of small items: A square box with a tube ending in a needle attached to it, with its only other notable feature being a small indent in which was set a piece of vesma.

The cadacus was carefully inserted into Kahli's neck, and as a small trickle of blood filled the indent it illuminated a tiny crystal, which started off with a dull glow that didn't last long before fading away. Pulling the cadacus out of Kahli's neck she shook it in a panic and checked to make sure she had placed it correctly. *"There can't be NOTHING in her blood, she killed two of the best women I know with little effort, the residue alone would have lasted for days!"*

Her mind clutched at straws to try and explain this reading. She didn't even know how to inform the Integra Pol that her fellow Natura had been killed, with no knowledge of who the attacker was or why she did it. Concluding the cadacus to be broken, she collected all the testing crystals she had and made a small incision on Kahli's arm. Passing Kahli's arm over the collection and pressing on the wound to quicken the bleeding she desperately inspected the pile of crystals for any reaction. Nothing. What the *futuo* was she going to report?

She was surprised when she got side-charged with enough force to throw her several yards, almost knocking her unconscious. Bruised and with a fresh surge of panic she looked back to see that the wija had taken up a post by the Maharaan girl's side and was giving herself its most menacing look. She sat still and questions about its strange behavior took second place to not wishing to further incur the powerful wija's wrath. *"Protecting mother are we?"* she thought to herself.

Standing back up she checked to see if she was okay. She wasn't sure when she would be able to make the trip back to the Integra Pol. She hurt. A lot. *"This place will become too dangerous soon, Mulat will just have to be happy with what information I have."*

Carefully circling the wija, she went to her fallen comrades and gathered any supplies she could for her journey home. There was little respect and ritual as she stripped her sisters of anything beneficial. She quickly nursed her own wounds and bandaged herself for the trip home — not once did the wija show any further interest in her and her doings.

Before she left she said aloud, "May your nourishment feed the land, and in turn all else."

With her prayer to the fallen uttered she waded through the lush field of green, intent on reaching Orbis.

Fetu would not live to see the Integrum again.

LAND OF THE GADORI

Toyo had been sent away by the short, fat hunter for reasons unknown, and a part of him felt that maybe it was for the better — maybe he was left alone on the ice for a reason — maybe him and other people just didn't get along. Regardless, his desire to not fare the world alone again, so far unwelcoming and unknown, was strong enough to stop him from making any real haste from the peculiar tree-village and its people. He tried to content himself with a child-like method of tearing out plant life that got in his way, of which there was plenty, that had the unfortunate frequent side-effect of smacking him in the face.

The muted peal of a horn blast penetrated the thick foliage, but he didn't notice it. His sense of uncertain guilt and thoughts, such as what he was supposed to do now, were constantly interrupted by a feeling of irritation creeping into his hands. "All this fuss over some stupid tree," he muttered to himself.

Eventually one of the horn blasts got his attention and the sound filled him with dread — it didn't sound like a celebratory thing. Had what he'd done been worse than he thought? Being sent away was bad enough, but why the commotion? Were they going to hunt him down?

Toyo's thoughts quickly turned to anger at Hoba. *"Why did that stupid fat guy have to interrupt our conversation? If he didn't get in the way then it would've been fine!"* All he could focus on was that the girl in the hammock was laughing and smiling at him, which had made him feel strangely charged, alive... and warm. Everything had been so cold up until now, both inside and out, that feeling warm felt better than he could have ever imagined. *"Maybe if I just go back and apologize,"* he wondered, looking deeper into the cold forest and finding it rather uninviting.

A small battle raged on inside his head, self-preservation on one side and his outrage on the other. He tried to think what swallowing his pride and apologizing to the old lady, the only person he'd met that he could talk to, would accomplish. *"What else am I going to do?"* He kicked the dirt under his feet around for a bit while he tallied up the good and the bad. *"But, if I go back, I can see that girl again!"* That was the thought that won the argument. Turning around to walk back, he only got a few steps before the irritation in his hands could not be ignored any longer.

He inspected his hands for the first time since leaving the camp and found a large glob of reddish-amber sap on one of them. He first tried to wipe it off on his clothes, and then scrape it off with his other hand, but the more he tried to remove it the more it seemed to spread. Looking at them with a frown he said, "I'll just... deal with you later."

Building up his nerve to make his way back and face the consequences he found himself fantasizing about what would happen with the girl. Too engrossed in his own world and feelings, he didn't notice until too late the loud crash of something large charging its way towards him. With a quick twist Toyo prepared himself in a hurry against an oncoming assault, only to find several blue lizard-like creatures a bit larger than his own head scuttle out of the undergrowth in a frenzied rush. Ready to fight he lifted his hands, only to be surprised when the creatures ran right by him with their long ropey tongues dangling out of their mouths to the sound of energetic snuffling — he found them to be almost cute, in their own way. Puzzled, Toyo watched them get only a few yards past him, when their energetic movements stopped, and they turned to face him.

Facing something unknown meant, given his life so far, trouble. He readied himself again for an onslaught — only to be caught off-guard by a long ropey tongue licking the back of his leg. He turned around to find another small batch of the creatures sniffing around him. It was one of the odder ten seconds of his life while he let himself be snuffled and explored by long tongues.

"Uh... friendly?" he said, brushing away one of the creatures' tongues with his hand. The one he'd touched began vibrating intensely, which made him worry. It looked at him and then squeaked out *meepo*, which started a chain reaction of shaking and excitement amongst the others as all their tongues energetically sought out his hand. "At least you don't have any teeth...." The more he fought the more excited they seemed to get. "Look, calm down okay?" They were getting on his nerves now. "GET THE FUTUO OFF ME!" he screamed at the blue lizards and began throwing them off him as far as he could.

A loud screech rang out from nearby and startled Toyo, but it didn't seem to have any effect on the small blue creatures. "*What now?!*" The day so far hadn't given him any rest or reprieve, but he felt that given the size of the sound he'd just heard he knew where he stood. "*Good, I could do with a fight.*"

Bracing himself for a proper battle, he grinned when he saw what burst through the foliage. A slathering, grotesquely muscled four-legged beast stood just a head taller than him, with a large horn protruding from a bloody mound on its forehead and a short split tail that ended in spikes. It gave him little time to admire it before it thrashed its tail wildly and made a crazed dash for him.

This creature was far smaller than that hachu thing Toyo had fought before so he thought this would be far easier, however his attempts to dispatch the new creature with some flair, failed. He was flung violently to the ground where the beast pounced upon him and latched onto his hands with a suckling motion. He tried to pry his hands free, but the beast was determined to suckle while upturning the ground next to Toyo with its horn's frantic thrusting.

Pinned down and wanting a fight, swarmed by strange blue lizards and this deformed mammal, Toyo began to feel overwhelmed. Being suckled at by a bevy of creatures like some brood sow while trapped under some slathering horned quadruped when he wanted something to kill, was not how he wanted things to go. A small part of him worried that he was going to be smothered to death.

Toyo started to feel claustrophobic and so took the offensive. He gripped the beast's lower jaw tightly and, bracing his legs against the beast's chest, began pulling and watched as sinew and muscle tore with ease. The beast screamed as large globs of saliva and blood splattered all over Toyo's face. Shuddering and flailing, the beast fell to one side as he heaved it off him with all the strength his legs could muster, completely ripping its lower jaw off as he did so.

He stood up and threw the beast's jaw to one side before turning his angry gaze upon the wounded animal and saw that it was screaming and thrashing around with crazed eyes. The throes were not of pain, and nothing in its body or face expressed that it truly registered what had just happened. It shakily got back up and walked forward with the impression that its mind and body were not in agreement as to what was more important: Survival, or suckling.

Three more screeches came from nearby foliage and more of the horned creatures burst out and charged Toyo, trampling some of the small blue lizards in the process. Throwing himself into the oncoming creatures with reckless abandon he reached the nearest beast, gripped its horn, and forced it through its own skull until the entire length was inside. The beast fell to the ground without so much as a whimper.

With one beast taken care of Toyo quickly lunged at the remaining two intent on tearing them limb from limb — his face flushed red with blood and covered in strange animal fluids. As he screamed at the two charging creatures he was surprised when they both fell to the ground with spears pierced through their skulls.

"<What the fuck are you doing out here?! >" shouted Tagai, taking in the scene of Toyo surrounded by the variety of dead beasts. A small part of him could not help but be impressed.

Toyo shouted back, "What the *futuo* are you doing following me!?" The fear of them hunting him for retribution was now revived.

Hoba was panting and not entirely happy at finding the boy. "<What do we do? This direction is not going to work either. >"

"<Then we will find ano —>" Tagai was interrupted by a wet mud ball hitting his face, and turned to see that it had come from the boy. He looked sternly at the insolent child until the boy began to look sheepish.

He then turned back towards the Ogagi and beckoned Toyo to follow. After a few steps in Hoba started to complain. "<Tagai! What are you doing?! First he wounds the Ogagi, runs off like a child, and has now doused himself in their scent! >"

Tagai calmly explained with a face set in determination, "<Hoba... he felled beasts within minutes that take us half a day to hunt. He is young, and perhaps stupid — or ignorant, I'm not sure which, either way he can fight, or, if it comes to it, be bait if we need him to be. Our luxury is not in removing either of those options right now. I assure you though, once we are clear of this feeding frenzy, we will deal with him. >"

"<Where do we go now? >" asked Hoba, trying his best to adopt the confident tone of his brother-in-love.

"<We are out of time to find a safe route. We have to head back to camp and just set out to the Gadori edge, then follow the tree line until we can safely make it to the next Ogagi. >" Tagai and Hoba gave one last beckoning gesture to Toyo before heading off into the forest.

Toyo waited a few moments before deciding to follow. He was internally debating as to why they would ask him back, but the memory of Nume made quick work of that too. Falling into step behind the two hunters Toyo began to feel like he genuinely would never understand anything that was going on around him. In deathly silence, and with the air of two guards taking a prisoner back on an invisible leash, the three made their way back to the Ogagi.

Ж Ж Ж Ж Ж Ж Ж

The short trip back to the camp was only several minutes of energy-conserving jogging for Tagai and Hoba, and a brisk run for Toyo, but the signal that they were close brought horror to all. Screams and chittering sounds sent Tagai and Hoba into full sprint, and Toyo tripping over his own feet as he tried to match the sudden change in pace. Scrabbling to get himself upright, he felt his stomach churn as the screams were cut off by the even more distressing sound of teeth crunching on bone. He found his legs and began running as fast as fear could carry him. Crashing through the dense underbrush he stood frozen, confronted by the hideous sight of the large tree with several large spider-like creatures, that looked like they could eat an average-sized man whole, crawling up its sides.

Toyo watched Tagai sprint around the camp trying to evacuate everyone and saw that the large tree had been abandoned. He thought, *"Surely the girl from before must have made it out already?"* but his legs didn't wait for him to finish that thought as he followed Hoba dashing towards the Ogagi. *"He runs fast for a fat man."*

As he neared the tree he saw Hoba and a small group of people as pale as him in strange garb frantically trying to uproot some sort of large tree stump that seemed well tended to, almost polished. They had pulled out four large roots from the ground and were placing the stump onto a big stretcher along with their equipment. Momentarily distracted, Toyo watched as they coiled the bottom roots around the stump itself, and he could've sworn that he saw the ends of the roots act like hands.

As he got closer to the tree he could see that people were still in the hammocks, and to his horror he watched as they began carting away the tree stump and made no attempt to help those in the healing hammocks.

Toyo watched the giant spiders' slow ascent and noticed they had a long tubular attachment hanging from their bottom with a spike attached to it. From what he could see they were using that spike to tether themselves to the tree. A sickly sucking sound could be heard from each spider, intermittently punctuated by a short scream and a stomach-churning crunch. With each noisy chittering slurp the spider's abdomen would glow brightly for a brief moment, followed by a shudder. He almost fell to his knees when he realized that the spiders were eating the sick and injured out of the tree like low hanging fruit.

Jolted into action by his memory of that girl who had waved to him he began sprinting with renewed vigor. As he got closer he could make out more of the small blue lizard-like creatures that accosted him earlier gathered around the tree, along with an assortment of other strange creatures he had never seen before. Each one mewling underneath a spider as reddish-amber sap wept from the wounds made by the hideous tail spike. The sap trickled downwards towards the frenzied beasts, who appeared to have lost all reason in their pursuit of the reddish-amber nectar.

In a panic Toyo tried to see if any could be saved, and noticed that some of the hammocks were untouched, however they were in danger of falling into the gnashing teeth and probing tongues of assorted creatures below. He was blindsided by a rush of more little beasts behind him that were filled with a single-minded clamoring to be the first to get to the tree. Swept off his feet and landing on his back, he was fueled with rage and stood up with fists swinging wildly as he charged towards the tree. His charge was interrupted by Tagai, who tackled him from the side and blew a cloud of white powder into Toyo's face.

"<Stupid child, you cannot solve every problem by swinging your fists, >" he said, as Toyo once again began to experience an overwhelming sense of obedience. Tagai jerked him to his feet and dragged him in the direction of the fleeing tribe. He muttered to himself, "<Whatever Ani wants you for better be worthwhile, or I will skin you myself. >"

Tagai eventually caught up with the surviving tribe members, moving leisurely in the certainty that now that they were clear of the Ogagi they would be of no interest to any of the horrors as long as the sap flowed. He quickly fell in line with Hoba and Ani in the lead — Hoba had to try his best to stifle his rage at seeing Toyo in tow.

"<Why is HE here?! >" shouted Hoba, jabbing an accusatory finger in Toyo's direction.

"<To answer exactly that same question, >" replied Ani distantly as she fiddled with a small trinket box on string around her neck.

"<… What? >"

Tagai had his own questions he wanted answered. "<This boy must be either exceptionally stupid or ignorant. He cannot be from

the Integrum — it is too far for him to travel alone all the way to the Gadori edge. Who would even take a child to begin with? WHERE is this boy from? >"

"<I do not know Tagai, >" replied Ani.

Tagai had little patience in the wake of losing more of his already dwindling tribe. "<He is not of our skin and he started the Ogagi feeding cycle nearly a month early! He could have caused a kusabana! I respect you Ani, but WHY am I rescuing a boy that is NOW responsible for the death of all our injured?! Have you already forgotten the last kusabana and what it did to our tribe?! How can you excuse him?! A STUPID CHILD SHOULD NOT BE EXCUSED JUST BECAUSE HE IS A CHILD OR STUPID! >"

Ani allowed silence to cool the air as the tribe slowed their pace and directed their piercing stares towards Toyo. Ani knew she had to defend her decision to all and that she had to do it fast. Hoping to capitalize on the emotions from the recent event she turned to address all. "<... This is not the time to discuss this, but it also is the time to do so. You all listen to me because of the wisdom I have imparted over the years. This boy is not exempt from his actions nor forgiven, but if you feel that I am no longer fit for my reasoning then kill this child now and I will find my own way in the Gadori. >"

Silence met her statement and the group began shuffling again towards the Gadori edge. With Ani's authority reasserted she turned to Tagai. "<Tagai I know you protect us, and have done for so long. I remember the wife you and Hoba shared and lost. I remember many things, and I will not ask you to forget the pain. This child will answer to us, but I fear what he would do out in the wild more than if he were with us. We can teach him to stop doing so much damage, but if he succumbs to the wild then all he would learn is how to destroy. I measure you and find you capable and honorable, I can only pray that you find me in kind. >"

Tagai was an honorable man — his wife Isetu had even once said it was to a fault. His tribe needed their Yohju now more than ever, and so he gave his nod of acceptance.

With purpose and in grief, the Gozuri trekked on.

INTEGRUM

A loud sigh echoed throughout Mulat's chambers. He was wracked with thoughts such as whose perspective was right, his or others, and debating whether or not he had made a positive difference. His people now lived longer, were fed well, and riots were not as common as before — but was that a good measurement? He was forever hard on himself for he knew that nobody else would or could be, and in that Mulat found — like all men with power — his harshest critic. But here he stood in a tower undefended and trying to control a city wracked by something the locals had come to call creba — a malformation on the name that the Quadra Logicum had given the drug of cremo faba, or 'fire bean'.

"Is it really better to leave them to decide for themselves? So many reports of brutal murders and strange deaths." He began to lament exiling the previous head of the Quadra Logicum, Erus Adsum. His quite literal genius in problem solving would have no doubt come up with something socially impractical as always, but whatever he came up with always at least helped lead them in the right direction.

The most valuable thing Adsum had ever said to him was, "The inefficiency of intellect is the capability of perceiving a multitude of pathways but not always having enough time or energy to synthesize all resultants." Mulat internally translated those words to, "Intelligence breaks down walls within — sometimes it helps to use others to lean against and catch your breath." Which was all well and good for Mulat as he had been using that trick on Adsum for years without him ever realizing.

As he turned from his window to poke and prod the strange long red bean pod that was sitting on his desk he idly mused, *"I suspect he is still wandering the Maharaan... probably dissecting babies or seeing if food can be ingested in some fashion other than orally."* He then sat down to begin reading his spies' reports on what the Quadras had been doing with the cremo faba. He had learned early on in his life that whenever there was a problem that threatened many that it was far better to investigate those in power rather than those on the streets.

Re: Quadra Culinum

Experiments involved attempts to enhance food flavor, results were subjects had no concept of a full stomach and died from burst stomachs due to overeating. Secondary attempts at enhancing diets for weight loss — results again fatal.

"I wish Erus Epula's pursuits weren't so predictable — I suppose the stronger the human need, the less thought required to pursue it. Then again I did not expect the prosperity I brought for the lower classes to have the subsequent consequence of their gaining so much weight."

Re: Quadra Logicum

Cremo Faba subjected to a battery of tests. Findings indicate the Logicum was the Quadra all others sought out for possible uses of the drug. Methods for liquefaction and granulation of the drug were initially developed here under Adsum, other findings confirm that this Quadra has had the drug for many years. No current or recent experiments found. Old reports indicate successful attempts to increase focus in humans. Further investigation required.

Mulat sighed heavily. *"Him again. Curse and cure this man seems to be, I wish he would cement himself as one or the other."*

Re: Quadra Lustrum

Drug was administered to charges at their request to enhance their 'sexual energy'. Charges came to almost kill themselves and their clients via physical exertion. Volunteers were eventually added to the 'Maenyr' room, a special room where the hyper-sexual charges of the Lustrum are kept. Fertility experiments were too successful and shut down when all test subjects became hyper fertile. All further experimentation has ceased.

"Erus Criso should have learned by now to tell me everything up front, I do dislike finding things out this way."

Re: Quadra Musicum

'Listener appreciation' experiment: liquified cremo faba was administered via the aural canal. Subjects clawed at their ears until restrained, ear drums needed to be perforated by spike before any relief was found — after which people fell into a deep depression, citing, "Where is the beautiful music?" Subsequently all subjects committed suicide within hours. No further known testing. Cremo faba was purged and banned from the Musicum immediately after.

Mulat looked down at the strange long red bean on his desk. "You are the source of a lot of trouble it would appear." Sighing loudly once more, he hoped that the next few minutes were not going to be as boring as he thought they would be and leaned back and began to think. *"I am surprised, I would have thought Erus Ictus would be one of the worst reports. I wonder —"* his thoughts were interrupted by a dagger that had traveled through his chair and was now pierced through his chest as well.

"Just so you know, there were easier opportunities," said Mulat without any difficulty before the blade was quickly removed and thrust again towards his neck. He caught the assassin off-guard by standing up very quickly and turning around without displaying any interest in the fact that he'd been stabbed. The assassin took several tactical steps back before reaching into a pouch tucked into his belt and threw a white powdery substance into Mulat's face, missing as the wind whisked it away.

Mulat looked at the masked assassin and said, "… Yes? Aren't you going to keep attacking? I somewhat thought —" he dodged the next strike with a slight twist of his body and brought a full-forced strike into the masked assailant's extended arm. Crippled and shaken the assassin lunged for a final attack at the rumored immortal man, eyes narrowed and filled with the intent of finishing his task. Mulat knocked him down to the ground with an almost imperceptibly swift strike to the throat.

Mulat turned his chair around and sat down to watch the assassin struggle to recover on the ground, and then rested his foot on the assassin's chest. He then looked up at the open window and smiled to himself. "I am impressed, it is not an easy task to scale this tower from the outside. As far as I know I am the only one who has, and even I have the benefit of actually having the tower to practice on. Your trainer is *very* good indeed and deserves my admiration, and most likely a job offer if I can ever find them." Mulat decided to table figuring out who could train someone to this proficiency for a later time and focused on the now.

While processing the situation Mulat failed to notice his blood dripping onto the assassin's clothes. "Look my good... man, I think, I would appreciate it if you would let the fear live elsewhere for a while so we can talk. I have no real intent of killing you — to be honest I have never killed anyone directly, and I would appreciate it if you kept that to yourself. Killing... It holds no real value to me...." Mulat allowed himself to be distracted for a moment while he thought on that. "I suspect it is because it is too easy? I'm not sure, but it is hard to find people to talk to so I apologize for the monologue. However, anytime you want to interrupt with answers to, 'Who sent you and why?' is encouraged and would be appreciated, but not wholly necessary." Mulat allowed the assassin a few moments to let his words sink in.

Reaching into a desk drawer behind him he retrieved an intricate transparent box containing a beautiful sand replica of the city of Orbis. "Let us take this transparent box and the intricate montage within. Quite masterful isn't it? It took a lot of time to construct, even more to find the person with the mind to create it." Mulat turned and twisted the box to let his captive see it in full glory. "Now, let us shake it and watch the powers of time and physical force rend this image to nothing more than a pile of sand."

Mulat shook the box gently back and forth in front of the prone man, and with each gentle swish the finer details of the montage were washed away. "We are all formless sand in the face of power, and time guarantees that we will all eventually meet that power. The most amazing thing about this box though is that for the entire time that everything in this box will exist, the montage you saw is but the briefest moment of it all. For years from now as this box sits on a shelf, or in a ditch, or until this box is destroyed, all it will be is an unformed pile of sand. That is what we humans are, the slightest glimpse of form and function in this box of a world."

Mulat gave the box a look of pity and set it down on the ground beside his captive.

He sighed again and looked into the assassin's eyes. "Did you know not many people like my lessons? Nor do they truly appreciate what it is I do. Responsibility is what a leader must embody. It is the ability to both identify and solve a situation — the ability to respond, and to be held accountable. Are you here because you find me lacking in either? Or perhaps you feel there is someone more suited to the task?"

Mulat waited for a response, but could see nothing but the assassin calculating ways to escape. To pass the time he looked around the room, and finally noticed that his wound had been dripping onto the man. He promptly waved it aside as an irrelevance and, feeling that he had given the man enough time, continued his one-sided conversation.

"You are welcome to try and escape if you like, but until you either answer my previous question or succeed in escaping you will just have to put up with me. Oh, how about an interesting fact? The... failure before me, for want of a better word, was a poor creature indeed.... There were many failures before me." Mulat shook his head in an attempt to not let himself get distracted. "Anyway, years ago there was a spate of horrendous murders, a powerful man had gone around and started torturing people. The first few were found alive, but shaken, and they claimed that a man kidnapped them and forced them to make a 'happy face' — when they did not comply, they were abused and beaten. You see, this man had observed that if you can force the action then the mind will follow, and that forcing it in such a fashion was easier than asking or torturing. So they began to find people with their faces altered permanently by stones and animal bones inserted under the skin, affixed in such a fashion as to maintain a permanent grin or smile. It was not long after that when people started to die."

He had hoped the masked assassin would at least ask some questions by now, or made an effort to escape, then again Mulat was happy to have someone to talk to at least.

"You see all Potentiates are taught to... obsess about what makes us 'human', we are driven to make people our passion and to learn how to read body language and faces. So this man who had committed these murders was what you might call my brother, a fellow Potentiate, and he had taken the face reading too far — so I had to lock him away. I had to hunt him down, show him his own face, and at his request cast it in iron and exile him so he could never see his or any other face again. He was quite distraught, as was I for someone so young to have to perform such a task. It is funny, the paths we take and sometimes miss... still that was his, and this is mine." Mulat noted that the assassin's mind was still on his job as his muscles imperceptibly flexed and tested for a weakness in Mulat's stance.

"Do you fear for your life?" asked Mulat. There was a professional but emphatic nod from the assassin. "I am not entirely sure why —" muttered Mulat and tore his shirt to reveal the wound the assassin had made near his collar bone, then leaned forward so he could show the assassin his back. An array of scars and welts lined his bare flesh, protruding like a poorly laid cobble stone street.

"Many have struck me in an effort to take my life, an action that I myself find little value in — violence begets violence, but perhaps I am naive and can only hold that opinion because there is little threat to me. Maybe if I had the fear of opposition I would think different." After a few moments Mulat covered himself back up and returned to the situation at hand.

There was now quite a lot of blood on the man, and Mulat decided that enough was enough and the blood dripping from his chest suddenly stopped. "Sorry, I should have stopped that earlier. Sometimes it is fun to scare people.... Would you do me the kindness of informing me of what Quadra you belong to?" Mulat inquired.

The assassin just shook their head.

"Is that a no to my request for information, or a no you weren't sent by any Quadra Erus?"

Again the response was only a shaken head.

"Well I know Tari didn't send you, her... rampant passions are quite quelled for now I am sure." Mulat called out, "GUARDS!" as he removed his foot from the person's chest and stood up. A second passed before a look of realization came over him. Mulat mumbled to himself, "Oh... right, they are at the Quadras now. How silly of me to forget."

He looked down at the assassin and saw that they had yet made no attempt to escape. "Well how about I just keep you for company? I am rather lonely you know, Juvorya has been away so long and now the guards are elsewhere. I just hope you don't mind listening to me rant — it does help to have someone to talk to I find," chirped Mulat as he grabbed the person by the collar and raised him to his feet, popping the mask they were wearing off in the process. The assassin was now visibly shaking and red in the face. "Well something is not quite right with you is there my good man?" said Mulat.

The shaking and redness became more and more pronounced, making Mulat feel a rare feeling of excited uncertainty. He leaned to the man's face and whispered into his ear, "You know what? This is kind of interesting. It isn't often I don't know what is going to happen next, but if you need any medical attention do just ask, yes? I am just assuming you aren't doing something so boring as poisoning yourself so you can't be interrogated."

The man coughed and spewed a large cloud of white powder speckled with blood directly into Mulat's face. As the assassin fell backwards, his body was wracked with violent spasms and Mulat watched the man's death throes with some regret.

"Oh... A last ditch effort at poisoning me. Look, I appreciate the dedication but really it isn't that hard for me to flush it out of my system. I thought that was common knowledge by now? If I couldn't then why wouldn't I have a food taster like the rest of the Quadra Erus'?" Mulat took some time to realize that he was talking to a corpse. "Well at least Epula didn't send you, he of all people would have noticed my —" Mulat began choking and a look of confusion came over his face. "*Hm, this is different,*" he thought to himself.

A heat began to rise in his chest, flowering into a most violent flame within — his thoughts were soon consumed by the heat, and, for the first time in Mulat's memory, he lost control.

Screaming in confusion as his mind went into a state of chaos, the usual checks and balances he kept in place so he knew that he was sane were stripped away. He tried to claw onto memories and thought patterns — all wiped away by this burning sensation that now filled him. He tried to cling onto his most favored memory of Juvo, of how she would stumble and fail but won him over by constantly standing up and trying. Of her flute and her songs... his most cherished person in this world... the only one that knew everything about him....

The room started to perform the impossible and began to slowly twist around Mulat, sparks from his mouth and eyes began to spring to life and die as quickly as they came.

The Integra Pol began to creak and groan while Mulat's mind was consumed. The room started to physically twist in synch with Mulat's heartbeat, and the race to the next beat slowed with each weakening ebb as he felt his heart and mind engulfed by the discord. Soon his heart stopped completely, and after a time Mulat just found himself on the floor — his mind returned to him, calm as ever, without heartbeat.

"Is that all the poison was supposed to do? How... exciting. I almost wish it went further." Mulat pondered all the events slowly to himself as his other faculties returned to him. When he felt comfortable that he could resume being himself he decided to regain control of his body and willed his heart to beat once more.

With that small throb of life the power inside him released, and the very center of Orbis, the Integra Pol, let out a piercing screech of mortar and stone as it twisted in on itself.

CHAPTER VII

"‹He is NOT useless! HE is my brother! Isetu chose him and me; I and Hoba chose each other. I will vouch for him. ›"
"‹And if he fails? What then? ›"
"‹He is my brother-in-love; he will not let me fail, and I will not let him. ›"

-The hunter's induction of Tagai and Hoba

THE MAHARAAN EXPANSE

A musty stench permeated Kahli's waking nose, it gave her the unmistakable feeling that she had smelled it before. Crazed memories ran through her head of the Jackals beating her with malicious grins and spitting on her face. Images of pain and degradation, along with the faint memory of weeks on end being placed in a simple bare room where all she did was stare at a wall, flickered briefly. In them there were no chains, no attempts to bind her, she just sat in that room, and stared at the wall forever and ever until she was told to do otherwise. Every now and then the door would open and she would be led somewhere for some task, never really feeling or thinking anything.

Kahli was eternally trapped inside her own mind whilst she was used by all, and beaten for entertainment.

Remember the truth...

There were days, so many days, toiling in the heat, performing the most banal of tasks. So many hours spent tending to wounds that she would not, and could not, defend herself from. Tears shed did little more than clear the dust from her eyes while she lived in a whole village filled with people who thought that evil was a sign of divinity.

"*I remember... drinking....*"

Kahli's brain kept processing the musty stench and memories, but was violently interrupted by a sharp stinging smell, forcing its way into her lungs, slamming them wide open and demanding her to breathe in deeply. Kahli's eyes shot open as her lungs performed the act of expanding without her consent in their attempt to fight the alien smell. Her body's panic was doubled when she saw that she was tethered to a stake in the middle of a fenced area. Backing into the nearest corner, she looked at the man directly in front of her and saw that he was looking at her as if she were an interesting specimen.

His skin was the same tone as hers and he wore clothing suited for long desert treks. It reminded her a little of her mother, the hunter. Looking around the enclosure she saw one of the women she'd met in that field of flowers from before — what was she doing here? She had an angry expression on her face and wasn't paying Kahli any attention, instead more intent on fighting off the two men that stood in front of her with eager eyes.

Kahli's vision became blurry and she began to wobble, what was happening? This felt different, weird. She heard shuffling in front of her and soon someone grabbed her jaw. Struggling against the man's hand and trying to escape, she bucked and kicked hard as someone brought a small bulb of something against her lips. The man quickly shoved the bulb up her nose and squeezed hard, shooting a scent that went directly to her head and chest, shocking her into full awareness. Kahli's entire body bucked and arched as she felt her sinuses and lungs rush to expand — her body responding as if it had no choice in the matter.

"Pull it out you fucking moron! You'll kill her," said a far off, unseen voice. The bulb retreated and soon she regained control. She wasn't going to waste this opportunity and swung up as hard as she could but hit only air. "See? You've given her too much now. Shut her up." A blow came and struck Kahli hard in the chest, doubling her over in pain.

Kahli retreated into her mind almost by reflex and now her brain registered only the mechanics of things, but nothing pierced through her consciousness. The sounds of grunting and groaning, the smell of sweat and grease went unnoticed save for the soft sobs and muted screams of the other woman who could not have been more than several feet from her. Another strike, but Kahli's body endured and she was sent further back into her mind, registering one final sentence before escaping completely into the recesses. "I was fucking sure she was fake!"

"*So, here we are again,*" said the strange voice that seemed to live within Kahli.

Kahli replied, "... we are?"

"*It would appear nothing has changed, and again I'm a prisoner.*"

"*I'm the prisoner! Not you!*"

"*What is the difference?*"

"*This is my body, not yours! What nightmare have you lived through!?*"

"*Countless.*"

As soon as the voice finished talking Kahli felt a jolt go through her. "I remember taking... care of people. My mother, the twins...."

"*Memories are not always honest, easily manipulated and can become whatever one wants them to be.*"

"But... my father...."

"*Is alive. A man that strong cannot die.*"

The voice sounded honest, but what it was saying couldn't be true. "... what? No, my father was a hunter... he died...."

"*He could be called that. What he is called though is irrelevant, I was still sold to Toka-Rutaa as an Orati.*"

"*An Orati?*" A sharp stabbing pain pierced her soul as a memory charged its way to the forefront of her mind.

A crying and muddied Kahli was paraded in the town center of Toka-Rutaa. People in animal skins and assorted feral apparel taunted and jeered at her as she was handed over to someone with great ceremony. The memory faded.

Kahli panicked. "Where are the Jackals? My mother?"

"*They were the family that bought me.*"

"But —"

"*I am an Orati.*"

Why was the voice talking like it was her? What was happening? "But... I CAN'T be! I am HERE RIGHT NOW talking to —"

"*Myself. Remember.*"

More memories returned to her. "But... I can't be. If I had taken the potion of living death, then I wouldn't be able to talk. I wouldn't even know enough of how to be human to even know how to be afraid like I am right now! I have seen Orati! They are lifeless beyond death, there is no memory or soul in them. *They are merely husks that perform the most menial tasks until they die! None live longer than a few months!"*

"All true. The Integra Humanus that passed through the village gave me a gift."

"Wait... what? Is that true? How do you know that?" How could this voice that was talking like it was her know something about her that she didn't?

"How do I remember?"

"Why are you talking like that? What do you mean?!"

"Whatever it was I meant, why question why I know what I know."

Kahli could feel the presence of the voice fade. *"... which part of me knows it though?"*

Bleak-faced and weary Kahli allowed her eyes to crack open to try and see what was happening around her. She felt like she was experiencing everything through a layer of soft, warm fur as she tried to open her eyes fully. It was a short reprieve as she tried to raise her lifeless body onto her elbows, only to be slammed back down by another blow, followed by a man saying, "Rasak said that everyone gets a turn to punish! Not kill her!"

"I am not dead," Kahli whispered inaudibly. "I am not dead," she repeated under her breath, over and over to the world in general.

"No, I am not dead," replied the voice in her head.

"Then what am I?" said Kahli out loud.

"What do I want to be?" the voice replied.

"Hey! HEY! She's talking to herself!" said a man in front of her. A stocky man shuffled into her field of vision before she couldn't keep her eyes open any longer. The hay underneath her was comfortable, at least.

An older voice said, "Then you can fucking wait your turn, if someone has hit her on the head hard enough they might've killed her in some other way already."

In tones low enough to not be heard the stocky man said, "... tell me to fucking wait. I'm going to take my revenge that's for fuck's sure."

Fresh screams near Kahli's head told her that the woman next to her was having problems of her own, but from the sounds accompanying they didn't sound like a beating. A male voice said, "Get up Integrum whore and bend over! I don't fuck no tired pig."

A familiar female voice, full of fight, said, *"FUTUO! I WILL KILL YOU!"*

"Demon's asshole!" swore the man who had called her a whore, "I hate Integrum pigs. So fucking rowdy."

"You're FILTHY! Raping an Integra Natura and beating a corpse?! YOU PEOPLE ARE —" the woman's screaming was cut off by a muffled thud.

The last thing Kahli heard before retreating back into her mind was the man replying, "What does the bitch mean a corpse?"

Her friend the voice welcomed her with, *"Don't worry too much about this. Like before, it will be over eventually."*

"Who... who is next to me?"

"Someone I didn't kill."

Kahli didn't want to kill anyone, what was the voice talking about? "... Where am I?"

"I don't know."

More games? "... What do I know?"

"As I can remember, nothing."

This wasn't right. If she was going to be locked away in her own mind then at least let her be locked away with the knowledge of what to do when freed! *"What do I do?!"*

"The sun always sets."

Kahli was getting irritated at the other voice's indifference. "Just wait until it passes?! What sort of advice is that? Then what?!"

"Wait until it sets again. There are many days for me that have been just that."

Faced with conflicting memories and the recent horrors Kahli rebelled. "MY LIFE WASN'T LIKE THIS BEFORE!"

"*Yes it was.*"

The confidence in the voice's response shook her. "*WELL! Well... WELL IT WON'T BE.*"

"*Yes it will.*"

"*Stop talking like that! Why don't you fight for me?*"

"*Fight me, for myself? How am I to do that?*"

"*I DON'T KNOW! STOP THESE MEN FROM HITTING ME! I DON'T WANT THIS!*"

"*I came to me this time. All I can do is keep me distracted here, so I don't have to be out there.*"

"*LET ME OUT!*"

"*I am too weak to do anything.*"

"*I AM NOT!*"

"*I can't even win an argument with myself, let alone defend myself.*"

"*SHUT UP! SHUT UP AND LET ME DO WHAT I WANT!*"

"*As I wish.*" Slowly her mind unraveled back into reality and the last thing she heard was, "*Needs and wants — learn the difference.*"

Kahli's consciousness snapped back, and with it came her screams. Screams of pain, of being bloodied and bruised. Screams of uncertainty, of the why of everything. Screams of rejection at how the world had treated her to this day. Screams that were swiftly silenced once more by a strike. As she lay still on the ground muffled sobs could be heard. For the first time in a long time, they weren't hers.

"*This is real,*" her mind called out as she continued to try and will her body into action. "*... hungry...*" she said weakly. A tremor had started in her legs, uncontrollable and filled with despair. Her hands began to shake and was quickly followed by the rest of her body spasming so fiercely that it felt like her very muscles were trying to claw their way further inside.

"*I did not do very well,*" said the strange voice.

Kahli started screaming and crying inside her mind. "SHUT UP! STOP THIS! MAKE THIS STOP!"

"*If I can't, then how can I?*"

"*WHAT ARE YOU!?*"

"*A stupid woman screaming at herself.*" Kahli began to feel that familiar heat deep inside her, a long way off. She felt like all she needed to do was reach out and touch it, and her problems would go away. "*And now I am a stupid person that will kill herself if she walks that path,*" said the other her as if reading her intent. Kahli tentatively reached out in her mind towards the warmth, and she could feel her physical body begin to thrash around violently the closer she got to it. "*I am not strong enough.*"

"YES I AM," screamed Kahli as she stretched her mind out further to it.

Before she could touch the flame Kahli was grabbed roughly by the shoulders and shaken — forcing herself back into reality, and she broke down crying as she felt her sanctuary slipping away from her. Bracing herself for the next assault she was surprised and relieved to find herself being lifted to her feet and supported to stand upright. A large clang rang out as a heavy weight fell onto her neck, and with no strength to break her fall she fell like a sack of grains onto the hay — making her lightheaded from the quick changes in prone, to upright, to prone again. There was much talking from many voices around her, but she could not decipher anything let alone wipe the tears and dirt from her eyes — the only thing her brain could register was a heavy weight being dropped next to her, followed by heavy sobbing.

The familiar female voice spoke out amongst her heavy tears, "You should be dead... you should be dead...."

"*Yes, I should be dead,*" said the other voice, dragging Kahli back to that mental room of safety.

"Why?! Why SHOULD I be dead?!"

"*I almost killed myself, three times over.*"

The voice spoke like it knew what it was saying. "... How?!"

"*Over-exertion.*"

Why wasn't it giving her answers? "*What do you mean?*"

"I know what the word means. I couldn't use it otherwise."

"That isn't what I meant!"

"I can scream all I like. I can't tell myself things I don't know."

"I didn't know I was an Orati!"

"Yes I did. How else would I?"

"How could I even know I was one? That doesn't even make sense!"

"Just because it doesn't make sense to me does not mean that there is not sense to it. It has to be true, otherwise I wouldn't be having this conversation."

A sense of dread came over Kahli. "Am I... dead?"

"No. I am very far from it."

"Then, what is this place?"

"... You."

"I don't... understand." She felt like sighing but realized she had no body to sigh with.

"No, I do not understand, but I can guess. My memories may be false, but who I am was never false."

That was strange, the voice almost made sense then. Maybe it wants to be helpful now? *"What does that mean?"*

"I used to be intelligent enough to figure things out, otherwise I wouldn't be able to. I did not always live at the beck and call of others, else I wouldn't have fought our captors."

Maybe more direct questions would give her the answers she needed. *"... How long am I going to be here?"*

"I can leave whenever I want. Getting back here is not so easy."

"Okay... what did that Integra Humanus give me?"

"Freedom."

Another answer with no real information. Time for a different tactic. *"I did not think there was any coming back from the Hidati drink. Once an Orati, you just exist until you die."*

"Apparently not."

"Then what about everything I remember?"

"*Even I know many of my memories are broken and incomplete. Do not trust them.*"

"*… can I trust you?*"

"*No.*"

Kahli went silent for a while and tried her best to think of what was important now. "What of the wija? Was that a lie?"

"*No, it exists.*"

"Where is it?"

"*I do not know.*"

"I… care about it."

"*I sound surprised.*"

"Yes… I thought it was important."

"*It was.*"

Kahli fought and decided that she shouldn't be caring about anything else other than herself right now and tried to be strong. "No, it isn't important. What is important is me, right now." She sensed the other voice in her head feel surprise at her response. "I am someone's prisoner… again," she thought angrily, feeling once more that warmth in the distance.

"*Do not touch that. I will not survive it again.*"

Kahli demanded answers. "You said I almost died several times, how?"

"*I am burning myself away with power, I have no more fuel to burn.*"

"I can do that?"

"*I always could, everyone can.*"

"I need more answers!"

"*I can't give myself anything more than what I already know.*"

"No, but that woman who gave me my freedom can," thought Kahli with a sense of determination.

"*Perhaps. At this moment though I recommend waking up.*"

250 | CHAPTER VII - THE MAHARAAN EXPANSE

Kahli opened her eyes to see a familiar young woman's bloodied and beaten tear-streaked face standing hunched over her with hatred in her eyes.

"YOU SHOULD BE DEAD!" she screeched, and brought down her shackles onto Kahli's face.

LAND OF THE GADORI

The Gozuri's journey to the Gadori edge was thankfully uneventful, but it was hindered by a collective hatred towards the young Toyo and the uncertainty of why he was with them. He didn't know why he was so hated, then again it was difficult to think of anything as Tagai kept him drugged, but the weight of their unmistakable rejection of him made him feel guilty regardless.

The farther south the tribe trekked the more distant Toyo felt from the world. It didn't help that nobody was willing to talk and he had to obey the most rudimentary of commands required to traverse the dense foliage, sometimes having to run in order to keep up. When he'd first started getting hungry he would ask Ani for food, but with each passing mile Toyo would ask less and less and with that his body began to suffer. It was tiring in more ways than one, his body walking the difficult terrain and his soul mired in the tribe's hatred.

They reached the tree line several days later at dusk, breaking through the forest and onto the wide open space they looked out at the lifeless and unforgiving frozen wasteland that stretched out before them. Some of the remaining Gozuri were frightened, they had never seen so much open and dead space nor had they been in Zobukiri territory before — the people of that tribe were almost as much of myth and legend as the Gozuri were to the people in the Integrum.

Meanwhile, Toyo's mind, still groggy from the recent drugging, tried to recount the last few days as best it could but found no comfort in what he could remember. His body was wracked from exertion and excitement at both being threatened by death and overcoming it, which had left his heart with an uncertain rhythm as he couldn't trust whatever would happen next. He didn't know what to do. All he had was one elderly woman who spoke the same language as him, and she had been less than willing to interact. The world as he knew it stretched out for miles as desolate tundra in one direction, and thick foliage in another — but neither felt like home and his desire to belong pawed at his brain.

The tribe took stock of themselves and everyone started resting up against any available tree or patchwork of grass that was available to them, none wanted to venture beyond the greenery. Being too worn to lament the dead the only thing the tribe had left was hatred and anger, and as small conversations began, there was the obvious undertone of blame echoing out from amongst the trees.

Ani, Hoba, and Tagai walked out of casual earshot farther into the frozen waste, leaving Toyo sitting near the medishi and the Ogaden they had carried to safety.

"<When will he return? >" asked Hoba.

Tagai replied, "<I gave him much less this time. I am surprised he hasn't returned already, unless his weakened spirit is keeping him away. >"

"<We need to find SOME way of restraining him, that boy almost brought down a hachu AND nearly began a kusabana! He is unpredictable and dangerous! >"

"<No, what we need is an explanation, >" said Tagai, and turned to Ani. "<We were not ready to leave Ani, the sabana was not complete and we had not harvested anything. I do not know if we even have enough to survive our next journey. Even if we did, I do not know if we would have much time at the next Ogagi, the next safe one on the flowering cycle is much too far away. We may very well die here. >" He pointed an accusatory finger at Toyo. "<So why does *he* live? >"

Ani kept moving her eyes between Tagai and Toyo, uncertain of how to respond. She was a Logicum charge, used to practical answers being the only required justification for any action. Knowledge in itself was valuable, and to know anything about this boy's power was tantalizing to a dangerous degree.

Tagai took her silence poorly. "<We took you in all those years ago, you and those... Integra Humanus — we even honored them with the name medishi. We accepted you, my FATHER accepted

you after being whittled down to a mere handful of us, after we had to try our best to defend ourselves from the last kusabana. We are here to protect this forest, and the world from it! WE made you our Yohju, only because there was nobody else! You repay us with this?! This... STUPID child that would destroy the last of us?! >" The remnants of the tribe and Hoba all looked at Tagai with fear as they had never known him to raise his voice to anyone.

Ani nervously fingered the trinket box on the string around her neck and took a step towards Tagai. "<I have not always been a positive influence, despite my desire for your tribe's prosperity, Tagai. I came to this land to learn, and in turn I have upset a balance. It has been a long time since, and in that time I had hoped to earn my penance. I do not ask for forgiveness as I was naive->"

"<YOU NO LONGER HAVE THE RIGHT TO SPEAK, >" barked Tagai, forcing Ani to take a step back. He marched over to where Toyo was sitting, grabbed his collar, and marched him out into the wastelands. Tagai began speaking to Ani in low and certain tones, "<You insult me by not answering my question first, and then give me more empty words. I will not insult you in the same manner. My decision is to banish this child and you. I provide and protect, but you manipulate and disrupt. I refuse to protect him, or you, anymore. >" Tagai stripped Toyo roughly of his heavy furs and shoved him hard out into the frozen wasteland.

A naked Toyo stumbled several steps but regained his balance and stood upright, bleary eyed and only semi-aware of what was happening. Tagai stepped forward and gave him one last hard shove, forcing Toyo several more steps — where he collapsed. Everyone watched Toyo lay still as Tagai turned to face Ani and stretched an upright open palm in the direction of the boy and said, "<You do not belong. >" The understanding that Ani no longer had any credibility with these people crept in, and she panicked. It made her realize that during the long trip, regardless of what happened, Toyo would be her best chance of survival.

There may have been many things she should be punished for but she felt no remorse. Her training led her to be ever curious and to seek a result regardless of what had to be done, or as Integra

Divinitas Stagnos had told her before sending her to the Gadori, "To regret the path is to regret the outcome — to regret both is to regret yourself."

Tagai turned back to the resting tribe and Hoba took one last look at the banished pair before following Tagai to the tree line. Ani watched them walk back with strong confident strides, their bodies reflecting the strength of their decision, and for the first time in a long time she felt naked and vulnerable without their ever constant protection.

Toyo started to shiver uncontrollably mere feet from his heavy fur clothing, while Ani concentrated on what to do next. Being banished and now having to first save and then somehow control this powerful boy was not a notion that brought her any great comfort. "*Live... then learn,*" Ani thought to herself, a mantra of her own devising from long ago. "*Then again this boy will die if I don't get him clothed soon.*"

She quickly gathered his clothing together and then tried to roll him over on his back, only to find him stuck to the ground. "*He's frozen to the ground.*" Ani panicked. "*Futuo! He can't die here!*" Her hands hurriedly tried to gain any purchase between naked skin and frozen ground, hoping to somehow save him from becoming flesh made ice.

Blood began to trickle out from his wrist. Jerking her hands away she watched in awe as the blood coursed down his arms from the gloves, congealing into thick red tendrils that wrapped their way slowly around his arms.

Then just as suddenly as the bleeding started, it stopped, leaving in its wake the red tendrils that seemed to throb slowly. Curiosity got the best of her and she tentatively inspected the young boy and was surprised to find that the tendrils weren't cold. After touching a bit more she found that there was no sensation of hot or cold to be found, no pain or pleasure, or even the sensation that she was touching anything at all. It was as if she was touching void.

Pushing that observation to one side she found a more important fact, that his hands were no longer frozen to the ground. There was a muted commotion happening behind her that she ignored — the tribe no doubt deciding to move onwards already now that they were safe from any marauding beasts.

Taking precautions she wrapped her hands in the furs next to Toyo, grabbed one of his hands hard and tried to leverage him off the ground. Pulling hard as she could her hands slipped and she fell backwards onto the ice. The chill crept into her spine as she lay there and several moments were spent fighting the delicious taste of abandoning responsibility to herself and everything else, but now wasn't the time for weakness. Not with something interesting this close.

She redoubled her efforts and scrabbled back over to Toyo's naked body. He was deathly cold... too cold to ever be alive again. She turned with a distraught face to the tribe and noticed that the commotion was coming from the medishi.

Ani sighed inwardly and thought, *"Well it is no longer my problem now. The Ogahigi was interesting research but near impossible to gain anything measurable from."* She had hoped that some of the so-called medishi might join her in her exile but knew that their Integra Humanus training would not allow for them to be anywhere else but with those that needed them most. One old woman on her own did not outweigh a tribe on the brink of extinction, and healers were always welcome everywhere.

Ani looked down at Toyo's stiffening body, she'd seen plenty of death in her life and was accustomed to it. *"Going to get very lonely with just a frozen boy to keep me company."* Sitting herself on his pile of clothes she began to fiddle with her trinket box. *"It has been... quite some time,"* she thought to herself fondly and opened the box with great care. From it she produced an intricate necklace with a large tear-shaped crystal hanging in the center. She said somberly, "Light... blue." She repeated herself several times, each time getting softer until she was just mouthing the words.

Tears began to fall as her thoughts from age, experience and confidence said, *"Everything fades with time, I am a fool for thinking that love would be any different."* There was a small part of her that wished that it didn't, and to somehow be rid of such childish sentiment. But no matter how hard she tried, she always looked forward to when the memories would surface. Even though they were painful.

The commotion behind her reached a crescendo, forcing her to find out what the *valde* was going on. Looking over she saw the medishi were all clamoring around the Ogahigi's trunk and making a large fuss while the rest of the tribe were rushing around. Ani stood up quickly and put away her trinket box. *"Futuo! The Ogahigi must be dying...."* To have the link severed between Ogagi and Ogahigi so suddenly and almost a full month before they were ready to would surely have caused it great harm. Being responsible for keeping the child around that led to the death of their Ogahigi would give them no pause in making sure she was punished. Her only avenue of escape was to head out farther into the wasteland — however the Gadori edge was no better an option than death at the hands of the tribe she had silently wronged.

She took one last look at Toyo and then decided that it was time to move while the tribe was distracted and started to make her way west along the tree line, hoping to disappear before anybody noticed, but her footsteps were stalled by the shock of what she saw. The Ogahigi was standing outside of her Ogaden. *"She's alive?!"* Ani thought, her face awash with sheer disbelief.

The few rare occasions that Ani had seen the Ogahigi in her home had not prepared her for the vision of her in full glory. The face of a young girl looked out at the world with the eye of something far older and alien. Broken vein-like patterns were visible where the roots had once connected her to the trunk on her bark textured skin, and her hair was straggly and looked like wispy vines. What was most surprising of all was the blooming flower that covered her left eye, it was a beautiful deep reddish-purple blooming flower with three large petals on the outside and a smaller three inside. These details made Ani see now that the Ogahigi was less human than she'd originally thought.

The entire tribe was in awe as they watched their Ogahigi take some wobbly steps. After five more her stride went from newborn babe to that of a seasoned hunter, and the progression stunned the onlookers as they found her to be... beautiful, in her own way. Tall and spindly, almost tree-like, and carrying the expression of something not used to using muscle and bone. Her face was set with a slight smile and purpose as she walked strongly towards the frozen Toyo. All gawped at the Ogahigi's emergence, she gave no sign of recognition in turn.

The Ogahigi looked directly at Toyo and straight through him. She then said, in a surprisingly normal voice, "You called out to me and I answered. Now I am to be invaded?" She waited for a response and then looked upwards. Everyone craned their necks skyward and saw the faintest of night-sparks that normally occurred during this time of evening.

"*She speaks vox?!*" For Ani there were a thousand other questions she wanted the answers to, but right now this was the most pressing.

The Ogahigi looked back down at Toyo, and her eyes seemed to focus on his body this time. "In time the others will come, but by then I will have grown beyond them. I will soon grow large enough to shelter all who asked for me... but, for now, it is time to grow." She knelt down alongside Toyo's body. "For that to happen though... it is time for you to wake up."

Ani looked back at the tribe to see they were as confused as she was, and though she wanted to run she felt certain that the safest place to be was next to their deity. Her fidgeting with her trinket box belied her genuine nervous disposition in the face of her calm demeanor.

The Ogahigi stroked Toyo with an almost puzzled look on her face. A few moments of silence passed, and she looked directly at a startled Ani.

"Is he dead?" asked the Ogahigi.

Not wanting to appear weak or unsure to this walking holy relic Ani steeled her face and replied with, "Yes." The Ogahigi seemed to be further perplexed by this reply.

"A juxtaposition of perceived states is occurring, it is creating a permutation of factorial complexity," said the Ogahigi to nobody in particular.

The exchange between Ani and the Ogahigi made the onlooking tribe gasp in awe, and in that moment Ani saw her chance to work her way back into their good graces. She was just thankful that they couldn't speak vox and had kept their distance when she replied with a very uncertain, "... What?"

The Ogahigi gave the impression that it was internally translating something with great difficulty before replying with, "I do not know what is going to happen next." Ani was completely baffled by the situation but positioned herself to make sure that the onlookers saw them talking.

Ani could see the color draining from the Ogahigi's face. She appeared to be mentally oblivious to the biting cold, her body however told a different tale — the beautiful eye-flower began to freeze and wilt as its petals shrank and closed. Soon her body followed suit and her movements and face grew ever stiffer.

"*Futuo! The cold... the lack of Ogagi sap.... She's going to die soon. I'm not going to wait around to be blamed for this too,*" Ani thought to herself. "*So much for my original plan, but if ever there was an opportunity, that time would be now. I just hope this works.*" She knelt in front of the Ogahigi and called out to her. "Ogahigi, could you please honor me by stroking my head?"

After a moment the Ogahigi replied, "Will this force my required super-positional event?"

Ani immediately thought, "*Can this thing tell if I am lying?*" but decided that this was no time to back down. She closed her eyes and said, "... Yes?"

The Ogahigi reached out her hand and stroked Ani's head with surprising warmth and kindness — almost like a mother's love. It momentarily flung Ani back to the memory of the child she once bore and the sorrow of its passing long ago. When the memory had passed the warmth from the Ogahigi had faded, but Ani could still feel her head being touched.

Too long had passed, and so Ani sneaked a peek. She saw that the Ogahigi's outstretched arm had frozen solid, with her face locked in the expression of kindness and love, and the eye-flower now crystalline with its colorful petals frozen. Stifling her own expression of wonderment, she gathered her wits and stood trying to make herself look proud and honored before swiftly making her way towards the tree line and away from the potentially murderous mob. She would not be able to make that reverent moment turn into trust again, but it would buy her some time nonetheless as they stood awestruck.

Ignoring the gasps and shocked silence when the tribe realized that the Ogahigi was no longer moving, she made her way to the tree line and began running for her life. Hoping to find somewhere safe a melancholy thought came. *"The death of a deity and child, that is how I will be remembered by them...."* All fear of what she would have to do to even survive the Gadori forest was replaced by the immensity of all she had witnessed.

Had she been paying more attention she would have easily noticed Hoba's less than graceful attempts at tracking her.

INTEGRUM

The Integra Pol twisted and buckled, letting out a sound bordering on a cry of emotional pain. Fear and awe stunned the populace into staring at the once revered monument that housed the Integra Divinitas, and they watched on as it distorted from an almost beautiful, proud animal's tooth to a hideously gnarled and twisted fang within moments. The final moment of the disaster was falling dust and debris, which collected on the surrounding Quadras as a fine film of bone-white powder.

The shock frightened those housed in the servants' quarters of the Integra Pol, sending them into a panic — their purpose had been threatened. Rushing to and grouping around what was now a twisted fang, many stood unsure of what to do as they tried to process what had just happened. The guards dispatched by Mulat to the Quadras looked towards the tower and to each other in sheer disbelief, unsure of what to do.

From the crevices and ridges of the tortured structure came blood, dripping and sloughing down the tower's side — the sign that confirmed the servants' worst fears, that the charges of the Integra Pol had been crushed to death. They were the sole witnesses, but still there were no tears shed — the rituals that the servants and guards of the Integra Pol underwent rendered them unable to feel anything other than yearn for a sense of purpose and need. In a state of solemn grace the servants of the Integra Pol looked out at their grounds and saw it speckled with dust. With an eerie communal understanding the servants congregated around the tower and began to methodically clean away the debris. Slowly they began to restore the grounds of the Integra Pol, and worked their way from the inside out.

Far off there was a crowd forming. All were curious, but none dared cross that undefined barrier of muddy streets and bone white ground that separated the Integra Pol from the Quadras. The wealthy and powerful who frequented their favorite Quadra, along with its charges and Erus', were now the only other people to see the true horror of what had happened.

The guards finally joined the crowd at the edge of the grounds and began to form a protective barrier, their final orders echoing in their heads to not return until they heard otherwise from Mulat. The reputation of Mulat and the reverence surrounding the Integra Divinitas washed through everybody as whispered conversations surfaced, and an air of fear increased as the volume rose.

Everyone could vaguely make out corpses jutting from the twisted fang while rich red blood flowed down its sides. The Quadra Erus' put their resources and efforts towards blocking off access to the public, as what seemed to be all of Orbis congregated in the First Ring. However the Quadra Erus' did not have power sufficient to hide the new visage of the tower, and what settled on the onlookers was the uncertainty of leadership and guidance — where would they seek arbiters of impartial judgment now? Who would rule the city? Who would protect them?

The guards went about settling the crowd with confident assurances that everything was under control and that there was nothing they could do. A patronized crowd responded with the feeling of being treated like idiots, and the cowards who were hidden amongst the most distant from the front began accusations of incompetence.

The Quadra Erus' then emerged onto the grounds, flanked by their flunkies, and upon seeing each other they nodded the nod of those in power — acknowledgment at the possibility of opportunity as a catastrophe unfolded. As cogs turned in their minds to capitalize on this surprising turn of events, each Quadra Erus turned to their respective patrons and charges. With a few quick sharp words of assurance, a few well placed lies, and the help of the guards everyone returned to their Quadras, unsure of what to think of but further reassured at each Erus' promise that their Quadra's services were on the house.

ЖЖЖЖЖЖЖ

The assembled Erus' understood the need to hide the meeting in the wake of a disaster lest they stir a panic — they also had a general personal distrust of each other. Being sat in a dark secret room in the Quadra Logicum to discuss the good of the public did little to foster trust between them.

"I despise meeting here," said a grumpy Erus Epula. The stocky man then mopped his brow with a small handkerchief and slicked back his greasy, wavy hair.

Erus Criso replied, "As do I, but wants are not needs when disaster strikes." Many would have been surprised at her unusually dull clothing and plainly bunched up hair — a necessity to not draw attention.

"What are we going to do about the crowd?" asked Erus Epula.

Erus Cogitans in his dull gray clothing and neat haircut replied, "Our options are limited, it is visible to all in the city that the Integra Pol itself has undergone structural deformation. We can keep other people from getting too close and explain away the discoloration, but if reports of the corpses reach saturation we will have a full-blown riot. As unpredictable as Mulat was I respected the man and his leadership, even if it was primarily derived from fear — the man knew how to motivate. Perhaps we should emulate in kind?"

"I'm not sure if he actually *knew* how to motivate," replied Erus Ictus. "A lot of the time it just looked like he did whatever he felt like doing. He caused a lot of havoc in my Quadra in his younger years." Ictus became distracted from the conversation and began mouthing a melody as he drummed his spindly fingers on the table in front of him.

Cogitans replied, "No need to divert. Public stability is key at this moment —"

"I have already disposed of anyone that would cause trouble," interjected Erus Criso.

Epula's expression of shock was accompanied by a cry of, "What?! ALL of them?"

"Yes. Out of ALL of us I have the highest flow of people, I cannot tempt them to stay longer — people have family and jobs to return to. As powerful as sex may be I can only serve so much. Even just one fantasy fulfilled is the effort of many, and my resources are stretched."

"How did you even get them all together?" asked Epula.

Criso replied, "I instructed the Integra Pol guards assigned to me that until Mulat surfaces that they are to answer to me. There seemed to be little argument about the arrangement."

"Good to see efficiency. I have already herded mine for further experimentation on the cremo faba," said Cogitans. A look of shock went around the table. With his face expectant and deadpan he continued, "Can we please dispense with the attempts at lying to each other? All your associated shame and guilt is somewhat unproductive at this juncture. Besides, you all have been sneaking further test subjects for your own purposes here and there. My charges may not be very good at guile but best all yours in deductive reasoning."

"Well I for one am NOT performing any experiments," said Erus Ictus promptly.

Cogitans coldly said, "Yes, I know." There had been little love lost between Cogitans and Ictus over the years.

"And MY patrons are still enjoying my Musicum. Unlike Erus Criso, a singer of mine can entrance an entire audience —" Ictus began.

"Would you like to guess what one of mine could do to an entire audience?" said Criso disarmingly and smiling slightly.

Epula chuckled at this little exchange before clearing his throat loudly. "We don't really have time to play. I have put mine to sleep for the moment so I could decide what to do with them later."

"So we have two Quadras' worth of people we need to deal with," said Cogitans.

Ictus was outraged. "My patrons are not so low brow as to speak of things they are asked to not speak of! And what of the guards?! How will you keep them silent? Or do you trust them more than my patrons?"

"The guards have been trained to follow orders and to die for this city, your clients have been trained to subvert orders for their personal gain and to profit from the city. It is not an equation I have difficulty comparing," said Cogitans.

Ictus burst out, "The nerve! They would NEVER —"

Epula interrupted. "Oh shut up, we are not here to discuss the *quality* of our patrons. We are here to deal with the problem of running the damn city without the Integra Pol!"

Ictus, visibly rustled, tried his best to quieten himself. "Some of my patrons are the most WELL known in the city! They cannot just *disappear* like yours could."

Cogitans took this into consideration. "This is... valid. Perhaps an outbreak?"

"An outbreak? How is that not lighting your own face on fire? Patronage would PLUMMET," replied Ictus.

"Hm, there is also the problem of when the benefits of the Integra Pol to the rest of the Integrum are noticeably absent..." mumbled Cogitans under his breath, his face deep in thought.

"I have already blamed the disappearances of mine on a girl who falsified her good health to my Quadra," said Criso.

Epula said, "Well I suppose that works for you, I can't go around telling people they got food poisoning from my Culinum!"

Roused from his thoughts of beyond Orbis, Cogitans said, "If we have too many catastrophes strike all on the same day I am sure even the dullest of people would suspect foul play."

Epula was not to be ignored. "We can't keep our patrons locked up forever! As it stands I will have a riot on my hands if I don't let some go home soon. We don't all have patrons who are entertained by eight hour operas. Even two hours is probably pushing it for the amount of time I can keep someone indisposed with a feast. We need a course of action, and quickly."

All turned to look at Cogitans, who took a few calculated moments before saying, "All we have left is Epula and Ictus' patrons and their low-level charges. The best option at this moment is to expose them to cremo faba, let them loose somewhere nearby, and have the guards quell the subsequent result. With that we will have the added clout of public trust through fear, along with the added bonus of decreasing public consumption of the drug."

Criso said, "Fear is not good for business."

"Public outcry at the lack of a leader would be worse, do you wish for your charges to be at the mercy of a leaderless mass?" replied Cogitans. The realization made the room fall silent as they thought on the plan, each Erus thinking of all the implications possible. The heavy leaden weight of responsibility felt crushing in this time of emergency and soon each Erus came to their conclusions.

Eventually Epula spoke in resigned tones. "We do not have time for much else. I will go make preparations. I will curry favor with the guards to become a permanent part of my Quadra, and will have quelled the 'drug induced madmen' by nightfall." With all he wanted to say said, Epula left. What was left behind was a very nervous Ictus looking at the remaining two Quadra Erus'.

Ictus pleaded. "I would lose so much... so many beautiful people. I have players of such great skill that saw it!"

"Then you should discipline your charges better, most of ours stayed inside," replied Cogitans.

"How can you expect my charges to ignore such a grand sound as the Integra Pol transforming?! Why should my charges be punished for being slaves to sound?"

"They are not being punished, they are simply paying the price for their obsession. Surely you understand that?"

A crestfallen Ictus reluctantly signaled agreement after some time and then made his way back to the Quadra Musicum, dejected and defeated.

Criso waited a moment after he had left then stood up to address Cogitans. "I will make sure he *complies*, Erus Cogitans," said Criso, who had always found it beneficial to entreat the alpha of the pack, and with Mulat gone, Cogitans was the next most powerful person she knew.

Personally Criso had always thought Cogitans to be cold and calculating, but nothing could be more comforting in a time of crisis.

Ж Ж Ж Ж Ж Ж Ж Ж Ж Ж Ж Ж Ж Ж Ж Ж

Erus Criso had already returned to her Lustrum and was stalking the halls of her Quadra to check up on the disposal of those unfortunate enough to require silencing. In her desire to keep moving forward she tried to focus but was distracted by recent events, and she still needed to devote time to the upcoming Ardeo Trial.

It had risen to the status of THE event of the year for her Quadra and was quite the cash cow for her from all the betting on if the Lovers would break and which Taker would succeed. Mulat had said to her some time ago, "If the young are stupid enough to tempt fate and the old stupid enough to pay then I do not see why you cannot profit from what is essentially a test." She could never quite figure the man and his motives out because either he was just a bastard, or a clever bastard and dangerous.

Looking out of one of the few hall windows facing the Integra Pol, she wondered what Erus Cogitans would come up with in order to explain away the twisted fang that now stood. The disaster along with the sudden gap in Quadra patronage would put the remaining charges on edge, so she had too much to do and little to do it with to aid in Cogitans' investigation.

Criso's thoughts were interrupted by one of her charges approaching and informing her of the rising tension in the main hall. She bit her bottom lip and sighed inwardly — this day was not going to end anytime soon, and she really wanted to just lie down for a while and pretend that everything was okay. There was still much more to do though, and as she made her way to the main hall balcony she readied herself with her best smile, and adjusted herself for maximum effect, before striding out onto the balcony.

As she spied the crowd below, to her shock she saw her daughter Tari in the middle, laughing and giggling like a twelve year old.

Everyone called her as beautiful and stunning as Erus Criso, both sharing the same flame-red hair and green eyes, the only stark difference being Tari kept her hair short while Criso embraced the grace of long flowing locks, but that would be as far as any comparison could allow. When it came to personality they might as well have been strangers.

Tari's parading of herself like some cheap harlot had always infuriated Criso, for she had worked hard to turn this Quadra from Erus Ardeo's parlor of cheap, vapid entertainment into a den of men and women who had the skill set and respect that would now rival the greatest chef or musician. She also had no guile and most of the time Criso ended up cleaning up after a mess she couldn't handle, such as her daughter's recent 'kidnapping' of Mulat. Although, secretly, she was deeply impressed — less so when she found out what Tari had turned her room into in order to achieve such a feat.

Tari had always craved attention and was a dangerous little thing to most men and women with the games she played with their hearts, and as daughter of the Erus of the Quadra Lustrum she brought little but shame to the title.

What infuriated Criso most about her daughter was that she had learned to seduce only the basest of needs, something that Criso found to be little more than a one trick pony. She blamed Erus Ardeo's years of grooming and the time spent taming her after he took her virginity — that man was a blight she was glad to be rid of. All Criso saw in her daughter was a child with a powerful weapon who wielded it without understanding respect or restraint.

"*Ah,*" thought Criso with a smile, pleased at the thought she'd just had. "Ladies and Gentlemen," she announced from her balcony overlooking the main hall with arms outstretched, pausing briefly to give the crowd time to quieten. "I am sure you are all wondering what that noise was. There appears to have been some sort of accident at the Integra Pol. We are investigating it as we speak but as it stands there is no cause for alarm."

Her daughter shouted, "Oh really, mother? What of the diseased lady and her clients?"

She was sure that only Mulat himself could have read her face at this moment as she fought the urge to shoot a death glance at Tari, but she did not get to where she was by not learning control and not having backup plans. "While unfortunate the event, let me assure you that it was not a 'diseased' charge of ours that caused the deaths of those clients. It was a group session, and a client had the gall to sneak some creba into a room. The result was... unpleasant. We have been deeply upset by the experience and would like to remind you all that the rumors that it enhances sexual potency are NOT true."

A man spoke up in the crowd. "But I heard from your very own charges that it was some sort of a disease!"

"That was one of our initial fears, but we have since found otherwise. Any reports of that no doubt came from someone in a panicked state of mind."

The anonymous man asked, "How can we believe you?"

Criso almost had to pinch herself with her self-satisfaction of her plan going smoothly and pointed to the man, two other random men, and three more women. "I ask that you be the ones to inspect the room used yourselves, and to conclude whether or not it is the result of a disease or man berserk. Do not worry, we have removed the bodies. Sadly we have yet the time and... resources required to clean up the mess." Those she had indicated seemed unsure at first but eventually allowed themselves to be led by some charges away from the crowd.

Criso waited until the group was collected and brought to the balcony before addressing the crowd one last time. "We will be back shortly," she said, then turned to walk away.

"Hold on a second! I want to come too!" Tari yelled out from the crowd, elbowing her way through the throng.

Criso turned back and gestured to her daughter. "Of course dear, you are welcome to join. In fact, I insist."

With the main hall calmed and awaiting the return of the group, Criso escorted the impromptu investigative committee through the Quadra to the upper levels.

"I didn't think anyone was allowed up here," said one of the group.

Criso replied with a warm smile, "Normally no, but if someone is an *extra* good boy we might invite them up."

As the group continued walking Tari started to look quite nervous, and all signs of her previous fun-loving self were now replaced with a solemn expression on her face when she realized where they were heading.

Upon reaching the room Criso announced, "Now, if any of you would like to open the door yourselves and investigate you are free to do so. I and Tari will wait out here until you are satisfied," and stood to one side, gesturing towards the door. Several members of the group were hesitant and Criso tried to comfort them. "Please investigate, I am counting on you to calm the nerves of everyone else in my Quadra. I am no stranger to expressing my gratitude to those that help me out in my times of need."

Bolstered by the promise of pleasure the group found its resolve. Two of the women from the group approached the door to open it tentatively — finding immediate resistance they became a little hesitant, and the three men backed away. The third woman, being frustrated at having her time at the Quadra interrupted, joined the other two and shoulder-charged the door in with a crackling sound, which was followed by the sound of stepping in something sticky. The whole group looked in on the room in shock and horror as every available surface appeared coated in near-fresh bright red blood.

"What appeared to happen was..." Criso began, and waited for the silence in her pause to be filled with their reaction. The entire group looked sick in the face and began to back away from the room while one of them quickly slammed the door. She gave them a few moments before continuing. "Would you like to investigate further?"

There was a unanimous shaking of heads.

Criso put on her best submissive face. "If you believe that is the work of a disease then please tell the people downstairs that is what you believe. I place the future of my good name in your hands. If and when you wish to take advantage of my utmost gratitude, merely ask one of my charges to seek me out and I will make sure that each of you are attended to personally." She gestured back towards the way they came.

Criso did her best to avoid Tari's gaze as the group weakly made their way back. It was only when the group had been dismissed that she finally addressed her. "Something the matter, daughter of mine?"

"You bitch!"

"I'm the bitch here? You create some sort of horrific prison for someone that could level our entire Quadra with little effort, and apparently 'I' am the bitch? You are lucky he did not plaster your room with YOUR blood to begin with, let alone that this very building still STANDS! Your stupid games almost cost everyone here their lives!"

"He couldn't have killed even if he wanted to!"

Criso took a deep breath to calm herself. "I'm not going down this road again. What I would like to know however is how the *valde* did you even get him up here?"

Tari grinned. "You think hiding him from everyone here and getting him to my room was the hardest part?"

Criso took another deep breath to center herself. "I am going to assume that you won't listen to what I'm about to say, but I am going to say it anyway. He is not a man that you should ever have trifled with." Her face now adopted an expression of hatred and rigidity that inspired fear in Tari. "I couldn't clean the blood off the walls, and it STILL looks as fresh as the day I barred you from it! Does this fact alone not prove something to you? I am tired of you screwing with me, and you have undermined me and what I have built for the last time." Her voice took on a sinister, biting tone. "You will play along, or you will find yourself in a very shallow pool indeed." In tones that brooked no argument she said, "Now follow, I have problems to fix, and you WILL help me with them."

The journey back to the main hall was silent as a chastened Tari followed. Walking out onto the balcony once more Criso was accompanied by her daughter, who did her best to put on a smile.

"Ladies and Gentlemen! I hope you will trust the opinion of those six chosen. I will not tell you what they concluded, please let them tell you themselves. Still, there is good news for all here! The Ardeo Trial!" There was a small and uncertain applause. Criso sighed inwardly, she had hoped to avoid using this tactic but the pace of the day did not allow for second thoughts.

"Also! There is an extra special treat this year, for you see my beautiful daughter Tari here," Criso gestured grandly towards her, "Will be one of this year's Takers!" Criso felt that she had been too hopeful in her tactics as this got only a response of shock from everyone in the room, not the excitement she had wanted. "I know traditionally the Takers are only made known at the Taker's Procession, but I trust you can all keep this to yourself? Sometimes I can't keep a good thing to myself. Do remember though in one week we will have the Lovers chosen and the Ardeo Trial underway, until then I hope you all enjoy my Quadra and never hesitate in your desires." She swept out of the room with her own style of grace, stern but subservient, and made her way back to her quarters.

Sitting at her large desk she looked angrily at the paperwork before her. *"The bloody best I could do with what limited choices I have,"* she thought to herself before being interrupted by her advisor. A skinny bald man with a very gaunt face, but many would have been surprised at his physique if they ever saw beneath his clothing.

"Erus Criso, a most excellent turn of events, electing your own daughter as a Taker this year will no doubt make it popular. However, I am sure that your mind has been preoccupied with other things, you still have yet to select the other Taker, but if you would like I have already compiled a selection of cand —" Criso waved him into silence.

"Who are our newest girls?" asked Criso.

"What for?"

"I need to select the other Taker."

"Erus Criso, if I may play advocate to the inverse, as you have assigned a female Taker already, it would very much be in keeping with tradition if the other Taker was male."

"No. I need a spectacle this year, and if I picked two men I would have to deal with far more outrage from the public, whereas women are used to bonding with each other. Besides, nobody seems to kick up a fuss over female homosexuality as they do male. Find me a female charge, the fresher the better — the prettiest one mind you! She has to look like she would win on looks alone."

"As you wish Criso, as it would happen I do have a very recent —"

Criso again waved him to silence and said, "Bring her to my quarters." The advisor stopped his shadowing and went to fetch who he had in mind. She stood up and looked out of her window which overlooked the Integra Pol and allowed herself some time to process the events of the day. Mulat had still not surfaced, and what was she to do when Tari retaliated? It had been a perpetual struggle with her daughter's attitude — Mulat had once called it the curse of privilege.

Seeing how her daughter had turned out made her occasionally regret pursuing Erus Ardeo's seed all that time — he was not the stablest, or noblest, of men, but was her being compelled to rise above what she had always known such a sin? Had Tari inherited her father's erratic mental state? The only thing stopping her from concluding that with any certainty was that Tari seemed much more focused than him and was not known for acts of cruelty, merely acts of manipulation. How she was not dead by some crime of passion was a source of constant amazement to Criso.

There was little time she could allow Tari to keep stealing from her, especially now with Mulat's and her own Quadra's fate uncertain. Keeping in good standing with Erus Cogitans would be easy, but she could not trust that he would be someone safe to follow for any length of time. His predecessor had been exiled for unspeakable experiments — in fact all of the Quadra Logicum heads had been eccentric to a worrying degree. Erus Ictus and

Epula alone would quickly find trouble with his recommendations, and it would soon be back to the ancient days of inter-Quadra war.

In her controlled panic she knew the city would stay united for a time, and the Ardeo Trial would perhaps extend that time of stability, but beyond? *"Who would destroy the Integra Pol? HOW could they have done it? The Integra Pol has stood for centuries!"*

A familiar short cough near the door made Criso roll her eyes. "Yes yes, come in already," she said without turning around. Her irritation with her advisor's constant polite approach to everything made her wonder why she ever put up with him at all. On occasion she would wonder how he never seemed riled by her treatment of him, but never for very long. She put it down to his history in the Integra Pol — those from there were a tad odd, but mostly harmless.

"May I present Clarus, she has only recently —" Criso walked over and ignored her advisor as she inspected the new girl. She was tall with flowing blonde hair, bosom ample and a face that could pass for scathingly beautiful with the right makeup. A body to make women envious and a confidence of stance to make men weak. She would do.

"I am... surprised. I don't remember seeing her before," said Criso.

"She is a very recent initiate into the Quadra, she hails from —"

"Do you know what the Ardeo Trial is, Clarus?" Criso asked. Clarus averted her eyes, nervous as a new-born and with an innocent expression that most men would fight over to defile. Eventually she gave a demure head nod as a reply. *"Oh, quite a new one then,"* thought Criso, worried that the innocence and naivety may be too much in her favor. "No, I don't think she will do. Go find me something el —"

"Please! I don't have anywhere to go and I have always admired the Quadra Lustrum! I want to be good, and I believe that I could make many a person happy!" Her words were brimming with neediness.

Criso offhandedly replied, "Then you can work the streets if that's all you want."

An expression of pure distress swept over Clarus' face, "Please no! I've heard the tales, and with this new drug going —"

Criso sighed loud enough to silence the room. "I never said you couldn't be a part of us, did my advisor not tell you what you are here for?" Clarus shook her head.

"The haste you expressed did not allow me time to brief her on the what and why," said her advisor.

Criso saw the misinterpretation and went into damage control mode, hoping to not lose this obvious unpolished gem. "Clarus, I am trying to find the next person to participate in the Ardeo Trial, I am not culling anyone. You would be a great addition to my Quadra, and I welcome you."

Clarus' eyes lit up at hearing her possible selection for the Ardeo Trial. "Oh really?! This is SUCH an honor! Thank you thank you thank you! I won't disappoint you!" Her eyes were so wide they were in danger of falling out of their sockets.

Criso was slightly alarmed at the overly energetic response. "No, wait, I did say I nee —"

Clarus blurted out, "I just KNEW I was going to fit in here! I have to go tell everyone right away." She did her best curtsy before leaving the room in an almost unladylike hurry.

"... She's an idiot," said Criso out loud in the wake of her departure, but she soon found herself thinking that perhaps this would work out after all. An innocent, virginal young man and a stupid pretty women would make for a rather effective, if not simple, show.

"I fetched according to your requirements," replied her advisor with the subtlest undertones of smug satisfaction.

Criso rarely showed her appreciation to her advisor, but felt that this was one of the times it was warranted.

"Well done Seconsulo," she said, finally calling him by his name.

CHAPTER VIII

The subtle shifting of one's own morals and rules over our life means we die a thousand times over, long before our bodies ever do.
From birth, to child, to adult; there are many deaths of self along the way.
A more alien creature you could never meet, than the person you become.

-Teachings of the Integra Humanus

THE MAHARAAN EXPANSE

Screeching like a banshee and with a face contorted into pure hatred the woman brought down her shackles as hard as she could. Looking into the woman's eyes Kahli saw nothing but the intent to kill, and Kahli was brought to the brink of fear and joy that her suffering might end soon. When suddenly she was saved by an elderly man, who gracefully directed her attacker backwards onto one of the piles of hay scattered about the pen. She quickly looked for any escape route with her spare moment of freedom but even though the sky was in full view the gate was blocked and the fences were not things she could have broken through.

Thinking that she would have to protect herself from this man too she scrabbled backwards and looked at him, but she could see no malice or harmful intent in his action. "Calm down," said the elderly man in neutral tones to the woman on the hay, holding her down with little apparent effort. "Oh... an Integra Natura. Rare to find this far north, what are you doing up here?" he asked.

"None of your damn business!" replied the woman.

"It isn't? Are you sure you won't reconsider?"

"YOU ARE ALL BASTARDS!"

The elderly man sighed heavily. "Very well then, it would have been better to garner information out of you in a kinder fashion — Mulat never did approve of my methods, but his never seemed to generate preferable results." He summoned two large guards to his side. "Please take her to my hut, she will have information most valuable, and inform Rasak that he will have one less woman at his disposal."

"We aren't your errand boys, Adsum," one of the guards growled. It was evident in their demeanor that they did not take kindly to this elderly pale-faced man.

"ADSUM!? The exiled Quadra Logicum Erus?!" screamed the woman, the fight in her now replaced with quaking fear.

"Is that a no?" said Adsum, addressing the guards and ignoring the woman's outburst. The two men begrudgingly complied and hauled the screaming and crying woman out of the pen.

Adsum was wearing clothes similar to the Integra Natura that Kahli had encountered but his had been altered to better suit the harsh desert environment. His hair was very neat, slightly graying, and he had piercing blue eyes and moved his body and hands as if they were under his complete control. He carried the expression of a person that found a passing interest in everything.

Kahli jumped when he turned his attentions towards her and began walking, only to deviate right slightly to a young woman who was lying next to her. Kahli was surprised to see another woman, she'd thought her and her assailant to be the only ones in the pen. There didn't seem to be much special about her — she looked like any other woman in the Maharaan, except for the far away look in her eyes and her body seemed built for breeding.

Adsum pried open the woman's eyes and began to stare intensely into them. "Yet again it would seem," he said to nobody in particular as he fumbled around in his belt and retrieved a strange needle. "Hold still or be blind," he said as he held open the woman's eyes and poised his needle just above her eyeball. Adsum then addressed Kahli. "Fascinating adaptations these creatures in the north have made, don't you think? Then again perhaps not, you are native to this region so I suspect everything has lost its wonder." As he eased the needle into the woman's eye, Kahli watched on as the young girl made barely a whimper when she was pierced. "I'm told that you aren't Habiak."

Filled with horror Kahli was unsure of what to do or who her captor was. All she knew was the pain from her bruises and the racing heart beating in her chest from the attempt on her life. She stammered, "I... uh... I'm not... I mean I might be. I don't know...."

"How do you not know?"

"I was... um... I'm an Orati, I think."

Adsum replied, "An Orati? The term is unfamiliar — expatiate."

"... Expatiate?"

"It means to give more detail."

"Oh... it's something like.... It basically means I don't remember anything." Kahli didn't want to explain it for fear of it being true.

Adsum had finally successfully navigated the needle to where he wanted it to be. He then placed a small saucer underneath it, lightly tapped the needle and liquid began pouring out of the tip. Kahli buried her shoulders deeper into the hay out of horror as he turned to her with a happy face and began talking while he was draining the woman's eye fluid.

"I find the chamu fascinating, don't you? Given the harsh environs of the vast tracts of dry ground and their extreme drive for water you would think they would have eventually migrated to other parts of Kasmah. I suspect it is due to their overdeveloped sense for water that they are somehow blinded to enormous deposits as they normally just prey on stragglers and oases — or it might be that they have some difficulty traversing ground that is firmer than sand, dry ground, or mud." Adsum saw that Kahli was only half-paying attention, but he didn't care. "Anyway, these little spider-worm-like creatures pretty much attack everything in large swarms, but sometimes a few stragglers get left behind and those that do go into a form of hibernation. Seeing as water is their primary focus they latch onto the first sign of moisture, which usually means they burrow into passing creatures and live there, slowly eating away at their host. Most Maharaan creatures have sacs full of moisture to sustain themselves but we don't, so they tend to find their way into our eyes mostly. Soft, easy to get into, and rather safe compared to the alternatives."

Adsum kept lecturing Kahli while she did her best to take in her surroundings. Everything he was saying however began to seep into her head and she then noticed that every time she blinked it went completely dark. *"I've been infested too!"* she thought. With horror revived she said, "Do I have the same thing!? I keep seeing nothing but darkness when I close my eyes! No light, no nothing!"

"I tell the men to be wary of where they lay the pen but they still do not like heeding my counsel." He checked on the needle in the woman before attending to Kahli. "Are you seeing any shadows cross your vision?"

"Uh... no, it... it just goes COMPLETELY dark when I close my eyes," she replied.

"That," he said as he grabbed Kahli's face and turned it to face the woman he'd placed the needle into, "Is because they just stained your eyelids black, like Ruzu here." He released his light but firm grip before continuing in his matter-of-fact voice. "One of this clan's punishments. Marks of shame, an attempt to 'blind' your sleeping eyes to what the Jara call 'The Dreaming', a sort of collective soul plane of all living things. They believe that the reason people with the mark always fall asleep easily is because it is their souls trying to reach out to The Dreaming and their souls get tired from wandering. They aren't interested in hearing about the difference between nocturnal and diurnal, to which either the absence or presence of light actually dictates activity. Interesting things, eyes — the necessity for light is far greater to our sleep than one would believe. I once tried to see if we were like plants, dependent on the sun, and all my test subjects would just sleep and fade away into their mind regardless of food and water — it was interesting to watch." The way he said his last words made Kahli wonder if this elderly man was mad.

Adsum checked on the woman and, satisfied with the slow rate of drippage from his needle, fished out another smaller needle from his belt and focused his concentration on the eye once more. He inserted the thin needle alongside the bigger one, and Kahli could hear a tiny inorganic scream like the scrape of bone on metal, and then pulled both needles out. A small amount of blue liquid came out with them, followed by a small black insect which he deftly caught and placed inside a strange container. After which he then took the saucer and collected it into another container.

"As always Ruzu remember to give your eye the opportunity to heal and refill, so keep that eye away from light as much as possible or else you'll go blind." He began to bandage up the eye and as he spoke the woman just nodded meekly. "That's the third time already now Ruzu. It is an anomalous probability that you have not yet been rendered blind by these infestations — I suspect your regular state of dehydration does not provide the chamu with much sustenance. I shall make a note to investigate chamu growth rate and water." He stopped to look at his specimen container. "If this one survives."

Ruzu turned her head to look at Kahli, and in the one free eye that Kahli could see there was only hatred.

Adsum moved her head back to look at him. "I also have to inform you that any attempts to kill your new pen-mate will have harsher consequences, and I do not mean death. I know you have argued that you are doing them a favor but Rasak says this one is special, and I do not want my only test subject for this Jara curse to be rendered useless." He looked into her eyes silently. "You are going to anyway, aren't you?" He sighed. "Well I may as well allow you a reprieve from the pen for a while and get what I can from you. Hopefully you will lose interest in your endeavor and I won't have to find another. Are you okay with this Ruzu?" Ruzu's nod was a tentative one, unknowing and fearful, and with a pause that indicated the choice made was whatever choice she had the strength to suffer today.

Kahli's inner voice was faint and far away the entire time the old man performed his task, but she could sense its presence nonetheless. Even though she could not make out what it was saying, she found comfort in hearing it — it distracted her from feeling that her own silence would be punished somehow.

"Good, I will go make the arrangements." Adsum stood up, collected his tools, then turned to walk out of the pen. His eyes fell on Kahli once more and had the expression of a man that had forgotten something. "Oh, yes you were here too. Interesting... if you have the inclination, can you tell me what an Orati is?" Kahli looked over and saw Ruzu had become limp and lifeless, having resigned herself to her fate.

Sensing that this man would cause her no harm so long as she was 'interesting' and accommodating she relaxed her bunched shoulder muscles and looked at him. After some more thoughts of what benefit she could get from him, Kahli finally spoke. "... It's a punishment."

"Really? What does it entail?" asked Adsum with genuine interest in his voice.

"I don't know. I know you take some vesma, turn it into a paste —"

The man interjected with, "Veneficium Kasmah is highly volatile, I am surprised anyone in this region has devised a safe method to change its form. What is their method?"

Kahli wracked her brain. "Um... I don't know. You take two plants —"

"What plants?"

"I don't know! I think one is poison, but I don't know what the other one is."

"I assume the other is what is presenting the amnesiatic properties of this 'Orati'. Continue."

Kahli felt jilted by his interruptions but remembered that she was a captive and had little choice in the matter — especially when this man obviously wielded some power, if not all of it. "So you take the paste and plants, mix them together then turn it into a drink. You then get someone to drink it, and then they become an Orati. It is called the living death and the person becomes an empty version of themselves."

"So their organs liquify?"

"What? No, I mean they lose their soul."

The man sighed, annoyed at other people's inability to be literal when explaining something. "Are they still responsive?"

"Well, yes and no? I think... they are kept on for hard work, but talking to them is a waste of time because they don't really talk back except for yes and no."

"So you mean that they lack emotive and expressive responses?"

"I... suppose so, yes."

At this point the pen gates opened and a large gruff man walked in, dirty and slick with sweat. He spied both women and tried to make his way towards Kahli before the old man waved him away without looking. The large man, now irritated, made his way towards Ruzu. Kahli's vision was blocked by Adsum, and the noises that followed made her grateful that it was.

"Hm... not something I have heard of before. I will ask around and see if there is anything similar. Where did you say you were from again?"

"Toka-Rutaa," said Kahli. Screams immediately followed from Ruzu.

Adsum said, in disarmingly neutral yet confident tones, "Leave, you are interrupting my conversation and Ruzu has just been cleansed of chamu infestation. You run the risk of killing her."

The large man continued unabated. Adsum said to himself, "A man that does not know that when I am in the pen that it is off limits, is a man that is not off limits to me." He stood up and searched his robes. "Hm... where did I put it," he muttered to himself. He began talking to Kahli again. "Interesting that you said paste. I can make it liquid or powder, but anything in between leads to results unstable and unpredictable. Here I was thinking that the people in the Maharaan had little to teach me."

The gruff man kept rutting as Adsum talked, and Ruzu's screams were now punctuated by sobs, but no attempt to defend herself was heard. "An old associate of mine, Erus Epula, asked me to research into whether or not temperature affects our diets. Amazingly enough I found —" his speech was interrupted by a smile indicating that he had found what he was looking for and placed the pouch on the ground, and began rummaging again. "That the colder it gets, the more we need to eat and vice versa. I concluded that a lot of our energy is spent generating our own heat, so I hypothesized that the Maharaan heat allows for less physical activity in hunting and gathering so more time and energy can be spent on thinking. I believed that heading north I would at least meet some like-minded people, but alas only brutish louts. However perhaps I have been too preoccupied with my own pursuit to bother investigating."

He found another pouch and placed it on the ground, along with a small wooden plank that he pulled out from the back of his belt. Pouring out the contents of both pouches into individual piles on the board he began moving various amounts around into a central pile and kept talking — it did not seem like much could ever stop the man from talking and that his belt was almost magical with what it contained. "I believe you may appreciate this actually. So many things are benign in their original form — they have to be, otherwise they wouldn't 'have' an original form — more because they would react with everything and 'be' something else. The usefulness of something becomes far greater in compounds — the reaction from combinations of original forms."

The old man formed a small pile of the powdered mixture and lowered a small piece of crystal into the compound. Twirling in between his fingers the powder began to dance around the crystal, lightly floating and orbiting it like water around a leaf in a pond. Slowly he reached out his hand and grasped the floating powder and crystal, squeezing his hand tight around it. "The human circulatory system is an amazing thing and I find that Veneficium Kasmah...." He shook his head. "Sorry, vesma, makes it rather messy. Vesma itself only seems to exaggerate the physical world, rather like fire — mere power for power's sake. But it has helped me learn some things about the human body that I would otherwise not have known." The elderly Adsum stood up and walked over to the rutting pair.

He grabbed the large man by the hair, pulling it back hard, and thrust what was in his palm into the gruff man's mouth and clamped it shut. After a moment's struggle the large man disengaged from Ruzu and rolled onto his side, clutching at his throat.

"You see for example there is quite a strong reaction between raw vesma and anything organic that doesn't match it's harmonic signature. Vesma exists in everything, but the accumulation and attenuation is so gradual that symbiosis can occur, however raw vesma obviously won't match anyone's signature — try as I might. One day I am hopeful to achieve a different reaction, but it is, as you can see, an experiment that requires more test subjects than I can acquire at this moment." Adsum merely watched his victim, with nothing in his voice to show that he cared in the slightest.

The large man stopped struggling and went deathly still. Adsum leaned in with a hopeful expression before quickly jerking his head away. The large man's mouth began to swell rapidly and the gums protruded from his mouth as they engorged themselves. Pressure kept building, until his teeth shot out with such force that they embedded themselves in the thick planks that made up the pen wall. Kahli screamed and several other men rushed into the pen to investigate, just in time for them to see the blood flowering from the mouth of Adsum's 'experiment'. The other men gave a look of indifference as they noticed the elderly man, looked at both of the girls, and then walked away. Adsum paid them no mind. "Hm. Different, but still more of the same." Ruzu gave only the subtlest of shivers when the man died but she had finally stopped sobbing.

As Adsum began to pack up his little kit Ruzu surprised Kahli by weakly saying, "You did not tell him everything about being an Orati, but what would a Dream Plague know?"

Adsum looked over at her and said, "Ah, so you know something about it then Ruzu," and crouched nearby. With his tools forgotten Kahli grabbed the plank and hid it under herself while trying her best to not make any noise. It appeared that this elderly man could only focus on one thing at a time like some sort of perpetually fascinated toddler without emotion.

"Please tell me," he asked Ruzu with intense eyes — her face by comparison looked far away and lifeless.

In a voice that indicated Ruzu's body was fit, but her spirit weak, she said, "To become Orati one must accept the evil they have done, for the Hidati brew does not work on people who think otherwise — guilt is the most important ingredient. The Hidati eats away at your memories, at everything you are, until one day you are nothing and become an Orati. The Orati are used for the lowliest of tasks and for the outlet of everyone's angst, rage and fears. That is their penance if they wish to find peace in the afterlife."

"It has no effect whatsoever without the guilt?" inquired the old man.

Ruzu replied, "No, in their heart they must accept their fault and go willingly into oblivion to find their redemption."

"Interesting — must require some sort of emotional state as a catalyst... is it only guilt? Has anything else been tried? Maybe anger?" Ruzu just shrugged her shoulders. "Do you know how to make this concoction?"

Ruzu just shook her head and said, "I do not know how to make the Hidati brew."

Adsum stood. "I will ask around and see if anyone does know, perhaps I could formulate something approximate. However, if any of this is true, then why is Kahli here functioning properly, and what did she do to earn such hateful stares from you?"

Ruzu remained silent. The old man shrugged his shoulders in response.

Adsum kept looking between Kahli and Ruzu. "I am somewhat torn between this new path and my current...." His eyes landed on Ruzu. "Well, I am sure this Orati thing can wait." Adsum began to walk out of the pen. "I will return shortly for you Ruzu so we can continue the experiments. Until then the pen is out of commission and if anyone violates this order please inform me. Also I would ask that you both refrain from killing each other." The old man slid the large wooden planks across the pen gate behind him — leaving the hulking brute's corpse for the flies and his stench to fill the girls' noses with the scent of death.

Kahli looked over to face Ruzu, only to see her already intensely staring straight through her. The look on Ruzu's face radiated the desire to kill Kahli on the spot with her hatred alone — that if she rejected the world hard enough, that something better would replace it. There had been many attempts on her life in such a short period of time, but this was the first time she felt someone wanted her dead for hating who she was. "*You can't hate someone this much and not know who they are,*" she thought to herself.

"... Who am I?" asked Kahli.

Both Kahli's inner voice and Ruzu simultaneously said, "The Curse." Ruzu's clenched teeth proved to Kahli that given a chance, she would happily kill her.

"But why? I don't even know you!"

"And you never should have! You split us! You destroyed our clan! We made you Orati and traded you away hoping to rid ourselves of the curse, but you are STILL here! I don't know how or why, but I promise you that you will not be alive for long. I will NOT give birth again!"

"What did I even do?!"

In lower tones Ruzu said, "You did not say that when you performed the Orati ceremony four years ago."

Kahli curled up and fell into a stunned silence, grateful that they were staked to the ground in such a way that they couldn't reach each other. She had been beaten by several men, her only sanctuary her inner voice, and had been called a curse by both herself and this stranger. *"How does she know me?"*

Ruzu kept staring at Kahli but she lacked the energy to fuel the anger her face wanted to express. "Why aren't you dead yet? How are you even thinking? You took the Hidati willingly —" Ruzu paused for breath, "I saw you being sold to the Heca clan, the worst that the Maharaan has to offer... we all thought it would be fitting that you be their problem...." Tears started trailing from her eyes. "Yet here you lay... free from the burden of knowing your crimes, and able to look to the future with hope." Ruzu sobbed softly as she turned away from Kahli and curled into a fetal position.

Kahli's words came out unheard and filled with sadness. "I... I'm sorry."

LAND OF THE GADORI

Toyo's lifeless body clenched as it was revisited by his first memory of pain, now refreshed by a new piercing and numbing kind. With teeth clenched and eyes wide, consciousness was forced upon him and he felt deathly cold as he tried willing his body to move. "... *Valde plaga,*" thought Toyo wearily before a fresh surge coursed through him.

Time diluted itself for him, and he felt like he could hear people near him, but not bring focus to the what and why of their words. The only thing he could focus on was the cold after each surge passed through him — all the while the conversations around him grew louder.

A lull from the pain came, and a bleary Toyo took the opportunity to look out onto a wasteland — a white sheet as far as he could see. "... *Again?*" The scenic calm was interrupted by what he felt to be a stick prodding him sharply in the back. "*Futuo, leave me alone you plaga!*" Toyo swore mentally at the offending sensation. The stick decided to leave him alone, which allowed him some time to wonder, "*How did I even get here?*"

When the surges subsided a wave of guilt crashed down upon him as the most recent memories flooded his mind — the tribe had cast him out and left him to die on the ice. Tracing backwards from those thoughts, Toyo's spirits sank as he remembered the spider-like creatures that feasted on the people in the hammocks of that large tree. The girl that had waved to him was gone... that fleeting moment of fireworks in his brain and heart from that chance encounter was the single most interesting thing that had happened to him in his life.

The stick decided to re-assert itself. *Poke.*

All he had in his mind was a fading memory of a pretty girl. "*She's dead....*"

Toyo could feel warmth in his wrists but was too dulled to register the sensation, and the voices around him started to become clearer. "<He's BLEEDING! >" shouted someone.

"*I can't understand you, you —*" Toyo didn't have the freedom to finish his thought as heat surged from his wrists down through his arms and straight to his heart, gripping it with a ferocity that made his body shake. His lungs slammed open as air rushed into them, and the breath marshaled the heat from his heart to his toes. Nerves began to register sensations once more beyond the bland cold, along with all the other prickling sensations of the world that crept in and demanded his attention.

The first thing he noticed was that he was wet, and further subtle probing with his arms and legs told him that he was in a shallow puddle. He could hear the frantic conversation in that strange Gozuri tongue behind him — the hurried conduct made Toyo wonder what was going on and decided that if it was going to be more bad, he wasn't about to face it on his back. With his newfound strength he leapt to his feet and turned around, ready to fight.

Fists raised and looking at the tribe that had scorned him, his urge to defend himself waned as the adrenaline subsided and guilt reasserted itself — the sight of the naked lady facing away and standing between him and the Gozuri also helped. He was not sure who the naked lady was but she seemed oddly pretty and reminded him a lot of a tree — her hair was scraggly like vines and her veins had the pattern of leaves about them.

That guilt came stronger and he lowered his fists, feeling that he had done enough damage with them already. A quick glance downwards made him wonder whose arms he was looking at, he then realized in shock that they were his — large red tendrils protruded from his skin that looked like they had crept out from the gloves and invaded him. Looking down his arm to inspect what else might be wrong he discovered that he was stark naked, and standing in front of everybody.

To which, he said, "Oh."

Next to the naked lady he saw his clothes. Tentatively, Toyo edged forward and gathered them up. Getting dressed with the muted hush of an audience made Toyo go from guilty to

LAND OF THE GADORI - CHAPTER VIII | 293

uncomfortable — were they expecting him to do something? Why did they all looked surprised? He turned to face the crowd after dressing and, after searching for a suitable response, bowed low in emulation of what he had once seen one of them do.

"I... I am very sorry for everything. I don't know what I have done wrong but... but I didn't mean it," he said with as much humility as he could muster. The tall hunter that Ani had referred to as Tagai walked towards him with eyes wide and an arm outstretched, holding a large stick. Toyo flinched expecting to be struck hard with it, and was surprised when all the man did was poke him, like a man scared to poke an angry creature on a dare. "Um... yes? Were you the one poking me?"

The tribe quickly crowded around both him and the naked lady. Why hadn't that strange woman moved? She looked cold and stiff, why was nobody helping her? He took off his heavy coat and thought that she needed it more than him, she looked awfully cold. Moving to drape the coat over her shoulders his glove brushed against the woman's skin and she gasped suddenly, startling him.

The woman began to breathe in and out, and with each breath more color seeped into her skin while her hair gained luster. Toyo noticed the whole tribe was in a state of shock, some falling to their knees while others muttered to themselves under their breath.

"Uh... hello?" The lady turned around, and he saw for the first time the deep reddish-purple flower in her left eye, surrounded by skin that looked both plant and human, wilting slightly.

"Hello Toyo," said the lady in a soft voice. Toyo's chest nearly exploded at the prospect of having someone else to talk to, but his excitement was tempered slightly by the strange vein patterns, vine hair, and petaled eye-flower that he was now face to face with. Silence brought to him the thought that one should probably do something when introducing oneself to new people — he was sure that staring at their breasts was probably not a part of the process.

"I... uh... hi. I'm Toyo," he stammered.

She replied, "Yes, I know."

"Uh... I come from," Toyo appeared stumped for a moment then rallied and waved his arm in a southerly direction before saying, "Over there." This got a smile, which in turn put a huge grin on his face.

"Hello Toyo, from," the lady waved her arm in the same fashion and direction as Toyo had, then said, "Over there. I myself am from," she waved at the empty tree stump with its crown of roots that the Gozuri had carried, "Over there. I have been waiting for you."

Toyo looked over to where she waved. "... That tree stump?"

The lady looked over, perplexed. "It shares the form, but not the function. It is now an Ogaden, my home."

"... Futuo..." thought Toyo flabbergasted, and a tiny thought came unbidden. "I... Uh... am I... the god of trees?" he asked sheepishly.

"No," she replied.

Toyo, slightly deflated, said, "Oh...."

Ж Ж Ж Ж Ж Ж Ж Ж Ж Ж Ж Ж Ж Ж Ж

In true Logicum style Ani had learned the theory of living in the forest with the Gozuri, but had opted to forgo the jump to the practical, which made it easy for Hoba to keep pace with her fumblings as she tried to make her way through unfamiliar terrain.

His disdain for her over all the years was now finally allowed to surface — the years of being ordered around and barked at like a sickly child who did nothing but fail, brought to boil his pent up feelings of malice. It was entertaining to watch her stumble through the dense foliage, barely avoiding dangerous plants, but his amusement was cut short when he had to intervene to stop her from walking right into a birthing nest of Ara'tai.

Throwing a looped vine he caught one of Ani's legs and pulled with force, slamming the old woman into the ground far harder than necessary. Striding up to straddle her he grabbed her hair, pulled her head up and clamped his hand firmly over her mouth.

"<If Tagai hadn't asked me to bring you back alive to face your punishment, I would have been tempted to let you walk into that

ara'tai birthing nest. >" Hoba pointed towards the unremarkable bush several steps away from her face. "<But unlike you, I respect him. Brother-in-love or not, I would not deny him the satisfaction of your punishment. He has done more to save us than you ever will. >" Hoba grabbed her hands roughly, bound them behind her back and turned her over. "<Scream, and I will leave you to whatever you summon, old woman. >" He released his hand from her mouth to find that she was smiling. Hoba's anger flared — it was the same smarmy expression she always had when giving him an order.

"<Saving someone you despise now? How weak-willed are you that you need listen to others? >" asked Ani.

A still certainty came over Hoba as a course of action revealed itself to him so clearly that he knew it would be the future. Stalking over to the nearby bush, he said,"<Then think of me as weak-willed, >" and peered into the nest and confirmed his suspicions. *"Ara'tai,"* he thought with a smile and walked back to Ani and straddled her again. Ani tried to struggle but Hoba's grip would not allow for any movement.

Hoba carefully worked his knife to cut through her clothes until he had made a hole large enough for his task. He reached into his large hunter's pouch on his belt and took out two smaller pouches, one that contained some white powder and another empty. He filled the empty one with a light dusting of powder from the other and then heavily dusted her left breast. Spitting onto the powdered breast he began working the two into a paste and kept massaging it until he saw her face lose all expression and felt her body go limp. Placing his knife gently against her left breast he whispered, "<You will be returned alive, and will remain so. In a fashion. >" He made a clean incision into her aged chest and cut out a large lump of flesh — no blood flowed from the wound, no screams from Ani were uttered.

Inspecting the small piece of flesh, he then took it and the other pouch with him as stalked over to the nearby bush. Peering into the nest he checked to see if it was safe before tossing the flesh into the middle of it and watched as the little creatures went into a frenzy. Noting which one struggled the least in the frenzy, he scooped up the obvious runt of the litter quickly into the powdered pouch and hurried back to Ani. Looking down at her, his face exuded a cold hatred and he thrust the pouch into the hole he had carved with little care for kindness.

From his hunter's pouch he produced a pod of Mihame and inspected it. The long, beautiful and slightly bumpy red bean was considered a scourge of the region because when it ripened the beans inside the pod would burn with a flame unmatched. That heat would cause the skin of the pod to expand and eventually explode, spreading its flaming seeds everywhere that would burn into wherever they could and take root. With no animals that could eat it and survive, and its reproduction self-reliant, it found itself in all corners of the Gadori. The Gozuri had found that they were harmless if you removed the beans and kept them moist — dry them out, and they became a source of fire.

Pinching Ani's skin together, he placed a cured mihame pod on her wound and began to softly blow. It took some time before a spark erupted, but once started the whole pod burned in a flash — scorching his fingers in the process. The pain was distant to Hoba due to the white powder residue that had numbed his fingers while Ani remained limp throughout.

After it all Hoba looked upon her scar with a look of satisfaction before dragging her to her feet and marching her in her stupor back to his tribe.

Ж Ж Ж Ж Ж Ж Ж Ж Ж Ж Ж Ж Ж Ж Ж

Toyo stood puzzled as he looked at the naked woman staring up at the sky — the tribe was doing the same but out of reverence.

"What are you looking at?" he asked, straining to see more than just the night sky.

The woman took some time before responding. "The attempts to penetrate me." Toyo went bug-eyed.

"Oh... yes, well I'm not trying to penetrate you if that... helps at all."

She plainly said, "You already have."

Toyo's brain stopped in its tracks upon hearing this. "So I... I've penetrated you, have I?"

"You are here, aren't you?"

"Yes, yes I am." Toyo was now thoroughly confused and decided to try a different tactic. "Is it easy to see?" he asked, pointing at her eye-flower.

"Is what easy to see?" she replied, looking at him.

"Um... anything? That... flower. It's very pretty! But, like, doesn't it make it kind of hard to see?"

"The flower is its own sight."

"Oh..." he replied, feeling sheepish at not understanding her. "Aren't you cold?"

She looked straight through him once more. "I was, now I am not. Thank you for showing my body the difference, it has been some time since last I needed to know. The last person... didn't, but he did teach me how to speak."

"So, like —" Toyo began.

"How did you do it?"

"... Do what?" he replied, fearing an inquisition about the accused penetration.

Silence followed.

The woman again looked deep in thought, then looked back up. "Ah, that is why: They are still trying..." she said to herself distantly. Toyo decided that it was not the right thing to leave a lady unclothed so picked up the coat off the ground and draped it around her shoulders. She seemed to not notice his gesture. Looking back at him she said, "You will serve my purposes regardless, I need a man to grow."

Toyo knew that he was not yet a man, he wouldn't even begin to know what one might be, and seeing that he did not know how to measure anything he felt it necessary to ask, "How do you tell when someone is a man?" This question went unanswered.

The woman turned to Tagai and pointed to her tree stump. "<My

Ogaden is dying, we need another Ogagi. >" What the woman said astonished the Gozuri, most were hearing their Ogahigi speak in their own tongue for the first time.

Tagai quickly responded. "<You will be tended to. I must inform you though that this boy was responsible for the last —>"

"<I know what he is and is not more than you. He is to be welcomed and trained as one of you, and the tribe will once again flourish, >" said the Ogahigi.

Honor-bound Tagai did not question the Ogahigi's words — he had only ever sought the best way to be. "<How? None of us can speak with him, Ogahigi. >"

"<Then find someone who can, but you must first save my home, >" she said, again pointing to the Ogaden.

As she surveyed the crowd she could feel a weight of unease in the air. "<The need for vengeance is great, >" she said softly. Her eyes fell upon the medishi and her expression changed from one of indifference to deep thought. Stretching out a finger she raised her voice so as to be heard by all and said, "<Kill them if it would sate your thirst — they have been deceiving you, selling the knowledge of this tribe to their masters, and the last kusabana that took so many was by their hands. >" Tagai's face went from subservient to stone as this news sunk in. He, like everyone else, had thought it was an accident with no malice or intent behind it, just pure accident all this time.

The medishi cowered together under the combined weight of the tribe's gaze. Two of the quick thinking ones fled into the trees whilst the remaining four stood still, locked in place by fear as they saw the tribe remembering everything in their life they had lost thus far.

Toyo merely stood there perplexed at what was going on, but seeing the focused anger towards the medishi made him feel both grateful and uneasy.

"Uh... excuse me but what's happening?" he asked the tree-woman.

Turning away from the angry crowd she faced Toyo, who

noticed that she had a lot less color than before. "<A cleansing for the tribe. >"

"Sorry?"

The Ogahigi seemed perplexed at its own mouth and tried to speak again. "A cleansing for the tribe."

"... It looks more like they are going to kill them."

"Yes."

"Why?"

"Law."

"Oh...." He felt a little confused again. "Are you okay? You don't look too... uh... healthy at the moment."

The Ogahigi inspected herself slowly. "I appear to be dying." The majority of the tribe had already reached the remaining medishi and bound them, save for the one that had already been beaten to death by those who hadn't the strength to listen to their honor.

"HELP!" screamed out one of the medishi.

"Wait... you can talk?!" said Toyo, startled by the revelation.

"Help us please!" screamed the medishi at Toyo as the tribe descended upon the cowering group.

Toyo began to run but fell to his knees, weak and unsure he looked up to the Ogahigi and pleaded, "If they go I won't have anyone to talk to!"

"All prices must be paid — this is theirs, just as being cast out on the ice was yours for almost causing a kusabana."

That word sounded familiar. "Wait, what? No! I didn't do anything."

"You injured the Mother-Tree Ogagi, her sap called out to the creatures — you are why they marched here, you are why many are dead." Toyo was on the verge of tears at hearing this. The Ogahigi tilted her head and said, "Am I not enough to talk to?"

His desire to not interfere with the tribe clashed with his desire to not lose anyone he might be able to talk to, but he did nothing as he watched them bind the medishi except obsess over his guilt.

Tagai meanwhile stood by the Ogahigi — honor and devotion were ever present in his mind, even in the face of revenge. He had also noticed her decay over time. "<STOP! >" he barked at the tribe. Respect for the man made his words infallible and he signaled for the Ogaden and medishi to be brought to him. "<Ogahigi you are not well, please return home, >" he said on bended knee. Looking down on him she smiled softly, then gently fell forward without making any effort to save herself. Tagai quickly leaned forward and caught her as softly as he could.

The Ogaden and the corralled medishi were rushed over, Tagai turned to the betrayers and demanded, "<Return her home. >"

Shaking from fear the medishi were speechless, save one who had a greater wish to serve his craft. "<Tagai, we have NEVER done this before — even if we were successful she would need constant monitoring to make sure that she —>"

"<Then do what you can, and I will ensure the rest, >" interrupted a stone-faced Tagai. Turning to the remaining two medishi he commanded, "<Help him. >" The tribe untied the three medishi and they quickly set to work like their lives depended on it.

Each member of the tribe sat and watched in expectant silence as the medishi busied themselves with their task — fetching strange balms and needles from their pouches as necessary. They gently curled the Ogahigi back upright into her fetal position inside the small alcove in the Ogaden. Once placed they tried to re-insert the roots she'd severed that connected her to the Ogaden, roots that had long ago grown into her flesh, but the freezing weather made it hard to perform any sort of delicate operation — the panic in their chests did little to aid them.

The inside of the Ogaden was alive and pulsing softly, and the medishi watched on as the multitude of roots tried to reach out to its former occupant with an eerie hand-like grasp.

When it appeared that nothing more could be done the medishi who had spoken before turned to Tagai and said, "<She needs

nutrients, the Ogaden has no nourishment. >"

"<Do you wish to live? >" he asked. There was a chorus of nods from the medishi.

He reached forward and carefully removed six of the many needle roots implanted in the Ogahigi. He thrust the bundle into the open hand of one of the medishi and said, "<Hold them. >" He then gently rolled up each medishi's sleeve, said, "<Now, join with her, >" and placed in each of them two roots to the silence of all. Toyo had no idea what was happening, but felt like something really, really bad was going on.

The medishi pleaded, "<You would condemn us to this unknown?! You know what the sap of an Ogagi can do! >"

Tagai said in calm tones, "<You were already going to die, how you die is now up to me. Here I decree: You have no value beyond keeping her alive, so I have bound your life to hers. Live well, live for her — or not at all. >"

INTEGRUM

The Erus of the Quadra Lustrum along with her near constant companion and advisor stood in the corridor in between the two Taker's rooms.

"Is this wise, Erus Criso?" asked Seconsulo.

Criso grinned while she played with an errant lock of red hair. "I do not know about wise, but it is at the very least entertaining."

Each Taker of the Ardeo Trial would usually be locked away in the Taker's rooms assigned to them for the fortnight before the Taker's Procession, to allow loneliness to foster their desire for company. In the past this had 'inspired' the Takers to be more enthusiastic when they were unleashed for the Procession, and also made for a more exuberant first few days with their partners. This year however, Criso wanted things to be different.

Seconsulo was not one to judge, but he was happy to always advise. "Traditionally we have always used both Taker's rooms."

"Traditionally it has always been male and female — Ardeo was somewhat close minded like that."

"The purpose of their solitude is to starve the Takers of human contact so they WANT to bond. How will they if Clarus and Tari are not individually confined?"

"Women have motivations beyond mere loneliness to want to bond, and they will bond to the couple just as easily by the desire to beat the other after a week of each other's company."

"Is it wise to place all your hopes on them becoming enemies?"

Criso rolled her eyes at this. "You have been here long enough to have noticed that every time there is a 'falling out' between my female charges that it is soon followed by a surge of productivity and profit. My male charges like to think they are competitive just because they are more outspoken than us, but they have never seen a self-made woman fight for her place — we are vicious creatures." Criso smirked at the thought. "And I would not be any other way."

"Whilst I applaud my mistress' replacing loneliness with competitiveness, tradition does state that —"

"What tradition states is that there is a room for a male and a room for a female, as there is no male I think we can dispense with whatever sensibilities of yours that aggravates."

The advisor merely shrugged, indicating both indifference and acceptance of the situation. "Our recent 'gesture' of showing the bloodied room seems to have had the desired effect and calmed our patrons, and our reputation remains... largely unaffected."

Criso sighed at her advisor's attempt at subtlety. Members of the Integra Pol tended to have difficulty understanding normal human emotion, but she thought that surely by now he must have learned something about them. "I assume the pause indicates some problem I am unaware of?"

"We have complaints from most of the districts about your announcement — ranging from nepotism, to forced homosexuality."

"So, nepotism because I assigned my own daughter, and forced homosexuality because both of the chosen Takers are female." She let out a restrained sigh. The damage to the public's sensibilities that Erus Ardeo had created was still causing her trouble all these years later. "'Forced?' Does nobody understand that the point of the trial is to test the bond of a new couple? We are not here to dole out free rides."

"Whilst true Erus Criso, most people remember what has happened before, more than the intended result. It is hard for people to discount that in the past most of the broken couples became infatuated with their Takers."

"Yes but —"

"There are also the riots."

Criso was slightly shocked by Seconsulo's interruption, a rarity it was, but the news was equally strange. "... Riots?"

"This morning. The Integra Pol's new shape has caused serious discord amongst the populace. Our Quadra still flows, but I fear that with the growing reports of the outbreaks of the cremo faba we will soon not have young couples who would wish to even partake this year. Unless something is done soon —" his report was interrupted by a loud crashing noise and screaming from behind one of the doors. Seconsulo glanced briefly towards the commotion and said, "I wonder if Erus Criso would entertain my idea of —"

Criso waved him to silence. "Either they will kill each other or not, either way at least one problem gets solved and right now I have more pressing matters. For example, cleaning up my stupid daughter's room." She began walking briskly to her quarters, Seconsulo fell in step without missing a beat while his Erus talked about more practical things. "When you parade Tari and Clarus for the Taker's Procession for this year, try to promote the Ardeo Trial in a specific light. Not as some sordid attempt to sexually pervert the innocent, but remind people that the tenets are to test the bonds of love. And downplay Tari — Clarus needs to be the one that shines through. Perhaps some pamphlets and announcers, we need to quash these rumors before the fear festers."

Criso reached the doors to her chambers and the pair passed through. On the other side she turned to her advisor with an expression of outrage. Seconsulo braced himself for the inevitable outburst, and was slightly surprised that she had held it in this long.

"The nerve of them accusing me of such! They would have never done so to Erus Ardeo! The man was known up and down for all sorts of perversions! Accusing me just because I am a woman — so what if the couple learns things they would not have in the normal course of things? The somewhat *inadvertent* sexual education is just an added bonus. It is not like we force their virginity from them, *futuo* knows that I myself would have preferred to not lose my virginity to another virgin. Such a messy ordeal, and it was years before I learned how to enjoy myself! If you want to learn how to play chess you play a chess master, you don't try to cobble the rules together from some half-truths and overheard conversations just to find someone as clueless as yourself to try and piece it together. Men bring their sons here all the time for just that reason! Forced homosexuality indeed!"

ЖЖЖЖЖЖЖЖЖЖЖЖЖЖ

Clarus simpered in the corner next to a smashed vase as an enraged Tari threw both furniture and her emotional baggage at the poor girl.

"Lock me in here will she?! Stupid old cow has no idea what I am going to do now! I'll just sneak out of here and —" Tari threw another vase hard at the door near Clarus, causing her to cower and look at Tari wide-eyed. "STUPID WOMAN." Tari strode over to Clarus. "Quit bawling! I have no time for weak-willed women! *FUTUO*, this is just so —" Clarus' face caught Tari's attention. "So..." Tari looked deeper into Clarus' eyes, "Do I know you?" she asked.

Clarus was shaking like a small puppy expecting to get beaten any minute. Looking for a way out she pounced on the question eagerly. She hesitantly said, "Uh... yeah! We're friends... remember?" A sharp slap was the reply she got.

"Don't play games you could never hope to win with me. Are you a spy for my mother?" asked Tari. Clarus shook her head violently, her body's shaking returned along with it. Tari's brow furrowed and thought deeply. "*Those eyes... she is also rather tall for a woman.*"

Watching Clarus leak from her eyes and nose made Tari feel sorry for women as a whole. Huffing into her face Tari went and sat on the bed. Patting it invitingly she cooed over to Clarus, "Come here beautiful. I'm so sorry to have scared you, but mine is not a happy family. That doesn't mean that we can't be happy, does it?"

Clarus' shaking hesitation made Tari's soul want to smack her again but she reigned it in and instead decided to make it easier for her and made her way over to Clarus. "There there," she said as she stroked her head. "Come on, all the anger is gone. And you are right, we are friends aren't we?" Clarus gave a muted nod, then Tari helped her up and guided her over to the bed and sat down next to her.

"Now my dear, do you know why you are here?" asked Tari.

"Um... yes. I am one of this year's Ardeo Trial Takers," replied Clarus. Her shaking began to subside.

"Well... yes and no. You are here because my mother thinks she is clever and is punishing me. You see my mother needed a way to keep me in the public eye so I could not have any fun. Do you remember that loud noise about a week ago?"

Clarus gave a blank expression. "Um, yes?"

Tari wondered how in *futuo's* name this girl didn't know what she was talking about, but it didn't matter. "Good, well you see I fear that something bad has happened to the man I love, and my mother wants to stop me from finding anything out."

"Goodness!"

"*Goodness?*" Tari repeated in her head in disbelief at such a soppy response. "Yes! Well anyway, it would appear you have gotten caught up in one of my mother's games. You were picked at random."

Clarus' face scrunched up in confusion. "But I am really good at what I do!"

"Well, I've heard that you've only been with us a short while."

Clarus' face fell in fear of being replaced or rejected. "Yes, but I impressed everyone!"

"Darling, that is just what they say as we are always in need of fresh female blood. We are in the business of giving people what they want to hear, see and feel, and variety is the greatest thing one can provide."

Clarus looked like she was about to burst back into tears. "But why would they lie to me?"

"*What the futuo did mother think in putting her up against me? She isn't even competition! Unless....*" Tari's face broke into a grin. "That is just how my mother does business I am afraid. I, on the other hand, do not believe in such things. You don't think I lie do you?" Clarus looked at her wide-eyed and shook her head. "Well I think you could easily win this year. I know you haven't been trained properly, but you see I haven't been either. You are also so much prettier than I am."

"Oh no! You have an elegance and grace that I could never hope to achieve Tari!" Clarus covered her mouth as soon as she spoke in panic. "I'm sorry! Uh, Lady Tari."

Tari was taken aback, she had never been referred to as Lady Tari with any sincerity before. Her past behavior and reputation had stripped people of the notion that they should call her 'Lady' and only ever did so if they wanted something from her. To be called it so candidly and honestly struck a chord in her heart. "Of course not Clarus, and please, just Tari, okay? Besides if I won, what would I gain? I already have respect, riches and the adoration of many. Also I am supposed to be paired with the Lover's woman this year, and I'm not really that much into women." Tari mentally added, "*That often,*" and continued in as self-deprecating a voice as possible, "So I don't know if my heart is in it to win at all."

Clarus blustered out. "But I don't want to win either! I don't think it is a nice thing to try and break up young lovers."

"Come come, we aren't trying to 'break' them up. We are just testing to see if they really want to be together, yes? If you don't try to win, then what if they just stay together for years and find out too late that they are unhappy? Isn't that worse?"

Clarus appeared to consider this quite deeply. "I suppose? It just... seems wrong somehow."

"Maybe, but that isn't for us to decide. It's not like we force the couples to participate," said Tari as she inched closer to Clarus on the bed. "Still, it is quite a boring game we are playing isn't it?" asked Tari, her voice now dripping with anticipation.

"Oh not at all! Every time I saw the Ardeo Trial I always found it fascinating and exciting. Don't you?" asked Clarus with an innocent face.

Tari was confused for a second before deciding to quit being subtle and just make Clarus hers. She reached out and grabbed Clarus' clothed chest quite forcefully and found bountiful flesh. A light moan crept out of Clarus' mouth and she began to tremble meekly. Her chest was heaving, and her flushed face did nothing more than show sure signs of arousal.

What lay before Tari was a clear course of action as she saw an overly eager beautiful woman in front of her, almost begging to be tended to. "*Wow, that is a very easy switch to flip,*" she thought to herself.

Clarus appeared weak and willing and Tari always appreciated her partners to be putty in her hands, with the one now before her the kind that could be sculpted quite easily.

"Well I have time to kill. *May as well enjoy myself,*" thought Tari, as she leaned on top of Clarus and kissed her passionately.

Ж Ж Ж Ж Ж Ж Ж Ж Ж Ж Ж Ж Ж Ж Ж Ж

The Erus' had a need to meet again in secret. Things had not been going well, and all wanted to voice their opinions.

"Erus Epula, I —" Erus Criso began.

Erus Epula's outrage paid no heed to politeness and the slight wobbling in his chin showed that there was more muscle than fat there. "Have you any idea what you have done?! The outcry alone is difficult to manage! Just because you have the next popular Quadra event does not give you free reign to do as you wish given the circumstances! Did you not think it wise to consult with us first before appointing your OWN daughter? We have a catastrophe to clean up after here!"

Erus Criso was not one to regret her choices and always defended them, regardless of if she had to clean up afterwards. "What is it your chefs teach again? 'Throw it in a pot — it'll either cook or spoil'? I did what I could. You make it sound like I had months to plan this bloody thing."

"It was an appropriate course of action," said Erus Cogitans, wanting the squabbling to stop. "The distraction has bought us some more time to investigate."

Epula bellowed, "How was it appropriate?! Have you not seen the complaints? Erus Criso has now become a prime target for —"

"Yes, detracting the focus from the Integra Pol and the missing people," said Erus Cogitans.

"But people aren't just going to forget!" said Erus Epula.

"As I said before, it has bought us some time. I would appreciate knowing what you have accomplished in that same said time, Erus Epula." Knowing that Epula was not a man who calmed easily all Cogitans had to do was wait for his brain to catch up to the questions.

Erus Ictus had a faraway expression on his thin face throughout the entire conversation as he explored the entertainment his own mind had to offer. The odd hunched man always found the rooms chosen for these meeting to contain little of interest to him in regards to lighting, decor, and conversation. All requests to try and liven the place up with some of his Quadra's charges were met with refusal, which Erus Ictus always felt was an unnecessary cruelty towards him.

Cogitans cast his gaze around the table and asked, "So nobody has come any closer to finding out what happened a few days ago?" An uncomfortable silence followed. He turned his attentions to the silent member of the group. "Erus Ictus?"

His eyes coming back into focus Erus Ictus returned from whatever fantasy his mind was occupying. "Yes?" he replied.

"Anything to report?" asked Cogitans.

"... No," he replied blandly.

"Well that's somewhat typical isn't it," sniped Epula.

Cogitans continued. "My informants have confirmed that virtually all of the Integra Pol's charges were inside at the time of the event. With their deaths we have lost a lot of the public confidence, I recommend that we devote a small force from each of our Quadras to perform the duties of those lost."

"How are people going to react when the people who come to deliberate on their legal issues or health are those from our Quadra? We don't have that sort of training to begin with!" replied Epula.

"I am already at capacity for my Ardeo Trial, I could not spare anything," said Criso.

"Then we should devote some of our charges to form a temporary Integra Humanus," said Cogitans.

"What of the Natura?" piped up Ictus.

"An irrelevance, we need our people healthy and lawful if we are to remain a city. Not to poke plants and prod animals," said Cogitans. "We have a need to restore order lest we ourselves become an irrelevance. The servants of the Integra Pol have already cleaned up the lower levels but it will be some time before we can confirm Mulat's death."

Epula, still raging, said, "He should have dealt with this creba drug problem sooner, I can't keep my patrons happy with cake alone. The stories of murder and rape are escalating and public rumor is mutating them into horror stories, what do you want me to do? Stuff my patrons' ears with cake?"

"Given my experiments and those of my predecessor I would have to say that the horror stories could be quite real," said Cogitans. "We have developed some lenses that will assist the guards in tracking down minute quantities of this cremo faba — that should help stymie the flow. I will distribute them to yours in turn."

"Lenses?" asked Criso.

"Yes. We were able to suspend some of the cremo faba and bind it to a lens. Wear the lenses and you should see where it has been, effective up to half a day."

Criso clapped her hands together. "You are indeed very clever Erus Cogitans, you must be very proud!" Cogitans chose to omit the fact that it was his predecessor who had developed the lenses long ago while he had only been able to piece minor parts of it together to form a makeshift copy of limited capability. Cogitans' only strength was mathematics, and he knew that. Everything else he either knew or did was merely a pale imitation of his predecessor, Adsum.

Ictus stood up silently and walked out of the room to the stunned silence of Criso and Epula. "Where are you going Ictus?" asked Cogitans.

"My music calls to me," he said distantly without stopping.

Stunned at the sudden certainty of Ictus' words and actions it was a while before Criso spoke up. "How are we going to fix all this without the Erus of the Quadra Musicum?"

"Perhaps it is time for his Quadra to replace him," said Cogitans.

"I knew the man was weak, but to walk out during a crisis?!" said Epula. An expression of shock crossed his face, "Maybe he's the one responsible for all this? That's why he is being all cagey!"

"Don't be stupid, the man is as harmless as a fly," said Criso.

Epula seethed. "Perhaps, but those musicians can be crafty bastards."

"And chefs are all sunshine and roses?" said Criso.

"That, is still the subject of discussion," said Cogitans. Both Epula and Criso turned to Cogitans with a confused expression. "The subject of what happened and why. Whoever did it is powerful enough to assault the most powerful person we know in his own home. If he is not safe, then how are we? Bickering will merely weaken our position. We will have some freedom until the Ardeo Trial is finished, but afterwards we had best be informed and ready to act. Mulat was a dangerous man, but I fear that his enemy would be more so."

ЖЖЖЖЖЖЖ

Erus Criso sat in her quarters pondering over her meeting with the other Erus'. Ultimately nobody knew what had happened to Mulat, along with the how or why. She wanted to devote her time to figuring it out but business before the Ardeo Trial was always so hectic that she could not spare anyone. The advantages of sex for information gathering however may still yield useful results.

"Perhaps Erus Ictus was right in washing his hands of this, I can't remember the last time I have had to think so fast," thought Erus Criso. *"I don't even have time to enjoy myself. The world keeps thrusting itself upon me and all I can gaze out of my own window to see is this... twisted fang."*

"Erus Criso, you have some visitors," said Seconsulo,

interrupting her thoughts.

Criso replied, "What visitors? Can't you see I am a bit too busy to deal with anything ELSE?"

"Those six that you asked to inspect the room have returned."

"... What, all together?"

"Yes."

"What the *futuo* are they? Some sort of committee now?"

Without humor Seconsulo said, "Coincidentally, yes. Since you anointed those people to oversee the room inspection, they have apparently deputized themselves to be the unofficial 'reporters of truth'. Since the other Erus' have yet to make any public statement of —"

"But that is the Integra Pol's responsibility!"

"... Yes," Seconsulo gave Criso a few moments to let the reminder sink in. "Now, seeing as the other Erus' still have yet to make any public statement, and with your grand gesture, the public appears to have taken the matter into their own hands."

"So these... six, are now spokespeople?"

"They have been approached by major heads of communities to report on the Ardeo Trial. Recent events and the rumors of the room —"

Panic spread on Criso's face as she sputtered, "What?! Only a few are privy to even the existence of the androcium! How did that get out?!"

With unerring patience Seconsulo continued. "The room that both Tari and Clarus occupy. I believe Erus Criso that they are more here to report on why you chose your daughter. It would do good to put to rest the public's concerns."

Criso's face went through many emotions silently before her face settled on professional calm. "Let them wait ten minutes and then show them in."

Seconsulo bowed and then left the room. *"Let your mind wander. When it returns, it will bring with it the answer,"* were the words that rang out in Criso's head. "We cannot all have such a peaceful state of mind, my dear Mulat," she said to herself.

The days had taken a toll on her and forced her into constant snap decisions and patchwork solutions that were far from ideal. More and more she felt like she was on a sinking boat with a hundred other people and that she was the only one plugging the leaks while others just watched. "*Erus Cogitans, Epula and Ictus are not going to help me here, the bastards. Could they do any better than I in this situation?*" Her irritation with the other Quadras rose as none seemed any wiser as to what was happening, nor showed any signs of even caring beyond their own walls. Criso squirreled away her thoughts as she set about to perform an inevitable song and dance of public appeasement.

Adjusting her clothing to amplify her cleavage, not too distracting, she turned, opened a drawer, and surveyed her assortment of lipsticks. An incredible array of red shades looked back at Criso, so many that to the casual observer the colors appeared to overlap ten times over. Criso had always believed that people never understood the concept of colors and sex — there is so much more to red than just 'red'. There was much argument over this from the seasoned veterans of the Quadra, saying that the point of always using a dark red was to make a man think you were always in season. To put the notion to rest though she and Erus Adsum made a particularly interesting discovery — that if you matched the shade you wore to where you were in your monthly cycle, the effects on others were significant. For optimum effect one should, from start to finish, go from lightest pink to a deep red.

Perhaps it was Erus Ardeo's old teachings that did not help her seasoned charges understand that looking at the same color always is both boring and misleading. "You are not a painting, you are a person," was what Criso introduced into the training of new charges in an attempt to dispel much of Ardeo's misplaced misogyny. Too much had to be essentially beaten out of her charges in order for new thoughts to trickle in, and forcing the training on the new girls rather than trying to train the old ones was Mulat's idea. It was difficult at first but eventually everything smoothed out much to Criso's relief. About the only thing that wasn't difficult to introduce was increasing the ratio of male to female charges for the Quadra, which she found somewhat odd. A soft knock indicating Seconsulo was at the door interrupted her thoughts.

Quickly applying the finishing powder to her face she scooped everything into a drawer on her desk. Walking softly over to the door she waited for Seconsulo to knock again. When he was part way through his pattern she gracefully opened the door, catching the assembled group standing outside off-guard. In a confident voice she said, "Hello my dear Ladies and Gentlemen. I am sorry to have kept you waiting, but things are terribly busy around here." Stepping to one side she curtsied slightly, held the door open, and invited everyone into her quarters. "Please excuse the lack of refreshments, I was unaware you were coming."

She noticed as the group filtered into her quarters that they did so with a sense of entitlement that was lacking confidence. Closing the door behind them she walked to her desk, allowing her heels to clack loud enough with each step to pierce the silence of the room. Sitting down carefully she smiled at the standing assembly and took a long, slow, deep breath before speaking, and paid special attention to those who watched her breasts rise along with it. "This is all very intimidating and sudden. I did not for a second think that you would all collect my gratitude simultaneously, but who am I to judge?" A few of the group seemed deflated and uneasy. Criso noted that they were each wearing what was most likely, for them, their best outfit. After a moment's silence she said sweetly, "What can I do for all of you?"

"We are here on behalf of the people to investigate certain claims," said one of the larger women in the group.

"The people? Did Integra Divinitas Mulat send you?" Criso asked disarmingly. The mention of Mulat made a few eyes widen in the room.

"No. Just the people," the large woman replied.

"Oh," said Criso, putting on her best crestfallen face. "Well my Quadra only exists to serve the people, so what are these claims you wish to investigate?"

"That you have rigged the Ardeo Trial in order to ensure your daughter wins by making the other Taker a newcomer with no track record."

"Well, my daughter has no track record with this Quadra either."

"Maybe not professionally, but she certainly has a public track record."

Being talked to so incredulously by the pudgy woman raised the hairs on the back of Criso's neck. She scanned the other faces hoping to see who else would speak up aside from this fat woman, but it appeared that she had silently become the leader of this group. *"So you think the law on your side?"* she thought to herself, and then calmly said, "May I remind you that the rule merely states that the Erus of the Quadra only has to select two Takers, and ensure that the couples entered are genuinely there to test their relationship bonds. My daughter being nominated does not break any covenant I know of, and I should know."

The large woman backed down, her temporary confidence weakened by the confrontation of both a calm Quadra Erus and a woman that she genuinely admired. Eventually a skinny man spoke up softly. "Yes, but she's a woman."

"I'm sorry?" Criso said with a look of innocent confusion.

"Your daughter is a woman."

"Yes... yes I believe that is what makes someone a daughter in the first place."

"I mean that your daughter is a woman, and assigned to the female Lover this year."

"I'm terribly sorry, but is there something I am not understanding?"

"Well, traditionally that Taker has always been male."

"I am sick and tired of hearing 'traditionally'! People speak as though it is somehow vesma incarnate!" Criso had a hard time not saying that thought out loud and instead opted for, "I also recall a tradition where Erus Ardeo would beat any charge he felt that was not living up to his standards. That was his decision and tradition to

make, but now you aren't comfortable with the head of the Quadra Lustrum making her own decisions?"

"No! Sorry, that is not what I meant. It is just that traditionally we are used to the Taker's Procession being a man AND a woman."

Criso allowed silence to blanket the room for a few moments before tilting her head and saying, with an expression of innocent misunderstanding, "Are you saying you would prefer my daughter to dress up as a man?"

"What? No, don't be silly."

"I'm not being silly, I am just having a hard time understanding here."

The fat woman had regained her composure and stepped back into the fray. "We feel that you are forcing a sexual choice on a young woman."

"How?"

"By not keeping it traditional!"

"I fail to see the difference."

"What do you mean?"

"Well, if picking a gender means I am forcing a sexual choice on someone, then regardless of what I pick I am essentially forcing a sexual choice on someone, aren't I?" Criso saw that a few members of the group were not following what she had said. "What if they both enjoy their Takers?"

"There is such a thing as what is right and natural for young couples, we —"

Criso stood up from her desk and tried her best to keep her cool. "This trial is not about you or anyone else other than the couple that chooses to partake. I am aware that past success has been somewhat less than ideal, leading some people to think that it isn't fair — many people thought how Erus Ardeo started it was unfair, and how he forced it upon people was unfair. Everyone has the freedom to make their own choice these days, and I am not about to tell my daughter that she cannot do it because others think she is not capable."

"We didn't say she isn't capable just that —"

"You're saying that she's not capable because of 'tradition'. May I remind you that sex is not the point of this trial — whilst it has always happened, there is no guidance to my charges that they should, or even have to, sleep with them. All they are to do is try, without malice or deception, to see if the bond between a young couple is easily broken. Nothing more. Do you wish to tell my daughter that she would not be able to test another woman?" Nobody had an answer for her. "Do you think my daughter could teach a young girl nothing of life or love? She is not some predator that I am 'unleashing' on a helpless person, she is to try and test a bond. Is sex the only way you think that is possible?" Criso allowed the information to settle into the group's mind before adding the final blow. "Mulat once said that tradition is just another word for habit and superstition, and that the only difference between them is the importance we place on those words." She sat back down. "If you feel that my daughter is not a good candidate for the role of Taker then please say so, but do not tell me it is because of 'tradition'."

"It has nothing to do with tradition!" said the skinny man.

"Oh?"

"Well it is hardly left to the powers of chance which Taker will win, is it? Your Tari versus some girl we've never heard of? People aren't even willing to take the bets even though the odds are ridiculous, they think this is a sort of scam. All we have is the name 'Clarus'."

"The couple might succeed." Criso was surprised at how uniformly the group silently expressed that this was as likely as all their legs simultaneously turning into pudding. "I have already disclosed one of this year's Takers, and somehow you have found out who the other is. You know 'traditionally' people would have to wait for the Taker's Procession to see who was selected, but if it would ease your mind I am sure I can arrange to have the other brought before you. Would that suit?" This got a look of approval, and she noted that two of the men present who had been listless until now perked up at this mention. She would not be surprised if one or two of the people in this group were spies from the other Quadras, but she had learned from the best how to deal with these situations. "I will take that as a yes."

She called out to Seconsulo, who was always nearby when she was conducting business, "Fetch Clarus, please." As soon as he left the room she readdressed them and said, "Please wait a moment, she will be here shortly. Is there anything you would —" Criso was interrupted by Seconsulo's soft knock at the door. "*That was... fast*," she thought to herself. "Enter."

Seconsulo opened the door and ushered Clarus to the front of the group. The tall and stunning woman attracted everyone's attention.

Clarus said, "Um... hello everyone."

While they were distracted Criso waved Seconsulo over and whispered, "You were a little too quick with that 'fetch' command. While I appreciate you being prepared, I do not appreciate other people knowing that WE are prepared."

Seconsulo replied, "My apologies Erus Criso." She silently sighed inwardly.

Criso watched as the crowd ogled Clarus, noting which of them found her desirable and attractive. The fat woman was not among that number, much to her irritation. "As you can see she is well worth putting on the poster, would you not agree?" she said to a chorus of dumb nods.

"She may be tall and skinny but that doesn't mean she can hold a candle to Tari's reputation. Perhaps she should perform for us?" said the fat woman to enthusiastic nods from her group.

"Oh, would you like that? I may not be good enough for everyone here, but of course I'd be happy to try!" piped Clarus. She turned to Criso and said, "I mean that is if you would like me to, Erus Criso," while bobbing frantically.

"Clarus you do not have to, these people merely wanted to see if —"

"We want to see her," said the fat woman confidently.

"*Valde,*" thought Criso in her panic. "*Has she even finished training? I don't know much more about this stupid woman....*" She looked at Seconsulo who gave her a silent nod of approval. Resigned to her situation Criso said, "Well if these people would like to see you, it would be best if we did not disappoint."

"Goody!" said Clarus with a flounce. She then splayed her arms out and looked like she was about to do something, then stopped and said, "What would you like me to do? I am a pretty good dancer but there isn't any music...."

"We want to see if you are as good as Tari," said the fat woman.

"Tari? At what?" said Clarus with a puzzled look. The group took a moment to realize that Clarus was not the quickest of bunnies.

"They want to know if you will be able to perform your duties as a Taker, Clarus," said Criso.

"Well of course I can! I mean, I wouldn't have been picked if I couldn't do it, would I?" replied Clarus with the innocence of the ignorant.

The assembled group began to feel a bit sheepish, save for their spokesperson. "It should be easy then to show us that you can," said the large lady imposingly.

"Of course! It's just I don't how you want me to do that..." said Clarus, her face now in danger of breaking into tears.

"*Oh good, I picked a wet blanket to shelter me from this storm,*" thought Criso. "Clarus, we were just talking about how they were worried about Tari's assignment in the Ardeo Trial not being traditional, and that sex might be —"

Clarus' face lit up instantly and said, "Oh, Tari's very good at that!"

Criso could feel her sphincter tighten upon hearing those words and through extreme effort moved no muscle on her face. She knew that nothing terrible would happen when she left those two alone, but she didn't imagine that Tari would prey on her so quickly. "Yes, I have heard that. People might think that you aren't any good at it either though."

INTEGRUM - CHAPTER VIII | 321

Clarus' face seemed to disengage completely, giving the impression that her brain required all her effort. When she came to a conclusion though it was as if you had accidentally looked directly at the sun from how fast her face changed expression. "Oh! Oh I see! I've never done a group before so I hope I don't make any mistakes but I will try my best!"

Her face flushed quickly to a shade of pink, and her breathing became very deep and heavy. Clarus reached out with her slender arms and brushed the rubenesque woman's face and stepped into her for a passionate kiss. Slipping easily out of her clothing, Clarus' hands started to roam about the woman's body. As the group watched each member looked slightly confused but found themselves becoming aroused at the sight as the once innocent looking Clarus passionately imposed her sexual self on another. Breaking from the kiss Clarus looked around at the group and said with a face fully flushed, "I am so sorry for ignoring all your needs, but I am here to take care of you," and she reached out to the next nearest member.

Expecting some sort of backlash Criso was surprised to find herself becoming increasingly aroused at Clarus' boldness and pure desire to please. It was a moment later that Criso was surprised to find how hot her skin had become while Clarus was snaking her hands through various clothing. The so-called 'wet blanket' soon had everyone attending each other with passion — no complaints or objections were uttered, only excited gasps and moans from Clarus' assault. As the lithe nymph bounced from person to person, she kissed each one deeply with an honest passion that pierced through Criso's normally composed attitude.

Stuck to her chair with lust Criso watched as Clarus performed her art and was transfixed on the proceedings. This new girl was demonstrating an understanding of the art that would match some of her most elite charges — no wonder Seconsulo chose her! Out of shock and confusion she turned to her advisor with an expression of pure arousal and confusion expecting some sort of answer, all she saw was Seconsulo with his usual expression of polite boredom. She knew that those wishing to become charges of the

Integra Pol had to sacrifice something of personal value, but she could never understand those who chose to sacrifice the joy of sex. Seconsulo however had... other qualities.

Her thoughts and worries were wiped from her mind when Clarus turned her gaze towards Criso, crawling on all fours towards her with lustful gaze and lithe body.

Regaining her composure Erus Criso stood to full attention from her desk as Clarus peered at her. "If there is to be an orgy in my midst, then it is my duty as Erus to see that it is conducted properly," she said, hoping to convey to someone that she still held some power over the situation. Those words fell on deaf ears.

The room had gone to a place where all stimulation beyond their own pleasure was ignored.

CHAPTER IX

*Hearts bonded; beating as one.
Unbroken by distance; undone by time.
Sacred; we are both, to each other.*

-Kahli's bond-pledge to her wija, Kasi

THE MAHARAAN EXPANSE

True to Adsum's word Kahli and Ruzu remained undisturbed until his return, but the sight of him gave no comfort to either when he walked into the pen and signaled for the removal of the now pungent corpse he had left behind. Avoiding all eye contact with him and Ruzu, Kahli hurriedly secreted away the plank that the old man had forgotten. In his absence Kahli had been trying to find a way to use the plank to escape, but her desperation and nerves rendered all attempts into stops and starts as every sound made her jump. She buried her face in the hay and could hear no resistance from Ruzu as someone undid her shackles and shuffled her out. Waiting to hear the gate slam shut Kahli began to feel fear creep over her as the sound never came, and risked looking up to see what was happening. To her surprise the gate had been left open and a quick look showed her that she'd been left alone.

Her spirit urged her to rise up, but her body rebelled at the idea and reminded her that food and true rest had not come for some time now. Fighting the opposition of herself her mind buzzed with thoughts of escape. Sitting upright and pulling out the plank she desperately tried to think of a way to use it to break her shackles.

"*I can't do anything with this,*" said Kahli's other voice.

"*Shut up! You are just words! AND RIGHT NOW I NEED MORE THAN THAT!*" she screamed inside her head.

Inspecting her shackles closely she saw that they were nothing more than cast iron, designed to hold a person in place with no greater complexity beyond plate and chains. At first she tried to whack the shackles with the plank, hoping for some sort of reaction, but reeled in terror at the soft *clink* they made when the two struck each other. It sent her curling into a ball in case anyone had heard her attempt at escape and she held her breath until she thought she was going to pass out. Moments passed and nothing could be heard so she checked to see if it was safe again and poked her head up.

"I expected more of you," said Adsum, standing in front of her. Kahli's heart leapt into her throat.

The old man appeared to talk to himself and said, "I had left all that you needed to escape, perhaps you needed more time?" Kahli had a surge of hope — the old man wanted her to escape! Maybe he was trying to help her? "Hm, perhaps you don't know much about alchemy. Both component powders on the mixing board are soluble and highly volatile as you saw yourself. I just used some vesma in order to introduce it into the man's bloodstream before, but even the dust left on the board would have made easy work of your chains." Kahli felt both abused and lost at his words.

Sighing loudly he said, "You can come out now, the experiment was a failure," and Kahli's hopes fell to the pit of her stomach as she saw two gruff Maharaan men come out of their hiding places.

"So... you weren't trying to help me escape?" she asked meekly.

The old man looked like he was doing some sort of internal calculation before he responded. "Should I have been? I am sorry, I was doing a *Captivus Accurro* experiment. In the past it has been a good measure of someone's intelligence or willingness to find new ways to use very basic items, but Rasak's requested limitations have reduced the effectiveness of it."

"That's what I am to you? I'm an experiment?"

"No, the *Captivus Accurro* is the experiment. I devised it based on the concept that when a human is incarcerated in adverse conditions the human mind goes into a heightened state of ingenuity — I have seen people escape with merely chicken bones and mud, that was a good day...." The man smiled fondly in recollection of that thought. "Still, I suppose the colloquialism 'old habits die hard' applies, even though the habit itself is in formulae that create non-static results. Nothing has really come of it since my time here in the Maharaan, people mostly just find creative ways to kill the guards to escape — I suspect perhaps the cells I built back in my Quadra did not pose any physical threat as such so did not necessitate that approach. Also, they had far more time to devise a way out, so I have to conclude error on my part for this particular failure."

Kahli bundled up her hatred at being tricked and merely waited for the elderly man to stop his rambling. "Anyway, Ruzu will be busy for a little while so I thought we should have a little chat before your meeting with Rasak."

"Rasak?"

He looked at her like she was stupid. "Yes... Rasak, Rasak Jara, the current Isti of the Jara clan. Do you know what an Isti is?" she shook her head. "It is like an Erus." A blank stare. "He's the leader — Isti means leader."

The way he was talking was beginning to rile her. "So, I'm just sitting here waiting for him to come and 'experiment' with me as well?"

"His propensity for experimentation I think is quite limited, so I doubt you will have to prepare for such an eventuality. I think his interest lies more in the fact that you were unconscious, covered in blood, surrounded by one dead wija and two dead Integra Natura in the 'sea on the sands', the largest chamu nursing ground. However now it appears to have become a field of a most surprising fecundity."

"Fecundity?"

Adsum wracked is brain. "That means 'flowery' in layman's terms." He sat down to her level while the two men took up station outside the pen gate. "Anyway, I can deduce that the Integra Natura were there to investigate the anomaly, and that they died in some conflagration that involved you, them, chamu, and the wija. Quite rare to see, wild wija. Rasak has forbidden me from any experimentation with their own wija sadly enough and has yet to share any knowledge regarding them. I do wish I had access to my Quadra's archives once more." Kahli's memories bubbled to the surface but she clamped them shut lest they lead her to say something stupid. "I was hoping to know what connected all those elements together, and if you help me I can be a good ally. I do hold some authority here from my helping Rasak with varied problems, so I am allowed what he calls 'flights of fancy' from time to time."

"*So that's all I am? Alive for a flight of fancy?*" Kahli thought to herself.

"The field is the primary anomaly, and I can put together why every other element in this conundrum was in the field save for the wija. However, given that you are apparently Orati there is little I could hope to extract from you as I would not even know where to begin. Ruzu however seems to be more accepting of my attempts at bartering with her as of late."

"*The girl that knows me.*" With those thoughts Kahli asked, "Who is she?"

"She is one of the Habiak. An original member of this clan actually, before they splintered into separate factions."

"What happened?"

"The folklore explanation is a tad tricky, but according to what I have been told — about a decade ago a man with great attunement to vesma passed through this region — I'm not entirely sure who. He was apparently slighted somehow by one of the women of this clan and cursed —"

"ADSUM!" Kahli jumped out of fright but Adsum showed no signs of surprise and merely stood to address whoever had made the noise. The booming word was heard before a rugged, middle-aged Maharaan man strode through the gate with dark brown hair, short and tussled, and the neatly trimmed beginnings of what could become a mighty beard and mustache. His face and eyes were strong and carried the sense that they once were kind things, but now they were older than they should have been — aged by a life hard and unforgiving.

"Yes Rasak?" asked Adsum.

Rasak replied, "Did you kill one of my men again?"

"Yes," answered Adsum plainly.

"I keep telling you to put them to sleep! I cannot keep replacing men you keep doing your weird shit to!" screamed Rasak.

"I was already in the pen, he ignored my requests to leave and was damaging my only test subject. You want a cure — educate the men to act better towards my only test subject, or get me more test subjects."

Rasak's rage seemed slightly cooled by this response but he display his rough hands. "Who lives and dies in my camp is not for you to decide. Take that power into your own hands again and I will REMOVE those hands." Rasak clenched a fist and seemed ready to strike Adsum down where he stood. "Get on with your stupid tests, but when you are done talking with this one send her STRAIGHT to me!" As he made his way out of the pen Kahli felt a familiarity that she couldn't place her finger on.

"Always a wasted attempt at aggression," said Adsum to himself before turning back to Kahli. "I would prefer to find out more but I suspect that I should hustle you along to Rasak now — he is a man of limited patience, despite his claims to the contrary." He clicked his fingers, summoning the two men posted outside who walked into the pen, unshackled Kahli and got her to her feet. "Take her to Rasak, and when he is done bring her back straight to me, understood?"

Kahli was too tired to resist and began to wonder if this was all her life was to be, from disaster to disaster and abused until she was no longer of use. Why had they beaten her earlier? What did she do that was so evil if THEY had found HER unconscious?

"You killed them all," said Kahli's other voice.

Kahli had no idea what the voice was talking about but everything she had experienced so far had dragged her desire to fight anything down to an almost imperceptible blip.

Too broken to even talk to herself anymore she was hoisted off to Rasak's hut with the desire that if only further despair awaited, her life may as well end there.

Ж Ж Ж Ж Ж Ж Ж Ж Ж Ж Ж Ж Ж Ж

"It really is quite fascinating, I wonder how —" Adsum kept muttering to himself as he inspected Ruzu, who was laid out on a table in front of him. He no longer talked to her in expectation of a response — she had retreated into her mind long ago.

Adsum paced and mused. After some time he squeezed a breast and waited expectantly. "Lactation still present, signs of early stage pregnancy are still visible despite hysterectomy. Several months have passed with no further gestation —" Adsum's notation was interrupted by heavy breathing and scratching from a nearby bench in the hut. "Adacio put that pouch of sand down."

"Rasak told me that I could investigate it," replied Adacio.

"And I encourage you to investigate things, but not when I need your assistance." Adacio reluctantly squirreled away his pouch but kept touching it out of a nervous compulsion.

The assistant granted to him by Rasak had been subjected to a remnant from Adsum's days of obsessive behavior modification through vesma. He had wanted to make the boy obsessed with human motivation in order to supplement Adsum's own shortcomings, however during the imprinting process the boy fell off his chair face first into the desert sands and imprinted that instead. Rasak was not accommodating to his request for another assistant after what he'd seen.

Adsum said, "Reports regarding her offspring?"

"Not all have come in. The Habiak were reluctant with giving us information about the pen offspring we provided them with," Adacio replied.

"Just give me what you have."

"All appear to be curse afflicted."

Adsum stood over Ruzu and looked her straight in the eye. "Subject still unresponsive. Fetch me Ruzu junior."

When Adacio had left the hut Adsum tried again to get information out of her the old fashioned way. "I am both interested and irritated by the fact that I am failing in getting the information I seek out of you. Habits are strange things, yes? Here I am with a brand new fascination and doing the equivalent of poking you with sticks. Highly methodical and strategic sticks yes, but sticks nonetheless. I AM trying to find a cure for you Ruzu, and I know you may tire of my attempts to talk with you, but if you could tell me more about the curse and this Orati you speak of I would be most appreciative." He allowed her some time to absorb what was said before continuing. "The difference between nature and machinations is that one made man, and the other man made. When it comes to this curse Ruzu I don't know if it is one, the other, or a combination of both." Ruzu responded with a blank stare.

Adsum sat back down at a nearby desk to begin jotting down his findings. As he finished writing and checked on her one last time he looked out of the hut at the scorched landscape.

"So many experiments sans results. If my Quadra hadn't made me so complacent I would be missing it, but then again there is so much knowledge wasted by that fool Mulat." What amounted to rage for Adsum almost bubbled to the surface. He was used to not relying on such base methods to reach conclusions — a whole range of his carefully crafted concoctions to elicit the most fine-tuned of reactions from people had to be left behind. Exile had not been kind on the elderly man — survival was easy enough, but the sheer boredom alone had nearly sent him insane. Many would argue his sanity departed long ago, but Adsum always felt that his experiments served a greater purpose. Why else would all the other Quadras seek his counsel? *"These emotions do me no good. Regardless, it will be safe to return soon."*

Adacio entered the hut with a swaddled piece of cloth and the look of a fool about to be beaten. "I overheard some of the men speaking of black sands close to the Maharaan edge."

"Black sands you say?"

Adacio's eyes lit up as he said, "Yes!" Usually all talk of sand resulted in what Adsum called 'behavioral adjustment'.

"That is interesting, I will petition Rasak for an expedition. Do you know how far —" a loud rocking noise came from Ruzu's table, dragging his focus back to the task at hand. Making his way over to the table he said, "Give me Ruzu junior."

Adacio crossed the hut and said, "Why isn't she screaming today?"

Adsum unwrapped the cloth and looked at the baby girl, then at

Ruzu, before handing the child back to Adacio. "Bury it with the others."

"Ruzu, if you do not breastfeed then I cannot measure anything except infant mortality. The men here are not well versed in child care." Silence. "If you will not talk nor support your offspring then how am I to garner anything? I tried to meet you halfway by calling her Ruzu junior."

Ruzu spat in his face. "You heartless bastard! You act as if I have a choice in the matter!"

"Noted outrage from infant death," muttered Adsum to himself before saying out loud, "You know if you just fed them they would live."

"Those things should NOT live. They are NOT my children — and while I may mourn the death of a child, I do not mourn the death of MINE."

"They did come from your womb."

"WHAT WOMB?! YOU TOOK THAT FROM ME!"

"Regardless, from you they are still birthed."

Ruzu fell back onto the table, tired. "You cannot cure this curse, and when my sisters come for me I will make sure that you will 'all' burn. The Orati has returned and ensured this camp's death."

"All I need to know is how you are still capable of getting pregnant, let alone birth, even after I've removed the relevant parts."

"Maybe you do not know what to remove, oh wise idiot."

"No... my parlance with Erus Ardeo and his requirements to abort unwanted children and prevent pregnancies has left me well versed in the matter. He was unhappy with the number of deaths that arose from their so-called home remedies and methods." Ruzu lapsed back into silence. "From my count you will birth again in five months' time. We shall try again then. If you let this child die after a few months again, and you will not speak, then that will be the last time we interact, Ruzu."

ЖЖЖЖЖЖЖЖЖЖЖЖЖЖЖ

Kahli was marched through the village, paraded by rundown huts, tired looking men, and saw nothing but a clan of men worn down to the nub. *"Where are all the women?"* she thought to herself while she was leered at by everyone she walked past.

Several older men who spied her had a look of shock and retreated into their huts. She kept walking and closed her eyes, allowing the black paint to blackout her vision so she could find peace in her mind. *"So this is to be my life? My family killed and people die around me."*

"They weren't my family," said Kahli's other voice.

"Shut up, what do you know? You're a hallucination," thought Kahli.

A strange change in tone and tense came to the voice. *"If you won't even trust yourself, then what am I supposed to do?"*

"I don't care! My life before was 'real', the Jackals and my mother! I loved them all... but all you tell me is that I am some sort of curse! I would never hurt anyone, and this is —"

"Then tell me the name of your neighbor."

"... What?"

"If it was so real, then what was your neighbor's name? Friends? Who taught you how to cook?"

"... I don't have to answer to you!"

"No, you don't have to answer yourself if you do not want to. You may want to answer him though."

Silence followed in Kahli's mind, and feeling that the other voice had left her alone she felt some peace in the solitude.

"I asked HOW are you alive Orati!" bellowed the imposing man standing in front of her.

Kahli's hadn't realized that she'd already reached her destination — a large hut that would have been quite the sight in its prime — but seeing Rasak standing in front of her with rage on his face quickly snapped her back to reality. The beating she received earlier had dulled her senses to any rough treatment but she vaguely felt that she had just been recently inspected like a pack animal.

She was too weak and ready to surrender, everything. "Kill me if you must... I don't really know what an Orati is, or why, or how! I am tired of people telling me what I am and what I am not!" Rasak gave a signal and the hut emptied, "There are many of my men who would gladly gut you given the chance. If you want to die then so be it, but I WILL have answers first. HOW are you alive?" Kahli shrugged. "Do you not remember anything?!" he shouted.

Angry at being accused of not remembering anything Kahli blurted out, "Yes! I remember my village of Toka-Rutaa! I remember my siblings! I REMEMBER MY MOTHER!"

Expecting a slap Kahli kept her face locked onto his, not wishing to show fear. A moment's silence passed before Rasak burst out laughing. "Really? You remember those THINGS? And what of the countless deaths of children that you caused?" His face lost all humor, and in a flash Kahli saw the man go from mighty warrior who could defeat hundreds to one who had no defense against the girl standing before him. "Or me?"

"I haven't killed anyone!" cried Kahli.

Rasak breathed in slowly and sat down in a large, decorated chair that was in the middle of everything. "No... no you didn't kill anyone, you made *us* kill them. Your own people! You brought to us a stranger death than if you had burned us all alive! Look at what has become of us!" Tears streamed down the man's face, and with each droplet coursing through hidden wrinkles she saw him wearing a face far older than he wanted to. "At first it was so beautiful — to be blessed by every woman in the clan with child. We thought nothing of it, even when every child born was female. And nine months later, again all would birth young women again... and again, and again and.... How could we feed them all? How could we handle all those pregnant women? The demands made by each child, withering their bodies away piece by piece." Rasak stood up and began walking around the hut. "The curse tore our once proud clan apart with the men fighting over whose children were whose — so many new mouths to feed with no end in sight. Cursed to be forever bountiful, BAH!"

Rasak turned to Kahli with a face of rage and sorrow. "Look at us! We were PROUD once! We ruled the Maharaan east of the Vios Ocean, and many held to our name proudly!" With each word his voice got softer and his face further downcast, "Now the fresh blood of the clan is reduced to a weak trickle of what we once were. Four years... in four years your childish ignorance reduced everything we built." A long silence followed his words.

Just when Kahli thought that his voice or face could not express any more sorrow, anger bloomed. "Nobody survives the Orati ordeal! We traded you away like cattle, hoping you would take the curse with you to that twisted clan, but NO! They remained unaffected! The curse stayed and rotted us to the core — mothers killed their own, many starved outright, and men were preyed upon. How was I to keep us strong? How was I supposed to fight my own people?! HOW WAS I SUPPOSED TO WATCH YOU DIE A THOUSAND TIMES?!" He gave himself a moment for calm. "My own Jagu left me, split my clan, formed the Habiak, and now we wage war with those we once called lovers and mothers. Now 'you' show up — you, whose punishment was to live out your days as their slave and be used for their sadistic pleasures. To have your brain eat away at your memories until eventually nothing was left."

Rasak went stiff and silent before his battle-worn face, scarred more by a hard life than steel, melted from hard to soft. Downcast he looked at Kahli forlornly and muttered, "I was wrong to send my desert flower away...."

The honesty in his voice and the passion of his speech made Kahli feel guilty even though she knew none of this. Was it true? Did she truly do such a thing? Worst of all she felt like she was failing him, but she couldn't tell why.

Rasak hardened his heart once more and looked straight at Kahli. "It is a father's responsibility... You are too dangerous to be sent away, I know that now." Rasak called out for the guards. "You deserve so much worse, and I will not cower from the duty ahead no matter how difficult it may be." The two large men that had escorted Kahli walked into the hut and stood to attention. "Take her back to the pen. All are free to punish her as they see fit, but none are to break her, end her life or lay with her. This is her punishment: Announce the return of the Orati."

The two guards each grabbed one of Kahli's arms.

Her face the entire time was going through stages of disbelief. Was nothing that she remembered real?

"You can believe what you tell yourself, or what the world tells you," offered up her other voice.

"… who are you?" said Kahli to herself out loud.

"I am the most important memory you have," the other voice replied.

"What is that?" said Kahli softly.

BREATHE

Time abandoned Kahli after the first week of the beatings all had wished to bring upon her and all her cries for answers or explanation went unheard. It would have been far more tolerable if they were simply cruel men, but too many had come into the pen crying and left the same. All those men with all their suffering etched on their face left marks on her soul that she knew she could never forget. She even tried to offer what little she knew of sex in lieu of being beaten but that only made them hit her harder and she soon stopped.

Left in the sun her skin would dry out while her body weakened from lack of nourishment. All she was given was a meal at the end of the day, which was also the only time where she was allowed to be free of her harness so she could eat. With her body ravaged and her mind attacked she found herself missing her fellow captive even though she wouldn't speak to her, but with Ruzu spending more and more time with that pale elderly Integrum man she had nobody to help her keep her sanity.

The only saving grace was a chubby little Maharaan girl with long black hair who tended to her — the only other female that Kahli had seen in the camp. Kahli wished she had the strength to speak when she arrived, but the girl would only come at the end of the day when she was at her weakest. That little girl was also the only one who would remove her harness to feed and clean her. She seemed unharmed and free to come and go as she wished, not a prisoner at all like herself. Kahli had also hoped that her mind would let her escape once again to that strange voice just so she had something to talk to, but it would not come. In the end all she had to talk to was herself and whatever gestures and grunts she could express to the little girl.

The whole world for Kahli was now the pen and nothing beyond it, what little she'd glimpsed of the camp was now hazy and the only thing she knew of it was that it was quiet during the day and loud at night. The campfires would be brightly lit, with men howling with raucous laughter, and Kahli's first few nights had her attempting to dull the noise by burying her head in the hay — a futile effort as the men would stream in, intoxicated and aggressive. At least the black tattooed on her eyelids would shut out all light and allowed her to retreat deep into her mind.

One day Kahli awoke startled, and to her surprise it was not another beating — the men had grown tired of what little punishment Rasak allowed them — but a croaking noise. Through bleary eyes she looked around and saw a rather large toad just sitting next to her. Confused by this she wondered what a toad was doing in the pen and struggled to roll onto her side to get a better look at it.

A nearby giggle made Kahli puzzled for a moment before she recognized it as the giggle of a child, and made the link to the only one she knew of — her carer. A weak smile crossed Kahli's face as the feeling of someone reaching out to her, even though a child, brought her some comfort — she had never come in the morning before. The little girl must have been hiding so Kahli decided to pretend that she didn't know the girl was there and reached out to the toad in the hopes of scooping it up and playfully throwing it at her. Straining to outstretch her arm fully, she found the strength to prop herself up on her elbows and crawled a few inches to get within reach. She darted a hand out in order to catch the toad before it bounced away and closed her fingers around it with a playful intent.

As soon as her fingers wrapped around the toad it began to secrete a sticky substance — instantly repelled by the sensation she tried to let go of it but found her hand unable. She thrashed her clasped hand in an attempt to throw the toad away, but it began secreting more and more, until her whole hand was covered in the substance. Her rapid breath and weak constitution sent her into a state of panic and she heard the giggles grow louder from behind her.

The toad under her fingers felt like it was drying out, as if it was excreting all of its fluids out of its body. Then when all she could feel was a small dried out husk of a toad the sticky substance flowered into a firm foam within a matter of seconds, trapping her hand within it. The little girl then burst out of the hay with a grin from ear to ear.

"Hi!" she said.

"Um... hello," Kahli said softly, unsure of what was going on.

"Daddy says that you are from here, but if you were you would not have fallen for such a stupid prank," said the little girl.

"Uh, okay," said Kahli.

"You really are stupid aren't you?" said the little girl.

"What?" replied Kahli, taken aback by the brashness of the statement.

"Oh, never mind," she said rolling her eyes. "Thanks for the fun! I will see you later tonight to feed you," said the little girl, and wandered out of the pen.

"Wait! WAIT!" screamed out Kahli.

The little girl turned around and asked, "What do you want?"

"My hand! What do I do?"

"Well you can wait for the Makatu to not feel threatened anymore and then it will just suck all the foam back in on itself. It's fun to watch."

Kahli began to sob. "Why are you torturing me too?" she asked.

The little girl again rolled her eyes. "Watch." She walked over to Kahli's hand and picked it up. "You are fine," she said and spat on the foam then took a large bite out of it and chewed. "See?"

"... What? What is this?"

"You really don't know anything do you? Wait... of course you don't. Well, when you startle or threaten a makatu they basically excrete all of their juices out of their body, which is kinda sticky, and then it quickly turns into foam that expands and hardens like stone. I've seen some animals with heads and jaws exploded because they were stupid enough to eat one, those ones looked funny. But if you don't try to eat them they are harmless. We use them as food on long journeys. The foam is good for those, but it isn't really tasty."

Kahli seemed bewildered why someone who had been caring for her for weeks would now choose to play a prank on her. "Why would you play such an evil trick on me?" she asked.

"Well daddy did say everyone was allowed to do what they want to you, and besides it wasn't THAT evil. I just wanted to see what you would do, people are saying lots of things about you so I just wanted to see some things for myself."

"Why... why not just ask me?" asked Kahli.

"Um... dunno." The child shrugged her shoulders and walked out of the pen.

Looking down at her hand she saw that the foam had a bite mark in it and looked a little spongy where the girl had spat. Kahli wondered if it really was safe to eat and concluded that her options were not many — besides, her hand was beginning to cramp and scratch against the stoney foam. Resting on her elbows she began to muster up whatever saliva she could in order to moisten it but couldn't bring up enough to make even the slightest difference. Some light spittle fell and she could see the pock marks it made, but beyond that there was nothing. She could start feeling her hand go numb and with it came the fear of never seeing her hand again.

Kahli softly whined, "What did I do that was so bad? Why do I deserve this?"

"*Does it matter?*" said the passenger voice.

Kahli said out loud, "YOU! Where have you been?!"

"*Where else would I be? I've been here all along.*"

"I've been calling out to you! Nobody else will listen to me! STOP ABANDONING ME!"

"*If you abandon yourself there is nothing I can do.*"

"STOP! Just... just... just talk to me please." Kahli began weeping.

"*I first talked to myself, and I didn't listen — then I talked to you, and you didn't listen. Learn to listen first, and we can talk much more.*"

"What do you mean?"

BREATHE

LAND OF THE GADORI

Toyo wasn't sure if the medishi were being punished while he watched them being hooked up to the Ogaden, but he was sure that they didn't seem too happy about it. That was until several minutes after when they all had vacant stares. Ani didn't seem to be around to explain things either, so he reasoned that given the way the tribe conducted themselves around plants that this might perfectly well be a good thing, or... maybe, a bad thing. At least the pretty woman came from a plant, which sort of made sense, and they thought she was important.

When all of them were being either attached or put into the tree stump all he could really think was about how he was going to make it up to everyone for the accident he'd caused. His guilt and the hatred they'd directed towards him earlier made him think about running away. Looking out onto the cold barren wasteland he was hit by how only not long ago he had walked out from there into this forest, and now between him and the forest the Gozuri stood. *"Is that who I want to be? I asked for people, only to run away when I do something bad? Do I really want to be alone again?"*

Caught between decisions Toyo looked aimlessly around and questioned if he would have to fight his way out, but everyone looked too preoccupied to care about him right now. In all honesty he wished that he could join in with whatever it was they were doing, or at least talk to the naked lady some more.

While Tagai oversaw the medishi being bonded to the Ogaden he wondered what the boy was going to do, and what Tagai could genuinely do to stop him when he'd decided. There was no doubting that he was both powerful and dangerous, and even death and the Ogahigi seemed to take note of him. The only tool they knew which worked on him were their herbs, but Hoba was the one in charge of it and he'd gone off to retrieve Ani. He was no match for the child with the iron hands.

When the preparations were complete Tagai walked over to Toyo, who quickly became defensive.

"Toyo," said Tagai.

Toyo replied, "What? Now you know my name? So you CAN speak my language?" His voice was hopeful and he lowered his defenses.

Tagai struggled with how to proceed — the Ogahigi wanted this boy to be a part of his tribe, but he could not see past what he'd done. The boy knew nothing of their ways, and the knowledge needed to impart to him would be an enormous effort. Why was he so special?

Putting the question in his mind about why a child would matter to one side he walked back over to the Ogaden — Tagai decided it was time to honor the Ogahigi's need, and to extend that honor to Toyo. It was not his place to question and he could not hold any claim to knowing better than others, but he could not accept being the weak root of his tribe's tree. Honor the tree from which all Gozuri are branches — honor yourself.

Moving the now limp medishi aside, Tagai grabbed an innocuous looking branch attached to the Ogaden and braced one foot against the Ogahigi's home. The entire tribe went mute as Tagai exerted a great amount of effort and pulled out a hefty wooden object, ripping bark and tearing roots as it came free.

"So... hello?" said Toyo, irritated at being addressed, ignored, and then forced to watch him vandalize the woman's home.

Tagai hefted his wooden trophy onto his shoulders and brought it over to Toyo, placing it on the ground with great effort and care as if it weighed as much as the Ogaden itself and was made of glass. Toyo looked down at what looked like a wooden sword confused — a tall, thin man, just pulled a weapon out of a tree stump that the lady he had just talked to lived in. "*Why was there a sword there in the first place? Is it special? What do they want me to do with it?*" His guilt brought a dark conclusion. "*... Do they want me to kill myself with it?*"

He bent down to look at the sword and he found that it looked like it had been grown rather than forged. Looking closer he saw that it was actually vines twisted on vines, wrapped tighter and tighter until it looked essentially solid — the fact it sort of looked like a sword was probably just a coincidence. He could see some fresh growth that was on the top, but there were cracks through which he could see the brown and drying vegetation underneath.

Tagai began a speech, which for Toyo only made everything even more confusing. "<The Ogahigi asked me to help you grow, to that end I offer you our tribe's Mogutougi. My father was its keeper, and I am its keeper now. See our lineage, and come to see that as the seed of the tree consumes the tree before it, neither will die, and both will become strong. >" Tagai knelt down low and placed his hands spread on the ground, and then his head. "<May we both grow strong. >"

"*So... a wooden sword? What am I supposed to do with this?*" thought Toyo. The entire tribe kept looking expectantly, making him now feel unsure instead of fearful. Wishing to show good manners he grasped the sword in his right hand and lifted it up off the ground. A chorus of gasps erupted from the members as if he had performed some sort of miracle, which did nothing more than make the tenuous smile of the uncertain creep across his face. Not wanting to offend anyone further he tentatively dropped the sword in the hopes to avoid doing something stupid with it, and jumped at the loud bang that erupted from it hitting the ground. Looking down he saw that the sword had landed with such force that it left an imprint of itself on the ground and the vines were writhing slowly across the surface.

"*It wasn't THAT heavy!*" He looked up to see if he had done something wrong yet again and saw a crowd of faces locked in wonderment. Turning to Tagai he implored, "Look, can you speak my language or not? Because to be honest I'm sort of not sure what I'm supposed to do here!"

Tagai just looked at Toyo and then down again at the sword. Reaching down to pick it up, his fingers clasped around the hilt and his arm jerked back in pain. It was intense, almost as if his hand was on fire, and he hurriedly went to soothe it in the cold dirt. He looked backed in confusion at the sword on the ground.

"*What the...?*" thought Toyo as he looked at the sword and

watched it melt slowly into the ground. Tagai shot him an angry stare, and, frustrated at the situation, Toyo shouted, "What do you want from me?! All I want is to stop being hated here!"

Tagai walked back over to the sword, ignoring Toyo completely, and tentatively touched the wooden sword again, testing to see if it would burn him once more. Satisfied that whatever had happened before was not going to do so again he easily lifted the sword back up, put it back into the Ogaden and began nursing his strange wound.

The moment was interrupted by Ani being shoved through the underbrush, followed by a stern-faced Hoba. As the whole tribe turned to look, Hoba smiled and said, "<I have her. >"

Ani stumbled for a few steps before falling heavy to the ground and remained there motionless. "<What of the Ogahigi? >" asked Hoba expectantly, resentful for having been sent away in the midst of their Ogahigi emerging.

Tagai pointed to the Ogaden and said, "<She has returned home. >"

Hoba saw the three medishi hooked up to the Ogaden with listless expressions. "<What happened? Where are the other medishi? >"

Tagai pointed to a corpse stripped bare for its parts and said, "<The other two ran away. >"

Hoba gestured at the Ogaden. "<What are those three doing? >"

"<Keeping her alive. >"

"<It is nice to see that some from the Integrum are noble enough to understand duty! >" said Hoba with some comfort.

"<They were the ones that caused the last great kusabana, >" replied Tagai.

"<WHAT!? >" said Hoba.

"<Calm yourself, much has happened. >"

"<WHY DO THEY LIVE?! >" Hoba demanded.

"<Because if they do not, the Ogahigi will not. >"

Hoba jutted an accusatory finger in Toyo's direction. "<And

him!? >"

"<We are to help him grow as part of our tree, the Ogahigi asked this of us. >"

The world that Hoba had left to fetch Ani felt very different to the one he'd returned to, and he felt that some divine being was playing a cruel trick on him — which added to the frustration of his keeping Ani alive. "<NO! I refuse this! We cannot forgive such pain! >" He withdrew a small hooked blade and knelt on Ani's back and held it to her neck.

"<STOP! >" barked Tagai, staying Hoba's hand. "<We need her, nobody else can speak to the boy, and we need to teach him the ways. >"

"<Why?! >" asked Hoba in frustration, shoving Ani to one side and pacing angrily towards Tagai.

"<Because the Ogahigi told us that he is important to us, >" replied Tagai, Hoba's face mere inches from him.

That statement made Hoba feel at odds — denied his desire for revenge and told to now accept someone as his own was causing him pain. Needing an outlet for his rage he leapt upon Ani once more with weapon drawn, pressing it firmly against her neck — his hands and arms trembling as his anger coursed through him. Nobody did anything to halt Hoba's actions, all had come to accept the difficult situation, but nobody could either deny or grant his desires at this moment — the stupid old woman's actions and the boy's recklessness had taken so much from him.

As his emotions climaxed his reason called out. He could not end this life, nor Toyo's — the boy's because he would not know if he even could kill him, and Ani's for the satisfaction he would derive from keeping her alive with the ara'tai inside her. He slapped Ani hard on the back of the head to sate himself for now and sheathed his weapon before roughly picking her up and dragging her over to the Ogaden and dumping her.

Tagai walked over, grabbed Ani by the jaw, and inspected her face closely. "<How much did you give her? >"

"<Three snuff's worth. >"

"<... That was too much, but she will live. >"

"<Well I thought I was bringing her back to face her crimes, not to act as translator for some useless child! >"

"<What is this wound on her chest? >" asked Tagai, fingering the scar on her chest.

"<She... fell. She's not used to the terrain. There was... a time where I did not try and stop her from herself. >"

Knowing that the purpose between his departure and return had changed, Tagai could not chastise Hoba. Placing a reassuring hand on his brother-in-love's shoulder he nodded gently, which is all Hoba needed to relax — the knowledge that he had done the job asked of him.

Toyo quickly walked over to the drugged Ani once Hoba had made some distance. "Hey, look I don't know what the *futuo* is happening but I'm glad to see you. Can you tell me what the *valde* is going on?" he asked.

Ani's head lolled from side to side, unable to focus on anything, and Toyo felt like he was never going to get a full conversation out of anybody ever again. He made his way towards the Ogaden and knocked, hoping for some sort of muffled 'Hello' from inside. Instead he got glares from the entire tribe. Flushed with embarrassment he quickly went back to Ani and sat down.

Tagai watched the events with indifference as his mind was no longer in the present, and instead fixed squarely on what had to be done in order for a future for his tribe to exist. Rearing himself up, he clapped his hands once loudly and drew everyone's attention. "<We have suffered much today, but the Ogahigi has once more blessed us with her wisdom. Toyo is to be accepted as one of our own! Ani will one day answer for her crimes, but until that day she and the medishi exist to serve us! I know we do not believe in slaves, but the thorn that pierced is best fit to stem the bleeding. We will grow strong once more, but we must now trek to the next Ogagi, The Withered Crone. I know I am not your Yohju, but I believe this all to be true. >"

Hoba raised himself up to full height and said, "<No, we have a

Yohju. It is time to be guided, not herded, and there is no man greater than you to serve that purpose. >"

Tagai's usually cool expression faltered. "<I do not want to lead the tribe — I do not wish to be the man who creates further burden, only one who strengthens it. We have all suffered too much. >"

"<Then I will carry you until you are ready, >" said Hoba with dignity, and knelt down low.

The tribe all looked at Tagai and followed Hoba in honoring the hunter that had given so much of himself when nobody else would or could. Through the times so harsh, he alone stood strong and raised everyone up on his shoulders. Unspoken and as one the tribe decided that it was time for Tagai to restore the Gozuri to their former glory, and to reclaim the Gadori and restore the hanraza.

Tagai found his words fail him, and he tried to see if there was anyone else he could answer to, anyone else he could make strong. Reaching inside he saw the signs, and everything that Hoba was saying was true: It was time to forge the tree with his own hands. Driven by responsibility and honor he then knelt down lower than anyone else, and kept going until his forehead touched the ground, with both of his hands placed on the ground near his temples.

"<I will always look up to you all in my duties, even if I have to get on my knees to do it. >" Words softly spoken, yet a promise heard by all.

Tagai knelt a hunter, and stood a leader.

Ж Ж Ж Ж Ж Ж Ж Ж Ж Ж Ж Ж Ж Ж Ж

As the tribe trekked from the outlining trees further back into the forest Toyo had little aid or comfort — they didn't seem to be angry with him anymore, but he was stuck carrying Ani, a sickly looking old woman who was incoherent most of the time. He hoped she would snap out of it soon and would actually give him more information than just snippets, if for nothing else than to have someone to talk to.

He'd been led on a whirlwind of experiences that had left him confused to the point where all he could do was follow. He felt awful in the wake of such death and destruction, and the once angry faces weighed heavily on his mind. Over everything as he marched on in silence, one question was the loudest: Were they going to let him make up for the mistakes he'd made?

Several times over the weeks trek to the next Ogagi, Ani said this one was called The Withered Crone, Hoba came and fed Ani some sort of drink — miming each time that it was *very important* with grand hand gestures. Toyo felt slightly patronized but kept entertaining the fat man in the hopes that he would be quicker about it each time. On top of that he could not help but feel some sort of pity for the medishi, and would've sworn that as time passed they were becoming paler. He did not envy their being leashed to the tree stump that housed the strange lady and being made to trudge through the unpleasant wilderness, carrying something that everyone felt important and fragile.

The journey finally came to an end when they reached another large empty space, which Ani told Toyo was actually called a grotto, and in the center of it was a rather sickly, spindly looking tree. It was not a proud thick trunk with flourishing leaves adorning it, more a gnarled husk of what a tree could be, or one that a giant had taken from the very ground and wrung dry of all its juices. It was still larger than most of the trees that Toyo had seen so far, but nowhere near the gargantuan size of the last Ogagi.

As the tribe set up camp Toyo was sequestered to a short distance from the Ogagi along with Ani and was told that he had been given a very difficult and important task: Sit still. It felt demeaning until Ani explained that for the Gozuri sitting still and taking everything in required great control of self, but even after that Toyo still felt slighted. He watched the medishi sidle up next to the gnarled tree that Ani had called the Withered Crone, dig up some of its roots and place them into strange holes in the Ogaden, and then sit very still.

He then saw some Gozuri planting things near the Ogagi but wasn't really sure what or why — Toyo would have investigated if he felt he had the right to, sitting still seemed like a waste of time when he could be helping.

Toyo began to get a little fidgety sitting still for all this time, not sure what he could or could not do, but tried his best to content himself with just observing and learning. The most interesting thing he observed was the array of spices and herbs in bags that they distributed amongst people, which they either sniffed or chewed as they worked.

Ani's mind began returning in full to her, which Hoba had been waiting for and made his way over to her. There was no friendliness found in his approach and Toyo instinctively stood up and braced himself but was politely shoved to one side as Hoba crouched down to look Ani directly in the face.

"<Whether you live or die depends on what I feed you from now on old hag. You are to live to teach this boy everything there is to know about us and you are to translate — if you wish to have a life beyond that role then you will do as we say. >"

Ani groggily nodded her head before saying, "<What did you do to me? >"

"<What I did is not an answer you will hear. >"

She looked at him up and down. "<If you are going to kill me then kill me, I don't have the patience for cowardice and stup —>"

Hoba interrupted Ani's ramblings with a hard slap and a shout of, "<SHUT UP! >" Regaining his composure he continued, "<You can accept this role... >" he pressed his thumb hard into where he had put the ara'tai inside Ani, "<Or you can find out what happens when I am no longer there to take care of you. >" Ani softly nodded her head, whatever he just did had made her body panic in a strange fashion. "<Very well, you answer to either Tagai-Yohju, me, or the boy. You have no duties beyond teaching him and translating. Do not fail us, or we will fail you. >" Hoba did not wait for a response and walked away sternly.

When he'd left Toyo got close to Ani and asked, "Are you okay?"

She coughed a little and replied, "Yes... yes I'm... fine I think," slightly dazed. "Wait... weren't you dead?"

"... Was I?" asked Toyo confused.

Ani took a second to notice that the thick red vein-like things sprouting from his wrist which crawled up his forearms had faded slightly, but were still visible. They were so... odd. "I...." She wasn't quite sure what she was supposed to say. Everything was still a little fuzzy.

He coughed. "Um... look I don't suppose you could help me out here? That tree lady spoke my 'tongue' and told me what I did. I haven't been able to say sorry to these people! Could you please teach me their tongue or at least tell them how sorry I am? I didn't mean it."

Ani weakly waved him into silence, "Think nothing of it."

"It's not nothing!" He shouted. "I thought they were angry at me for no good reason before I was told what I'd done! I'm not a bad man, and I refuse to think that I can't be good!"

"... How much do you want to know, boy?"

"I'm not a boy!"

Ani tried to not let her exasperation show. "Fine, man, what would you like to know?"

"Well... everything."

An answer that wasn't an answer — Ani rolled her eyes at impetuous youth and cursed her situation. At heart she was a charge of the Quadra Logicum — not a Yohju, savior, or some damn child's mentor — however she resigned herself to accepting that if she was to live, this was the latest role she had to adopt.

"Just let me rest a while and I will answer your questions," said Ani weakly.

"No! Tell me NOW!" Toyo screamed.

"I have to talk to other people first! I don't know everything, only what I know. So I have to ask. Maybe YOU should learn to ask questions."

"I am! You are the only one that can hear them, and I want answers."

Ani sighed heavily to herself. Her recent drugged state had not helped her mental faculties, leading her to opt for honesty rather than her usual cunning — mostly in the belief that it would be the faster route to shutting the boy up.

She shook her head in hopes that something would come back to shut him up, but not a lot did. "I am no longer the Yohju, I tricked the tribe and many lives were lost. Much in the same way you did back at the last camp."

"But it was such a tiny mark in such a huge tree! Why would it matter?"

"It is more to do with timing than size, you pierced the outer layer of the Mother-Tree and let its sap flow — all creatures of the Gadori can sense it, especially when it is so close to its flowering. That is what the Gozuri do, they go from Ogagi to Ogagi in hopes to siphon off enough each time through their sabana ritual to stop a kusabana."

"Then why don't they just chop all the Ogagi's down if they're so dangerous?"

"You would destroy something just because of the one dangerous thing that you see within it? It is only through the kusabana that an Ogagi can cause chaos, otherwise it is good for the forest."

There were those words again. He wasn't really interested in listening before, but he was now. "Kusabana?"

"Its approximate translation is 'chaotic flowering' — the term is mostly used when an Ogagi becomes so laden with sap that it essentially explodes."

"Why does it explode?"

Ani shrugged. "The sap has high concentrations of vesma inside it, I'm not sure why but I am quite sure the accumulation of so much is what causes it to do so. Also when a kusabana occurs many strange creatures are born, plants uproot themselves and eat one another, the simplest of creatures turn into the most horrid of beasts — events of that nature."

"And... I did that?" he asked uncertain.

"No, you just started the cycle early. The Gozuri siphon the tree to feed their own plants and their Ogahigi — I'm led to believe there are other uses for the sap but a lot of knowledge was lost in the last kusabana. Anyway, when the Gozuri have siphoned enough safely they either use it or dispose of it, and then the cycle starts all over again."

"But... why do they do it?"

"They have been doing so for as long as the history of their tribe and they believe that if they did not do it then all of Kasmah would be overrun."

"So they are protecting the world?"

Ani looked directly into Toyo's eyes like he'd said something truly alien. "Yes... I don't think I've ever thought of it like that, but you could put it that way." She was doing her best to retain her composure but could feel tiredness grasping at her body.

"But... I didn't make anything explode. I just nicked a tree."

Ani wanted to ask, "*Do you even KNOW how tough the bark of an Ogagi is?*" but knew it would be a wasted question. Instead she said, "If Hoba hadn't been there when you did then we wouldn't have had time for emergency measures." Toyo opened his mouth to ask what those were but Ani preempted him. "We used the Ogahigi and her Ogaden to drain as much vesma from the Ogagi as possible through their link." Her mind connected the dots. "*Ah, that must be why she was walking and talking before.*"

"But what about —"

"I am sick Toyo... please let me rest," implored Ani, hoping the change in tactic would stop his line of questioning. If she were in her previous position of authority she would have slapped the child for imposing questions on an obviously sick person. Doing that now however would mean she would be at the mercy of Hoba, or worse, the impulsive reaction of a child that did not know its own strength.

Toyo tried to push the limit and asked a question that had been bugging him, "... Why are we pale skinned? Are we rare or something? I hadn't said anything because it didn't seem important, but... we seem sort of hated."

Her patience was wearing thin. "We are hated for what we did, not our skin. We are pale because our parents were pale, and there are plenty of us in the Integrum. Now, please, GO AWAY."

Toyo felt jilted and gave a gruff, "Yeah, whatever... I'll go and check if anyone wants anything." Rising from their secluded spot, Toyo went to investigate the camp while Ani got a good look at the red tendrils on his arms stemming from his iron fists as he readjusted his clothing.

"*Futuo! What in grace's name is he!?*" she thought to herself.

ЖЖЖЖЖЖЖ

Toyo wandered around the camp trying to constantly gesture that he was willing to help, but other than polite, and some begrudging, smiles, not much else got done. Surveying the landscape he was surprised to note that the environment seemed sort of lackluster and not at all flowery and dense at the edges like the last campsite. He spied the flowering plants near the gnarled tree and saw that they had large orbs of all colors sprouting from their branches.

Seeing the myriad of ways the Gozuri used plants made him think, "*I wonder what they use them for?*"

An old man was tending to the plants and noticed the nosy Toyo and quietly sidled up to him. He caught Toyo off-guard as he was too used to being either ignored or feared, and this was the first time he could remember where he'd been approached in a non-threatening manner.

"<Would you like one? >" the old man asked, pointing towards a plump orange and red bubble of sorts.

Toyo's experience with solid food, let alone vegetation, was minimal at best. To date he had only been fed a variety of liquids and meager rations, which had made his belly yearn for something more substantial. His mind caught onto that thought and wondered what the last solid thing he ate was — he remembered throwing up something, but that was quite some time ago. The old man saw the distant expression on his face and just shrugged his shoulders, plucked the strange item from the branch, and handed it to the boy.

Toyo looked at the gift with renewed intensity, and then up at the old man offering it, who rolled his eyes and took a large dramatic bite out of it and chewed exaggeratedly. Toyo's face went the way of the starved — wide-eyed and salivating. Not wanting to wait he shoved the food into his face as quickly as he could and bruised his lips in the process. Oblivious to his self-harm and not remembering the strength in his iron hands he pulverized the object between his fingers and smooshed it all over his face until there was nothing but large chunks of sticky pulp all over him. His new-found friend jerked back from the spray of juice and looked at him in that familiar way Toyo found infuriating, as if he were weird.

Before Toyo's anger of feeling alienated could be ignited the old man let out a hearty laugh and began wiping the juice from his face. Several onlookers joined in with a chuckle, making Toyo feel a little stupid, but relieved, and his heart concluded that it was far better to be accepted than rejected, no matter the circumstance.

Picking another piece of the plant the old man offered it to Toyo, who now took a much gentler approach to eating it. Biting into the offering, he found that it was sweet and succulent with a bitterness that pierced right through to his brain — his face contorted into a look of uncertain disgust before acclimatizing to the flavor. Toyo had a big grin on his face while everyone looked on, taking comfort in seeing his smile, but they were still wary as they saw how his fingers dug deep into the food with ease. The sweetness of the food ran straight to his head and he immediately wanted more, rudely snapping another off a branch and biting into it savagely, devouring it as fast as possible.

As Toyo reached out for another the old man slapped his shoulder abruptly and waved a cautionary finger at him. He was unsure of what he had done wrong and tried again to reach out for the tasty treat, and was again given a slap on the shoulder.

"<There are others to feed, >" said the old man.

"Um... I'll just go see what else needs doing..." said Toyo sheepishly, unsure as to why he kept engaging in pointless conversations. He did his best to clean up after the mess he'd made before continuing his wander around the camp.

The next thing he came upon was a large wooden box with what appeared to be steam coming out of it. Intrigued he closed in and peered around it, and saw a thin slit with a wooden panel on the front and a tiny fire underneath — he hoped that they were cooking something. Sliding the wooden panel open he was almost overwhelmed by the cacophony of smells that invaded his senses. A rush of scented spices, rich and full, filled his nose and forced into his mind an image of a great steel tower in a great body of water, followed by a sense of deep longing. After the strange yet familiar feeling subsided his brain finally registered the naked lady curled up inside looking back at him.

"<You are letting the cold in! >" she yelled.

Toyo spluttered out, "Sorry!" and quickly shut the wooden panel. When he turned around embarrassed he saw that he had five people watching him. He tried to keep his plea brief. "I didn't mean to! Accident!" There were no looks of anger or disgust amongst them, more of interest and polite acceptance.

Suitably stressed out by the happenings of the day and the inability to communicate with anybody else he tried his best to excuse himself and went back to where he'd left Ani — filled with the hope that she'd rested up enough to answer more questions.

Ж Ж Ж Ж Ж Ж Ж Ж Ж Ж Ж Ж Ж Ж Ж

Freezing cold water splashed onto Ani's face, waking her with a shock. Spluttering and panicked she looked around wide-eyed to her surroundings, and noticed Hoba standing over her.

In very certain tones the fat hunter said, "<We must talk. >"

"*Futuo!*" she swore, "<You could have just woken me up nicely! >"

"<I don't have to do ANYTHING, nice OR nasty, but if you want me to do nothing at all we shall see how long you live. >"

"<... What did you do to me? >"

"<Something that only I can fix — leave it at that. You have had a night's sleep, that is enough for now. The boy has been bumbling around the camp and I am getting irritated at him getting in the way. Others may accept him, but I have not. >"

Ani knew when a man was not joking and Hoba exuded the confidence of a man that held her life in the balance. "<Well then where is he? >"

"<Tagai is trying to show him how we hunt. >"

"<Fine. Let me have some food first and I will help —>" Ani was interrupted by Hoba shoving a pouch of strange pasty liquid into her mouth.

"<Drink. >"

Ani spat it out of her mouth and pushed him roughly away. Hoba casually threw the pouch to the ground, spilling some of the mixture. "<I do not need to feed it to you like some belligerent child, I have enough of one on my hands already. You will drink what is in that, or you will die from within. If you run away, you will die, but I feel that the forest will take you long before the rot inside you grows. >" Hoba's dull tones were more threatening than shouting. Ani reluctantly took a few swigs and offered the pouch back to Hoba, who attached it back to his belt. "<There are some basic rules here Ani: Translate for the boy, and help him learn our ways — that is your role. >"

Ani nodded slowly — her old body had taken too much rough treatment to even warrant the desire to fight but she couldn't help her mind from saying, *"You've already told me that you moron."*

"<But before all that you are going to come and tell me and Tagai the truth of your past. On your feet. >" Hoba roughly hauled her up.

As Ani was led through the camp she now saw the medishi look at her with a sense of revulsion, and found herself making the same face when she saw them hooked up to the Ogahigi's home. The once normally healthy medishi now looked malnourished, and their skin was turning brown and flaking — she did not know if she could call them comrades anymore, let alone human. Passing all the way through the camp they made their way further into the spindly and spiky forest until they came to an unremarkable set of trees, save for one that had indents all up the side of it. Ani's eyes followed the trail to the top to see Toyo sitting high in the branches above smiling and looking down at her.

"Hi!" he shouted and threw a stone hard at Ani, hitting her on the bridge of her foot and causing her to wince in pain.

"*Valde!*" she swore, Hoba giggled.

Toyo began his descent down the tree with loud crunching noises. As he reached the bottom Ani saw that the indents had come from where his gloves gained purchase.

Toyo said with a beaming face, "You're up! Thought you were going to sleep all day. Tagai and I have been playing!"

"Why did you do that!? What are you? Mentally deficient?!" screamed Ani, rubbing her foot. Toyo looked at her confused. "It means STUPID, you STUPID boy!"

Toyo sheepishly replied, "Stupid? But... I didn't miss."

Ani looked at him dumbfounded before being shaken by another stone that whizzed by her face, and landed mere inches from Toyo's foot. He spun around and shouted, "Ha! MISSED ME!" before darting back off into the bushes.

Ani sat down and rubbed her foot. "<What are they doing? >" she asked Hoba.

"<Training. >"

"<Well I've never seen this before! >"

"<We haven't had anyone to train. >"

"<I was with you for years! I've seen other people hunt with you! >"

"<To hunt and be a hunter is not the same thing. >"

Ani was disgruntled from her rude awakening and sore foot — Hoba's new confident stance with her was also taking some getting used to. "<Looks like a bloody stupid children's game to me. >"

Hoba shrugged his shoulders. "<Everything is a game to a child,

and in games you can learn the world without fear. We place rules in the safe haven we make for people to learn, and when they are ready to leave and face the world they will find that the game is not so childish. >" He spoke as if he were quoting some distant memory.

"<I don't think I've ever heard you be so... reverent, >" said a surprised Ani.

Hoba solemnly replied, "<I don't think you ever listened to me. >"

Ani wanted to get on with her task already — she needed to find her routine so her mind could find its peace once more. It was something that her lover from long ago taught her and one of the most valuable lessons she had ever come to learn: In routine you can find safety, for knowing where you now stand makes your next step ever sure. She exhaled loudly through her nose. "<I see that you have at least given him something to wear other than those furs. >"

Hoba brusquely replied, "<Tagai's idea, not mine. >" They waited in uncomfortable silence for a while, until Hoba said, "<Call for them, it is time to talk. >"

Ani sighed inwardly, hating the regression to errand girl, but she had lived long enough to know that nothing is permanent and if you are patient enough change will come. "Toyo!" she called out. Moments of silence passed. "TOYO!" she screamed.

A loud crash and rustle of a bush produced an exuberant Toyo. "Yeah?" he asked, face flushed from exertion.

"Hoba has asked me to talk to you and Tagai so we can 'explain' some things."

"FINALLY!" he said with his arms splayed wide and was quickly pelted in the foot by a stone. Tagai stepped out from behind a tree to a sour faced Toyo hopping on one foot and swearing.

"<Never give away your position, Toyo, >" said Tagai. He turned to Ani expectantly.

Ani translated, "He said to never give away your position."

"<What did you say to him? >" demanded Hoba gruffly.

"<I just told him what Tagai said! >" replied Ani.

"What did he say?" asked Toyo.

Ani rubbed the bridge of her nose hard and took a deep breath. This was much easier when she'd had nobody else to answer to. "<I am here Tagai, what is it you wanted? >" she said tersely.

Going from a playful to confidently threatening tone in a very short time span, Tagai said, "<Adopt that tone with me and I will ensure that your hands will be the only way you can communicate with the world. >" There was something very different about how he carried himself now, and Ani could not put her finger on it. "<Tell the boy to wait and not to interrupt. >"

Ani turned to Toyo and said, "Toyo, we are going to have a no doubt angry discussion now, and Tagai has asked me to tell you to just stay put and not interfere. Can you do that?" Toyo nodded his head in agreement and plonked himself down on the ground where he stood.

"<Why? >" asked Tagai.

"<… Why what? >" replied Ani.

"<No more games, why did you lie to us all these years? >" demanded Tagai.

"<I did not 'lie' as such. >"

"<You would dishonor my desire for the truth with more lies? An enemy can be honored, for all they are is someone who defends what they believe to be right, but you could not even be considered an enemy. You are a cancer that wormed its way into our lives. We taught you much, and withheld more, but now we are at a split in the branch. >" Tagai leaned in very close to Ani's face, "<Either you are cut out here and now so we can grow free of your corruption, or you honor yourself by respecting us. >"

Ani's mind did the mental gymnastics that only one of the Quadra Logicum could perform, but found no way out — either she would provide them the truth, or she would die. If she were to run away from her guilt and shame she would die, if she were to continue it here she would die. It was time to tell the truth. "<Very well... we will need to sit down, >" said Ani.

Both hunters squatted in front of Ani, who sat down cross-legged, and gave her a stare that showed that she had their full attention. Feeling slightly uncomfortable at being inspected so closely she unconsciously began to fidget with the trinket box hanging around her neck. Hoba held up his hand and said, "<Before anything, what is in that box? >" Tagai nodded, giving Hoba's question permission to be answered.

Ani froze and took a second to register that she had even touched it in the first place.

"<A... memory of sorts, >" said Ani.

"<What kind of memory? >" asked Hoba.

"<A memory of love. >"

"<Open it. >"

Ani's face sagged slightly and she then removed the trinket box from around her neck. Undoing the tiny latch she opened it for Hoba and Tagai to see. "<A necklace with a clear stone in it? That's all? >" asked Hoba, taking it from Ani.

She had to do her best to suppress lashing out at him. Her usual cool command of her body was temporarily shaken by the emotion. Breathing in deeply she regained her composure and continued. "<In vox it is called a *cupla mola*, a bond stone... it is a way for two people to remember each other, a thing that was quite popular in my youth. It is an assortment of vesma crystals that grows strong chromatic bonds with the observer over time — basically, the more you look at it, the deeper the color you see. >"

Hoba turned it around in his fingers and noted that it had been crafted and honed, not something plucked out of the ground. "<How does that work? >" he asked.

"<It was explained to me once by a member of the Quadra Logicum that each person has a unique frequency of vesma inside them. The more you look at the stone the better attuned your body and the *cupla mola* become. It starts for everyone at deep blue, and goes through all the colors to a blood red. >"

"<Why? >" asked Hoba.

"<Why what? >" replied Ani.

"<Why do you have it? >"

"<... I had someone I loved long ago. >"

"<That was not my question. I do not understand, why would anyone want one? >"

"<It was the symbol I and my lover chose to forever remember each other by. >"

Hoba handed the bond stone back to Ani. "<So if we look at it more it will change color? >"

"<Yes, but nobody else can see the same color you do. >"

"<So it is a deep red to you and clear to us. >"

"<... It is light blue for me, >" said Ani sadly.

"<I thought you said —>"

"<My love was a long time ago, and the stone does not retain the bond forever. >"

Hoba kept his gaze on the stone with a look of concentration. "<Why isn't it changing color right now? >" he asked.

"<It takes a little longer than just a few moments. >"

"<How long? >"

"<To reach red? Three to five years, give or take. >"

"<So you have to stare at a stone for three years and it changes color? That seems very stupid. >"

"<IT IS NOT STUPID! >" screamed Ani, she couldn't hold herself back any longer. Tagai placed his hand on Hoba's shoulder, expressing to him that his line of questioning was over. She recovered and said, "<I'm... sorry. No, you only have to see the stone every day for it to keeps its color. It is used more for people to measure their own love and memory, you wear it as a necklace so your lover sees it every day and remembers... that.... >" Ani fell silent, she couldn't bear to think of what she'd forgotten and didn't want to give anyone the satisfaction of her sorrow.

"<You have loved and lost. You have also taken our loved from us. Now is the time you tell us why, >" asked Tagai with a face that brooked no argument.

Toyo was deeply annoyed by having his fun interrupted. Of his short memory of life nobody had ever played with him before, and while he did not quite get the point of hitting someone's foot with a rock it was enjoyable anyway. The old lady had come again and taken away his fun but still he was tethered to her by the sole fact that she was still the only person he could talk to.

At that moment the naked lady in the tree stump flashed across his mind and a great desire stirred in him to see her again. While they talked he saw their faces grow ever more serious and focused, which to him seemed like the ideal time to slip away and see if maybe the naked lady would like a visitor.

INTEGRUM

The doors to Mulat's chambers were opened gently and several people filed into the room. Looking out of the window Mulat said, "Erus Adsum," without turning around.

"Integra Divinitas Mulat," replied Adsum blandly. "You have interrupted crucial experiments and my Quadra's charges cannot continue the work without me, so expediency would be appreciated."

"You stand accused and convicted of crimes against the population of Orbis, the Integrum, disgracing your Quadra Logicum, and shaming yourself. This will be the last time we speak, so I recommend you make it interesting," said Mulat, admiring the weather from his view.

"Accused and convicted? I do not recall standing trial," said Erus Adsum with a confused expression.

"Nor do I recall giving you permission to mutate vesma in order to alter the body or behavior of our citizens."

Adsum adopted a confident stance and said, "I demand a trial, I know the law."

Mulat waved the guards outside and turned around. "Do you know the law?" he asked.

Adsum stood proud in his gray clothes of office, with shoulders and back straight he had no weakness in his stance as he tried to educate the young Integra Divinitas. "Yes, each citizen of Orbis is free to do as he or she chooses, so long as it does not clash with the consent of others. All infringements of this will be brought to an arbiter to determine the outcome."

"No, that is not quite right."

"Excuse me Mulat, but as Erus of the Quadra Logicum I AM privy to the laws and apply a rigorous scrutiny to them. I do not see how you of all people can fault me on this."

"I can fault you for the exact same reason I can do this," said

Mulat and thrust a fist with his thumb pointing out with such a speed and force that it lodged neatly between two of Adsum's ribs. "Because you do not have the true knowledge or power to understand or enforce the law."

Adsum felt blood trickle down his mouth but paid it little mind — too many experiments on himself that resulted in pain had left him interpreting it as a sensation like any other. The Erus of the Quadra Logicum had never gotten the hang of assigning 'good' or 'bad', even when it came to himself — finding the categories when self-applied too limiting.

Mulat then twisted his thumb, cracking the ribs apart and forcing Adsum's body to gasp for air. "The human body is an amazing device and your pursuit of exploring it I will admit I approved of — but these reports?" Mulat dislodged his thumb and walked back to his desk, and Adsum sagged slightly.

Spreading out some documents he began to read while standing, "Efficiency experiments batch numbers one to three: Basic task optimizations. Each subject programmed to dress and undress repeatedly, each batch to perform its task differently as prescribed in notes attached, and timed." He looked up at Adsum. "Like most of your experiments, the result was death. Whilst your desire for knowledge is commendable, do you not feel that perhaps some restraint is in order?"

"If you are referring to the deaths, that was the human result. This so-called 'restraint' would have denied the true result, which is that with a small apparatus clothing oneself could be performed within three seconds. This would lead to a decrease in —"

"The human result is my domain, Adsum — do you think those lives were worth that knowledge?"

"If you multiply the number of people by the time saved over the average minute you would have days' worth of productivity in the city." To Adsum everything was merely interesting, and more often than not used his goal as justification for the path he chose to take.

"For some perspective: What of the time and energy it took to get those to a state where you could even use them for those experiments? Does it outweigh that? And what of the relative versus absolute emotion experiment? Is there value in opening a man's skull to directly manipulate his feelings?"

"Yes, there is value in finding that 'feelings' are conclusively a morphable, relative concept. We could elicit the same emotional responses from different acts," his voice became excited, "And actually the most interesting was the banal versus the dramatic. A man could experience the same emotional response from walking up the stairs, as he could from his wife leaving him for someone more rich and powerful!" Adsum always got excited when talking about his work. "But why are you stopping me now? I have yet to complete my terminal velocity experiment, which could save lives — if that is the point of contention regarding my experiments."

Mulat's face rarely showed what he was thinking unless he made an effort, and this was a situation where he did not want Adsum to not have access to all of his thoughts. "That is because your attempts to measure fatal heights for humans, and then alter them with vesma to accommodate for their weight and terminal velocity to a ratio of their impact thresholds, is not knowledge worthwhile. Whilst the knowledge might be interesting, this is not what a people or city is to be made of."

Adsum felt like some complicated puzzle was being presented to him and he wasn't being given any clues — he attributed some of the confusion to his body's response to the recent injury. "But why would you want inefficient people? You keep saying people need to live 'well', and 'well' in this instance would mean reduced risk of fall damage."

"The definition of 'well' is not a judgment to be made by you, being human means having the freedom to live as one sees fit."

Adsum pondered. "Then why did you give control of the Sanitarium to me?"

"I gave that to you because I felt the others would abuse it — either from neglect, or through using its occupants to serve their own purposes. You of all I expected to understand the necessity to leave these people alone."

"What value is there in maintaining those that others do not want? I do not see those that reside outside of the Integrum performing such charity."

"They are not as powerful or as wealthy as us. We support those that cannot support themselves with the excess of our wealth and power."

"Why waste it on them and not ourselves?"

"To breed good relations and to give hope to those that fear others' power and wealth, and if they were to be similarly indisposed that they would be taken care of. The hope of our people is what keeps them going. If these reports ever got out it would destroy much of the power we hold and I do not wish to regain that control by force. I've spent enough time trying to restore the damage done by Stagnos' apathy, and you of all people should understand the necessity of restoring the southern Integrum lands on both sides of the Vios Ocean."

Adsum had a quizzical look on his face and looked down. "Why did you stab me?"

"Oh, sorry I forgot about that lesson. Because I am more powerful than you, and the law of man does not supersede the law of nature. That is to say, both can be dictated by the person with the biggest stick." Mulat rummaged around his desk drawers for something and made his way towards Adsum.

"The danger within you, is that you cannot be reasoned with," said Mulat.

"I am the epitome of reason!" retorted Adsum, uncharacteristically flustered.

"Then do you believe reason personified brought you before me? You thought your experiment to peer into the mind of the mentally ill was sound reasoning? Removing all their facial features, smoothing the skull down, and transplanting muscles to every inch of skin on their head, would be sanctioned by me?"

"Why would I seek your sanctions when I had all the authority necessary? I thought you of all people would understand what I tried to achieve."

"Which was what, pray tell."

It was rare for Adsum to feel that who he was talking to would be able to understand his experiments, let alone the true value of their results. "I have noticed that the majority of human expressive muscles are in our face, I believe that it is tied to the singular fact that our brain does all the processing — the closer the muscle to the brain, the more expressive it is. How expressive is a foot? Not very. The mentally ill do not know how to communicate with means that we find natural — so by removing it, and transforming all available surface area of skin with close proximity to the brain, we might augment their expression and communication."

Mulat raised an eyebrow. "And the fact that all the notes pertaining to this experiment say that all the skin on the skull rippled like waves on the Vios, followed by what seemed like the entire head screaming and writhing in pain. This demonstrated to you that they were getting close to 'natural' expression and communication?"

Adsum waved dismissively. "All experiments run risk until the method is fully developed. I thought you would have wanted me to help us understand their minds, where is the harm? I tested them prior for any cerebral Veneficium Kasmah malformations, and I concluded that all test subjects were mentally ill as a result of their biological failings. I would have thought you would also want to understand what goes wrong when vesma's pervasiveness is not involved — don't you want to know the truth of the world without vesma's interference?" Mulat could now see that Adsum would only delve deeper into acts that would harm the city and that this misguided attempt at salvaging one of the finest Quadra Logicum Erus' was in error.

In a voice as heavy as stone Mulat said, "**The world is what you don't understand, vesma or no. Therefore, I will make this easy for you to understand.**" Mulat slapped his hand over Adsum's face leaving a large sticky glob that quickly hardened to cover his nose and mouth. Gasping for air as his consciousness faded Adsum felt panic and hatred towards the man that did not understand the purity of his work.

"Exile."

When Adsum's struggling stopped Mulat called out for his guards. "Shackle him, put him on the next trading sortie north, then apply the *deprimo os* dissolving agent," Mulat instructed, and then returned to his desk to ponder who to appoint as the next Erus of the Quadra Logicum.

ЖЖЖЖЖЖЖЖЖЖЖЖЖЖЖЖ

Naked and glistening with sweat, Erus Criso awoke on the floor of her chambers underneath some bedding. The last thing she remembered was writhing around with Clarus and… someone else? "No… *there was definitely more than that involved,*" she thought to herself as the scent of the room wafted into her nose.

A light cough brought her attention to Seconsulo sitting at his little desk near her own. She looked at him blearily and tried to stand but her legs wobbled and buckled, making her ascent more that of a newborn foal. Grasping onto the edge of the desk she asked, "What the *futuo* happened last night?"

Seconsulo replied, "You entertained some guests, Erus Criso."

Criso composed herself as best she could and sat down. Her head throbbed and her hair was matted to her body from sweat. She caught a glimpse of herself in the mirror on the wall and her eyes widened in surprise. "Get me some water!" she barked. Having some already prepared he merely looked to a corner of her desk and made no movement as she downed it with alarming speed.

"You are going to run a bath, and THEN I am going to speak with Tari and Clarus. I have no idea what trick my daughter pulled last night but I will find out. And then I think I will punch her. Quite hard."

"Very good Erus Criso, I shall return shortly." Seconsulo made his way to the door to carry out his mistress' orders.

"WAIT! What of the… committee, or whatever it is they were calling themselves."

Seconsulo replied, "I escorted them out earlier while I let you rest. They left feeling satisfied and indicated to me that their report would be a positive one." Criso waved him away and he left to perform his tasks.

Something did not sit right with her regarding last night. Nobody is capable of arousing *every* single person in a room within seconds of meeting them, especially to those heights — even a damn orgy could be notoriously difficult to organize what with the wide variety of people's preconceptions and insecurities. Last night reminded her too much of her Quadra's experiments with that creba drug — had Tari gotten a hold of some? Criso knew she was disruptive and impulsive, but had the Integra Pol's destruction sent her over the edge now that she'd lost her obsession? Tari was starting to become dangerous — perhaps she meant to be picked for the Ardeo Trial? A multitude of possibilities ran through her mind, but she had to give up quickly as her head still throbbed.

Turning to look out her window onto the Integra Pol, she made a mental note to meet with Erus Cogitans and find out what he had so far discovered about the cause of the disaster. There were no threats or further destruction beyond the events of a week ago, which puzzled her deeply — why destroy the most powerful person known and do nothing else? Perhaps the would-be assassin was waiting for proof before their next move. But the servants had already cleaned out up to his chambers and no body in sight, where else could he be?

Since the destruction of the Integra Pol the Quadras had become increasingly segregated — best demonstrated by their meetings now holding less discourse and more bickering. Without a unifying force Criso feared that the old days might return — where the Integra Pol was merely a symbol for the people while the Quadras fought bloody wars of power.

Criso had thought that all Integra Divinitas' before Mulat felt that dealings outside of their precious Integra Pol were beneath them, but it wasn't until Mulat disappeared that she realized those Integra Divinitas' were smarter than she gave them credit. It was that they knew what would happen if they interfered, and then one day weren't there to help maintain the changes they'd made. She still couldn't help but miss Mulat as he did help end Ardeo's horrendous practices and allowed Criso to rise from his personal concubine to replace him as Erus of the Quadra Lustrum.

Criso pushed the hatred of her past from her mind and tried to drown the voices with the plans for the Ardeo Trial on her desk. The usual fanfare and rules to be posted in the public spaces and the accounting and legal work stood as a stack but she left that to Seconsulo, the Ardeo Trial was far more than paperwork. After all people came for the spirit of the thing, not the numbers, and if Criso knew one thing it was how to put on a good show.

Her thoughts and planning were interrupted by Seconsulo. "My Erus, your bath is ready."

Looking up from her desk she said, "Good. Now fetch me my daughter, I will speak to her beforehand. Actually, before fetching her you are to fetch a guard to accompany me."

"Is something wrong that I should know about, my Erus?"

"If there is something wrong we shall find out *now*, one way or another."

"As you wish Erus Criso, however I should perhaps remind you that —" Seconsulo was silenced by Criso's usual hand gesture and he left without argument to fetch Tari from her joint accommodation.

She went about finalizing the plans while waiting for Seconsulo to return, and being left to herself brewed a growing fear inside her chest about her ability as a mother.

There was never a great love for Erus Ardeo, and Criso worried that her bitterness towards him might have poisoned the relationship she had with Tari. "*Did I send her over the edge?*" she thought solemnly. Too long a time with that thought passed, and with it came irritation — she hated to be kept waiting for reasons unknown, especially with her demons. She was not however about to operate on Tari's schedule and rang for one of her personal charges to go and see what was taking so long.

As irritation turned to aggravation her emotions reversed in quick order when she heard Seconsulo's familiar knock at the door.

"Come in!" she barked.

Seconsulo opened the door and was followed promptly by one guard, Tari, and Clarus in tow. Clarus looked absolutely radiant with her tall figure and simple smile, jerking Criso back to thoughts of the night before.

"What is this? I asked for Tari, not HER," she demanded.

"Tari did not... seem to wish to come without her," replied Seconsulo.

"I do not care what my daughter wants."

"Hello mother," said Tari distantly, with puppy dog eyes fixed squarely on Clarus.

The complete and utter lack of animosity or strained deference was missing from her daughter's voice, and that was disconcerting. "... Hello," replied Criso.

Clarus was just standing in the room idly looking out the window at the Integra Pol — not demanding attention from anyone, but seemingly commanding it from all.

Moments passed before Criso's anger surfaced again. "Tari! What sort of stupid prank did you pull on Clarus?! I am tired of you being so disruptive, but you are now damning this Quadra to a reputation of one lower than that of a mentally challenged rutting pig! I had thought...." Criso trailed off when she noticed that Tari was off in her own little world. Her anger came to full flower and Criso sternly walked over to Tari and slapped her as hard as she could, knocking her to the floor. Being so close to Clarus once more gave Criso a minor shiver of excitement, amplified further by the rage she felt, all of which confused her.

For the first time Clarus took her eyes off the Integra Pol and after a cursory scan found that everyone was looking at her. "Oh... oh, I'm sorry," she said sweetly. "Am I distracting everyone?"

Criso had mentally prepared a speech for Clarus for when she would next see her, both about last night and the dangers of spending time with Tari — it all seemed to wash away when she looked at her smiling. Clarus said, "I am, aren't I? Sorry I'll stop," and seconds later she was no longer tall, elegant and radiant, but more plain and dull. Everyone in the room breathed out, and their faces were no longer filled with interest. Criso was almost knocked off her feet by the speed of the change — from fear, to rage, to lust, to empty — her brain did not know where that left her.

Criso opened her mouth to say something but she was struck once more by that glamorous feeling as Clarus walked by everyone, ignoring all, to the window and looked in earnest at the Integra Pol. She had everyone's attention but none had enough of their senses about them to think — it was as if a fog had descended on the minds present. She reached out and touched the transparent pane with a fondness and the room remained speechless as Clarus turned and breathed in deeply, life appearing to flow into her face from the inside out as she bloomed with energy.

Whispering low so that only she could hear, she said, "Yes… yes I think it is time to go home now. I have been gone too long, and no doubt Mulat is missing me."

Ж Ж Ж Ж Ж Ж Ж Ж Ж Ж Ж Ж Ж Ж Ж

"*I will NOT be the weakest!*" screamed Erus Ictus inside his own head. "*They think I will let my Quadra go back to what it once was? Players playing for unappreciative morons, audiences without any ability to judge how perfect a sonata or fugue can be! Compositions used to wipe the public's collective cultural ass and spit on the tones of joy my charges play! No! Not again!*"

Erus Ictus' thoughts were filled with rage and fear when the hope of any sign of Mulat dwindled as the weeks stretched on. The situation was deteriorating too fast for him to keep pace, and with each Quadra now having their own personal Integra Pol army tensions rose fast. Inter-trading had now become near interrogations rather than pleasant lunches between equals, with each side demanding more and offering less, and scuffles between different Quadra charges became more commonplace.

Erus Epula had removed the Quadra Musicum charges from his establishment, only Erus Criso and Ictus had retained theirs — whilst Ictus deplored the notion that one needed a pretty man or woman to sit next to during a concerto, he could not doubt results.

Ictus understood the concept of sex in a distant sense, but did not appreciate it himself — he believed the flesh should have no part in the love that came from the heart and soul, for love was pure and unyielding.

The sparing few charges that Mulat had imposed upon Erus Cogitans were returned... changed, and Ictus despaired at their new demeanor, but there was no love lost between the Musicum and Logicum — ever since Erus Cogitans claimed music to be 'boring and repetitious patterns' Ictus knew there would never be a love between them.

The event that saved both Logicum and Musicum mutual destruction was Mulat's intervention. Ictus remembered the argument that silenced both parties to an almost mutual, yet begrudging, understanding.

ЖЖЖЖЖЖЖ

"Erus Ictus, Cogitans, please sit," said Mulat. The two Erus' looked at each other with disdain and Mulat wondered what it was this time that had gotten them so riled up. One of the better methods to diffuse a situation was flattery, so he looked at Ictus and said, "I see you are still having trouble remembering pants, but you have done quite well today." Ictus was wearing a gown designed for a figure far more feminine than his, but Mulat chose to ignore that. He then turned to Cogitans. "And gray, loose-fitting robes. Most perfunctory, I congratulate you on your practicality."

Neither seemed to care much for Mulat's attempts. Cogitans said, "Why have you summoned us?"

Mulat pointed at them both. "To resolve 'this' — the animosity between your Quadras is becoming disruptive. You are neighbors, so why can't you —"

"Then tell Ictus to cease banging his sticks and stones and tricking the public away from my Logicum. He's the one denying people a valid education."

Filled with a rage too pure to be denied Ictus could not hold himself back — Cogitans called his Quadra a bunch of people banging things together! Lunging at him with his ever accompanying violin bow he placed it across Cogitans' neck with such fierce pressure that the man gasped for air. Cogitans quickly retaliated with a hidden knife and plunged it deep into Ictus' arm — the ferocity and suddenness of the attack did not allow a better target. As the two struggled Mulat watched on silently and idly from his desk, vaguely sensing both of them wanting to use their vesma, but unable to.

"Will neither of you relent?" Mulat asked.

For a scrawny wild-eyed man Ictus was surprisingly strong, but what Mulat found more interesting was the contrast in their hairstyles — Ictus' was white and wild, while Cogitans' was black and flattened against his scalp. It was an entertaining spectacle for a while, but when Mulat saw the blood from Ictus fall and Cogitans' face turning purple he sighed and sang out a single note which he held for a few seconds. The doors to his chambers opened, and in walked several people with expressions on their face that indicated their minds were experiencing things that were not wholly happening inside the room they occupied.

Mulat sang out another single note again for a few seconds, and a woman began to sing harmoniously alongside him and moments later the others joined in accompaniment. Ictus was stunned by the beauty of the vocals and became momentarily distracted. Cogitans took advantage of this and repositioned his blade for a killing blow, and was stopped mid-thrust by Mulat's open palm being placed in front of the blade.

As it pierced him Mulat did not wince or shake, he merely looked deeply into Cogitans' eyes and asked, "Are we capable of talking now? Or shall we let this situation escalate to a fatality." He slid his hand off the blade and his blood dripped onto the floor. Ictus backed away, enraptured by the music, and calmly sat down, while Cogitans allowed himself time to catch his breath by holding onto the chair.

Mulat coughed, silencing all, and allowed both men some time to regain their composure. "I am sorry. I would have used the baritone, but I had no wish to kill either of you."

Ictus and Cogitans looked at Mulat, then at the women. Ictus eventually asked, "... Who are they?"

"I decided to name them Devotarecalis, however I can appreciate that word might be a bit of a mouthful so I welcome any alternatives you may feel better suited." He pointed to the woman who had sung alongside his own voice. "That lovely lady you heard sing was the first of her kind, and while she sought me out what she has become is more an idea formed from both your Quadras — so I thought she would perhaps be a good demonstration of why you two would benefit from each other."

Cogitans replied, "The man tries to garrotte me and you think some warbling notes will deter him from future attempts?"

"No, I think what will deter him is the same thing that will convince you: Reason," said Mulat in calm tones. "The link between you both is patterns — one seeks to use patterns to better understand the world, and the other uses patterns to understand oneself. For example a rather interesting logical statement provided to me by Erus Adsum long ago was that zero is more a 'state' than a number. It is only a value until you are able to assign it to something, which then makes it a group." Mulat noticed Ictus appeared slightly lost and decided to change his wording. "You can have zero bananas but what if the banana did not exist? There is quite a lot of difference between 'zero' and 'banana'." Mulat waited for Ictus' face to indicate he had caught up.

Leaning in closer to them from his chair he said, "The truly amazing thing I found though is that if you can count to two, then you have broken free of the chains of either existing or non-existing. That is what our brains do, we categorize, assign, and find patterns." Mulat turned to Cogitans. "Your patterns, Erus Cogitans, allow you to calculate the tax required to make the city function cleanly, to have waste disposed of, and how best to police the city. You find the patterns of the world and make them more efficient." Mulat then turned to Ictus, "You, Erus Ictus, find the patterns of the mind through music. What if there was no such thing as B flat? Or F sharp? You can conceive of a piece of music not having those notes, but can you imagine the world that did not contain those notes, but all others?" Mulat gave this notion time to sink in before continuing.

"It is the same as if there was no city to tax — you both find the patterns to your own ends. Music is a grouping of notes we hear, aural grouping — logic is the grouping of numbers, mathematical grouping. The human mind is far more amazing and not as limited as you both wish it to be, and I fail to see the difference in your Quadras' methodology — merely your focus." Mulat saw that Ictus again was drifting away from the conversation and decided to move to more practical applications.

"Erus Ictus, can you play for me the least played song of this year in your Quadra? And you, Erus Cogitans, can you please recite to me that fascinating number pi?" he asked. Both looked at him strangely. "At the same time, if you would be so kind."

Both Erus' felt stupid at having to silently nurse wounds and entertain what they always felt was a madman, but complied. As they recited the devotarecalis could not help but harmonize along with Ictus, filling him with slight excitement. After fifteen seconds Mulat held up his hand and said, "Stop!"

Ictus was trying hard to not look at the devotarecalis and asked, "What was the point of that?"

Mulat smiled. "What you both did I found as exciting as the other. Your brains and the patterns they find will forever amaze me, and I hope you will in time find each other's amazing also." Mulat stood up and walked in front of them. One quick glance told him that they had heard his words but not the message and he wondered if it was because they were unable to process things in tandem like he could.

Beckoning to Cogitans he said, "Recite pi to me — or as you call it, 'an irrational number', and keep going until I ask you to stop."

Cogitans decided to show off and began. "Three one four one five nine two —"

"Now skip all numbers that aren't prime."

"Five three five seven three three three three — "

"Now express the distance between each prime digit as a percentage of the whole value of digits traversed, rounded up."

Ictus had no idea what Mulat had said but was enjoying watching Cogitans beginning to sweat.

"Eight percent, seven percent... thirty-three percent, thirty-two percent, thirty-one percent... fourteen percent... three percent... three percent...." Cogitans looked like his forehead was about to explode from effort and Mulat waved him to silence.

Turning to Ictus, Mulat said, "Your turn now," and stood up, gesturing both to follow. Leaving his chambers they walked down a short corridor and entered a smooth room that had no harsh corners to it. In the middle stood the grandest of pianos that Ictus had ever had the pleasure of seeing in his life. Mulat gestured towards the seat in front of it and Ictus sat down with giddy glee, while Cogitans merely waited.

"Now play the last 'popular' piece that your Quadra has played, Erus Ictus." Being given such an easy task seemed boring to Ictus, but he was not about to let Cogitans show him up, and began playing. As the chords and cadences bounced around the smooth room Ictus was amazed at the harmonics and again was gladdened at Mulat's appreciation for his art.

All of a sudden Mulat said, "Second species contrapuntal, now." Scoffing at the task Ictus launched into matching chords for the fairly simple tune with little effort. Playing on for a bit he was only a quarter away from finishing before Mulat said, "Third species."

Ictus did his best to comply but his fingers staggered as his brain tried to do the mental gymnastics required for such on-the-fly composition. With brow sweating all the way to the end of the piece Ictus' heart soared — this is what separated him from every other charge in the Quadra Musicum.

With a subtle finish and lingering chord Ictus beamed at the pair, but quickly scowled when he saw that Cogitans' face did not register any appreciation whatsoever.

Mulat sighed, they had not even bothered to try, or was it his own fault for failing them through reason? "I tried to show you the beauty and value you both have through reason, but you still do not see it." Walking out of the room with the Erus' falling in step,

Mulat talked while they made their way back to his chambers. "So instead you are to both send three of your charges to take up residence in each other's Quadras, until I see it as no longer necessary. Just remember that power is not what you seek — it is patterns, and I hope you learn each other's." Upon reaching his chambers the Erus' noticed that the singer was still where she was before, eerily unreactive to her surroundings — the others however had all gone.

After some time organizing the specifics of how the charges were to be distributed and overriding the Erus' objections, Mulat concluded their business and gestured for them both to leave. Cogitans stood up to leave with a cold expression, but Ictus had other interests and remained seated. Mulat said, "Hold a moment Erus Cogitans, it would appear Erus Ictus has something else on his mind." Cogitans stopped short of the door, turned, and stood still.

"Yes... yes, I would like one of those... devotarecalis. I have never heard such beauty, I must have one for my Quadra!" said Ictus with mounting desire.

Mulat allowed silence to settle in Ictus' mind so he could think back on the words he had just used. "You would like something from me? Something of mine?"

Ictus defensively threw up his arms and said, "I mean no disrespect but... but they must be heard! There are such things that should be heard, and new music to be written! How could you deny me such joy?"

"They are not for musical appreciation in the sense you are accustomed to."

Ictus cried, "How can they not be!? They are divine!"

Mulat pondered for a moment. "Very well." He walked over and took Ictus' violin bow with a speed that caught him off-guard. Then taking out a thin sliver of vesma from his pocket Mulat began to draw the bow across it, playing a harsh high note. A pattern began to emerge as he played and soon after the devotarecalis joined in — it was a simple little tune, but it evoked such feeling in

Ictus.

Mulat's piece began a crescendo, and with it Ictus' heart swelled. Reaching the pinnacle of the piece Mulat sharply dragged the bowstring across the crystal, and a force ripped through the room from the devotarecalis that destroyed Mulat's desk and blew out the window behind him, stone and all.

As the debris settled and the Erus' composed themselves Mulat gestured once again for them to leave and said, "Patterns are interesting to you both, so surely in time you could find some interest in the patterns the other one makes. I wish you both a pleasant day."

Ictus had a wide grin on his face and Mulat could tell that Ictus saw only beauty in what he had just witnessed. Resigning himself to fate, Mulat said, "Co-incidentally, this one wishes to return to her Quadra Musicum, so you are welcome to take her home — if you will care for her. I will be checking up on her."

Even with Mulat's constant attempts to soothe the strained relations over the years, sadly the animosity between Ictus and Cogitans never diminished.

☼☼☼☼☼☼☼

As Ictus stared out from his chambers at the twisted fang that was once the Integra Pol he could not help but wonder what it would now sound like if it were music. Before it was smooth and proud, almost pristine and filled with power — now it imposed, standing there as if a single tooth were now mangled and rotting from the inside with all the little servants running around trying to save it.

"*Something with... yes. I think predominantly strings to express the harsh emotions, and given the extreme change the Integra Pol underwent the piece should be chromatically modulated. Major key, shifting to augmented. I think we can skip the minors.*" He began humming a tune to himself, and after a few bars he shook his head and cursed letting himself be distracted.

Ictus was beginning to miss Mulat — the man might have been difficult to pin down on exactly where he stood or what he liked, but he did provide his Quadra with what was necessary. Ictus never knew he had something he COULD protect, until Mulat, because until he came along: if the Quadras were a litter of pups his would have been the runt of the litter. But now... now was the time to ensure his Quadra's safety, now was the time to remind people that music was a force as great as anything else. With his heart strengthened Ictus made his decision, and left his chambers to enact it. That day with Mulat and the devotarecalis had given him silent inspiration — Mulat may have only tapped the voice for power, but he did not have the training or obsession for music that Ictus did. Years of quiet tinkering and neglect of his craft led him to finally perfect something of his own devising.

Fusing someone with raw vesma was difficult, this Ictus knew, but his goals were far grander than mere power. Having to bond the body then their minds as one, to think as a single piece of music always playing, and to follow each other's improvisations and responses to the environment was a task suited only to the most vehement of fanatics. Many that he had secreted away to experiment on, some of his most talented singers and musicians, died.

There were many times that Ictus feared being found out and exiled like Adsum was, but if Mulat ever knew he never said anything of it. It gave Ictus a misplaced sense of accomplishment and confidence, which led him to cockily composing a piece for orchestra entitled *'idea rubata'*. He hosted a huge event where Mulat and all the Quadra Erus' were invited to attend. Ictus was on the edge of his seat delighting in flaunting his achievement in the unknowing faces of his guests. A part of him was expecting retribution, for someone to stand up and oust him, but all that happened was a round of applause — everyone was congratulating him for being so clever!

With that confidence came dedication, and devotion towards his experiments.

When the time came he would make Erus Cogitans and the others rue the day when they tried to take his Quadra from him.

ЖЖЖЖЖЖЖЖЖЖЖЖЖЖЖ

"What did you say?" asked Erus Criso, shaking her head and wondering what Clarus was doing standing at the window. When did she get there?

Clarus turned to Criso with her usual lighthearted smile and said, "Oh nothing! Sorry, please continue."

Feeling derailed Criso turned back to Tari, who was still fixated on Clarus. Something strange had just happened, and now she was faced once more with her daughter's peculiarity. It was all very, very tiring, and her daughter's games were reaching a point where the thought of killing her seemed a practical solution. "This... this is not something I understand. What is going on here?" Criso demanded of anyone that could answer her.

"Love, mother. Just love," said Tari wistfully.

"LOVE?!" shrieked Criso, taking forceful steps towards her daughter. "Do not speak to me of LOVE you ungrateful child! You have corrupted everything and brought my Quadra to disrepute! You WILL participate in this Ardeo Trial, or you can join the Maenyrs until you are withered and gray! Whatever you have done to this poor girl will CEASE and —" Criso noticed that Tari wasn't paying attention, again. She walked over to Clarus, pulled her hard by the hair and slammed her to the ground — she finally had Tari's attention. Clarus gave no resistance and complied fully, and didn't react like it was a painful experience.

"Did you hear everything I just said?" she asked Tari. With a look of fear Tari nodded her head. "Are you going to be a good girl?" Tari nodded her head again, tears welling up in her eyes. Criso grit her teeth at seeing her daughter with such a soppy expression. "I tell you what Tari... if you can beat the odds on this year's Ardeo Trial, I will allow you to keep Clarus for yourself." Tari's face lit up like the sun. "ON THE CONDITION, that you cease your games." Tari again nodded mutely.

Criso looked down at the blonde-haired Clarus and wondered what it was that had entranced her daughter so. Admittedly last night's orgy was unexpected and lent some credence to the unbelievable effect Clarus had on people — the passion involved was more than any other she had attended, but it seemed quite alien from this strange devotion Tari now seemed to exhibit. This was a mystery she had neither the patience nor time for.

"Guard! Take Tari back to her room, and Seconsulo take Clarus to the other Taker's room. They are not to see each other again," Criso commanded, keeping her eye ever watchful on Tari's expressions. Her daughter gave away nothing that would indicate disobedience but she could see the despair at being separated and the silent longing on her face.

When Seconsulo returned from delivering the girls to their respective rooms it was to Criso sitting as cool as ice in her chair, and that worried Seconsulo more than any shouting could hope to achieve. She was given to outbursts of emotion, something they both believed came with any position of power, but her demeanor indicated something far more serious.

"My Erus?" he inquired.

"Yes?"

"You appear stressed."

Criso took her time before giving a very deliberate, "... Yes."

Seconsulo nodded his head knowingly, breathed in deeply, and calmly walked across the room to a nondescript cupboard. Opening the doors to the cupboard and selecting an elegantly made riding crop he walked over to Criso and placed it in front of her. "I offer you me, to clear your mind," he said, and bent over the desk. Over his time served with Criso he did not waste it by never learning to read her needs and wants, and what she needed now was to be free of her stress.

Criso took some time to register her emotions again, having locked them away in an attempt to save her sanity — but as always her dear Seconsulo had offered her an outlet. With a great impulse she took the riding crop and began to beat him without mercy or desire less than that of breaking the man in front of her, all the while screaming obscenities.

The first time Seconsulo had offered himself like this to her she had treated it more like she was entertaining his fantasy while indulging in a little of her own stress relief. Over time she saw that he felt no animosity towards her, or even acknowledged the pain she inflicted — he was as a doll made flesh, one that did not understand what flesh was for beyond being beaten. Eventually the beatings became more brutal and relieving, and her guilt of hitting him faded while the ferocity increased until it became a practice of necessity in her mind. Switch after switch and blow after blow she gorged herself on her rage, letting it flow through her until on one stroke she violently threw the riding crop across the room and collapsed crying onto the floor. "No! NO! NO NO NO!" she wailed.

Seconsulo got up from his position to comfort his Erus as she broke in his arms. "It is all going to die! Everything I've built! My men and women will be regarded once more as chattel, forced to walk the street to earn and all skill lost! My charges will either become victims or abusers without being able to have others recognize their skill or trade — there will no longer be any passion or art to my Quadra! All the years of building up the art of mental arousal and spiritual sexuality, of demonstrating an orgasm through the eyes of both sexes! The art of the male and female body's sexual movement! EVERYTHING!" Criso sobbed heavily. "It will all again be reduced to the crude ruttings of base and vile people who would not see that sex empowers themselves and those they engage, but as a form of sinful release and control."

Seconsulo held Criso until the tears subsided. It was some time before she regained her composure, and stood up to stare longingly out of her window. She softly said, "I, who have enriched the art of my Quadra a thousand times, will not let it shrink back to a loveless, beaten mongrel."

"My Erus?" asked Seconsulo.

Criso spoke to herself. "The wars will start again."

"My Erus it is a tad premature to believe —"

"The guards Mulat gave us all have now taken sides, they serve the Quadras and wear patches to show their fealty — perhaps they are just used to belonging to something greater than themselves.

The Erus' are withdrawing inter-Quadra charges, and less and less do the Erus' respond to my messages or deal with the reports of fights. We are all becoming withdrawn, and I had hoped to stop it by making my daughter make this Ardeo Trial an event to remember for decades!"

"The alternatives —"

"Alternatives?! I've sent waves of lovers at them all, and all were returned untouched! I am being looked down on again Seconsulo, but I will not let my Quadra suffer! I promised each and every person who became a charge of the Lustrum that they would not fear for their practice. Mulat may not approve of my actions, but he is not here to stop anything — so it is now time... If the Integra Pol is dead, and the city at unrest, and my army is not enough to protect us — then I will amass the best army there could ever be."

"And what would that be Erus Criso?" Seconsulo inquired.

She turned to Seconsulo and said, "The love of Orbis."

Ж Ж Ж Ж Ж Ж Ж Ж Ж Ж Ж Ж Ж Ж Ж

Looking out from one of the buildings the servants occupied on the grounds of the Integra Pol, Mulat took in the view of his once beautiful spire and felt the remnants of guilt. He had, even though indirectly, caused it to happen, which was more than enough to send him into a depression. His whole life had been spent trying to use as light a touch as possible to help others, to be a good man and someone all could look up to. He didn't want to be like Divinitas' past, locked away in the tower too afraid to do anything. But now the beauty within the Pol was lost, its history and knowledge now residing solely in Mulat and the few straggling survivors that made it out along with those who were posted in places outside of Orbis.

The hardest part of wasting away the weeks as he watched the servants clean up was that there had been no sign of Juvo.

"My Divinitas, the reports," said a hooded figure from behind Mulat, and placed the documents on the bare desk. Turning around to the sparse room, pasted bone white and with nothing more than a basic bed, desk, and table, Mulat picked up the pages and read through them — the hooded figure had already gone. Retrieving the Integra Pol's archived documents had been difficult with the warped passages and rubble blocking the way.

To overload an Integra Divinitas' power with cremo faba infused with vesma, what was his enemy thinking? Had Mulat not twisted the power in on himself it would have flattened the entire city, and more. Whoever had organized this was far more clever than he had anticipated, and in a different mood Mulat would have welcomed the challenge. But his enemy was not threatening just him, they were threatening Orbis, and Kasmah.

As he flicked through the reports of the cremo faba he soon found the tale behind it in a Logicum report — the sortie sent out to investigate the troubles at the trading post Abrotonus. He had thought the party destroyed as the small army Mulat sent to secure the south found no trace of them.

"So... someone called Ani sent Adsum an interesting little Gadori bean, and some fabled Ogagi sap," thought Mulat. The Ogagi sap from the Gadori was known to the Integra Pol as the purest form of living tissue infused with vesma but little else was known as the exchanging of information between Integrum and Gozuri died long ago, and what little information they had garnered since was of little value.

A week was not enough to uncover everything as reports from his spies indicated that the Quadras were dissolving their co-operations and utilizing the guards for their own purposes. Mulat was despondent at honoring their request and now seeing that they only kept to the rules he put in place because he was there to keep the fear alive. They had stopped trying to curb the creba, and ever to Mulat's confusion petty rivalries prevailed in the wake of obvious destruction.

But now trouble was upon the people of Kasmah. Too many years had passed since the last Deaspora, and with his recent plans disrupted Mulat feared that his enemies' interference had damned the city to a slow death. Arrogance, pride, and greed — these were the things that would bring down everything he desired to cherish and nurture.

Mulat was at a loss. Knowledge was power, but nothing was being brought to light for him, and he was still so weak after his exposure caused him to discharge everything in one burst. He would have to keep biding his time until something else reared its ugly head.

At least then he would have a boil to lance to save his city from festering.

CHAPTER X

*Providence and prophecy, order and chaos;
the great Nujah walks between them as he sees fit.
The power of his floods, the gentleness of his rain;
tools in his need to cleanse the land of sin.
Praise Nujah, for he shares our love:
Life.*

-Prayer to Nujah, Keeper of the sky-river

THE MAHARAAN EXPANSE

Kahli's eyes opened wide as the blackness that the other voice had taken her to was ripped away, while her lungs fought to take in as much air as possible. She looked around and saw that it was late in the evening with just the last remnants of light soon to fade, but she had no recollection of time passing. She was alone save for the little girl who'd been startled by Kahli's quick change from comatose to conscious. Breathing in and out heavily, Kahli first looked at the little girl before looking down at her own hand again — it was still encased in foam. She tried to control her breathing and calm down but when she tried to wiggle her fingers she found all sensation from her hand had gone.

The girl timidly moved forward with food and water almost trembling, when she got close enough Kahli noticed that she had a bruised eye. At first she was thrilled to see the little bitch in pain, but a larger part of her wanted to take care of her. Reaching out her arm felt the dead weight of the hand in foam and her desire to help faded quickly, replaced by bitterness. The little girl placed the bowl in front of Kahli along with a water bucket and sat down hugging her knees to her chest. Kahli grabbed the bowl with her other hand and began scarfing down whatever was given, all the while glaring at the little girl in her submissive position.

"You've never sat and watched me eat before." Kahli said between mouthfuls. "What do you want?"

The little girl just shook her head softly with a face full of fear. Refusing to let her heart be melted by the plight of a child she quickly finished her meal and noticed the bucket of water. She kicked it over hard and it splashed on the ground — the little girl gave out a yelp.

"What? Another stupid prank?! GO AWAY!" Kahli screamed.

The little girl began sobbing and cowered. "I'm sorry, I was just trying to help."

Kahli shouted, "HELP?! My hand is dead because of you! I can't feel anything and you say you were trying to help?!"

A large man with a strange tattoo on the side of his face entered the pen upon hearing this commotion — silently and calmly he looked at both girls. When he saw the little girl crying he started to make his way towards Kahli, but was stopped just inches away from her by the little girl saying, "NO!" The man stopped in his tracks, and Kahli seized the opportunity. Lunging forward she swung her dead hand at the man's head with all the force she could muster. A satisfying crunch came and some blood splattered onto her hand and face, softening bits of the foam and warming her skin where it landed.

The man looked down at her with no expression, grabbed her foam hand, and reached back with his other to punch Kahli with a force she knew would kill her. The little girl screamed out, "NO!" again, and his body was sapped of all aggression. He lowered Kahli down, looked at her glaringly, and walked over to where the little girl was. Kahli could overhear whispers and a hurried discussion.

Kahli refused to back down though, she'd had enough of being punished and refused to be pushed lower than the dirt and hay she'd called a bed. So long at the mercy of this clan's punishments for things she had no knowledge of and nobody to explain it to her, to be beaten so consistently and by so many felt like it had broken something inside of her. It had driven her to the brink of suicide, and the only thing that brought her back was the voice that lived inside her.

When the two finished talking the large man just sat down, blood trickling down his face, and the little girl scurried over to Kahli. "Wait wait! Look, I'm sorry okay? Just listen, don't you think it is weird that you aren't wearing your harness?" Kahli stayed resolute and showed no signs of backing down. "I forgot to put it back on you last time when I pulled my prank, and I am REALLY sorry for that, but that is why I was punished. I was... punished for... for not being a good girl, and I try really hard to be." Tears began welling up in her eyes.

Kahli lowered her fist, when faced by a crying girl there could be no malice in her heart. "I can help you escape, but you have to promise to take me and Sasara with you!" she said, hurriedly pointing to the large man Kahli had just hit.

Kahli however was not about to let her emotions get the better of her. "Who is he, and why would I take EITHER of you?!"

"Because I don't know anyone else except you that wants to get away from this camp either, and you aren't going to get away all by yourself, and Sasara is a... friend."

"I am not listening to anything you say, you little bitch!" said Kahli as loudly as she dared and stared directly at Sasara, challenging him to rush to her rescue again. He made no movement and never uttered a word, he merely sat and watched.

The dull throb in her arm from her dead hand gave her no reason to forgive the child, but the promise of escape was too tempting to risk hitting her for her own satisfaction. *"Maybe she's in just as bad a situation as me... this can't be a good place for little girls,"* she thought to herself as tiredness further sapped some of her rage. Kahli eventually said, "I'm not leaving until I have some answers." The little girl's face brightened right up and signaled to Sasara, who went and stood watch outside the pen. "You said he wants to leave, what's his story?" asked Kahli.

The little girl crouched down and began talking as if she was telling an amazing story, forgetting for a moment everything that had just happened. "He's a hunter from the Calu-Jedde, but he did a bad thing a long time ago which made his people take the strong letters from his name, leaving him only with 'Sasara' so that his name has no power. Then they cursed him to only speak truth so he could not hide behind words. He didn't like any of that, so he exiled himself and he found his way to us. He's been my friend ever since."

"The Calu-Jedde Mountains? That is a long way, why would he choose to exile himself?"

"One day he saw that his words only caused pain and that made him really sad, so he left his people so he couldn't hurt them anymore and vowed to never speak again and cut out his tongue so he couldn't hurt other people. That tattoo on his face is his symbol for the last words he ever spoke."

Kahli could not help but be carried away a little by the child's story. "What were his last words?" she asked.

The little girl quietly said, "My tongue is a knife, with which I shall strike no more."

Kahli felt a strange small pang of sympathy for the large man, but not enough to make her trust him. She had to tell herself that she was the only one she could rely on, but at least she could get some help. "... Tell me how we get out of here."

The little girl stood up and said excitedly, "Sasara can start a fight! He's HUGE, and nobody can beat him! If he starts taking challengers everyone will flock to either fight him or watch. While he's doing that I can undo your chains, then when we escape, Sasara fakes losing, and then he meets up with us!"

"... Whose idea was this?"

"Sasara's."

"... How? He can't speak."

The little girl looked at her like she'd asked a stupid question. "He can read and write, can't you?"

"Well yes of course, but... but he looks like he could barely understand anything beyond pointing and punching."

"Well, not everything is what it looks like."

The little girl's smart-ass response inflamed Kahli's irritation at her. "Like stupid little girls that think it's funny to kill my hand."

"I didn't mean for that to happen! I really thought you would have just eaten it all off by now."

"How could I! I am out in the sun all day! I can barely make enough spit to even swallow my food!"

"Well I brought the bucket! If you hadn't kicked it over then you would be free by now!"

"It's a bit late you stupid little cow!"

"That's not my fault!"

"Yes it is!"

"Look, we can't keep arguing! We have to act fast if we want to do this. Today was a big day for hunting so there will be a feast, and that is the best time for everyone to be in one place so Sasara can get all their attention." That made a lot of sense to Kahli. "After they've eaten and drunk and fought with Sasara, you and I will be far away from here and the hunters will be too tired to catch us."

"What about Sasara? Won't they hold him when they notice you gone, or follow him when he tries to 'sneak' away?"

"Nobody cares about him anymore."

A nagging doubt ate away at her mind. "Why aren't you a prisoner?"

"I'm small and people don't pay much attention to me — I'm just a kid," said the little girl with a smile. "And I'm not a prisoner because my daddy is important — I love him but he doesn't treat me very well... I think that is because he knows when a girl grows up here everyone wants to throw her out or kill her."

Kahli was shocked to hear this. "But, why?"

"Don't you know about the curse?"

"Oh... yeah," said Kahli solemnly. She concluded that it must be the only reason Ruzu was still alive or... might be still alive. She had no way of knowing as her coming and goings had become less frequent and all her time was spent with that Adsum. "Well what's your name?"

The little girl balked a little as if trying to catch the words coming out of her mouth. She quickly recovered and said, "Jatah." She smiled, but it was a smile on a chubby face that seemed to lack respect or pleasantry.

Kahli ignored her observations and asked, "Well Jatah, why am I here?"

Jatah just shrugged. "I don't know, all I know is what I am told. Mostly about how lucky I am to still be here and how daddy always protects me and that I was too young to remember. All I know is one day you left for your cleansing, and after you returned the curse has been around. So you didn't do the ritual right, or something." She began to fidget and looked very uncertain with herself. "Can I ask a question?"

"What?"

"So you really remember nothing?"

Kahli felt uncertain at answering the question, both out of trust and how unsure she was of her own answer. "I... remember these three women. I think I... killed some of them. And my family or... what I thought was my family, and the whole village I think is dead. Also a wija, but I think that's dead too," said Kahli with a tear forming in her last words.

"So you don't remember anything else except dead stuff?"

"Nothing that I'm sure of."

"That's kinda weird," said Jatah. Cocking her head to one side she continued, "Look your hand isn't dead okay? I had someone play the same prank on me a long time ago. It has just gone to sleep. I'll go get another bucket of water, but then we have to go okay?" Kahli just nodded her head. "OK, I'll go tell Sasara to start and I'll be back soon."

Kahli still felt unsure about everything but decided that uncertain freedom was better than the certainty of staying in the pen. "*Where would I even go?*" she thought to herself — she could escape where she was, but to go where? Every time she traveled it was only to a place where horrible things happened. Was that her lot in life? To be punished? To continually go from place to place experiencing the worst of the world? At least this Jatah was starting to show some sort of kindness.

"*The world does not always have to be bad,*" offered Kahli's other voice.

Why was the voice talking so much now? She had begged it for weeks and now she was getting it twice in one day. "*... I don't want it to be.*"

"*Then don't let it.*"

"*How?! How am I supposed to fight EVERYTHING?*" The voice was calm, why was it always so damn calm?

"*All you need to do, is listen.*"

Why didn't it ever show emotion? "*I want to listen!*"

"*Yes, you 'want' to listen. I said you 'need' to.*"

"*Why don't you ever just answer my questions?! I don't understand what you're saying!*"

"*Yes you do, you do because I do.*"

"*Then explain it to me!*"

"*Explain to me how I killed those Natura.*"

The question caught her off-guard, how did she? "*I... I don't know. It just happened.*"

"*And you being in this pen, being beaten and bruised, just... happened?*"

"*This is nothing like that!*"

"*Why not? If both this and that just 'happened', then what control do you have over either?*"

"*I HAVE CONTROL!*"

"*Then why are you here?*"

"*Because I don't have the power to be anywhere else!*"

"*Why ask me questions if you won't listen to the answers?*"

"*I'm listening!*"

"*Get up!*"

"*... What?*"

"I said get up! It's time to go!" Jatah said hurriedly and plunged Kahli's hand into the bucket. "Look, just swish your hand around in it and it'll melt."

Kahli blinked a few times to come back to full consciousness and began to notice a strange smell coming from the bucket. She looked down at her hand and saw that the bucket was filled with some sort of thick slime. Remembering that the foam dissolved with water, she swished her hand around and saw something float to the top. Revulsion crept into Kahli's arm as the sludge became thicker as she doused her hand and whole chunks of foam came free.

"Quick, undo my chains!" said Kahli. The smell got stronger and began to fill her nose and throat, choking her. Doing her best not to gag and splutter she looked at Jatah and said, "Damn this stuff smells foul when it melts, I don't remember it doing that when you did this." Jatah began giggling her irritating giggle from this morning again, and she just sat there without showing any sign that she was going to do anything else.

Kahli's sense of unease grew greater at hearing that sound and looked closer into the bucket, and noticed that the lumps floating on the top were not chunks of foam, but excrement. Jatah's giggle turned into a full on belly laugh as she flung the slop bucket into Kahli's face. Kahli fell back onto the now sodden and soiled hay that had housed her for so long, never once freshened and filled with her sweat and blood. Kahli fought with her mind's desire to both retreat into herself and lunge at the stupid little girl — torn between the two she lay there paralyzed by the shock.

Jatah's voice changed. "Daddy was right, you are kind of stupid. Who would want to save you, you stupid pen pig!" She spat on her. Kahli reached a decision and lunged at the little bitch with both hands, falling short by mere inches. Jatah fell back a little scared, but still smiling. "I just wanted to see how dumb you were before I let Sasara play with you. You really do belong in this pen, you worthless pig."

"I am here when you need to listen," said Kahli's passenger voice.

"SHUT UP!" screamed Kahli clenching her fists, and she felt the foam crackle.

Hearing the commotion Sasara wandered back into the pen and looked at Kahli. Jatah took a long look at Sasara and said, "Mount her, no need to be gentle."

"What are you doing?!" Sasara silently began to undress and Kahli pleaded with Jatah. "Tell him to stop! Why are you doing this?! YOU'RE JUST A CHILD!" she screamed while trying to find refuge in the foul hay.

Jatah made herself comfortable in a far corner and said, "A child who will be Isti one day, with Sasara as my Jagu. While daddy said I didn't have to ever worry about you becoming Isti, I never liked you anyway." She started throwing tiny stones at Kahli. "Besides, what do you care? Kasi went missing one day, and then we find her dead next to you with you covered in her blood. Your wija went to find you after all that time, and all you could do was kill your other heartbeat?!" Jatah began throwing the rocks harder and harder. "She tried to help you, YOU of all people, and you killed her! How COULD you?! You are nothing but a curse, a curse that doesn't feel the pain of her half-beating heart! Daddy was right to punish you!"

Kahli's thoughts stumbled. "*My... wija? Did I kill... wait... Kasi?*" She felt strongly towards the wija that had saved her, stronger than she thought she should have. Weren't wija solitary though? Didn't they avoid people? Jatah's words now had finally unlocked a memory, and it was one that made Kahli grab her chest and wonder what had happened to the rhythm of her heartbeat. "Kasi..." she whispered. Tears streamed down her face as all the feelings came to her at once, and the feeling of a heart-bond between person and wija broken. But no memories of true things past came, only the feeling.

Jatah laughed. "So you CAN remember! Good! I hope your heart BREAKS, I would never do that to my Jasah! My wija is my best friend, and I love her almost as much as daddy!" She threw the last stone as hard as she could. "I'm his only TRUE desert flower! I LOVE HIM THE MOST!"

Sasara had removed what clothing he deemed necessary to get the task done and walked slowly towards Kahli, while his future Isti enjoyed the growing look of fear on Kahli's face. Not much ever crossed Sasara's mind, however he felt unease as he approached a trembling female covered in feces. He had no wish to disobey, but he also had no desire to mount what he would call, in every sense of the word, a filthy pig. Sasara wasn't sure if Jatah would truly be sheltered from Rasak's wrath this time when he found out what had happened — this was going a bit far, even for her.

Jatah saw his hesitation and asked, "Would you prefer to clean her up before you mount her?" He stopped for a moment, turned to his future Isti and nodded his head. Jatah softly replied, "... No." Turning back to the task at hand he pushed all thought of repulsion to the back of his mind and reached out for Kahli. Fear rose in Kahli's throat from the knowledge that she was about to be raped, and then killed. In that moment of terror a part of her soul broke free, but this time the voice said nothing to drag it back into place.

Sasara turned her over, held her in place, and spread her legs forcefully. As he was crouching down she felt a familiar flame burn inside her, desperate to be free. Acting on reflex she lashed out at Sasara once more with the stone foam fist — expecting no real resistance Sasara made no effort to avoid the strike, believing the hand to be nothing but sodden mush. As her hand smacked him in the face it did nothing to deter his descent, and each further sloppy fist to his face did nothing more than cover him in filth. Kahli smeared both of her hands, one open palm and another semi-clenched fist, all over his face and did her best to push him off her while she squirmed as hard as she could, but she made no progress beyond helping her panic rise further.

He shook her hard against the hay. She felt how strong he was and knew it was a pointless battle, but when he began to descend upon her once more a rush of heat came into her heart and her hand broke free of the foam prison. Her face went blank and her eyes bright, she screamed, "**BURN!**" and shoved the dried up toad that had lain at the center of her numb hand this whole time into his mouth. Her arms pulsed for a moment before she went limp and Sasara went still as a statue.

Jatah screamed, "What are you waiting for?! MOUNT THE PIG!" Sasara fell to the side clawing at his face as the revived toad expanded, forcing his teeth up into his gums and tore his jaw apart. Further and further it grew until Sasara's head burst, splattering Jatah and Kahli with bits of skull and brain matter.

After the moment of shock passed Jatah said, "But... what? HOW!? GUARDS!"

"There there, that's enough for now I think," said Adsum walking into the pen with a dazed Ruzu in tow. Kahli roused herself and upon seeing his piercing blue eyes, braced for what was to come. He always seemed so in control of everything, himself or others.

"Adsum! Go fetch daddy!" Jatah commanded with all the rage a spoiled child could muster.

Adsum replied, "My apologies little princess, but it is time for me to move on to, as they say, greener pastures."

"What? What are you saying?!"

"Are you asking me to repeat myself?"

"But... but you helped me with all this!"

"Yes, preying upon the weak is what a member of the stronger species does — either physical or mental strength, both are prey to natural selection. Cruelty is indeed a special form of stupidity."

"But I am your future Isti!" Jatah cried indignantly.

"Aside from the fact that I am not bound by Jara Law, nor considered one of you, I would find considerable objection to following the rule of someone so easily manipulated."

"Just wait until daddy hears of this!"

"I would be surprised if when 'daddy' Rasak hears of this that he will be able to articulate much."

Kahli thought, *"Rasak is her father?"* Jatah made a dash out of the pen, only to be blocked effortlessly by Adsum.

"Sisters fighting is a rather inefficient modus operandi for species propagation," said Adsum as he restrained Jatah, pinning her arms behind her back, and pushing her firmly into the ground.

From her position in the stained hay Kahli weakly asked, "Wait... wait, she's my sister?"

Adsum appeared to notice her for the first time. "You are quite filthy it would appear," he said to nobody in particular. "Yes, she is your sister. Thankfully I've had enough time to find out more about everything, so it is time for you and I to escape."

Kahli felt apprehensive about this seemingly genial offer. "Why are YOU helping me?"

"Am I? Altruism is for those who feel they have exceeded their limits, however I will always have something new to learn. That isn't to say that I am not helping you though."

"Why are you doing this?!" screamed Jatah.

"For an optimum explanation I would recommend experience over hypothesizing," said Adsum, and reached into his robes to produce a beautiful and intricate crystalline sphere which he looked at with great love and care. He then applied a light pressure, breaking some of the surface, and threw it as hard as he could up into the air and ducked. Unsure of what was going on everyone else looked upwards, and were almost blinded by the light that followed.

"What the fuck was that?!" screamed Rasak, jumping up and scanning the night sky as the flash lit up everything. Virtually all were gathered outside the Jara hut for the feast, and all were startled by the sudden brightness. They looked to their Isti for guidance. "What the fuck are you staring at!? Where did it come from?!" he yelled. Some of his men pointed towards the pen where Kahli was being kept.

With only the slightest of hand gestures he commanded some men to take up guard positions and for a small group to follow him and investigate. When he reached the pen at a run, he slowed down when he passed through the gate and saw inside. Sasara lay dead, his daughter Jatah sat in a corner looking around in fear, and Adsum stood over Kahli with Ruzu trailing behind him.

"What is going on here?!" demanded Rasak.

Adsum replied, "Oh, Rasak. I had not expected you to be here already."

"Well I am, so what the fuck is going on?!"

Adsum replied in calm tones, "If you would just give me another minute or two everything should become apparent."

Feeling that Adsum was acting like he was in control of the situation only irritated him. "Where is your assistant, Dabuk?"

"Oh, you mean Adacio?"

The aged Integrum bastard's constant categorizing and questioning got on Rasak's nerves at the best of times, and now seeing his best hunter with his head all over the place did not help matters. "Shut up! I don't care if you think giving him a different name means anything. Where the fuck is he, and what the FUCK happened to Sasara?"

"He's dead."

"I can see that!"

"Sorry, I meant both are dead."

"How?!"

"Well, both, directly and indirectly, by my hand."

Rasak felt derailed by the frank admission before he unsheathed his weapon and advanced on Adsum. "What did you say?"

"What I want to say is that they are taking much longer than I expected." Adsum quickly brought up his hand, opened up his palm and blew black sand into Rasak's face. Rasak became enraged from such a childish trick and saw Adsum back away, hurriedly wiping his hands off onto his robes. "Strange stuff Adacio found, that black sand from Toka-Rutaa — I should really investigate it proper one day. Anyway, the fascinating property is that it appears to be super-hydrophobic." Rasak was having difficulty breathing and his eyes began to shrink. "Oh, right, layman's terms: That means that it hates water, a lot. It repels any moisture it finds, with quite a significant amount of force I might add, so breathing it in is fatal. It finds its way into the bloodstream quite efficiently and —" Adsum's rant was interrupted by choking sounds from Rasak as his face contorted into one of confusion and pain and he dropped to his knees.

Taking a step forward Adsum said to himself, "Now as for the guards —" he was interrupted by three hooded figures that appeared behind Rasak with long thin blades — one pierced his heart, the other his skull, and one his throat, all in perfect unison. "Oh I say, most effective," said Adsum distantly. "Still, you took too long and I had to waste some interesting new product...

anyway, remember our deal." He pointed at Kahli. "If you want any hope of finding a cure then she is mine." The hooded figures expressed nothing and left swiftly to kill others, having already silently taken care of the guards that had followed Rasak.

A low horn blast roared throughout the Jara village and was soon followed by the sounds of an all-out war — blades and screams were plentiful in the cacophony of violence. With the noises of battle Kahli felt strangely comforted by feeling too pathetic to even be killed and succumbed to the desire to retreat back into her mind. What she did earlier had drained her more than she thought possible, even though she was still trying to figure out what it was she'd done.

"Now that we are alone —" Adsum was again interrupted, this time by Ruzu uttering a guttural scream and pouncing at Kahli. Swiftly, Adsum struck her on the back of her head, dazing her. "Ruzu, predictability is my life's work, even my saying that brings no comfort," he paused a moment before saying, "Predictably."

Ruzu's staggered back and forth while she muttered, "She must die."

"Whether or not she must is not for you to decide anymore." There was a soft rustle of hay, without turning around Adsum said, "Please don't try to escape Jatah. Thinking that I have forgotten you would irritate me, so please respect my —" his last words were lost to Jatah as she darted out of the pen. "Oh well, I had no real need for her. However, rushing out to certain death is somewhat silly."

"Am I going to die?" asked Kahli — half there, half not.

Adsum replied, "I have no plans for you to die if that is what you meant to ask, so long as you stay in here. The deal was that all who were in the pen were to be free from harm."

"But... she's my sister," Kahli said weakly.

"You would want to save someone who showed you no love or compassion?" Kahli hated herself for nodding but felt there could be no other way. Adsum sighed heavily. "Very well, I suppose I can spare some *phrenesis clavus*." He retrieved three strange looking spikes swiftly from about his person and walked over to Ruzu. "Are you physically fit?" he asked, a nod was his reply. "That is good to hear. Now —" he violently jabbed the three spikes deep into Ruzu's chest, and then quickly struck the spikes with his open palm to drive them in deeper. He then grabbed both sides of her head and loudly said, "Protect and retrieve Jatah."

Ruzu's body jerked like it had been hit by lightning and she ran out of the pen. Adsum then turned back to Kahli and said, "There, see? Your sister should be back soon enough."

The extreme change in Ruzu scared Kahli. "What... WHAT DID YOU DO?!"

"Oh, a new delivery method I've devised to carry out some experiments that require people. I grind up the required vesma along with some blood and clay, and then dry it all out to form a *clavus*, or spike if you will. Essentially you stab the subject, then apply enough force to splinter the spike after it is lodged in them, and their blood will carry away the vesma and powder — it is as effective a delivery system as I could manage given my limited resources. Not nearly as effective as an intravenous —"

"Wait... no, what... why is she going to get Jatah?"

"Ah. The *phrenesis clavus* basically gives the injected a surge of energy and an intense impulse to follow their first command — my attempt at mixing my obsession experiment with body enhancement. I haven't had very many test subjects, and so far the fatality rate is one hundred percent — interestingly though I believe that if I were to use a chimeral *clavus* that —"

"FATAL?!"

Adsum looked at her. "Yes, is this some sort of problem? I do not see any friendship lost, if that is important to you."

"But.... I don't want anyone to die."

The sounds of battle pierced the conversation.

"Do you think that nobody will tonight?"

Kahli was being rubbed raw by Adsum's apparent indifference. "BUT NOBODY MORE SHOULD HAVE TO DIE!"

"Yes... aside from grammatical errors in your speech, you do know that merely saying what you want does not make it immutable? Besides —" Adsum kicked the fresh corpse of Rasak, "It is a bit late for that sentiment."

Their conversation was interrupted by a group of five hooded figures pouring into the pen. Adsum seemed unfazed by their arrival so Kahli assumed that they meant her no harm and relaxed slightly. They advanced on her with an alarming pace — quickly replacing Kahli's light relief with immediate fear.

Adsum shouted, "STOP!" and they all turned to him. "Just because I do not partake of emotions does not mean that I cannot understand them. We had a deal, so calm yourselves, or you may never see an end to your plight." The hooded figures restrained themselves, and one of them spoke up.

"She will answer eventually," said the figure closest to Adsum. It was a woman as far as Kahli could tell.

Adsum replied, "Eventually, is the important word in that sentence, because it is the NOW in which our deal stands." A figure broke away and strode right up to Kahli and grabbed her by her hair. Adsum then spoke with slightly more haste than Kahli was accustomed to hearing from him. "There is a battle to tend to — I gave you this opportunity to strike back at those that shunned you, you AGREED to this price! Renege and there are acts in this world far worse than what you have experienced so far that I can inflict."

Throwing Kahli back down on the ground the figure walked up to Adsum, "YOU WOULD THREATEN ME?!"

"Do not think them said idly out of emotion. I would also recommend subduing Ruzu, I have *clavumed* her and the results may be unpredictable," replied Adsum calmly. The hooded figures hesitated a moment before they left silently.

Adsum walked back over to Kahli. "No need to inform them what Ruzu might do to them, yes? Let us hope they can rescue her before her heart explodes, she has been useful to me so far and I would prefer it to continue."

"What do you want with me?" asked Kahli.

"As with everything, to learn."

"You... you only came to see Ruzu, and left me here to wallow in this nightmare. Why would I let you learn anything if you would be so cruel to me?"

"Cruel? Leaving you be while I orchestrated all this is not, I believe, something that would be construed as 'cruel'. I did not talk or experiment because Rasak did not allow it, and I did not interact with you because these past few weeks you have not always been *compos mentis*. I also needed to know more about you, and you were hardly going to be the one to tell me. I am pre-empting a lot of questions here so we can move beyond the asking phase. Is there anything else?"

Kahli felt the weight of her unwanted ignorance weigh heavily on her, and she asked, "... Why me?"

"I have some theories I would like to test." The true question in Kahli's words was lost on Adsum.

"... Did you really kill a guy?"

"My assistant? Yes, in a fashion. He was a botched experiment in the first place. The black sand was an interesting find, fatally so for him it would appear. I had no real need to kill or keep, so natural selection ran its course."

"That's... evil."

"In your current state you still find it prudent to hold a moral and ethical perspective on the world? That is indeed peculiar."

"Just... get me out of here."

Adsum unlocked Kahli's chains and raised her up. She felt weak as the blood tried to reach her head upon standing, and Adsum barely caught her as she slumped back down to the ground.

"Ah, atrophy. They did not really let you do much except lay on the ground and be beaten. Well, come on I will carry you, we must go before the battle is done."

"Why?" Kahli whispered, with tiredness and hunger getting the better of her.

"Because if we stay here I doubt they will honor our bargain given the unstable emotional balance fighting brings. Besides, it is time for me to return home, and it does not look like you are welcome in your home either." Kahli weakly nodded her head in agreement and let the old man carry her with surprising efficiency — he was not as frail as she originally thought.

Kahli and Adsum made their escape from the camp and with each step covered, the sounds of battle dwindled. As she looked up, she marveled at how the night-sparks could be so beautifully bright and colorful on a night so dark.

Ж Ж Ж Ж Ж Ж Ж Ж Ж Ж Ж Ж Ж Ж Ж

As the unlikely pair made their way through the sparse land with only the odd dry bush for scenery, Kahli wished that the old man would shut up. She wondered if he talked so much because after looking at parched ground for so long he had gotten bored.

"Interestingly enough the only three things necessary for a human to learn are utilization of objects, relation of objects, and limitations of objects — that is why we can do anything from painting to crafting furniture. I tried to educate the other Quadras about this immutable fact and they responded by telling ME it was more a philosophy! It is hardly anything so amorphous and the facts are quite...." Kahli constantly drifted in and out of paying attention as he ranted and raved about any thought that seemed to pop into his head. He seemed obsessed about the world, about laws and reality, like a giant toddler that could find nearly anything 'interesting'.

Kahli was sick to her stomach of the cruelty of the world, both natural and man-made, but eventually came to find some comfort in her traveling companion, Adsum — although a part of her was willing to admit that may just be because he appeared harmless enough, at least to her. Even though he'd killed in front of her she didn't find him that scary. He always had a reason for things and that was oddly comforting when most of her life felt so nonsensical, half the time she couldn't even trust her own thoughts or why she was even alive. Adsum's approach to everything had given her a sense of acceptance of things, which was something she had been desperately looking for ever since the reality of who Jatah and Rasak might be to her came to light. Why should she have to worry about her past? Surely she couldn't have meant anything by it. *"Like it even matters that I don't remember! How can I be the same person now that I was before?"* she thought.

Days passed by, filled with only meager rations and sparse patches of trees and various greenery as they traveled to a destination unknown to Kahli — she didn't even know how they were going to survive, or had done so for so long. While Adsum seemed to rarely eat or drink his knowledge of extracting nutrients, not always palatable, from the environment was impressive at times, but right now she was hoping he would just keel over and die so her ears could have some peace. Where was he getting all the energy to talk?

Today had been more lacking in food and water than the others and Kahli had finally reached her breaking point from exhaustion, hunger and thirst. "Just shut up! Why do you keep talking?! Can't you see we are in the middle of a desert trying to survive!? What do you have to say that is so important that you have to waste your breath with this!?" she screamed at him.

Adsum stopped walking and looked directly at her. "Not all words are for your ears. Sometimes I like my brain to hear what other parts of my brain are thinking, and the only way that can happen is if I say it out loud. Also, whether or not something is of importance is not a factor of time — whatever happens WILL be important when the causality of inter-connected repercussions collide." She gave him a blank stare. "For example, the fact that you are pregnant now, is not important enough to make an impact on your behavior, but it will be." As if to demonstrate his point, he added, "Sooner or later."

"What?!" Kahli felt blindsided. Nobody in the pen had touched her like they had Ruzu, so what was he talking about?

"Where was I? Oh yes, my theory that everything is a recurring circle. You see a circle is unique topographically as it is the only shape where any edge you want to travel to from the center requires the same straight line of equal length. Given this we can deduce that a circle is a structure that we can mathematically derive, but not structurally create — a circle is our best approximation of the formula to say all edges of this shape are equidistant from a central point. This leads one to conclude that a circle is the more 'perfect' shape because its curvature variance can be infinite in relation to its size, whereas a square of any size would only have four angle changes. The propensity for a circle's infinity means that in truth everything must be a circle. My Logicum...." He went quiet for a moment and looked up at the sky. "Do I thank Mulat or curse him for exiling me? I do have a predilection for becoming preoccupied and distracted, but maybe if I had stayed in my Logicum I could have found peace." He looked down at the ground. "Then again being exiled has helped me..." Adsum prattled on.

Kahli was too busy thinking about what he'd said about being pregnant. How would he know? How would it even be possible? The only reason she gave this more weight than usual was because Adsum was not one for lying, in fact most of his honesty was grating, and that it made as much sense as everything else up until now.

"*There is one way to find out,*" said Kahli's other voice, breaking its long silence.

"*How?*"

"*Listen.*"

"*I have been listening! It has been almost impossible to not listen to him rant on and on and on and on! I may have to pray for death before salvation if I have to put up with his rantings.*"

"*If you are hearing things you don't want to listen to, then ask the questions you would want to listen to the answers of.*"

"Adsum," said Kahli. Adsum was too entertained with his own thoughts to register. "ADSUM!" she screamed, finally getting his attention. "I want answers."

"Then I want questions," he replied. Adsum enjoyed having his mind focused by questions.

"What did you do with that Natura woman? The one that you saved me from."

"Fetu was a boisterous woman, but she was fresh blood and ended up where all the others did: The cleansing pens."

"Is that where I was?"

Adsum shook his head. "Yes and no, you were in a pen reserved for special purposes — hence you and Ruzu. The cleansing pens however are a recent construct. The Jara men needed outlets for their sexual needs and a way to feel like their seed would live on. The clan cannot keep many women and those they do can't be kept for any significant period of time before they succumb to the curse also. Interestingly enough I found that they used to believe that sex was a sacred thing."

"I don't think there was any comfort to be found in those Jara."

"You speak like you aren't one of them."

"I'm not!"

"From what I have gathered you are the curse template, Kahli Jara. Rasak and many others have confirmed it, and seeing you now leads me to many questions. For example do you know how many times I've seen your face? I've experimented on your exact body a hundred times — I've watched it be beaten, raped, rot. The number of Jara that have been party to those actions I could safely assume to be in excess of half."

"What are you talking about?! I'm the ONLY one of me I've ever seen!"

"Those people who killed Sasara, if they weren't hooded you would have had visual confirmation."

She didn't want to believe any of this. "If there are so many of 'me' running around then how could anyone tell if I was the original? For all I know I might not be the real me!"

"You have a mark that the others do not apparently."

"Even if what you are saying is true then why didn't everyone just come to love me?! If every mother and father saw me as their own —"

"That is not how the Jara function. The father of the child is the husband of the wife who birthed it, for he would have been the only one who could possibly dream it — sex is otherwise considered a recreational activity. It all has to do with what they call the 'Dreaming'. It is their belief that merely being awake is not all of reality and that the dreams their minds encounter are what forms the bedrock of what reality bases itself upon. So everything from their children to where to hunt was formed in their dreams first — a fairly comforting ideology, don't you think? They quite clearly understood the difference between recreational and procreative, but I am quite surprised they never found the link between —"

"Stop getting distracted! You talk as if they used to be some advanced culture and not some brutish, backwards bunch of bastards!"

"They were not always so 'brutish', but they believe the 'Dreaming' has been cursed and all the men's ability to dream has been taken from them. The men believe that if they dream enough and put all their dreams into one or two women that they can take back the dreams to have children again."

"*Calm. Do you want to listen to his words or your own rage?*" her inner voice cautioned. Kahli did her best to regain her composure as she still had many questions to ask and finally someone to give answers. "Why was Jatah safe? Why did my father protect her and not me?"

"He did protect you for as long as he could, from what I know it was 'you' who chose to save him by becoming Orati — Ruzu informed me that you chose it because people were starting to suspect that maybe your father was the cursed one instead."

"How would SHE know?"

"All Habiak are told of everything to do with their separation from the Jara."

"Habiak?"

"The Jara women who chose to exile themselves, the original batch of women that became pregnant and started the wave of births — they went and started their own clan. Ruzu was a captive from them, one of the original Jara, and I needed someone to experiment on. I am still curious as to how those cursed-born age to the point of sexual maturity so quickly though."

Kahli was determined to not let the man get distracted. "Were Jatah and Rasak really my family?"

"Yes, from what I could tell. The time-line fits and I cannot find any evidence to the contrary."

The earliest memory she had was of how loving and caring her father was. Did she really bring down the Jara? What did she even DO to make that possible? "So... everyone blames me for poisoning their dreams?"

"Well, the women blamed the men — believing them to have corrupted dreams. The men blamed the women — believing they were denying fresh blood to the clan, for reasons I'm not sure of. In a short period of time there were a lot of theories for hate, but after they got over those initial wild accusations, everyone blamed you."

"But how?! How did I do ANY of this?! I couldn't have meant it!"

"That is what I'm hoping to find out along the way to the Integrum. I have my suspicions — there are very few people who could affect such a change on this sort of scale."

Eager to see if Adsum could shine some light on the darkness of her mind, Kahli asked, "If you know so much, then tell me why can't I remember anything? Why are my memories false? What IS this Hidati, Orati thing?"

"Orati is the person who imbibes the Hidati — which I suspect is more just a special form of poison with some tribal beliefs added in."

"I know all that! I want to know how it's possible that my mind can do that to me."

"Do what?"

She threw her hands up in the air. "My whole sense of time! I can't FEEL how much has passed! All I know is that only recently I have clarity — a defined, clear line of time that I can follow. Why?!"

"Time is quite a relative concept — an hour can pass like a minute, and vice versa. If you would like a more pertinent example, going by the tests I performed on you whilst you were unconscious you have been pregnant for approximately five years, far beyond the norm and —"

"That's... that's not even possible!" Adsum just shrugged his shoulders, expressing that her belief did not change the facts presented.

"I must admit that informing Rasak did have its appeal, but at the time your death would have probably been brought forward with expediency."

"Kill me? Why would he kill me just because you say I'm pregnant?"

"I believe because killing you remains the most plausible cure to their predicament."

Kahli walked in silent shock and looked down at her waist. "*Is... is that who you are?*" she thought, trying to call out to her other voice — silence was her response. Her face now downcast and spirit weakened she asked, "Are you going to kill me?"

"Me? That would be counterproductive. I am far more interested in how this came to be. It has been a welcome distraction to my primary focus of returning home, so I am hoping to satisfy two of my life's greatest curiosities with a singular course of action."

"Sorry? How are you going to do that?"

Adsum stopped walking and sat down in the middle of nowhere. "By waiting here."

Kahli looked around, expecting some trick. "How is that going to achieve anything?"

"Well timing is quite important, and judging by my calculations we are due for..." Adsum peered north into the vast desert. "Ah yes, right on time I see."

Kahli looked to what Adsum saw and a panic rose in her chest as a small group of mounted warriors were now charging their way towards them. "What do they want?!" screamed Kahli.

Adsum looked at her as if she were stupid. "To capture us, obviously."

"But the camp! They were attacked! How could they already be seeking me out?!"

"It is not the men that are chasing us, it is the Habiak."

"Those exiled women?!"

"Yes."

Kahli turned to run. Adsum called out to her, "Are you going to try and outrun them?" but his words went unheard. She feared what they would do to her, especially if her own father would have condemned her to 'purify' the dreams. *"No! Not another prison! NOT AGAIN!"* she thought as she ran, and ran, and ran.

It was not long before Adsum was trotting alongside her on his own beast looking down at Kahli. "If it is not obvious enough they are not here to harm you. They are here to honor our arrangement," he said to an exhausted and frightened Kahli.

Adsum dismounted and walked towards her. "Had you asked instead of acted I could have explained to you that if we had stayed at the Jara camp the Habiak warriors would have killed you out of spite — escaping allowed for the more level-headed of the clan to find us. My deal with them was you were to be spared for a time, and that I would provide them with a cure for their curse." He saw no acknowledgment of his words on Kahli's face and merely sighed and turned to the head of the scout pack. "Is the deal to be honored?"

The hooded figure looked at him a good long while before responding. "Yes."

"Excellent. Now, you have been honorable enough to provide me with your excess children all this time, and as requested I will tell you how to relieve your curse."

"Speak it," demanded the hooded figure.

414 | CHAPTER X - THE MAHARAAN EXPANSE

Adsum pointed a finger directly towards Kahli and said, "All you need to do is kill her."

Kahli fell to the ground trembling as a hooded rider dismounted and descended upon her with weapon drawn, the strike was stayed by what Adsum had to say.

"However, that will merely relieve 'this' instance of the curse — if you wish for it to never return, you should join me. It is Mulat and the Integra Pol you need to destroy, and without her I do not think that will be possible."

The hooded figure looked at Adsum and knew his reputation for deranged honesty, then looked at Kahli and felt bile rise in its mouth. Sheathing its weapon it bound Kahli with rope and put a bag over her head, and once more Kahli found herself hooded and bound, fearing for her life.

LAND OF THE GADORI

Toyo walked through the forest back to the large gnarled tree and wandered around in an attempt to find where they had put the Ogaden. Along the way he noticed that everyone seemed more accepting of him — had he been forgiven somehow? He returned all the friendly gestures with an uncertain smile as he walked.

Upon reaching it he noticed that the three medishi attached to it seemed a lot less like men now and a little more like strange trees. Their hair had faded and flattened, skin dried and flaked, while their faces possessed a vacant stare. He tried to say hello and get their attention but nothing moved their fixation on the Ogaden — Toyo wondered if they were even alive at all. He looked around the stump and found a large root going from it to the gnarled tree and felt creeped out when he saw it pulsate slowly. Unsure of what to make of it he inspected the Ogaden and wasn't quite sure what to do next. He decided to try and knock on the stump in the hopes that the lady wanted to come out.

A few raps on its top got a rustle of its root crown followed by a synchronized head jerk from each of the three medishi and a never-ending stare. "Hello?" he called out nervously.

"Hello," the three medishi replied in unison.

"Uh... can...." Toyo had just remembered that he did not know the woman's name. "Can the lady inside come out and talk?"

"I am," they replied.

That didn't make any sense. "No, I mean I want to talk to the lady inside."

They replied once more, "You are." Toyo moved over to one of them and gave it a tentative poke, to which all three of them said, "Do not do that."

This was getting silly now. "Look can she come out and talk or not?"

"If you want to talk to her — speak, she is listening."

"But I... kinda need her to talk back."

"She is."

"What... are you talking for her?"

The three medishi looked at each other and the Ogaden perplexed, "Is there a difference between us and her?"

"Of course there is! And I want to speak to HER, not 'you'."

The three medishi again looked at each other, then back at Toyo.

"Oh, I see. You wish to see a naked woman."

Toyo's face went bright red. "No, I just want to talk to her." Suddenly and silently the three medishi each gripped a nondescript part of the Ogaden and pulled gently.

A portion of the bark rippled and began to curl back into the trunk with a sickly sucking sound, to reveal the naked lady curled up inside. Toyo had expected the woman, but not the insides of the Ogaden to be some sort of soft, greenish-pink color. It looked very warm and inviting, but quite a strange color for a tree.

Toyo just shrugged and concluded that he wasn't sure what a good color of the inside of a tree was, given that the last tree bled some sort of red. At least she seemed to have a lot more color than she did before. He smiled and said, "Hello!"

"Hello," responded the three medishi.

Toyo was beginning to get irritated with their interruptions. "Look, can't I just talk to her?"

"You wanted the body, you have the body. You wanted her words, these are her words."

Toyo had to think about this for a moment. "So... she is speaking to me through you?"

"It can be seen as that, yes."

Toyo kept peering into the Ogaden. "Isn't she cold?" he asked.

"You showed me warmth," they replied.

He wasn't sure what to do with that answer and instead looked around. "Why is this part of the forest so different from the last?"

"Different how?"

"Well, the last place was full of huge trees and plants with big roots, thick leaves and... just everything seemed so big and healthy. Even when we were making our way here from the ice the trees just kept getting smaller, thinner. Lots of bramble, vines, trees looking like..." he looked at the Ogagi and pointed. "Well, like that. Is that what these Ogagis do?"

The medishi followed his finger. "The Ogagi does not change the land, it represents it."

Toyo'd had enough of the cryptic responses and shifted his mind to just get everything he wanted off his chest as he wasn't sure how long he could be gone before they noticed. "Look do you know who I am? Why I am here? I feel like I'm lost but... I don't think I have a home."

"You are an invader, you are here to invade, and your home is not here."

"An invader? I don't want to attack anyone!"

"Yet you do, all the time."

"What? No I haven't!"

"So you are claiming that the things dead by your hands were accidental?"

"But those were just animals!"

"Can humans be the only things to think of something as home? Can you not invade theirs?"

"I'm not here because I want to kill things!"

"Yet you do."

He didn't approve of being told what he was and wasn't, but wanted to prove that he was more than what she was saying. "Fine, then I just won't kill again!"

"Then you will die."

"What? Why?"

"That is what life is, kill or be killed."

Toyo thought about this deeply. "I don't believe in that."

"The next thing you meet may not share your beliefs."

He felt like he was listening to answers and questions that he didn't quite get and tried to ask something simpler. "Do you know who sent me here?" The three medishi each pointed a different direction. Toyo chose to ignore what was obviously a useless response and tried not to think that he was being made fun of. He sighed and said to himself, "Where is my home...."

"Where would you like it to be?"

Toyo wasn't expecting a response and blandly said, "... I don't know."

"Then let me be your home."

He was surprised. "But nobody here accepts me! I keep making mistakes and —"

"You are a child. They can help you be more than just a child, if that is what you want."

"I... but... why is nobody angry at me?"

"I asked them not to be."

"Why? I don't understand."

"Then don't, but the words to understand should you listen: They aren't angry because I asked them to stop being angry."

"Why?"

"Was my answer not simple enough?"

"How is it simple?"

"How is it not? Did you ever try asking them yourself for an answer? Or did you just react on impulse, acted as you pleased without seeking confirmation?"

"How could I?! I couldn't talk to anyone!"

"Are words all you have?"

"I... I...." Toyo began to feel a presence and turned around to find that a small crowd had gathered behind him. Feeling like he might be on the verge of making another mistake he got up clumsily with an odd mixture of nonchalance and hurried exaggeration. He then saw the medishi begin to lock the woman away again and he decided that it was time for him to leave.

LAND OF THE GADORI - CHAPTER X | 419

As he walked away the medishi called out to him. "Find something to love if you feel like you have no home. If you can rest your heart, then that is where your heart belongs." These words went unnoticed in his hurry — driven by fear of what Ani would say when she noticed that he had been gone too long.

He quickly made his way back to the trees where he'd left them and found that they were still talking, and that none of them seemed to have noticed his absence. Sheepishly sitting up against a nearby tree he mulled over in his mind what the tree lady had said.

Ж Ж Ж Ж Ж Ж Ж Ж Ж Ж Ж Ж Ж Ж Ж

"<We were part of an expedition to investigate what we called a mass infestation from the Gadori, it wasn't until later I discovered that you had a kusabana that broke free of the forest. The sortie was me and my partner from the Quadra Logicum as the heads of the investigation — accompanying us were six Integra Natura, a dozen guards, and an Integra Humanus. On Erus Adsum's orders we were to —>"

"<Wait wait, who are these people? I don't even —>" Hoba began before Tagai waved him into silence.

"<We have traded with the Integrum enough, I know these names Hoba. I will explain later, but for now be quiet. >"

Feeling a slight pang of pain Ani rubbed her chest before continuing. "<On Erus Adsum's orders we were to find cause and solution. As we traveled farther south the reports from each town got more disturbing until we finally reached the southernmost trading post, Abrotonus. As we approached we saw everyone just walking the streets in a stupor, so several of the guards were dispatched to investigate while we hid nearby. When they got close, the inhabitants as one noticed the guards and like they were puppets on strings ran towards them. Fighting several off they were quickly overwhelmed and then all the bodies just... exploded. >" Ani sighed heavily before continuing.

"<We waited a long time before attempting a retreat when that foolish Integra Humanus demanded we investigate. We inspected the dead and found that the bodies had only exploded from the

inside out in certain places and that the guards were lightly wounded, but had some sort of slug attached to them. It appeared to be 'feeding' and sapping all the strength out of them. The men were comatose the entire time, until we found out too late that the next step in the slug's life cycle was to find the nearest living thing and explode in order to germinate. >"

"<I do not care about those details, >" said Tagai gruffly.

Her chest began to hurt more and Ani had to push through the discomfort. "<My Erus Adsum charged me and my partner with finding out as much as we could. We set up base at Abrotonus for excursions and research purposes. One day a member of your tribe stumbled upon us as we were conducting experiments and eventually you took us in, but by that time the only members left were the Integra Natura and myself, the rest had been taken by the chaotic creatures of the forest over time. We lost the guards too early for us to safely return home, so we went with you. >"

Tagai's face went to stone as he asked, "<Why the kusabana? >"

"<We did not know! >" Ani said with pure honesty. "<When we sampled the Ogagi sap and found that the vesma content was so intense, I HAD to study it further. The Integra Natura saw you all use it to cure people of illnesses and bring them back from the brink of death — the value in understanding it would have been immeasurable. >"

"<Why meddle with things you don't understand? >"

Ani sniped back, "<How can you understand anything if you don't... meddle. >"

"<How did the kusabana happen? >" Hoba asked, making a mental note to bring to Tagai's attention that Toyo had left and returned.

"<We were all wanting to send a sample back to Erus Adsum, along with some of the plants you use to make hunting tinctures, so they could better research it. I... bore a hole into the Ogaden and tried to take a sample from the Ogahigi. >"

"<You WHAT?! >" shouted Tagai, standing up and making Toyo jump.

Ani hurried to try and explain herself. "<You have to understand that the creatures were encroaching on our lands! At first it was trading posts, but as the months of our research passed, and you showed us more and more horrifying things, we did not know how soon it would be before it was our cities that would fall! >"

"<We protected you, and you would interfere with OUR Ogahigi!? For years we thought she was silent from trying to recover from that kusabana, but it was YOUR fault?! >" screamed Tagai.

Ani raised her arms defensively. "<We did not know! I went to take the sample and the Ogahigi and the Ogagi seemed to... I don't know... breathe together. There was some sort of surge and the Ogagi expanded until it exploded. >" Tagai looked at her with a ferocity to burn the world, but stayed resolutely still.

"<The medishi are not the ones that should be attached to the Ogahigi, you should be, >" said Hoba with a damning voice.

"<The years we hunted, the people we lost in order to destroy the abominations that were born of that event... all to send something to the Integrum for research? >" asked Tagai. Ani nodded her head. "<And what did they learn? >"

"<I do not know. The Integrum could be a wasteland for all I know as there are plenty of creatures we missed. I waited a year for a response from my Quadra, some sort of rescue party or request for more resources, but nothing ever came. >" Tagai was silent, and in that silence Ani's mind came up with a hundred different ways he could punish her. Her guilt surfaced roughly and almost made her regret everything, but she wouldn't let herself succumb to that feeling.

"<Why the Ogahigi wants this Toyo to become a man in our eyes I do not understand, I do not even know if she has now been tainted somehow by your meddlings all those years ago. But I have been asked to lead, and lead I shall. I would personally have you both exiled for what you both caused, but I will honor that something greater than me has asked me to be greater than myself. >"

"<If you don't trust the directions given, why walk at all? >" The question escaped Ani before her common sense dictated that it was a bad idea.

Tagai replied, "<I do not need to believe in a tree for it to give me the richest fruit. >"

Ж Ж Ж Ж Ж Ж Ж Ж Ж Ж Ж Ж Ж Ж Ж

The time that Toyo spent training with Tagai, while filled with Ani's translations and Toyo's misunderstandings, was the best time of his life. The Gozuri now seemed so willing to move on with life and look towards tomorrow that Toyo took on a form of optimism, which lasted even after he had been sequestered to an isolated part of the camp after one too many 'accidents'. It was a small blow to feeling like he belonged, but he just pushed through and kept trying his best to make amends. It didn't help though that the accidents had only rekindled their fear of his iron hands.

Tagai had come to understand Toyo well enough that he knew what was bothering him today when he saw the boy's usual enthusiasm quickly give way to anger and confusion.

"You have to hold the spear *lightly* Toyo, otherwise how are you going to learn to throw it?" translated Ani. Toyo looked at her in response and threw the broken spear, smashing it against a tree.

"<I told you to tell him to keep a hold of the spear! >" said Tagai.

Ani replied, "<I am telling him your words exactly, but how do you expect me to make him? >"

"<How is he going to hunt without learning our tools? How can I teach him our ways if the most basic of things he refuses to grasp. >"

"<Him grasping seems to be the problem here, >" said Ani, gesturing to the pile of splintered wood. "<Look, he just cannot hunt the same way you do — his hands don't seem to register anything, I mean... anything at all. He puts his hands in fires and ice-water, like he doesn't even understand that they could be dangerous things for a person to put their hands IN. >"

"<It is not about the weapon! It is about discipline, and the boy

does not have it! >"

"<Well how do you expect him to? You've seen him die and come to life and take down hachu that would take weeks for you to hunt with a team of five! What discipline can be given to one without fear? >"

Tagai looked at Toyo and saw that he was upset. It still surprised Tagai that Toyo would so readily look like a beaten puppy — the boy could rip his ribcage apart without a single grunt of effort, yet he still responded like there was something Tagai could do to hurt him. He breathed in deeply in an attempt to collect his thoughts. "<He is... not one of us but must become one of us, >" thought Tagai. He told Ani, "<Ask him why he is here. >"

"He wants to know why you are here," Ani translated to Toyo.

Toyo responded, "Isn't this training? *Valde*, was I supposed to be somewhere else?"

"No... he means, why are you even staying."

"Well you told me that he wants to train me to be a better hunter."

Childish ignorance, or stupidity, was not something Ani had ever learned to cope with. "Look... just FORGET about the training bit. Why haven't you left?"

"What... left the tribe?"

"Yes."

"<What are you talking about? >" Tagai interrupted.

"<Just give me a moment, >" sniped Ani.

Toyo continued, "Why would I leave? You told me that the Ogahigi asked me to become one of them."

"Toyo, you don't even seem happy." The boy just shrugged his shoulders, and Ani sighed before continuing. "Tagai wants to know why you are staying. Should I just tell him you are staying because someone asked?"

"Well, yeah. It's the truth."

Ani turned to Tagai. "<He said he is staying because we told him that the Ogahigi asked him to. >"

"<That is not good enough, there has to be more. >"

Ani turned back to Toyo. "He says there has to be more."

"Why?"

"I assume to Tagai it doesn't make much sense, and I'll admit it doesn't to me either. What if someone else asked you to stay with them? Would you just leave?"

Toyo gave her a shocked look. "Of course not!"

Ani hated trying to herd a conversation but kept the course. "And why is that?"

"I... I have done some pretty bad things. It wouldn't be right for me to leave."

"Who could stop you, Toyo?"

Toyo's patience at being asked stupid questions was wearing thin. "Well what's stopping YOU? You are getting treated worse than I am! I remember when we first met you were barking orders at people all the time."

Ani panicked, knowing that she could never tell him everything. Without thinking she went on the offensive, "This is just what happens when leaders fail, and I failed because I did nothing to stop you!"

Toyo looked like he had been punched in the stomach and was about to cry. "I didn't mean to! I keep telling everyone I didn't know! You don't know what it's like to wake up not knowing anything and only having some boring old woman to talk to!"

Tagai was watching the exchange with interest but belted out a hearty, "<STOP! >" when he saw it getting too heated.

Toyo looked at both Ani and Tagai through the beginnings of his tears and stormed away from the conversation. Ani turned to Tagai and lined up a string of words to defensively explain herself, but was silenced by Tagai's glare.

"<What was his answer? >" Tagai demanded.

"<He... he says it would not be right if he left. I think he is lonely. >"

Tagai looked at the retreating Toyo. "<So, he is human. >"

"<He has been through a lot but still no memories are returning to him. >"

"<The boy knows right and wrong at least. I don't think he knows how to do either though. Perhaps I should teach him that first. >" Tagai then picked up a nearby stone and broke into a short dash, darting through the gnarled trees to find an ideal spot. With ease he pegged the stone at Toyo's foot, and struck it with surprising accuracy and force.

Toyo yelped and looked towards where the stone had been thrown from, only to find nothing except the odd, twisted batch of trees and vines that surrounded him. While he searched in earnest several more stones hit his feet, and the constant pelting from places unknown was really starting to get to him. Eventually he screamed out in frustration, and then Tagai stepped out from behind a tree and walked slowly towards him, pegging him harder and harder with his small handful of stones.

Toyo however did nothing to defend himself — using each fresh pang of pain to bring his blood to boil, daring the hunter to keep going and then they'd see what would happen. They couldn't push him around forever!

Ani was watching the whole time in silence and her eyes almost bugged at the stupidity that Tagai was exhibiting — was he trying to get himself killed? The boy looked ready to kill!

Tagai kept a steady pace, and when he reached Toyo's face he slapped it hard, all the while keeping his own calm. Toyo just stood there, red-cheeked and angry as tears rolled down his face.

"<Why do you not strike back boy? >" Tagai asked.

Toyo's labored breathing and clenched fists made Ani worry — if Tagai were to die then she would surely follow not long after. Tagai slapped the boy hard once more, and did not hold back this time.

Toyo's tears stopped, and only anger was left. "WHAT DO YOU WANT!?" he screamed.

Tagai looked over to Ani, who translated, "<He wants to know what you want. >"

"<I want to know why he does not strike me. >"

"He wants to know why you aren't hitting him."

"Because it's wrong!"

"<He said: Hitting you would be wrong! >"

"<Then ask him what the right thing to do would be. >"

Ani said as calmly as possible, "If that's the wrong thing to do, then what is the right thing?" Toyo's rage subsided and was replaced with complete puzzlement at Ani's question.

While Toyo was still trying to figure out what Ani had meant, Tagai asked, "<Ask him why he wants to be one of us. >"

Ani felt the situation too emotionally charged for interpretation, so translated as direct and literally as possible for the two. Her usual subtle manipulation of words to make conversations go a certain direction was definitely not an option here.

"Because I... I don't want to be alone. I don't want to hurt or kill anyone again," said Toyo.

"<But in time you will have to, that is the nature of life. >"

"Maybe... but if all I can do is kill then I'll be alone! I don't want to be alone!"

"<Then help. >"

"I want to help! Nobody lets me!"

"<No, you wanted to feel useful more than you wanted to be useful. >"

"What does that mean?!"

"<I am sorry to say that only time and reflection can answer that for you. >"

"What? I could just help carry things! Go on hunts! Do what everyone else does!"

"<You aren't like other people, you cannot keep trying to help them in the same way they help each other. Stop forcing yourself to be like them, and stop forcing your help on them. >"

"How can I be one of you if I don't try and help?"

"<You are more powerful than any of us, but that does not mean you have to be alone. >"

LAND OF THE GADORI - CHAPTER X | 427

"Then tell me how! I don't know how to be anything except me? Where do I belong? What is my purpose? What can I DO?!"

"<Protect us, protect everything, and protect everyone. If you do not want to be alone, then protect those that cannot protect themselves. >"

"But... but then I'll just be the boy with the iron gloves."

"<So? I was just the tall hunter who has lost his wife, and now I am just a Yohju — who knows what else I might 'just' be. But all we 'just' are is what people see — do you think how we are viewed is so limiting? There is more to us than what the eyes of others will see, but what is more important is what you want them to see. What do you want them to see, Toyo? >"

"I just want people to like me...."

Tagai sighed and sat down. He offered a place on the ground for both Ani and Toyo and waited for everyone to get comfortable. Without warning he then launched into one of the fondest tales he was told as a child.

"<Before there was life on Kasmah there was only the sky, where lived two great giants — Atmos, the ice giant, and his brother Tiyaou, the fire giant. These two brothers had never gotten along and so fought ferociously, destroying and recreating the land of Kasmah below endlessly through battle. One day Tiyaou wounded Atmos so greatly that it forced him to flee from his sky home. Too afraid to return, Atmos wandered the mountains and valleys for an age, and found peace upon the mountains we now call the Calu-Jedde. Without their constant battle, life began to bloom, and from atop his mountain home Atmos was witness to all its miracles. Trees and birds, insects and worm, man and beast — all were wondrous and beautiful to Atmos, and, in time, he came to admire the land, and the creatures that he would watch be born, grow old, and die. >"

"<Atmos' peace was not endless, for one day Tiyaou saw that his brother had grown weak from living on the ground and began to hurl searing bolts from the sky and laugh. The mountains were no longer safe, so Atmos ran. The ice giant now walked the land, and

as he did he froze the trees, the birds, and the insects as an endless cold descended upon all life. There was nothing that did not suffer from his mighty frost and fear-filled footsteps, which would come crashing every time he thought his fire giant brother had found him. It was tiring, so tiring, to be so filled with fear. It saddened him that all the life that he had found comfort in for so long would flee from him. >"

"<One evening, while Atmos was resting after running again from his brother, a little old man with the thickest coat you could ever imagine caught his attention and asked the giant to look at the land he had just walked upon. 'Why can you not give up your fear?' The giant replied that his fire giant brother in the sky would destroy him, and that he had every right to be afraid. 'You cannot be that powerful if you are ruled by fear', said the old man. >"

"<Angry at being talked at like this by something so small, Atmos said, 'I have more power than you could imagine! Who are you to tell me what I am or not? What have YOU done that is so great?' >"

"<'Do you think that the size of your heart means you have lived or loved more than me?' >"

"<'I have seen your life, and many before you like it. To sit in one place your whole life, rooting yourself to a landscape. Building a home? Tending to the braying and whining of animals' needs? Working tirelessly, only to sleep? Every day the same thing! So that is everything you lived for? That is everything you loved?' >"

"<With a voice filled with sorrow, but never breaking, the old man said, 'I did not live for me,' and gestured for the giant to look at a nearby grave. 'I lived for her. You could stand there and kill an old man, and I see no problem if that is what you want to do, because we all have to make choices. I chose to face my fear and talk to a giant who could crush me on a whim. I also chose to build a home for those that I loved, and I lived with those I loved. I did not run from my fear like you did, I did not kill an ant out of fear. I have heard the tales that you admire this land, but a land that will only want to shun the winter death you bring will not love you in return.' >"

"<The giant Atmos felt in his heart that the man was right and looked high up at the sky and watched the red night-sparks. 'But what if my fear is all that is saving me, or you? What if my brother finds me and destroys me?' >"

"<The old man put on a brave face and replied, 'Do you think your brother finds pleasure in your death, or your fear?' With that the old man reached out his hand. 'Give your brother what he desires most, your fear. Send your fear home, back to the sky, and let an old man try and teach you to love the land, and I promise that we will love you in turn.' >"

"<Atmos looked up at the sky, then down at the old man. >"

"<The old man put on his strongest smile. 'My wife's grave is one of many that you have made, but still I gave to you my fear and anger. I give it to you so you know who I am and know that I do not want your death, I do not want your fear. I want your love, Atmos. All the land does.' He then reached out his hand, and waited. >"

"<Atmos was unsure of everything, he'd been alone with his fear for too long. But, he had finally found a friend. In him, Atmos found the strength to let go of it all, so he took the old man's hand and, sent his fear and powers back to the sky. Soon after, the long winter ended, and many found peace. >"

"<In his grief at losing his brother Tiyaou did not know what to do and simply watched the new life that his brother had chosen. Atmos came to learn love from the old man, and when time claimed him, even Tiyaou let out a mighty cry that burned the lands. The pleasant warmth all had felt, now became scorching, and Atmos saw the things he had loved live in fear once more. >"

"<What Atmos then realized though was that his brother was living in fear of never seeing his brother again, fear of being alone. Sadness filled his heart, so he returned to the sky and became the ice giant once more to save himself, his brother, and the lands below. The brothers tried to work out their differences, however they would still fight. But now they had learned they both had fear, and they would need to abandon it when they fought too greatly, so all below could feel the love of the sun and snow. >" Tagai ended his story with a heavy sigh and a long stare at Toyo.

Feeling that something was expected of him Toyo could only reply with, "I... think I understand."

Ж Ж Ж Ж Ж Ж Ж

After Tagai's story Toyo was excused, and Ani pounced on this opportunity to bring something to light that had been worrying her.

"<We have another problem, >" she said.

Tagai replied, "<Do we? >"

"<He is attracting the attention of some women. >"

This hadn't escaped Tagai's notice and he actually welcomed it as it meant that he was becoming accepted — Toyo had even learned rudimentary greetings, yes and no, good and bad. What he didn't know however was that Ani was intentionally stopping Toyo from learning too much of the Gozuri's tongue lest her own value to them dwindle to expendable. "<Power is attractive Ani, something I am sure you are familiar with. >"

"<You need to think like a Yohju and not a Gozuri man! I know your women get all the say in who they want to be with but you saw how he handles tree climbing and tools, do you really want this young boy to fumble his way through the opposite sex with those hands of his? >"

"<I see your point. But what would you have me do? There are so few women left and we need all the seed and strength we can get. >"

Ani noted Tagai's deference to her returning in the way he talked and wondered if the stress of being Yohju was affecting him. "<Scare them away from him. >"

"<I will not tell my people they are not allowed to interact with him, that would be against the Ogahigi's wishes. >"

"<You have to do SOMETHING. He is a sensitive child and his outbursts have caused a lot of damage whether he meant to or not, what do you expect will happen when he is full of passion for a girl and accidentally rips her arms off? >"

Tagai mused over the possibility and didn't like where it led him. "<Do you truly know nothing about those gloves of his? Or those red... things on his arms? >"

"<I already told you that it is nothing like I have seen before, and he has no information regarding them either. The best I have gotten is that he has said he can't feel anything, that the world seems to move out of the way for them. >"

"<There must be some way — I've seen him use a light touch. >"

"<That apparently requires him to actively think about them 'turning off' in a sense and he can't keep it up forever, you've seen him when he gets worked up. >"

"<Then we will just guide him through it, talk with him. I'm sure he can learn how to control himself properly given time and teaching. >"

"<Or, you could induct him. >"

"<Induct him? He's not even a man yet! >"

"<How else are you going to curb your women seeking his favor and the boy's own natural curiosity in women? >"

"<You would ask me to force upon a child a Hunter's Induction, just so he could not explore what even I was given the good grace and time to do? >"

"<You need to think like a Yohju. What is best for your people? >"

"<I... >" Tagai felt somewhat lost.

"<The boy would become more a part of this tribe if he were to be inducted. >" Tagai digested this information slowly. "<You would be protecting the few women you have left, a boy from heartache lest he destroy something out of passion, and satisfying your Ogahigi's wishes. >"

Tagai's face indicated he was approving of the idea, but his code would not allow him to accept it. "<No, we do not even know if he could handle it. Our stories and ways will show him the path to be one of us. >"

"<And what of his physical needs? >"

"<I am sure the boy knows how to cope with his urges on his own. >"

"<My two problems with that statement are whether or not he even knows what they are yet, and, that if he does, how he would actually satisfy himself. However, if you have any information to satisfy my curiosity I am happy to listen. >"

Tagai replied with, "<... Shit. >"

Both turned their heads to the sound of nearby hurried footsteps and were surprised to find Hoba, panting. He cried, "<He opened the Ogaden! >"

"<What?! What happened!? >" said Tagai jumping to his feet in a panic.

Hoba replied, "<He... talked to her again, and that's it. >"

"<He wouldn't dare! >" Tagai said, outraged. "<What did they say?! >"

"<How would I know?! I don't speak vox! >"

Ani said, "<And why wouldn't he? All you do is teach him how to hunt, so what guidance does he have in being a young boy? >" Ani gave Tagai a look that he had seen many a time before over the years — one of smug acceptance that the world had proved again that she knew the best thing to do.

"<Then YOU can guide him! >"

"<How? I am hardly young anymore, or a boy. >" Her proposal was now looking to be more and more attractive to Tagai. "<If you induct him at this age now, what would be the problem? >"

"<The problem is that I would be robbing him of one of life's joys! He has not even been on a hunt yet, and now I am supposed to make him lose all sexual desire and channel that passion into hunting? That is not a choice HE can make without knowing what he is sacrificing, and for that he would need to experience BOTH. >"

"<If he does not yet have it, then what is he sacrificing exactly? >"

"<But —>"

LAND OF THE GADORI - CHAPTER X | 433

"<I agree, >" interrupted Hoba. Tagai was surprised at hearing this as Hoba had shown only the most rudimentary of courtesies to Toyo, and now was willing to extend this? Wishing to win her argument she pushed onwards. "<You will honor all your obligations this way Tagai. Who knows? With his fresh focus he could eradicate the kusabana spawn. >"

Tagai looked at both of the people he had known and trusted more than any other for so long, and felt trapped for choice. With a voice of defeat he said, "<But what of honoring him? >"

"<All the boy wants is to be accepted. I am sure if you explain the situation to him that he will accept it — you do not have to lie, and all are happy. >"

Hoba and Ani began to throw argument after argument at Tagai, and eventually he held up a palm, silencing them both. "<No, I have been asked to treat him as one of us. He should be given all the respect as we would another of ours. Only if there is another accident that causes true concern will I offer him to be inducted. >"

Ani and Hoba began to argue back but Tagai shot them both the intense stare of a man decisive. "<This is a decision — recognize it for what it is, >" he said with an air of finality. "<Ani, go and accompany Toyo — Hoba, come with me. It is time we gave Toyo some experience. >"

Ani wandered off with a sour look on her face and rubbing her chest. When Hoba felt like she was far enough he said to Tagai, "<We have only just started our new camp and are hardly prepared to risk —>" but he was waved to silence once more.

"<The Ogagi's flowering will bring dangers to us regardless of our wishes, and if we have any hopes now they lay in the boy. We must ready him. >"

"<Why can we not just let the hachu fight amongst themselves? It has worked for us so far. >"

Tagai sighed. It had been a tiring day and it didn't look like it was going to get any easier anytime soon. "<I will not leave our survival to chance, and our people need some hope. Prepare some Seibutsu-Mihame for a hunt. >"

Hoba knew the signs and stopped pestering his brother-in-love. "<Understood, I will go prepare our rations. >"

"<Make enough for three. >"

"<What? You are seriously considering taking the boy out already? You said training! >"

"<What better training is there beyond the real thing? Besides, his body doesn't need training, but maybe the fear of some creatures will force him to think better. Also, the boy has a name, it's Toyo — it is time you came to accept him already. >"

"<He has no training! And what do you think is going to happen if we give him some seibutsu-mihame?! Giving him one of our most powerful concoctions to join us on a hunt that he has NO skill for is tantamount to stupidity! >"

Tagai casually said, "<Would you rather him stay here and explore our women? >"

Hoba had seen how Toyo looked at Nume as she lay nestled in the Ogagi, and knew his desire to pursue a woman would come soon. He nodded his head in acceptance of the task, fighting back his snap response and deciding that perhaps it would be best if this outsider were to join them, and who knows? Maybe he'd die out there and then there would be some justice. It seemed far more appealing than dealing with the stress of Toyo's interest in women.

Tagai then asked Hoba, "<Why does Ani keep rubbing her chest these days? Is she ill? >"

"<I don't know. Old age, probably. >"

Ж Ж Ж Ж Ж Ж Ж Ж Ж Ж Ж Ж Ж Ж Ж

"*OK, so... so I'm a big scary... thing,*" thought Toyo as he walked around the camp trying to pay careful attention to everyone to see if they needed anything. Tagai's story rattled around in his brain and whenever he thought he understood a part of it, it slipped away from him as if refusing to be caught. It didn't help that the few girls near his age that were there only seemed to giggle at him and run away when he tried to help. That hurt him most of all, as he was reminded of Nume's death, and all he wanted to do was be able to talk to her.

Toyo sat down, unable to stop his downward spiral. *"Why are they so afraid of me? I'm helping now aren't I? I know I did bad, but now I'm doing good! I'm really trying! It isn't fair!"* His thoughts turned to anger, and just as he felt like going to his tent and punching the ground to relieve his stress, Ani spotted him sitting near the Ogagi garden and wandered over.

"Hello Toyo," said Ani.

Toyo snapped back with, "What do you want?" The old lady was not someone he really wanted to talk to right now. She never had any good advice unless it was something she deemed 'practical' and talked in such a specific way that made him feel stupid.

"Thought you might like a conversation, can't be that easy finding people to talk to around here can it?"

"Well for your information I CAN go talk to the lady in the tree, and she is much more interesting than talking to you."

"Yes, I heard about that. I would advise against repeating that."

"Why?"

"The Ogahigi is sacred to them. Though they won't stop you, it still upsets them."

Toyo threw his hands up. "Like everything else I do! I have brought food for people to eat, helped with cracking open animal shells and hides, removed trees — I'm not hurting her! It's just talking!"

"Yes, but they don't know that."

"All they can understand is that some pale boy with iron hands is talking to their most sacred person, not what is being said."

"But they can SEE that I'm not doing anything else!"

Practicality. That's what Ani needed. Looking around the garden she saw the wide variety of fruits the Gozuri would plant at every Ogagi for their own sustenance and got an idea. "Let's take this garden for example. Have you ever seen its caretaker?"

"The old man? Yeah, he gave me something from here to eat once. He was nice."

"Good, now have you ever seen him burn, rip out, or cut any of the plants here?"

"Not up close, but, yeah, I've seen him do things."

"Do you think when he does those things that it is good or bad?"

Toyo shrugged. "I don't know."

"There, see? Unless you can ask it is very difficult to know if someone is doing good or bad, and the Gozuri don't know what your talking with the Ogahigi 'is'. She is *very* important to this tribe Toyo, do you understand that?"

"Well yes, but that —"

"That means that she was here before you, and they were here before you. You can't just go around doing whatever you like."

"But I'm not! I'm just trying to not... be alone."

"Why? Being alone isn't so bad — you can get used to it."

"My first memory I have of being alive is waking up scared and alone and dying. I thought I was the only person that existed! And then I met these people, then I thought I was the only one that could speak my language, and then you spoke to me. What is so wrong of me to expect the next thing to happen is for me to find someone to be a little closer than that?"

Ani dreaded her next question but had to ask it. "Are you talking about sex?"

"What's that?"

"... Are you joking?"

"Why would I be joking?" said Toyo, his face radiating innocence.

"Well... yes." Ani recalibrated her approach. "Are you saying you don't know why all the girls are running away from you?"

Toyo'd had enough of feeling stupid. "Look I don't really get what you are talking about and I don't see why it is so important. You get to talk to everyone so of course you don't feel alone like I do."

"I'm far from the most popular person in the tribe at the

moment."

"So? At least they don't run away from you!" Ani considered Toyo's position and almost felt a sort of pity for him. "It would just be nice to be able to help people."

"Well, you can help."

"How? All they do is run away!"

"Do you remember those creatures at the last Ogagi?"

Toyo's mind went to a dark place. It was still hard to ignore his regret, and the creatures that he had seen that day kept cropping up in his mind from time to time. "Yes."

"Those creatures are unnatural and should never exist, and were the reason I even left the Integrum in the first place. The Gozuri's life revolves around ensuring those creatures are snuffed out from existence." That last statement stuck to Toyo's mind and he wondered if there was something he could do about that.

"You... you keep talking of this Integrum place. You keep talking about a lot of things, but you don't TELL me anything. I thought you were supposed to teach me?"

"Well yes, but we have been rather busy. If *you* don't remember, we have had —"

"Look, I know! I did something bad! But... but I just want to know things now. I can't help people if I don't know anything, can I?"

Ani sighed heavily. "What do you want to know?"

Toyo looked longingly towards the Ogaden and pointed. "What is her name?"

"I do not know, I have only known her to be called the Ogahigi."

"Ogahigi? But that's not a name."

"I do not think they name their Ogahigis, and if they have... well, nobody here has ever talked to her before."

"Why did she choose to live in that stump?"

"There used to be many Ogahigis, there still might be some lost. But everyone who chooses to become an Ogahigi has to live in that stump."

"Why? Did she do something bad?"

"No, she is a sacred thing. But also I don't think she can survive outside the stump or fend for herself, that is why everyone lives to protect her."

"Why? What does she do?"

"In all the years I have been here, nothing that I am aware of. I have asked countless times but nobody ever told me, and the one time I tried to figure it out for myself ended with a poor outcome. The only information I've ever garnered from the Ogahigi is that she asked YOU to be accepted to be a part of this tribe."

"How can she be sacred and do nothing?"

"How can you have legs but not be running right now? A function is a subset of you, *non vice versa*."

"... What?"

Ani shook her head, realizing that talking in vox after all these years was making her fall into the old patterns of the Quadra Logicum. "Sorry, forget I said that."

He shrugged his shoulders and brought up something that had been nagging at him. "If the Gozuri's life is about killing those things, then why haven't they done any of that so far?"

"They have had more important things to tend to, such —"

"Such as training me, you mean."

Ani waved her hand dismissively, hoping to derail him from that topic. "More importantly, I brought up...." Ani's voice trailed off as she noticed Toyo had a faraway look. She waved her hand in front of his face. "Hello?"

Toyo turned to look at her directly. "So people will like me if I kill all those beasts?" he asked with a naive desire that made Ani feel sorry for him.

"Well if you want it put so bluntly, yes —" Ani was interrupted by Toyo walking away all of a sudden. "You know it is quite rude to leave a conversation mid-way!" she shouted out after him. He didn't respond so she tried to jog after him, but the pain in her chest caused her to cough and splutter. "Where are you going?!"

"To belong!" Toyo shouted back in excitement as he ran off into the thick forest.

She screamed after him in vain. "You stupid boy! That's not how this works!"

INTEGRUM

Erus Criso sat in her chambers of office, growing increasingly worried at Seconsulo's news. "My Erus, there have been some minor riots in the streets. We will need to ask for help from the Quadras if we wish to quell the rabble."

"No. Violence is how Ardeo handled things, and there would be no love gained from a punch. People are expected and encouraged to be excited before the Taker's Procession — are the girls ready for their appearance yet?" replied Erus Criso.

"Almost."

"Who is this year's favorite in the betting pools?"

"Tari."

"Hm... I would have thought Clarus would have been, given her demonstration to that —" Criso summoned as much venom as she could before uttering, "Public committee."

"People are sometimes difficult to persuade."

"You'd be amazed at what you can achieve with a pair of tits, Seconsulo."

"As you say Erus Criso. Shall I calm the crowd with tits?"

She inspected his face for any sign of humor. "... If I didn't know you any better Seconsulo I would say you were attempting to make a joke." She waved her hand dismissively. "It is not a wholly stupid idea, but, no — they can just sit and stir and let their emotions build. They'll have their outlet soon enough. Go now, make sure the girls are ready on time. If they don't start their procession at noon I will hold YOU accountable."

"Very well," said Seconsulo, and left to make swift the preparations for the day ahead. It had to go perfectly and without a hitch, and there was no doubt in his mind that he could deliver for his mistress that perfection.

The day of this Ardeo Trial had begun like those before it — with grand streamers and banners galore, and with the First Ring of

Orbis filling with people who were there to lap up the air of celebration. This year's turnout was far more than expected — numbers bolstered by those who thought news regarding the Integra Pol would be released, and many just to be comforted by being part of a group and feeling safe during these troubled times.

But the Taker's Procession was not until noon, and that was time for all the other Quadras to get as much attention as possible. Musicians would play, bakers would bake, and professors would lecture all outside their Quadras to their own fanfare in the hopes to entice people inside and while away the hours. Normally it was a battle between the Quadras for attention, but the huge crowd made it so all were brimming over with people eager to forget about their worries.

The Taker's Procession, the time when each Taker would be paraded around the First Ring of Orbis in full glory, was going to need extra guards to create a wide enough berth through the throng of people and did cause some delay. An irritating, but necessary, delay. Criso just hoped that everything would go smoothly enough so that afterwards there would be enough candidates, who were young and of their first love, who would come forth and register their desire to partake.

In Ardeo's time the Takers were objectified and locked in cages for all to see, a spectacle only for the most cowardly of spectator or cruel of heart. The Lovers themselves had no rules to ensure fairness or safeguard against the wiles of expert Lustrum charges.

Criso had gotten to make what she felt to be the most significant change, which was that nobody entering the trial could be a virgin — Ardeo had cared little for such particulars and thought it funny that some would be deflowered. An indifference that had led to many Lovers leaving the trial with souls broken after being subjected to things unknown. From a cruel spectacle for the wealthy elite to watch young love die — Erus Criso transformed it into what it should have always been, a way for the young to know if their love was real.

It had taken years, but eventually Criso made the Ardeo Trial an artistic and beloved spectacle for all to respect — if only she could just change the damn name without public opinion thinking that the trial would be 'softer' somehow.

Today was not the time to gripe about that however, and Criso surely had enough on her plate of 'now' to complain about the past or the future. She was at least thankful that public fear of the drug creba, reports of which had been increasing steadily, and questions of what happened to the Integra Pol were washed away in light of the festivities. Something that had been aided by the collusion and insistence from all the Quadras that everything was under control and that there was nothing to worry about.

Ж Ж Ж Ж Ж Ж Ж Ж Ж Ж Ж Ж Ж Ж Ж

Mulat found a simple pleasure in cleaning up after the disaster alongside the servants of the Integra Pol, but it did not take long for the work to disappear. He tried to indulge himself in the listless servants, but with nobody to occupy the Integra Pol they had found themselves without purpose. Many soon began to splinter off to serve a nearby Quadra, usually chosen by proximity when the notion struck them, and filled the Quadras' ranks with docile and obedient servants. The few who remained and knew of Mulat's survival meekly urged him to take command again out of despair at how abandoned and lifeless their once proud tower stood. Mulat however was reluctant to occupy the tower again — his assailant was still unknown, and the reasons for the attack he only half understood.

All he could do was spend his evenings idly watching the night-sparks, lost in his thoughts — most of them dark. He wondered if Stagnos was right to create him in the face of everything that had happened, and how quickly everything had fallen to pieces without him. Perhaps Stagnos was right to do nothing all those years, to let the Integrum east of the Vios Ocean fend for itself against the Gadori incursion. Maybe all Integra Divinitas' are destined to be a figurehead and nothing more. People should lead people. The reports of public opinion that reached his ears did not indicate that they missed him or the Integra Pol in any real sense and only of minor confusion as to the events.

Then again perhaps the upcoming Ardeo Trial was simply occupying public interest. Criso was no doubt giving all her attentions to ensure that was the case, and she had proven time and time again that she was a most adept Erus of the Quadra Lustrum.

ЖЖЖЖЖЖЖ

"My Erus'! I am to be the new Integra Divinitas," Mulat announced loudly. Everyone gave him a stare of combined awe and pessimism from their seats around the table. "I have chosen this place for this meeting as it is a neutral place where you can all feel at ease." Many of them wanted to point out that the decor certainly matched — everything from the floor to the ceiling was bone white.

What held their attentions however were the ornate boxes placed in front of each of them. Were they gifts? Since when did an Integra Divinitas give gifts?

"I am aware of your doubts as the time between Stagnos' recent passing and my succession to his stead has been quite lengthy, along with the fact Stagnos' years were, in many regards, self-indulgent and reclusive. Still, I am the new fork in the road and I wish to inform you all of my desire to break the cycle of the Integra Pol's mostly superficial role." The Erus' weren't expecting this and they all raised their eyebrows in surprise.

"This is my sincerest wish, but, as tradition dictates, I am not Erus of the Integra Pol or an Integra Divinitas if I cannot be accepted by you all. So, to each I will provide the two most powerful things imaginable — knowledge," he paused briefly, "And perspective." He scanned the room's reaction with excited expectation.

The gathered Erus' looked at each other with expressions of uncertainty — yes, tradition did dictate how things were done, but the Integra Divinitas' were always the ones that dictated tradition! Furthermore they had heard Mulat was more powerful than all who had come before him, so why was he bothering trying to win them over? Why the show? The fear they all shared from his spectacle and invitation was that he was going to turn out to be another madman, and nobody wanted to deal with that.

Mulat pressed on. "The best thing that combines these two elements is, simply, time." The room returned blank stares, but he was unfazed by their lack of response. Patience was something he had learned very early on, and patience was easy to have when he knew that if he was so inclined he could destroy anyone here with little effort. Everyone else knew it as well, and he still hoped that they would accept him on merit and value — not from fear or tradition.

Turning to Erus Ictus, Mulat said, "The Quadra Musicum! For the lovers of sound and its form. Many find joy in percussion before growing to a love more refined of instruments complex — audiences start with shanties, and age to love arrangements. This is how time, music, and people grow together, but here I gift you the knowledge that the love of sound lies in more than just us." Mulat opened the box in front of Erus Ictus and from it produced a small green frog that he placed on the table. It sat there comfortably while the weight of all the available attention in the room bore down on it. It went *ribbit*.

The Erus', while collectively experiencing both fear and interest, felt even more lost than before. "Now, if I show it..." Mulat reached over to the box closest to Erus Ardeo and produced from it another frog. "The opposite gender they will, as you can hear, sing." The two frogs *ribbited* excitedly to one another and lazily hopped around the table.

"So... my gift is a frog?" asked Ictus.

Erus Ardeo quickly said, "I... uh, like my frog," eager to please the biggest dog in the room. His attempts to be slick were no different than how he styled his hair: overeager and unnecessary. Ardeo had been handsome his whole life, with his cut jaw and strong features, but he somehow always had the need to be more, like some fear always hung over his shoulder.

Mulat gave them both a look of pure perplexion. "What? Oh, no, not quite. Just listen." He then took out a strange sphere with a seam along its middle and placed it between the two frogs. As he gently began to turn it he kept talking, all the while the frogs' ribbits began to slow down. "You see everything lives in, and experiences, its own time. It is hard for a person to escape their own perception of time, let alone experience the time of another, but all life shares a pattern. That is why we grow from percussion to performances, Erus Ictus — from when a child first beats a drum, to the mastering of the viola or clarinet. That is a thing you have seen many times before, but to you, my Erus Ictus, I show you the music of these frogs."

Mulat then gave the sphere a hard, sharp twist and let go. The sphere began to spin faster and faster, all on its own. The *ribbits* of the frogs slowed as if in opposition and soon a before unheard melody began to reach everyone's ears. It grew slowly until it began to sound like a strange foreign singer bellowing out a hymn, low and sonorous but with intricacies that felt both enchanting and alien for them all. Ictus was mesmerized by the sounds and leaned in closer in amazement, but then Mulat gripped the sphere, stopping it instantly, and soon the song was gone, replaced once more by *ribbit*. Ictus looked at Mulat with pleading wide eyes, why did he stop the beautiful music?

Mulat was pleased with Ictus' reaction — he wasn't quite sure how he would have taken it. "We hear music in our own way, because we experience time in our own way. I wanted to show you the time of other things and the music within them. Time measures music in the heartbeats of everything — I showed you the heartbeats of these frogs." Ictus looked at the frog and sphere with a look of extreme focus and concentration — Ardeo meanwhile was beginning to get excited at what his frog would do for him.

Mulat then turned to Erus Epula and said, "To you, Erus Epula, I wish to give you," he placed in front of him the frog from the box that was in front of Ardeo — whose face turned into a scowl like a child seeing someone get a toy he really wanted, and thought to himself, "*Why did he put it in front of me if it wasn't FOR me?*"

Epula eyed the frog suspiciously. He was a proud, stout man, and wasn't about to let some fresh-blood educate HIM about HIS specialty. "... This? I already know every flavor you could get from this, and which breed would give you the best one! There is no man that knows better than me how long you should roast anything — from a fly to a goat. What so-called 'time' of this creature can you show me? Or are you going to make me 'taste what it can taste'?" Epula's arrogant tone caused a wave of shocked expressions.

"Erus Epula, there is little I could teach you about food, nor any here about their chosen profession. I am only here to prove my value."

Epula deflated a little, both from relief and seeing that he was wrong. "... So what does the frog have to do with it?"

"Oh, nothing. Ardeo just seemed smitten with it so I wished to redirect his attention to you." Everyone tried very, very hard to not look at the Erus of the Quadra Lustrum, while he himself coughed loudly and smoothed the front of his shirt with practiced nonchalance. Mulat reached over and grasped the frog from Epula's hands gently and clasped his own hand shut on it, slamming with such force that a loud bang startled everyone. He then rolled his palms together and formed a small ball out of what once was frog and placed it in front of Erus Ardeo, who perked up. "Please, wait your turn Erus Ardeo." He coughed a little.

Returning his focus to Epula, Mulat said, "I have heard that you have neglected the people more and more over the years. As Erus of the Quadra Culinum you are charged with ensuring that the public knows good and bad food, how to prepare it, and why."

Epula wasted no time defending himself. "What of it? We have our basic information available to all and we make it available as required. I have broken no rule or law."

Mulat began to pace around the room and spoke as if trying to understand a concept in a foreign tongue. "Yet, you beat a man that did not... appreciate a meal that you had prepared for him."

"The impotent buffoon had the audacity to say that my meal was not," Epula shuddered, "Tasty."

"This warrants you beating him to within an inch of his life?"

Epula stood up and banged his fist on the table. "The people are idiots! I cannot sacrifice MY life's passion on people who cannot appreciate the elegance of both the creation and consumption of a galantine!" The Erus' visibly pressed themselves into the back of their chairs, each not wanting to associate themselves with this suicidal man.

Mulat allowed Epula the time to realize that his outburst was most probably ill-advised before gesturing for him to sit down again. When Epula had returned to his seat, Mulat once more paced and talked. "I only consume the most basic of foods and do not indulge in the senses, which may lead you to believe me to be ignorant of greater things — of the love people have for the sweet and savory. One might also conclude that the richer the food, the finer the palate must be in order to appreciate it. For example the more layers to the sauces and marinades you have then the more your brain has to process, and if you haven't experienced so many layers before one cannot appreciate all the nuance." Mulat paused, distracted by a thought. "I believe this is why the expression 'Death by chocolate' exists." He shook his head. "Still... simplicity is powerful, and some people pervert simplicity by deifying 'complexity' without remembering that something complex is merely a lot of simple put together."

Epula'd had enough of his rambling. "What ARE you talking about?"

Mulat stood still and looked at him. "I fear your palate has grown too complex to understand what you would call 'the commoner'. You have forgotten that food is a fuel first, and a pleasure second."

"So? It is only natural to grow to aspire for greater things!"

"Yes, it is. Sometimes though we forget our station, and in our growth we lose sight of purpose...." A long silence hung heavy in the air. "Do you wish to remain as Erus of the Quadra Culinum, Epula?"

Roused, Epula leaned forward and asked, "Is this a threat?"

"No, I have no need nor want to threaten any of you. I said that all these were gifts — this is only a question."

"Of course I do!"

"Excellent news! A Quadra Erus serves the people of the Integrum through their charges, and perfects their own art via their own passion — know that I would never change that. My gift, is perspective." He then gestured to Epula to open the box in front of him. Inside it Epula found a simple slice of bread, and a cup of water. "Do you reject my gift?" asked Mulat. Epula hesitantly took the items from the box and placed them in front of him. As the gaze of all those in the room bore into him, he decided to go along with the stupid charade and ate the meager slice of bread and washed it down with the cup of water. Mulat smiled. "Thank you Erus Epula, I trust you will serve your Quadra well in the future with your new-found perspective." What was the man prattling on about?

Mulat addressed Erus Adsum next, and Ardeo began to grow impatient — why was he being taunted so? "My Erus Adsum, your gift, I trust you will appreciate more than anyone else here. I will not bore you with a diatribe of words, your thoughts and conjectures surpass most, and no doubt you got bored several minutes into this meeting. However, you are Logicum, your experiments and constant pursuit to improve on what we know and to strive for things we do not is immutable. I cannot give you knowledge nor perspective, so to you I merely give that which your Quadra Logicum enjoys bearing witness to most: change." Erus Adsum merely nodded his head in acceptance, giving nothing away about what he was thinking or feeling. "Please, open your box and accept your gift."

Adsum opened the box and found inside a vial filled with some sort of liquid. Mulat saw Adsum attempting to analyze its contents, and decided to help him out by saying, "My gift to you is not complete unless you pour it onto the frog-ball I made for Erus Ardeo."

Adsum took the mixture and inspected it — being unable to deduce anything of value from it he went over to the frog-ball in front of Ardeo and coated it with the liquid, then went back to his chair and waited patiently. Ardeo was slightly nervous — he had long known of Adsum's experiments and lack of empathy, but as this was all Mulat's doing there was no way Adsum could play any trick. Even with that assurance in his mind, he was still a little uneasy. Mulat finally turned to Ardeo. "My Erus Ardeo." He fell silent and Ardeo wondered if he was supposed to say something. "Out of all the Quadras, yours is the one that needs my help the most, and so I will grant you the hardest gift it is for me to give." Ardeo grinned wildly, this was more like it! "As Erus of the Quadra Lustrum," Mulat gestured to the frog-ball, "Will you accept its gift?"

Ardeo nodded with as much grace as he could exude and excitedly grabbed for the frog-ball, wondering what amazing thing it could be. Upon first touch he was deeply surprised at the texture — it was very familiar. After rolling it around in his hands and squeezing it a while, he realized that it felt exactly like the inside of a woman. Mulat said nothing and simply watched Ardeo investigate the strange object. Probing the ball with his fingers Ardeo found it to be very elastic, and that it got warmer the more he fondled it. A dark curiosity got the better him and he plunged a finger inside — he found it to be a pleasurable, moist, and warm experience, and immediately thought of four different ways he could use this in his debauchery.

Mulat interrupted his playtime with, "Thank you, Erus Ardeo, for accepting this gift on behalf of the Quadra Lustrum." Ardeo looked at Mulat confused as he kept playing with the ball, he wasn't quite sure if this was all there was to it but wasn't about to confront him like Epula had. All the while Adsum was watching him intently and trying to analyze the changes.

"Now, to the rest of the Quadras, I gift a second chance. I know what you have all done in Stagnos' apathy, and how you have used his name to defend your actions and choices. Ultimately you have all, bar one, served your Quadra in the capacity that your Quadra required you to." Epula didn't enjoy feeling like he had been put on the spot but said nothing as he was a little distracted by Ardeo now shaking his hand hard. The frog-ball appeared to be stubbornly stuck to his fingers.

"I hope all of you approve of your gifts, and accept me as Integra Divinitas." There was a hurried chorus of approval, tinged with slight confusion as to everything that had just happened. "Thank you. So today I say: I will endeavor to restore you all to your full glory — heal the Integrum lands ravaged from the Gadori incursion, and repair the relations damaged with the Integrum lands east of the Vios Ocean due to Stagnos' lethargy in sending aid — and renew trade with the Maharaan Expanse. While I may do these things in a style you are not accustomed to please understand that I will do my best."

Ardeo couldn't handle it anymore and started to swear as he slammed the frog-ball onto the table in the hopes to get it off. He screamed loudly as the ball viciously contracted around his hand and clamped down hard, its form shifting rapidly against his skin. It bored under the surface of his hand, and the gelatinous form quickly traveled up Ardeo's flailing arm as terror crossed his face. It burrowed its way up his elbow, across his shoulder, and from there straight into his heart. His head fell heavy onto the table, and all the Erus', save for Adsum, backed away from the table and watched the horrific scene unfold.

"Yes… change," muttered Adsum when Ardeo's screams had stopped. Looking at Mulat he said, "Thank you for the gift."

Mulat replied, "You are most welcome, Erus Adsum."

"My apologies Integra Divinitas Mulat, but what was the knowledge and perspective for Erus Ardeo?" asked Adsum.

"His gift was that sometimes time cannot redeem a man and a new perspective must be granted, but as I said the gift was for his Quadra. As my first act as Integra Divinitas, I appoint Lady Criso as the new Erus of the Quadra Lustrum."

Adsum nodded his head lightly, while the other Erus' finally clued in that Mulat was not the idiot he appeared to be.

༄༄༄༄༄༄༄༄༄༄༄༄༄༄

Tensions rose in the high noon sun as the heat and proximity of others began to rub the public nerve raw. Respect for the celebration stopped it from getting out of hand, as all had turned up to do their best to enjoy and cheer on the young lovers that dared enter this year's controversial Ardeo Trial.

A peal of bells rang out from every Quadra. The conversations and arguments of everyone in the streets were pushed out by the sheer weight of the noise but soon the bells themselves were drowned out by the legion of feet, shuffling their way to get a good view of the Lustrum. Another loud peal rang out five minutes later and Erus Criso stepped out onto the outer balcony, garbed in such fashion that would make any vain person proud. A third peal rang out, silencing the crowd completely.

With grand hand gestures Erus Criso addressed the crowd. "Ladies and Gentlemen! This year I present for your approval the Taker, my own flesh and blood, Tari Scor!" The large front doors to her Quadra swung open, and all could see Tari standing proudly naked on her platform, raised high. She was carried out into the main street to the cheers and whoops of the crowd. Tari smiled and flaunted herself as much as possible as she was carried off left to circle the Quadras, and the doors closed behind her.

Erus Criso allowed herself a few minutes after Tari was out of sight before ringing her personal bell — small though it was, the crowd fell silent once more. With her public speaking voice, Criso said, "And a newcomer to our Lustrum, proven to be a potent mixture of passion and beauty, this year's Taker." Erus Criso paused briefly for effect, before saying as demurely as she could, "Clarus Prae."

This time the doors were opened gently, revealing Clarus sitting naked on her platform, but holding a grace that Tari could only ever hope to achieve. Very little was known about Clarus to the public compared to Tari, so many did not know what to expect, but all were blown back by the poise and innocence that this woman exuded — almost too pure to touch. Silence followed in her wake as she was carried off to the right to circle the Quadras, and the doors to the Quadra Lustrum closed once more.

With both Takers dispatched Criso felt some relief, but the day had just begun. "Today is a day of celebration, and to prove to the world that there is love pure! I trust that you will all in kind show each other the type of love you would want in the spirit of today." She turned to leave the balcony, paused a moment, turned back, and said, "If however you don't know what kind of love you would like to experience, I hope you will all allow me and my charges to show you every kind of *love* there is." As soon as she finished talking the doors to the Lustrum opened once more, and a large number of her charges walked out onto the streets, stroking and grasping the hands of any willing to be led into the Lustrum. Unsurprisingly, very few resisted.

Once again Criso saw her male charges highly sought after amongst the crowd, by both man and woman, and felt a sense of pride. She would have loved to have seen the look on Ardeo's face when she openly promoted male charges, and watched his smug face turn to confusion when it turned out to not only be highly profitable but welcomed — after the public's slow coming to terms with it. That man held little esteem in love, only himself and his debauched desires. Criso understood that there was little difference between a man or a woman and when it came to sex all had desires both mental and physical, but ultimately all merely wished to be desired and express their own freely.

She recalled a conversation once with Erus Adsum who had said, "From a body mass perspective gender difference would account for less than one percent of a human. Interestingly though from my tests that one percent contains approximately seventy-five percent of the pleasure nerves associated with sex, but I have yet to find any true gender specific reaction to sexual stimulation." Criso had thought that a fancy way of saying, "Fingers and tongues have no gender in the dark," and for a moment thought the man's renowned brilliance to be warranted, but it was still the kind of intelligence you could never feel safe around.

Both Tari and Clarus were carried around the Quadras three times before being returned to the Lustrum where they were taken directly to be confined in the Taker's rooms — where they would wait until a brave couple would dare test their affections. After the procession Criso made her way out onto the First Ring where a special area had been set up for prospective couples to express their interest. Sitting in her designated chair and protected from the sun, she felt it strange that there wasn't the usual long lineup, in fact there was nobody. She did her best to fret quietly and kept smiling as invitingly as possible. A few of the usual attempts from older couples and others who obviously had no innocence left presented themselves in vain, but she humored them as long as possible in the hopes that anyone who was truly eligible would be encouraged by the bravery of others. The few times that any promising couple did come close they merely hovered near with their hands clenched tightly together, but ultimately walked away.

The day passed by quickly and now it was nearing dusk, and as she watched the sun sink her hopes followed suit. She wanted to find comfort in her constant companion Seconsulo, standing by her all this time with a dull expression on his face, but there was none to be found. What was happening? Normally there would be dozens of valid applicants and it would come down to a raffle to see who would be chosen as the Lovers of the Ardeo Trial. Silently she cursed and wondered if youthful desire to prove oneself to the world may have been diluted by the recent reports of violence, Mulat's death, and the vacant Integra Pol. The reach and influence of the Quadras was far, but information would always be a slippery fish to hold tight. The crowd had grown bored and thinned long ago when they saw so few applicants and instead had chosen to fill the Lustrum or amuse themselves with the other Quadras' attempts to capitalize on the big day.

Finally some hope arrived in the form of a very young couple — who to Criso looked like they could not have been any older than sixteen. Stepping nervously forward, the young man and woman announced their intent to participate — Criso had to stop herself from lunging forward and bursting into laughter from the tension she had bottled up. She put on her best face and gestured for them to come forward. She asked the usual bevy of questions, but in a far kinder and gentler fashion than usual, while Seconsulo dutifully wrote their answers down.

"May I know your names?" asked Criso.

The young girl scooted slightly behind her man's shoulders while at the same time trying to give off an air of confidence. The young man said, "I am Laris." It was a while before he realized that his partner was not going to say anything. "And this is Ilia, she is my true love."

Criso ignored the bravado. "Wonderful. Please tell me Laris and Ilia, how old are you?"

"We are both nineteen," he replied, with all the false confidence and machismo a young man could muster. Criso was slightly surprised at hearing this and decided to quickly kill her follow-up question — even though she was sure they were lying she had no time to be picky.

"Are you two first lovers?"

"Yes, we are. We do not want to be with anyone else." Criso noted that Laris had become the spokesperson for both as his Ilia clung close to his shoulder, demure as a fawn.

"Have you celebrated your love?" asked Criso.

A blank expression crossed Laris' face. "... What do you mean?"

"I'm sorry, I meant to ask are you both virgins?"

"No."

"Did you both watch the Taker's Procession?"

"Yes."

"Do you understand what you risk to lose and gain by participating?"

"Yes," he replied again with youthful ignorance.

"Then please explain it to me."

"We... uh... we get separated, and then —"

Criso shook her head and waved her hand. "That wasn't the question, I asked do you understand what you risk to lose and gain." Both of them remained silent, unsure of how to respond. "You risk your love being found false, and what you might gain is knowledge that nothing can break it. What you risk and gain is each other. Do you understand and accept this?"

"Um... wasn't there some sort of... prize?"

"You are competing for the money?"

"No! Well, not just for the money. We want to start a life together, and our being together isn't really approved of, so this... seemed...." The boy's confidence waned and he wafted into silence.

"Oh, I understand. Of course there is a monetary prize and lifetime access to all the Quadras and their teachings, but that is only if you succeed. In order to pass you have to stand before me one month from now, after you have spent your time separated in the Taker's rooms with your respective Takers, and prove to me that you both feel the same about each other." They both looked at each other uncertainly. "Do you still wish to enter?"

Laris confidently replied, "Yes."

"Very well." Criso turned her focus directly to the girl trying to paradoxically both hide and show strength. "You have said nothing and let your man speak for you. I cannot accept you as a couple if I do not have understanding and consent from you both. Your Taker is a woman, a first in the history of this trial, and my own daughter. Do you understand and accept all the information that has been placed before you today?"

"... Yes," said the girl meekly.

Criso sighed heavily. She could see their story written all over their faces — two people brought together by rejection of their home and environment. A love that she knew would always end in tragedy. With the slightest hint of remorse in her heart she said, "Then I congratulate you both and wish you the best of luck. You are this year's Ardeo Trial Lovers. Please follow Seconsulo."

The pair were shocked. "Wait, what? Isn't there some sort of test or something?"

"Yes, you passed."

Laris' brow furrowed. "... What was it?"

"Something that you passed. The only way to do that is for me to find your relationship to be genuine and true. I see no fault in you or your partner's claim that this is your first and only romantic relationship. I am the only test you need pass."

"Oh... but... last year there —"

"Do you really wish to question your acceptance further?"

Defeated, Laris said, "Um... no."

"Excellent! Please follow Seconsulo. We must announce you as this year's Lovers, after which you will be separated. One month is what we ask — we will provide everything for you, and ensure that whatever job or responsibility you sacrifice to partake in this will be looked after in your absence. If at any point either of you wish to abandon the trial, just say so and your Taker will make themselves scarce, however regardless of what happens or what you want you will both spend the month in your room. I only ask that you should remember that at the end of all this there is no judgment from us — you alone will judge yourselves more than enough. In either case you will be seen by the public once more, lovers or not, for all to witness." The couple bowed nervously, then were led away by Seconsulo to be prepared for display to the public on the grand balcony of the Lustrum.

Watching them be escorted away brought Criso some hope, but she still needed to wait until the sun dipped low — the signal thatced the time for applicants had ceased.

When the time came Criso quickly made her way to her chambers and did not allow any expression of relief until she got inside, and even then only one long drawn out breath was all she could afford. She couldn't let herself fall to pieces now. Freshening her makeup and putting on a new dress she hurried to make herself presentable for the Lovers announcement, and she gave herself a cursory inspection before rushing back to the grand balcony. The public of Orbis had grown bored! On the day of the Ardeo Trial! All her planning to secure her Quadra's future would be for naught if she lost the public's interest. She needed this to WORK.

Pacing behind the doors to the balcony overlooking the First

Ring, Criso impatiently asked, "Where are they?"

"First time jitters, My Erus. They are almost ready," replied Seconsulo.

"Damn it man, bring them here NOW!" she demanded, and he rushed off, hastened by his Erus' agitated state.

Haggard and nervous, the couple were swiftly brought before Criso, who quickly gave them a look over to ensure presentability and nodded her head in approval. She gave the signal to rouse the bell ringers, and she felt calm when they sounded off the first peal. "*Just wait...*" she said to herself, and soon she could hear the crowd behind the doors. The second peal rang out and Criso could hear the crowd outside start to increase in volume.

Laris said, "Aren't we supposed to...."

"Just wait a moment dear, anticipation can be as good as the release," replied Criso.

Laris gave Ilia a look of confusion and they exchanged a nervous smile while they held hands.

When the third peal rang out she whispered to herself, "And now for the release," and flung the doors open wide.

In her finest garments and arms stretched wide, long red hair flowing in the wind and wide grin, Criso bellowed to the crowd, "Ladies and Gentlemen! May I present to you this year's Ardeo Trial Lovers! Laris and Ilia!"

There was the usual bevy of cheers and chants, and then a hushed anticipation came over the crowd. Criso smiled lightly, and then said with a flourish, "Can our Takers make them undone, or are these Lovers forged as one?"

Ж Ж Ж Ж Ж Ж Ж Ж Ж Ж Ж Ж Ж Ж

Insulated from the happenings of the outside world, Laris sat uncomfortable on the large plush bed in the enormous room. It was a nice room, far nicer than he was used to anyway. The bed was large enough for three, with large pillows and fine silks that adorned everything, it room also housed a bathtub for bathing with a partition for privacy, but it was empty for the remainder —

which was a LOT of empty in this large place. The other thing that made him uncomfortable was the window that opened to a large outside balcony which overlooked the Integra Pol, a sight that brought him little peace.

He was curious about where the other doors in the room led to, but his worst fear was that if he was going to spend a month in this room with just his Taker for company he might go insane from boredom. He had been told that if he wanted to change anything for any reason to just summon one of the charges and everything would be taken care of — food, furniture, entertainment — anything he desired. Still, a month of luxury and pampering with only one other person for company did not strike him as terribly stimulating.

This trial would be difficult, but he had made a promise to Ilia — so long as at the end in their eyes they only saw each other, that was all that mattered. However, even with his lover's blessing, he fought over even looking at this vision of beauty — Clarus had been kneeling before him, her face radiating innocence and never once taking her eyes off his face. For quite some time now.

Clarus finally spoke. "Would you prefer me to hide?"

"I'm sorry?" replied Laris.

"You are nervous and look sad. If I'm the reason I can just go hide in a corner or my room until you feel better."

"What? That's terrible!"

She cocked her head to one side. "Why?"

"I could never tell you to do that!"

"But, I offered."

"But —"

She pouted. "I am here to make you happy — if me hiding away makes that happen, then I am happy." Laris gave her a look of confusion as he wrestled with the concept.

"Look, I know you want to be the person that wins, but me and Ilia are going to succeed! Our love is strong!"

"I would not know, and would never dare think you would lie to me. I am not here to see if your love is strong — I am only here to make you happy in whatever way you see fit. Do not feel sorry for me, or ashamed of asking for whatever you want. It makes me happy to be useful."

Laris deflated slightly. "Well... you don't have to hide in the corner."

"Then I can go to my room."

He looked at the number of doors in the room and assumed that what lay behind one of them must have been one set aside for her. He wasn't ready to be alone in this huge space just quite yet. "No, you don't have to go."

"What would you like then?" she asked doe-eyed.

Laris had been fighting everything in fear of failing, but found it difficult to fight someone who he could see only wanted to try to be happy and make him happy in turn. Before his very eyes she turned from an unknown enemy, into a person. "What can you do?"

Clarus smiled and, misinterpreting Laris' intentions entirely, calmly opened her gown to reveal her chest. The boy gawped.

After some moments Laris finally pointed and said, "Uh... that...."

Clarus looked down and her eyes brightened, "Oh, that is a conducutis — it's like a magic promise that I can't break. It hurt getting the tattoo, but I'm okay now."

"Why do you have one?"

"Didn't you read the rules?"

He sheepishly said, "No. We were kinda rushed."

"Well the rules state that I am allowed to do anything except leave the room. Oh! And that I am only allowed to do things to you with your permission. That means I can't kiss or even hug you, unless you want me to."

"... Really?"

"Yes."

"So you are bound to the rules. I thought like... I thought people basically had their brains fucked out in the Ardeo Trial."

"I don't know what other people think, I only know the rules I was told. Maybe back in the old days that is what happened. I have heard that Erus Ardeo was not a nice man."

Laris began to feel uncomfortable with Clarus just kneeling there with breasts exposed. "So like... okay." He looked around the room. "Um, is this it? A whole month of just us?"

"Uh-huh."

"It's going to get pretty boring isn't it?"

Clarus shrugged and her ample breasts heaved with her shoulders. "It might. We can ask for anything we like from the outside, and I will always do my best to keep you entertained."

"Look, you are a..." Laris could not help but fixate on her chest, "Beautiful woman, but Ilia is the only person I will love. I mean we did talk and we both knew we would probably end up having sex with our Takers but —"

"I am sure I can entertain you with things other than love."

"What do you mean?"

"I could tell you a story, or sing if you like."

"Oh... right. Sure! Um, tell me a story please."

"As you wish, this story is one of —"

"Um, could you... like sit on a chair or something, and perhaps cover up? I don't feel very comfortable with you kneeling in front of me."

"As you wish." Clarus repositioned herself next to Laris on the bed and began her story.

However, she had forgotten to cover up, and so Laris had a hard time paying attention to her mouth or even opening his own to remind her.

Ж Ж Ж Ж Ж Ж Ж

Sitting on her own large bed with Tari besides her, Ilia said defiantly, "I don't really have any interest in girls."

Tari replied, "Now now Ilia, don't be shy. It is not like I am going to bite you. We have to spend a month together, so why not make it fun?" She had cracked far tougher nuts and enjoyed every single one, but the innocent did grate on her at times.

"But you aren't a very nice person."

"Now who said that?"

Ilia regretted saying that. "... Everyone."

"Well you can't believe what everyone tells you, can you? Besides, I don't think I would be allowed to participate in this trial if I was a bad person."

"... I suppose."

"Oh come come, don't be so nervous. We are just a couple of girls who have to spend a month together, it is not like we ever have to DO anything naughty. My only goal is to make you happy."

Tari's words got Ilia's hackles up. "You can't tempt me away from him!"

"Why would I want to do that? Do you think the point of this trial is for me to take your lover's place? No. It's just to show you that perhaps your first love is not the right one."

"You don't know that! You can't possibly know that! How dare you say that!"

Tari's voice remained calm. "You are arguing with someone who isn't fighting you right now. Besides I don't have to make you love me, we can just talk. About anything. Like Laris for instance, what is he like?"

"Oh... well... he's... he's just wonderful!" Tari jumped a little at Ilia's abrupt change in tone. It was so sickeningly... nice. "He helps me out all the time, and always checks up on me. He makes sure that I am happy, and is always asking me if there is anything I want...." Tari decided to mentally check out of a conversation that she had heard a thousand times before and just nodded her head as Ilia prattled on about how wonderful her man was. "*I wonder how Clarus is doing....*"

Tari fondly remembered the few days she got to spend with her.

She had thought that she would never feel as strongly as she did about anyone other than Mulat, but Clarus was just so pure and innocent and made Tari feel that drinking from her spring of purity was an intoxicating honor. The sex too was mind blowing — she had always believed men to be more fun in bed but Clarus had blasted that particular notion to smithereens. Her reminiscing was only interrupted by her brain's cues to say things like 'Really?' and 'Uh-huh' so the soppy girl wouldn't get offended.

When it seemed like Ilia was never going to shut up Tari thought, *"This girl really is gullible... stupid too. Hm... maybe I should have some fun."* She stalked closer to Ilia with a predatory grin — interrupting her mid-sentence with a deep and passionate kiss — Ilia didn't fight back much. *"Nice and submissive I see, this will be much easier than I thought,"* thought Tari, and continued her assault. As her fingers slid down Ilia's body a stabbing pain pierced her heart, freezing her in her tracks. Falling down and clutching her chest, she scrabbled to the farthest corner of the bed with her face flushed red. A few moments passed and Tari screamed, *"Futuo!"* as she raised herself up on her arms.

"Wha... what happened?" asked Ilia, her own face flushed with lust and confusion.

"My *futuo* conducutis."

"... What?"

"My conducutis! All Takers have them, weren't you told any of this?"

"... No," said the girl meekly. "Um... are you hurt?"

Tari rolled her eyes and sighed heavily. "Yes I'm fine, it's just pain — it doesn't do any real physical damage. It binds me to certain rules, such as I can't touch you in a sexual way unless you give me permission. I also can't leave this room — otherwise I get to experience the *delightful* feeling of being stabbed in the heart. My mother's idea of 'ensuring fairness'."

"I thought conducutis was only for, like, special promises?"

"Yes, well, we use them for business too."

"I... well..." the girl then remembered an important fact about her situation and became angry. "Serves you right! You should never touch me, and I will never let you touch me at all!" she cried, strengthened by the knowledge that she could hide behind the conducitis now that Laris wasn't around to hide behind instead.

Tari sighed loudly. "Fine fine, I won't touch you. Was just trying to have some fun."

"Yeah well... well, don't!"

CHAPTER XI

"‹Toyo, do you want your anger, at this very moment, to guide your next action? ›"

"But, Tagai! How am I supposed to NOT -"

"‹The feelings in your heart; your actions upon this world.›

‹Which lasts longer? ›"

-Tagai's teachings to Toyo

THE MARAAN EXPANSE

"*Hello again,*" said Kahli's strange passenger voice.

Kahli indifferently replied, "*... Hello.*"

"*You did not listen.*"

"*... I don't know what you're talking about, or even care.*"

"*It is going to hurt more if you don't listen.*" The voice carried the tone of a promise attached to its words.

"*What is going to hurt?*" asked Kahli, worried.

"*You did not listen.*"

Kahli tried to humor the voice by responding in its own bored tone. "*You said that already.*"

"*You did not hear it the first time.*"

"*I just... don't care anymore. Why do you bring me here? What is the point of talking to me? Why do you keep DOING this?*"

"*To get you to listen.*"

"*TO WHAT?! AND DON'T JUST TELL ME TO BREATHE!*"

"*... To know when it is time to push.*"

Kahli was awoken by a tender hand caressing her face with a damp cloth, but she did not dare to open her eyes. She was beginning to hate the voice dragging her into some dark corner of her mind where time didn't exist. It came when it wanted and left for reasons that seemed arbitrary, and sometimes it released her into another dream. To her surprise she heard the soft words of, "Wake up." She opened her eyes, wincing as they adjusted to the harsh light. Looking up she saw an old lady, wrinkled and kindly with dark, dark skin, and hair whiter than bone, looking down at her.

"Hello Kahli," said the old lady.

Kahli weakly forced a plea from her mouth. "Just kill me already."

"I do not think you would like that, little girl."

"I am NOT a little girl!" Kahli'd had more than enough of people talking down to her. If they wanted to kill her or hit her then they should just get on with it already!

"Ah, found our strength have we? Well anger is as good a motivator as any to fight death."

Kahli got up on her elbows and looked around at the inside of the makeshift tanned hide tent. Aside from a small fire pit in the center with a shell-pot sitting on top of it and another bed there was an air of gentleness, of a home well-loved somehow. She turned her head to the old lady and saw nobody else, and that for the first time in a long time she had not woken up tethered to anything. "Where am I?"

"From what I've heard it wouldn't matter if I told you that, you wouldn't have a clue," the old lady chided.

"WHERE AM I!?" Kahli screamed.

The old lady looked deep into Kahli's eyes calmly and waited for the rage to drain from her face. "I would have thought a question you would rather the answer to was, 'Am I safe here?', but seeing as you aren't smart enough to think about yourself or even guess where you are I'll tell you: You are safe in my tent." The old lady shook her head, and again Kahli felt like she was being treated like a child. Silent judgment passed under the old lady's gaze before she got up and walked out of the tent with a heavy sigh.

Feeling the opportunity of escape Kahli quickly rolled out of bed and tried to stand, only to find her legs had decided to remain sleeping. Through sheer willpower she hobbled, and after falling over crawled to the entrance of the tent out into the blinding desert sun where she saw an entire camp full of tents, and women looking directly at her. The old lady was sitting on a stool just outside and had watched Kahli's attempts at escape with some amusement and said to herself, "I did say you weren't smart enough, but I didn't think you were actually stupid."

Kahli shot her a death glare and weakly said, "Fuck you."

"Now now, that's enough of that." Helping the weak Kahli back into the tent, the old lady tucked her in and made her comfortable.

"You haven't eaten or drunk enough in quite some time — also please pay attention to the fact that nobody here has clapped you in irons or threatened your life. If you want to walk away from the camp you are welcome to try, but be warned you'll just be brought straight back and you'll feel pretty stupid for it. As your carer I cannot stop you, but the least I can do is let you know that without fuel for the legs you won't get that far."

Kahli wanted to fight the old lady for tucking her in and what she'd just said, but she knew what she was saying to be true — she had been operating on borrowed strength for far too long. The best she could do to express herself was gruffly turn her head away.

"How about I tell you some stories? Everybody likes stories," said the old lady. She took up a seat next to the bed and handed Kahli a leather pouch of water, but it was clear as day to her that the girl was going to continue to act pig ignorant and stubborn. "Well I will just leave it here then shall I?" she said, placing the pouch close to Kahli's hand. Leaning back in her chair, she smacked her lips and looked up at the ceiling. "So, what story… how about the tale of the screaming caverns? Or the fog of a thousand voices…?" No reaction. "Ah, how about the story of the Maharaan clans, the Jara and the Harat? Of Suta Jara, the first of Jara? Would that be something you'd like to hear?"

Kahli slowly turned her head so she could hear better, her interest piqued at knowing something more about her supposed family name. The old lady smiled when saw this and opted to use her grandest story-telling voice she saved only for her own kin.

"In the first days of Kasmah, long before the Vios Ocean had carved itself in Kasmah, there was only one large clan that spanned all of the Maharaan, and they were called, the Nujah, after their great unifying leader. People of peace and skill they sought only the betterment of themselves and to foster good will with all. But! Life was difficult for many, and traveling large distances was hard, for water was scarcer then it is now. Nujah knew the secrets to finding water in the ground, the plants, he even knew how to extract water from the air! But he saw that life was too hard for his people, and so he summoned up all his strength to give birth to the great Vios Ocean. It is where Nujah now calls home, and from there he blesses the land with life-giving rain."

Kahli inched her head closer and closer as the story unfolded, but still wasn't willing to give the old lady the satisfaction of her attention.

"With the Maharaan split by the great ocean and no way to cross it, there came a divide in its people. Without Nujah to lead, those in the west wrote down Nujah's laws and teachings of peace and spread it freely. They came to call themselves the Harat, and even as they splintered and shrank in size all kept to the teachings and could find safe haven in another Harat's camp."

The old lady saw that her guest had finally relaxed her shoulders and she smiled, but kept it hidden — lest youthful rebellion render her storytelling all for naught.

"Those to the east of the Vios however had not written down these teachings, for the creatures in their lands were far too dangerous to live a life of words, so they became great warriors and hunters. There was much fighting between themselves, and little else. One day, Suta of the family Jara found a stone in the desert lying in a pool of water, and he remarked that it looked as if the stone was weeping tears. Suta Jara was dying of thirst from being lost in the desert, so he sucked on the stone for its water so hard that it slipped past his lips and went straight to his stomach!"

It must have been how the old lady was talking or something but Kahli couldn't resist tilting her head a little away from the wall.

"For days and nights he saw the dreams of how great his land and clan could be, and through them his strength and conviction grew. The stone told him its true name, Tabu, and that his family would unite these lands for Nujah and bring peace once more. Suta found his way home, to the delight of his family, and they soon saw that their beloved Suta Jara had changed — his face was set in stone, and in his face there was a purpose far beyond the day's hunt. As the years passed there was much love shared, many children reared, many battles won, and for generations the clan of Jara was strong. It was not always easy though for many grew jealous of Suta's strength, and having heard the story of the Tabu, coveted the crying stone for themselves. Many clans attacked, but all were repelled by Jara's prowess! In time Suta rode out, and not long after all the Maharaan east of the Vios Ocean swore fealty to the great Suta Jara. He had finally brought the memory of peace... but peace still found a way to be forgotten."

"One day an assassin reached Suta in his old age and struck the great man down, a man who had shown nothing but love and compassion to those under his care. The greedy assassin disemboweled him in the hopes of finding the crying stone, and when he had it he quickly gobbled it down. As the assassin strode out of the hut and proclaimed his rule over the lands now that he possessed the Tabu, he fell over dead, and everything inside the man ran out of every hole he had until the Tabu could be seen on the ground. It was there on that day that all gathered saw the myth come true — the stone began to cry and washed itself clean of the assassin."

"Amongst the crowd was Suta's daughter, Adu, who felt the stone call out to her. Everyone was afraid after what they had just seen, but Adu showed no fear as she walked over, brought it up to her mouth, kissed the stone to her lips, and drank the Tabu's tears. She drank so much that she seemed fit to burst and fell to the ground. Not long after, all saw her stand and knew as one that Suta's offspring had become the first Isti to guide and rule them — as it has been for generations, all the way to Rasak Jara." Kahli faced away again upon hearing Rasak's name and stared intently at the opposite side of the tent.

With the old lady's story told, she leaned in and wondered if in its telling it had helped bring Kahli's memories back. The change in the young girl's body language told her all she needed to know, but she also needed to say what Kahli should hear. "Rasak was once a benevolent and proud Isti, but the curse of his clan took its toll on a man bound to responsibility too tightly. He descended into a pit of despair, from which his own wife or even his two desert flowers, Jatah and Kahli, could not bring him back. The tale of Jara, while sad for now, does not need to continue being so."

No reaction, just more tensing. The old lady shrugged her

shoulders and relaxed in her chair. Waiting for the girl's childishness to pass she amused herself with her own thoughts.

"*No! I AM NOT KAHLI JARA!*" screamed Kahli inside her own head. Enough of being captive! Led around! Forced into things and told what to do! More importantly, she'd had enough of people telling her who she was and where she came from. The world had come to reject all her memories, and the people within had rejected her body and soul. So she planted a truth in herself then and there: It was time for the world to listen to Kahli.

Sitting herself upright with defiance on the edge of her bed she drank and ate her fill of the sustenance provided. All the while the old lady smiled.

"*Never again! I'm not going to listen to all these lies!*" Kahli lay back down. The strong and tall woman who entered next was flanked by two women, who were the spitting image of Kahli herself. She was shocked to see that what people had been saying were true, there were other Kahlis running around. If she wasn't so surprised by seeing two of her standing in front of her she may have recognized a familiarity in the face of the strong woman.

The strong woman then said with both confidence and relief, "Hello daughter, welcome home."

"No... no, no more," said Kahli. This was someone she would never have thought existed, couldn't have existed. A mother should love and protect her daughter from what the world had done to her. Why were they torturing her?

Kahli's mother replied, "No more what?"

She screamed, "No! YOU ARE NOT MY MOTHER!"

The woman sighed. "Yes, I am. Why would I lie to you? I know that you have been through much, but I know the girl I raised —"

"YOU DID NOT RAISE ME!" screamed Kahli. She jumped up off the bed and kept screaming.

The woman slapped her. "Yes! YES I DID! I raised you when your father broke! I know what my hands —"

Kahli backed away. "Leave me alone! YOU ALL HATE ME!

EVERYONE HATES ME! I DIDN'T DO ANYTHING!"

The voice in her head responded. *"Yes... You know you destroyed that town you called home, you killed everyone and everything within it. You killed the Integra Natura, and they all deserved it because they didn't love you. You were reviled and hated, feared and loathed. Listen to what the world is telling you Kahli, this world is rejecting you...."*

Fire began to flow from Kahli's mouth as she clutched her head, while her so-called 'mother' shouted out for the guards.

"It is time to push Kahli, it is time to push the world away. Remember to breathe...."

Kahli looked up and, in a voice imbued with certainty, strength, and age far beyond her years, she said, **"Why does everything reject me?"** She looked around the tent with eyes that hinted that they took in more than simple light. **"I have tried to be me, but every time I try to think, or do something different, or survive, I encounter only people and places that tell me what I was, or am. Even the voice in my head wants something from me...."**

Kahli's mother, visibly trembling at the change in her daughter, tried to reason with her. "Now... listen my little Kahli, there is —"

"Yes... listen. It is time for me to listen. It is time for me to —"

BREATHE

Whips of flame erupted from Kahli's very being and wrapped themselves around those nearest to her. From upright and solid, to gelatinous and half-formed — they melted quickly into sloughing masses of cooling flesh. Feeling the rage against the world build inside her Kahli's flames grew larger, and soon the tent was consumed in flames. The whole camp ran to the commotion only to find an enraged Kahli enveloped in righteous fire.

"No more controlling me! I tried to listen to who people said I was, and still I was punished — I tried to accept your truths! You, who would sacrifice me a thousand times over!"

Kahli picked up the weapons from her mother's fallen guards and began flinging molten metal at everyone she saw, dropping people to the ground branded and dead with flesh and iron fused. The whole camp dropped everything and fled from the devastation — save Adsum, who watched in awe at the display of sheer power. He was conflicted between having his assets summarily wiped out and wanting to see the limits of her power. It did not take long before he believed that she could rival Mulat himself. Thinking quickly on his feet he wondered how he could turn this to his advantage, and knew the one thing that she would want more than anything.

Tearing his shirt off he revealed his upper body to be covered with tattoos, intricate and varied. As he walked closer to the vortex of power that Kahli exerted, his tattoos began to glow brighter and brighter before bursting into flame on his flesh. Knowing that he did not have much time he worked fast, he had to reach her so he could speak lest he lose all he had worked for.

Adsum cried out, "KAHLI!"

"You... why do you not burn?" asked Kahli, turning her full attention to the strange glowing elderly man.

"I can teach you the why, but I have something more important!"

"**What is it?**"

"If you calm yourself I can give you the man that cursed you!"

"... **What proof do you have?**"

The tattoos were in full flare and the burns left in the old man's skin were rending his mind from coherent thought. "I... know... what happened," said Adsum, and then collapsed. She looked down at him, then up at the camp that was fleeing from her in terror. He had been the only one so far who hadn't lied to her, who had answered her questions when asked. She reached her decision. Kahli let out a wave of fiery destruction that devastated the camp and burned every last person alive, save one old man.

Her rage sated, she began to cool and calm herself, but the fire of hate within kept burning. Walking over to the unconscious man she yanked his head up from the ground and growled at him, "**Tell me!**"

Kahli noticed that the burns on his body were not from her, but were in intricate patterns that followed the lines of the tattoos she had glimpsed on him — what power did this old man have that saved him from her? She had destroyed villages! People from the Integra Pol! Mighty warriors!

She leaned down next to him and whispered into his ear, "**I will save you this once, for you have shown me respect at least, but I do not trust you — I do not know what I will trust again. All I do know is that I am listening now, and now I realize that I have never heard anything but hate. If that is what the world will give, then that is what I will give back.**"

Ж Ж Ж Ж Ж Ж Ж Ж Ж Ж Ж Ж Ж Ж Ж

"Please Rasak! NO! NOT THIS ONE! PLEASE! IT IS YOUR OWN CHILD!" screamed the cowering woman as she slid to the floor, clutching the child swaddled in cloth and starting to sob.

"I asked all the women of this clan to do what needed to be done." He breathed in sharply. "And not long after, you all said that you could no longer listen to the last screams of pain of your children, then you called YOUR husbands, fathers, and sons, barbaric for doing what you could not. Do you think they have no hearts? That they are creatures of stone? Two years and this curse sees no end, do you think WE are not tired as well? There are too many mouths to feed — this child would starve like the others, and you along with it." Placing a gentle hand on her shoulder he bent down on one knee and said, "You have not gone mad like the other women, nor have you tried to take your own life like some. There is some strength in you, so you must be strong enough to witness this and tell the others how to be strong so we can survive."

The air in Rasak Jara's grand tent was heavy with the knowledge that all who were present were to witness something that would bring them all pain. Rasak stood and spoke coldly. "You know what must be done, and this is the punishment for your actions." His words said, he took the child easily from the unresisting woman, and then took a needle from the woman's mending pouch. "The weakness of the sexes is known to both. Men must resist the urge to fight for everything — women must fight the urge to care for everything. The mistake hidden by weakness you could not overcome, must end — if not by your own hand, then by what your own hands use best."

As he stared into the woman's face her resolve weakened. Rasak walked and placed the child in the center of the tent. Kneeling once more over a baby girl, he saw the face of his favorite daughter peer up at him. Steeling himself he pierced the needle into the baby's heart, and held it there only for a moment before withdrawing and handing it back to the woman. The little human shuddered softly, and an expression of pain and confusion crossed its face as the blood flowed out with an almost beautiful thickness and color from its chest. There was no cry of anguish, no scream of pain — just a tiny gasp of air, and a crushing silence.

"No... please no," cried the woman softly as she scrabbled with tear-streaked face and shaking hands towards her child. Putting her smallest finger into the open wound of the child's heart, she put as much pressure as she dared in a desperate attempt to fight death. But with each beat, the child's heart got weaker, and each pulse that she felt through her finger ebbed with her own, until she could not feel it anymore. A mother's heart, beating in rhythm with the last of her child's. When the thrums of life stopped the woman lay cradled over the child, still as a statue. Soundless.

Rasak looked down at the woman and almost broke, but kept his resolve for his people. Even though he had done this many times before a small part of him withered away when he witnessed his daughter's body die. To find the strength to make an example got harder each time, but the women of the tribe had been hiding more and more children. The day he could not find the strength to lead his people to better choices was the day his clan would fall.

He knew that his clan was suffering at the hands of each woman birthing only girls every nine months, without husband or failure. No stillbirths or miscarriages, no abortions took, and nothing would stop the flow of mewling children and mouths to feed. Eventually they ran out of teats for the young to suckle and food to make swollen breasts — the clan was being flooded by birth, and all of them were Kahli.

Watching his daughter be born again and again, only to die a thousand ways, took from him too much of his own soul. His eldest desert flower would bud, bloom and wilt in such a short time and in so many different ways. Something had to be done.

Rasak looked down at the woman and wanted to say sorry, to cry right alongside her, but instead gruffly commanded, "Take my Jagu back to her chambers and make sure she is seen to. And bring me my daughters!"

Kahli and Jatah were escorted into the tent — Kahli with the look of a puppy beaten, and Jatah with that of a fattened calf. Kahli was roughly thrown to the ground as Jatah bounced along with sibling glee at seeing her older sister being mistreated, while outside there was the baying of a crowd heavy with unrest.

Rasak breathed in deeply. "The time has come, Kahli. I can no longer stop them from wanting your head, but what I can do is give you a choice. You can become Orati and be exiled to satisfy their rage, or you can let them tear you limb from limb." The clan of Jara, armed only with the fact that Kahli was the only one incapable of rearing a child and that all born became her, had passed judgment that she was the source.

The time leading to this moment had been almost too difficult to bear for Kahli, who so far had experienced public humiliation to an extent where she had twice tried to take her own life and failed. Seeing so many women born and growing rapidly to her own age before stopping, seeing her face a thousand times over day after day. Those 'false' Kahli's had become like chattel to her clan, and at times people mistook her for one of them. The mark that her father had given her to identify her as the true Kahli did stop people's anger before it came to blows, but the words of hate they left in their wake bruised her spirit far more than their fists could.

Kahli saw a fresh blood stain on the ground in front of her father and knew that another child had been dealt with — as the Isti he was to be the strongest and perform the hardest tasks, but she feared her father was killing himself in the process. He had done so much for everyone and hardly took anything for himself, who was she to make things harder still?

"I love you father..." said Kahli, attempting to emulate his strength by facing him head on. "If it appeases them, then Orati I shall become."

Rasak lowered his head to hide his face for a moment, while his daughter did her best to not shake in her stead. "Very well," he said and lifted his head. "Today we accept defeat, so that one day we can accept victory."

He wanted to walk up and hold her, tell her everything was going to be fine, that he would fight every man and woman that would dare take her from him. Instead, he walked out of the grand Jara hut and addressed all standing outside. If they were going to take his most cherished desert flower from him, then all would have to be present for her acceptance to become an Orati. They should all know the sacrifice he had made, they should all become stronger for it. If he was not allowed to be a coward, then neither were his people.

Days passed and preparations were swift, and Kahli found herself deep in fear at how quickly it went from mere words to ceremony. But she would not run from her choice, she would be proud and strong like her father. A Jara stands by their word, a Jara is strong.

The ceremony was held out in the open and all were in attendance. There were no special songs sung, no colors flown. All there was, was silence as everyone stared at Kahli walking into the center. Rasak soon walked into view with the Hidati drink, and he placed it down on the ground in full view of everyone.

Kahli began to cry as she looked at the cup, and Rasak crouched down low and lay his forehead on the dry ground in front of her in a gesture of complete submission. Not of a man, not of an Isti — but of a father to his daughter.

"May my head help you on your path," he said aloud for all to hear.

Kahli tentatively collected the drink and walked to stand in front of her father. Raising one foot and placing it softly on his head she whispered, "I love you," and drank deep.

LAND OF THE GADORI

Toyo ran through the scraggly forest, filled with the energy that only youth could bring, in search of something to kill that would make everything right and finally give him the acceptance he craved. Making his way through the paths shown to him of the surrounding area and pouncing on every possible sign that there might be something nearby led him to a very fruitful... nothing. His limited experience had shown him that wherever he went, something would want to kill him — so why was it being so hard?

After a few false starts Toyo's enthusiasm began to wane, and after several more still his feelings reached the boiling point of a full-blown tantrum and he screamed out loud, "IT ISN'T FAIR! I JUST WANTED TO KILL STUFF!" He huffed and puffed and carried on, punched a few trees and generally let everything within earshot know that he was well and truly wanting to battle. The only things around him to absorb the sound were some gnarled trees, a few rocks, and a large number of strange looking brown mounds. It was the most space he'd seen between plants ever since the Ogagi.

Spying one of the innocent looking brown mounds, he decided to smash it. Punching through it, he found there to be a colony of strange looking worms living inside. Curious, he poked and prodded them for a bit and in response they crawled all around his gloves — they looked like they were trying to bore into his hands, unsuccessfully. Remembering Tagai's warnings of how dangerous the creatures in the Gadori could be no matter their size, he shook his hands free of them and backed away to watch them from afar.

Looking onwards he saw them try to rebuild the mound with surprising speed, and then he looked around at the trees and vines surrounding him and again marveled at how different everything was from the first Ogagi he was at. There was life here, different from the other place. This Ogagi, the Withered Crone, must reflect or affect the landscape somehow, he thought. Isn't that what the medishi said?

Then, an idea struck him. *"The creatures must all be at the old Ogagi!"* he thought excitedly and decided to think of how to make his way back there. Tagai had taught him enough to survive on his own, and he was confident that he could kill everything there — he might even be able to kill those huge spiders that no doubt killed Nume!

With hope renewed, he looked around to get his bearings and tried to figure out what direction the old Ogagi might be in. His only problem was that after all his aimless running around he really wasn't quite sure where he was in relation to the camp, let alone anywhere else. Being able to tell east from west by sunlight made him feel confident that at least he knew he was lost. Despondent, he had to conclude that the idea was nothing more than that, and thought, *"Well, if I can't find something to kill, then I'm sure if I just wait that something will come to kill me eventually."* To best carry out his new plan he slumped against a tree.

With the impatience of youth, Toyo soon became very, very bored — it had seemed so simple when he'd run out here, why was it taking so long? Without the distraction of the constant need for approval from others he began playing with his hands, and finally began to wonder about them. Whenever he saw anyone else try to lift or push things their muscles would bulge and sweat, nothing like that happened when he did the same. It still didn't make sense though, because pushing his body off the ground still took effort, as did trying to climb a tree.

It felt more like nothing in the world wanted to touch his hands, so everything moved itself out of the way. Even when he tried to help, imprints of his hands would be left on poles and planks — something that did not endear people to him as he had hoped. The only thing he felt from using his hands was the tugging of his shoulders as he pulled on things, or when the two hands touched.

"Why do I have to be so different? Am I really some sort of freak?" he thought while inspecting his hands. He still didn't know what to make of the strange red latticework on his forearms. They didn't hurt or anything and everyone had just come to accept the sight of them, but WHY were they there?

A lot of weird stuff kept happening to him and at the rate he was going he was afraid that he would just get weirder and weirder, until even trees would not want to spend time with him. Ani had told him that people were just afraid of his power, but that didn't make sense to him. *"If I am SOOOO stupidly powerful then why do they avoid me? Knives are dangerous, but they don't avoid them. I just want to help them cut up their food! I don't want to stab them... But maybe... But maybe I can change that."*

For the umpteenth time he grasped his hands together and gave an experimental pull to see if the gloves would come off. The red vine structures on his arms began to pulsate as he increased his effort but he didn't get anywhere beyond feeling like he was pulling his own arms out of their sockets. Feeling despair he placed his face in his hands to hide from the world and was surprised to find his face coated with a sticky, strange smelling substance. He hurriedly tried to wipe it from his face only to feel stupid at coating himself with even more of the stuff.

"What the *futuo*?" he said, trying several more times to wipe it off before giving up. "This is just brilliant. Lost, and now my face is sticky and smells awful." He hunted his surroundings to find some leaves to wipe the substance off his face but even with the leaves each attempt at wiping did little more than smear it around. What was weird was that with every wipe he would have sworn that every leaf he tried turned less brown and more green.

Toyo began to wish for things to be different for the hundredth time, but as he had those thoughts he wondered what he could actually wish for — there did not appear to be any great alternative to the life he had lived so far. For a moment Nume and her long hair flashed across his mind, bringing with it a surge of mixed emotions.

He felt frustrated at feeling stupid and guilty — his frustration found his fists, and his fists found a nearby gnarled tree. After a healthy dose of expression, he sat down near the now unhealthy looking tree to try to stop caring about everything.

A great deal of time passed as he sat and fumed at everything but he could not stop his frustration from his sticky and smelly face, and his attempts to further ignore it just made his face itch. Standing up, he was determined to find a way to wash it off and he tried to stalk off further into the jungle, only to find the path blocked by trees. Fearing that he had gotten lost to the point of ending up somewhere from which there was no return he looked around him and found that all available paths looked to be blocked by strange rocks and trees.

Puzzled by the change in the environment he looked around trying to find any way out. *"This is bloody stupid, I couldn't have fallen asleep in some sort of prison!"* As he gently ran his hands over the wall of trees and rocks he noticed that life seemed to spring forth from where he touched. Living things became greener and the rocks started sprouting a strange kind of moss, and on closer inspection there was a hint of some green sticky stuff. What was happening?

"Hey this is... is kinda interesting." Entertained by what was happening he began to paint his surroundings with his hands, and he found in it a sort of joy as he watched his little private crèche spring to life.

His fun was interrupted by a familiar muffled shout and without a doubt Toyo knew it was Tagai — he must've followed him or something. Feeling stupid that he had gone off to find his acceptance, only to have to be rescued, made him feel indignant, so decided to not give Tagai the satisfaction of pinpointing him. More shouts came, closer this time, as if Tagai knew where he was, and they had the distinct feel of being directed at him rather than trying to find him. He quickly stopped his self-pity and decided it was time to climb the trees and get out of his prison.

As he plunged his hand into a nearby tree to gain purchase, a loud crack came from one of the other trees and a thunderous howl erupted from everything around him at once. In shock he pulled out of the tree and fell backwards onto the ground with a thud. He stood up and tried to will the air back into his lungs after they had decided to evacuate themselves, and then the howls turned to screams. Whipping his head around to see where it was coming from he saw creatures strange and horrific spew forth from the edges.

Rolling towards him were wheels of corrupted piles of flesh that seemed hollow — save for bone, teeth, skin, and sinew. With each flex from the flesh-wheels they would heave themselves a step closer to Toyo, accompanied by a large crunching sound of bone and cartilage competing, followed by a scream. Bones and teeth stuck out everywhere on them — they had no real form or structure, and appeared to be something built rather than born.

A smile crossed Toyo's face and his heart swelled with joy as he thought, *"I'm surrounded! Something wants to kills me! FINALLY!"* and leapt towards the nearest creature. Gripping two separate parts of it, he pulled and watched as the skin and bone tore with ease. The ear-piercing scream went unheard by Toyo as he was finally, in his mind, earning acceptance by eradicating what looked to be horrific creatures from a nightmare.

As one the creatures moved closer towards him in their tortured, pained manner while Toyo kept ripping the first one apart. Several had now clamped onto his hands and legs, but again he just ripped them apart and beat several to death with whatever his hands were full of at the time — sometimes it was another creature, sometimes just another part of the same. There was no blood however, and soon the little crèche became draped with skin and littered with bone.

With each death enacted by his hands his resolve to kill grew stronger, and as his resolve grew the number of creatures seemed to match — which suited Toyo just fine, his guilt was large and needed an equal amount of atonement through violence. He had found his blood lust, and sating it was... good, real good.

As the screams and sickening sounds of the flesh-wheels he tore asunder continued his ears began to hurt, but he was able to tune them out and began operating on instinct. There was no real challenge save for their persistence and numbers — the whole crèche was alive with a cacophony of crunches and scrapings, like some gruesome orchestra.

An enormous scream pierced through the air, and Toyo looked around to see one of those large chittering tree spiders with a spiked tail that had attacked the last camp, and to him it felt like he had just been given a present from the forest directly. The only difference he noticed was that this beast's abdomen was not swollen like the others. The vivid memory of those creatures eating the sick and injured at the Mother-Tree in one bite came back to him, and Toyo screamed at the charging beast, yelling, "ARE YOU STILL HUNGRY!?"

Diving right at the spider's face, Toyo met a clamping jaw that reached over and under him and bit down. It could not complete its bite as he had grasped both top and bottom of the beast's maw with each hand and was holding it open without effort. It was a horrible stench, but its gross body only made him feel like its death would be all the sweeter.

"You BETTER be hungry," shouted Toyo, but had to jump out of its mouth when another flesh-wheel lunged at him. He quickly grabbed it and threw it at the spider's face and watched as the spider crunched through it.

Toyo then got an idea, and began a systematic approach to removing the spider's legs one by one — all the while the mighty beast thrashed around as it tried its best to kill him. Ripping out each leg he worked his way down the abdomen, merely latching onto the spider's body and shifting himself as needed, blocking each strike with a hand and throwing away flesh-wheels when necessary. When he was finally done the spider lay helpless and he noticed that the flesh-wheels had begun to gather around each severed limb, from which came the sound of gnashing teeth.

Moving to the front of the spider, Toyo's face was twisted with anger. "HUNGRY?!" he screamed loudly as it tried to crawl on its belly towards him with chomping maw. He then went and got some flesh-wheels, and shoved one into its mouth. The spider thrashed around and tried to fight back, but to no avail, even its attempts to vomit were interrupted by Toyo shoving with more and more force any flesh-wheel he could find down its gullet. It convulsed and gasped, but Toyo showed no mercy. Even when the creature's shudders had stopped and he was merely forcing corpses into what was now a corpse itself.

Seeing the easier prey, the flesh-wheels began to heap themselves onto the spider with only a few making cursory attempts at attacking Toyo. As he watched the spider being eaten by a massive flesh pile he admired his work for a moment before climbing the wall that had surrounded him, and perched on the highest tree branch to watch from a safer place. With nothing left to attack him, he looked around and saw the devastation he had wrought and felt that this surely should be enough to earn his place.

"Plaga spider got what it deserved!" he said happily. A harsh smack to the back of his head disoriented him and he swung his fists behind him but stopped short when he saw that it was Tagai. The tall hunter seemed different, far more full of energy and alertness than usual, and was wearing strangely thin garments that Toyo had never seen before. After a brief recovery Toyo merely smiled at him and pointed at the spider below. "See! I did that!" he said proudly. "I don't know why you guys have such a hard time hunting these things."

Tagai merely shook his head and sighed heavily at what was a child's boast. He took out from his pouch a small bean pod, and a small sack filled with a strange gel. Tagai coated the pod and popped one of the beans from it into his mouth, quickly afterwards he closed the rest of the pod by crushing it in his hand. He then took off his wafer thin torso garments.

"So... having a snack?" Toyo asked.

Tagai pointed again at the spider and Toyo replied, "Yup! All me!" Tagai rolled his eyes and kept pointing at the spider. "What? What's wrong?" Toyo asked as he watched the slow eating process. "Am I supposed to be learning something here? Is this a lesson?" Unsure of what else to do, he watched. Soon he saw the spider and the flesh-wheels rise as one — it looked as if the spider was resurrecting right before his eyes. "Hey! HEY! I KILLED YOU!" he screamed, and was met again with another sharp smack as the spider focused on the sound.

Toyo couldn't help himself and again screamed, "Stay DEAD!" He went to jump from his perch, ready to kill the spider as many times as he needed to, but was caught by surprise when Tagai streaked down from the tree with unnerving speed towards the spider. Toyo recovered as quickly as he could to join him but was stunned by watching Tagai dance deftly between the spider's strikes and make his way to its tail. He grabbed it, and with a great grunt of effort, forced the tail-spike into the closest tree. As the beast swung around to strike at Tagai, he dodged the swing with only moments to spare. Again dancing through the beast's attacks he returned to Toyo, and stood before him with a flushed red face and breathing hard and fast — it looked like standing still would cause him to explode. Tagai pointed in a direction that appeared random to Toyo and sped off, not giving him any time to respond.

A bewildered Toyo watched on as the strange beast seemed now to be fighting the tree. As he looked he saw it was not really a spider, at least not anymore, but more something wearing a spider's skin. From its tail he saw roots spring forth that wrapped around both tree and beast, bursting forth and flowering through the spider and flesh-wheels — he fought both disgust and confusion as the scene played out before him.

Eventually the beast collapsed as the tree roots overran it, turning it into nothing more than a part of the land itself.

Shaking his head, Toyo decided it would be best to follow Tagai as fast as his legs could carry him.

ЖЖЖЖЖЖЖ

When Toyo reached the camp he was confronted by a sombre Tagai, enraged Hoba and an indifferent Ani.

"Look I —" Toyo began.

Ani quickly replied, "If you think talking right now without being spoken to is a good idea I would advise against it."

"<Why did you leave? >" Tagai asked Toyo.

The passing days had brought to Ani an increasing weakness, but she had to keep up her strength and do her duty of translating.

Toyo replied, "Because you don't accept me! Ani said that you guys are here to destroy those creatures, and if I destroy them then you'll accept me!"

"<Let us assume that path you see is a true path — do you think you killed the hachu? >"

"You saw me! I tore it apart! I don't see what else it could have been if not dead."

"<Do you know which one was the hachu? >"

"Well... all of them were! First there were these strange flesh-wheel thingies, and then a spider —"

"<Hachu are creatures that pose threats to the hanraza. They are not born of the forest nor do they live in harmony. So I ask again, which one was the hachu? >"

Toyo thought it was an easy question. "That giant spider." Tagai shook his head. "The flesh-wheels? But they were easy to kill!" Tagai shook his head again.

"<The things you call 'flesh-wheel' were simply the remains of other creatures found by the hachu Odang, they have been around ever since I can remember. The story told of them was that they were just seeds of a common flower, but the kusabana transformed them into seeds that would seek root in living flesh. When they did they would eventually consume beast after beast in order to flower. The only way to destroy them is to return them to the land and remind them of what they once were. Had you known that you would not have wasted your time tearing apart pointless flesh. >"

"Well how was I supposed to know that?!"

"<How did you expect to learn by simply running off without asking any questions? >" Hoba and Ani were amazed at Tagai's patience with the boy.

Toyo's calm demeanor broke down into tears. "I just... I just want to be accepted," he sobbed heavily.

"<Then start by accepting that you do not know better than I. >"

"I don't know better! I just hate being looked at like I am some sort of evil thing. Why can't I eat with anyone? Why does nobody want to play with me?"

"<Learn to wield your power wiser, learn restraint. People

cannot play with you if they fear for their life. >"

"HOW can I learn that?"

"<How do you learn to walk? >"

"That isn't fair! That doesn't even feel like an answer, and you had a father! You... have a history, I don't have anything! I can't remember a life ever being lived — all I can remember is this past month! Just teach me!"

Toyo never got Tagai's reply as they were interrupted by Ani falling to the ground unconscious.

Ж Ж Ж Ж Ж Ж Ж Ж Ж Ж Ж Ж Ж Ж Ж

Many days had passed, and Ani had yet to recover — a fact that made Hoba worry as it was getting harder for him to sneak her the medicine while trying his best to honor his brother-in-love.

While Hoba and Tagai were on patrol, Hoba asked, "<What are we going to do now? >"

"<About? >" replied Tagai.

"<Our translator is unconscious and the boy is getting worse now, too frustrated at not understanding what is expected of him. You have been asked to lead, do you really believe that we can continue like this? >"

"<I have been asked by the Ogahigi to make him one of ours, and that is what I shall do. >"

"<Yes, but really how can we do that now? And why? All to help a child that ran away? >"

"<The boy merely wants to earn his place. >"

"<He is killing us all in doing so! How can you ask everyone else to accept the time and effort you are putting into him? We NEED our Yohju, WE your people need you. >"

"<Ani will —>"

"<Ani is recovering slowly but still cannot speak, and the boy has been moping around the camp. I cannot babysit him forever. >"

"<Then don't. Stop fearing him, and let him find his own path with us. >"

"<But he keeps speaking with the Ogahigi! If we keep —>"

"<Hoba, an old friend and brother you are, but I am Yohju now. Be quiet and allow the boy to follow this path, if the Ogahigi thought him a threat I am sure she would have told me. >"

Hoba gave a hesitant scowl in response but decided to remain by his brother-in-love's side in silence. The man had been through enough already, and Hoba would forever be by his side to help him stand. The only true problem for him was that Tagai took to his new role with such grace, that he felt that his own value was lost.

Ж Ж Ж Ж Ж Ж Ж Ж Ж Ж Ж Ж Ж Ж Ж

Toyo paced despondently in front of the open Ogaden. "They are never going to accept me," he said.

"Who?" asked the Ogahigi. The eye-flower was a small distraction for Toyo and he tried his best to ignore it. He was happy though that she now looked healthier, fuller, and he found the eye-flower oddly expressive whenever she talked.

"These people! You said that I belong here, but I don't feel it."

"I never said you belong here."

"What? But you said —"

"What I said was for them to treat you like one of their own and from what I have seen, they have."

"Then why do I get ignored? Why can I only talk to you now? Even THAT they hate me for."

"You do things that they don't understand."

"Like what?"

"Do things that for others would require strength unimaginable."

Hold on, how did she know what he'd been doing? "I thought I was the only one that talked to you?"

"Yes, you are. That does not mean you are the only person I listen to."

Toyo noticed that the three medishi had become less human as time had gone by. They now seemed planted in the ground and unmoving, keeping an ever vigil watch over the Ogaden. Every now and then Toyo would feel a little creeped out by them, but after the Ogahigi's explanation of why it must be he thought that it was probably what they deserved.

"... Why do they call you Ogahigi?" he asked.

"It means 'little Ogagi' in their tongue."

"... So you are a tree?"

"I am, and not."

"Don't you have a name?"

"Yes, Ogahigi."

"Isn't that like, a title? Like Yohju? Don't you have like a name, name?"

"It has been a long time since I have heard it and I have never had a need for it."

"Why?"

"For humans, a memory only lasts so long."

"So... either you are human and you have forgotten it, or you are a tree and remember it?"

The Ogahigi chuckled slightly and the eye-flower pulsed softly. "I am no different, time takes it from me too. I did not find it so important after a while."

"Well I can't just keep calling you Ogahigi, it doesn't sit right. So... I'm going to call you... um... Anumarbor."

The Ogahigi was stunned for a moment and the eye-flower froze in focus on Toyo. "Does that name mean anything to you?"

"I just like the sound of it."

"You wish to name me purely by phonetic aesthetics?"

"... Sorry?"

"Ah, sorry. I am still getting used to how you speak, the last one to speak to me was far more.... It is a bit too long for a name don't you think?"

Toyo smiled wide. "Then... what about Anma? Anma... Yeah! I like that." And just like that, she had a name. "I kinda wish they would let us talk longer Anma. Ani is still not talking, and I really don't feel like I'm learning anything at all."

"Then learn to listen."

"Yeah okay…" he dismissed this advice like he did all others that seemed easier said than done. "Why do you want me around here anyway?"

"Because you are important."

"Yeah but… why?"

"Some answers only time can bring."

"<What is the meaning of this?! >" interrupted an angry Hoba.

The three medishi turned to Hoba in unison, "<The meaning of a conversation? >" replied the Ogahigi.

"<You shouldn't be exposed like this! You risk too much to entertain a boy! >"

"<And you risk nothing in your attempts to teach him as I asked. Am I allowed to be disappointed in you also? >"

"<He does not listen! >"

"<You do not speak. >"

Toyo stood between the shouting Hoba and the softly spoken Anma in an attempt to defend her.

"<What? What is this? >" asked Hoba.

"<You do not understand his expression of respect? >"

"<What?! >"

"<You are yelling at me — the boy feels you are threatening me. >"

"<I would never threaten you! >" screamed Hoba.

Toyo adopted a fighting stance, but was quickly calmed by assurances from Anma. He lowered his fists, but that didn't stop him from still looking at Hoba in anger.

"<Hoba, all you bring is anger whilst the tribe suffers while your brother-in-love carries a great burden on his shoulders. Do you wish to chide the child, or help him? >"

Feeling unappreciated and belittled, Hoba stormed off.

"What was that about, Anma?"

"Some people have difficulty finding their place when their emotions get in the way."

"What do you mean?"

Anma gave herself a long pause before responding. "Your emotions led to the destruction of the old camp. Not intentionally, but it is making it difficult for you to find your place."

Toyo felt guilty and looked at the ground. "Yeah I know."

The medishi pointed at the direction Hoba had stormed off in. "It is no different for him, his emotions are threatening himself, and he does not know how to find his way back."

"Oh... okay...." A question that he'd been dreading to ask bubbled to the surface. "Do you accept me?"

"Of course Toyo, I accepted you long ago."

"... You know, I tried to go fight and earn my place. It didn't go so well."

"Then learn to listen."

"I am listening! I just want people to accept me, isn't there anything to prove that I want to be here?"

"Yes, there is. It would be the wrong way to go about it though."

"It can't be any worse than this. Please tell me."

"You can be inducted as a hunter."

"What's that?"

"A ritual that diverts the sex drive towards hunting and working. Tagai and Hoba both went through it, and are the last of their kind."

"Sex drive?"

"Yes, the desire to copulate."

"Oh... okay." He wasn't quite sure what she was talking about but any path was a good path at this point. "So, if I do this then everyone will accept me?"

"It would prove your commitment to them. My people put great stock in commitment and honor." Toyo knew all too well how self-disciplined and strict the Gozuri were.

Embarrassed, he asked, "… Would you like it if I did it?"

"What I would like Toyo, is for you to grow as a man and stay with us."

A stupid grin crossed his face. "Okay."

He couldn't help his thoughts of how much he wanted to crawl into that warm pink tree stump with Anma and find comfort there.

ЖЖЖЖЖЖЖ

Toyo was excitedly leading Tagai by the hand to the Ogaden and upon reaching it gestured to the woman curled up inside of the trunk. Tagai bowed his head low as a sign of respect. The Ogahigi had not spoken to him much, and he had no idea why she would want to speak with him now. "<What can I do for my Ogahigi? >"

"<Induct the boy. >"

"<Is… that wise? >"

"<Yes, >" replied the Ogahigi.

"<How does he even know what it is? >"

"<I told him. >"

"<I will grant your desire Ogahigi, but I must speak my mind and say that it feels rushed. >"

"<It is not my desire, it is his. The boy only wishes to please us. >"

"<Then why does he spend all his time talking to you? You rarely speak to others, even me. Are we not worth your time? >"

"<He is helping me grow. When I am strong enough, then I can give you protection and guidance once more. Until then, all my strength has to be placed into him. >" Her voice took on a different tone. "<Why has he not been taught more? >"

"<Ani has been consistently unwell, and I have been very busy trying to ensure that everyone is safe and doing as necessary. I do not always have time to tell him what and why. >"

"<Words are not what a man needs, he needs to be shown what to do. If you cannot let him be by your side while you work, then why has Hoba not come forth? >"

"<The loss at the Mother-Tree weighs heavily on him and he too has to work hard to make sure all are taken care of. >"

"<If you cannot perform as I have asked, then do not question what I choose to use my strength for. You have to accept that time will give you the answers you seek. >"

"<I accept Ogahigi — I did not mean to offend. >"

"<You did not offend. >" The Ogahigi paused a moment. "<I would appreciate it if you called me Anma from now on. >"

"<... Anma? >"

"<Yes, Toyo named me. I find it rather pleasing. >"

"<He NAMED you?! But you already have a name! >"

"<No, I had a title. Is it such a sin to want a name? >"

"<Of course not, but —>"

"<Then it is settled. >" Tagai balked at being cut off and tried to accept this change as best he could. "<Will you induct the boy? >" asked Anma.

"<I will honor the wish. >"

"<Good, prepare as soon as you are able. I must rest now — this Ogagi is not fully ready to nourish me as I need. >" Anma looked at Toyo and said, "It is time for me to rest now. He will induct you as you wish. Speak to me again when you have recovered."

The wooden entrance to the Ogaden was closed by one of the statue-like medishi — leaving an excited boy and a tall man looking at each other, each unsure of what was going to happen next. Tagai exhaled slowly and gave the signal for Toyo to follow and set out to find Hoba. The only other thought in his mind was the change in color of the Ogahigi's eye-flower, it seemed richer than before.

The pair found Hoba nursing a conscious Ani, who appeared to have made a miraculous recovery, and both were somewhat surprised at the care Hoba had rendered. After inquiries of her health and recovery, Tagai informed them both that Toyo was to be inducted. Hoba's face visibly froze and Ani appeared to panic — both expressions went ignored by Tagai, but confused Toyo as he thought everyone would be happier to hear this.

"<Tagai wait! This is not —>" Hoba began.

Tagai replied, "<Be quiet, the Ogahigi told me it was his wish. He has the power to make his own choices. >"

Ani joined in. "<Now?! He is a child! Does he even understand the decision he is about to make? Can we even spare the time and resources? Look at how thinly stretched you are already! >" Her outburst startled Tagai as this was a complete about-face from her earlier proposal.

"<Listen to her Tagai! The boy will still sap strength from the Ogahigi over —>"

"<Anma, >" interrupted Tagai.

"<... Anma? >" replied Hoba confused.

"<She wishes to be called by the name that Toyo gave her. It is Anma. >"

"<HE DID!? >" chorused Ani and Hoba.

Ani didn't think that her suggestion would have been taken so seriously and acted upon so swiftly. There had been little time to endear herself to him, and as soon as the boy had the acceptance he so craved there would be little need for Anicula Amo anymore. Desperation forced her hand. "<Tagai please listen... let me take the boy. >"

"<Take him? >"

"<Yes, to the Integrum. The... Anma, wants him to grow yes? You and your tribe are weak and will need much time to regenerate. Even a few days ago the boy threatened AGAIN the livelihood of this camp when he ran off and you had to retrieve him. I can take him to where he will feel a part of things and can learn everything his heart desires — your language, customs and history. Anma just wants him to be a man, correct? I can take away the dangerous boy and bring you back a man. If he can survive the

journey then that too would be training and experience for hunting, yes? >"

Hoba liked Ani's idea more and more as she explained, but in his mind he pictured the old woman dying without her medicine, with the boy following soon after, far away from here. He decided to join in the argument. "<Yes! We can take care of ourselves now, and when they return we can induct him! You said so yourself that you do not wish for a child to sacrifice something they do not understand. Let them both go, and they will return later, and we will all be better for it. >"

Ani was shocked to hear Hoba's approval of her plan, then quickly realized that he obviously wanted to be rid of two troublesome outsiders.

Tagai looked at Hoba in surprise. "<Hoba? You approve of this? How do you even know they will return? >" He felt like he was being attacked from both sides.

"<Well... >" stumbled Hoba.

"<Do you not have faith in us? >" said Ani innocently.

Tagai replied with a cold, "<No. >" It was really boring for Toyo to watch the three of them talk, so he passed the time by counting how many times Hoba scowled at something. "<No more from either of you. You are to stay here and I will gather the tribe. I will honor our Ogahigi, and Toyo's wishes. >" Tagai allowed them no response and stalked out of the tent.

Hoba began to shake with rage. He was so close to being rid of these two! His tribe had done nothing but suffer by the hands of these Integrum folk, and now they were going to become a part of his people?!

Ani noted his shaking and worried, what was he going to do?

Hoba had hoped to go about this differently, but time had now forced him into a corner. He quickly scanned the ground for any nearby rock, picked it up, and turned to Ani. "<You will leave NOW, >" and swiftly smashed his head, making him bleed profusely and fall to the ground dazed.

Ani panicked at the suddenness of Hoba's actions, but he had

LAND OF THE GADORI - CHAPTER XI | 497

now forced her hand. Tagai would not trust that he had done it to himself, and while Toyo might be given the benefit of the doubt, she doubted that she would be. With haste she set about gathering what little she owned, all the while Toyo stood slack-jawed. After grabbing what she could comfortably carry, she began searching Hoba in hopes to find some of whatever it was that he had been forcing down her throat to make her chest stop hurting.

"What the *futuo* just happened?" exclaimed Toyo, wondering why Hoba had clubbed himself.

"*Valde,*" she thought. "*He doesn't have any!*" She turned and said, "Come on Toyo!"

"Wait, what? Aren't I going to be inducted? Why did he do that? What were you doing?" The panic in his voice was something that Ani would have to deal with, but she wasn't quite sure how that was going to play.

She slowly asked, "Do you know what you have to do?"

"Well, no, I wasn't really told —"

Her mind kicked into overdrive. "You have to go on a journey first to prove you are a man. Hoba... rejected you, and this is their custom to prove that opinion — it's weird I know. And, as you know, he is a very important person here, so you have to go and become a man and then maybe when you come back they'll accept you. It's a ritual! The boys who want to prove themselves always go on long journeys alone and come back men, it's a very old tradition! Tagai also rejected you, that's why he walked away. If you stay long then they will be offended, so we need to leave quickly!"

"But this is —"

"You have to become a man first! Do you want to be inducted or not?!"

"Of course, but —"

"Then COME ON!" Ani shouted and dragged Toyo out by the arm, rushing past everyone and running a straight line to the dense forest.

"Where are we going?" asked Toyo.

Huffing slightly, Ani said, "Home."

ЖЖЖЖЖЖЖ

After spending some time preparing himself mentally and gathering what was needed, Tagai walked back into the tent with the intent to educate Toyo of what he must do over the next week and how difficult it would be. Instead, he found Hoba nursing a head wound with blood trickling down his face.

"<What happened!? >" demanded Tagai.

"<The boy... struck me and then ran away with the old woman. >"

"<What? Why?! >"

"<I don't know — Ani pleaded with him not to. She told me it had something to do with not feeling like he would ever belong. >"

He couldn't believe this, it seemed so strange for him to return to this! He could have believed Ani to have done this, but Hoba wouldn't lie to him. "<But.... >"

Hoba weakly shrugged his shoulders and waited until after Tagai had left to inform the Ogahigi before allowing his angry thoughts to flow. "<*That decrepit old woman... I wish her all the luck in the world to reach home. Maybe then we shall know peace from those meddling Integrum people as the creature inside her consumes them all.* >"

Tagai felt angry — a pure rage coursed through his veins at this betrayal. The Ogahigi had been wrong, and the boy had almost killed one of the most important people for the tribe, his brother-in-love.

Striding out of the tent and straight to the Ogahigi he demanded an audience with her. Weakly, the panel opened, and she looked up at him.

"<Yes? >" she replied.

Throwing honor and ceremony aside, Tagai sternly stated, "<Your precious boy has decided to run away. >"

The Ogahigi was silent, and then the Ogaden began to shake and pulsate.

With the backing of Kasmah itself behind her voice, flower fully splayed and turning an ardent red, the Ogahigi cried, "<NO! >"

INTEGRUM

Being in Erus Cogitans' chambers of office was always a rather dry affair for Erus Epula. There was no soul in the Quadra Logicum, and the only way Epula could describe the room was 'meticulously gray'. As he looked out the window at the twisted Integra Pol he said, "I hear that Criso's Ardeo Trial is proceeding well."

"Yes, I was asked to vet the betting odds," replied Cogitans.

"You? Why?"

"I assume Criso merely wanted to consider a second opinion as it is difficult to identify suitable odds given all events as of late. Tari's reputation both works for and against her, while Clarus has the backing of some public committee."

"What's the payout for the couple to pass this year?"

"A ratio of one thousand to one."

Epula turned to see Cogitans still mulling over paperwork on his desk. The man seemed to live for pencil and paper. "That high?"

"The figure is accurate."

"Yes... I suppose it is." It was time for him to get to why he was here. "Tell me Cogitans, have you heard much from Erus Ictus as of late?"

"No, he has removed my charges from his care and sequestered himself to his chambers as far as I know. Reports are that he is hiding in fear now that Mulat is no longer around to protect him."

Epula always had to rewire his brain when speaking with Cogitans and his blunt manner — at times it was harder than dealing with Mulat, but perhaps that was only because Cogitans was not as clear a danger as Mulat could be.

He walked around the room and fiddled with the buttons on his clothes — he would've preferred something else but Cogitans did not care much for knickknacks. "And does he need protection?"

"Given that someone has rendered the Integra Divinitas

incapacitated I would conclude we all do. I removed my charges from the Lustrum — Mulat's silly idea of 'exchange' has no clear benefit at this juncture. I know you removed your charges from everyone except the lowest ranking providers of food, and you know my movements. All convergence points to all-out war as one of us struggles for power."

"Why such a pessimist?"

"That would imply I choose to employ less than accurate data when making estimations and predictions. I solve problems, and the largest problem now is that without a central seat of power for all to aspire towards or fear, Kasmah may descend into the wars of old. The solution is fairly obvious, even to you, which is why you are here to suggest an alliance."

Epula was momentarily stunned. "I... how did you know?"

"I am the strongest of all of us. Erus Criso has the public on her side from the Trial, and Erus Ictus has sequestered himself and therefor rendered himself irrelevant. Why else would you be here if not to ensure the safety of your own?"

"If you have it all figured out then why should I bother talking at all?"

Cogitans looked up at him and smiled in satisfaction of a plan going smoothly. "I am glad you understand your position. I intend for my Logicum to occupy the Integra Pol, after the public's high esteem for the Lustrum is lowered when this year's Lovers are announced as failures. We do not need bloodshed if I have your cooperation. Together we can confront Erus Criso and Erus Ictus, and inform them of what we feel is the path of least resistance."

Epula had indeed already thought of all that, but there was something he wasn't getting. "... Why?"

"Why what?"

"Why do you want to occupy the Integra Pol?"

"Knowledge is power. To know where to place which lever grants a person might greater than any muscle. There is much of interest to me that I wish to explore, and if I have even the remnants of the Integra Pol at my disposal I will be able to explore that much more."

"But what of the city?"

"What of it? It can do as it pleases."

"It needs a ruler! Who will rule?!"

"We do not need a ruler of the people — we need someone that will keep the Quadras in check, who in turn keep the people in check. The one to keep the Quadras in check will be me, I believe that has already been established." Cogitans returned to his paperwork. "Is there anything further, Erus Epula?"

Epula felt like he had been talked to rather than engaged in a conversation. "... No."

Cogitans gestured towards the door without looking up. "Farewell then."

Ж Ж Ж Ж Ж Ж Ж Ж Ж Ж Ж Ж Ж Ж Ж

Mulat's spies' reports on the Quadras were sadly predictable as he could see where everything was heading. Perhaps Stagnos was right — when you are so powerful that your breath alone can change the course of the weather, you cannot breathe around the things you love. It seemed unjust and surreal to Mulat that so soon after reports of his death that his beloved city would descend so far, and who knows how long it would take for the other cities in the Integrum and regions of Kasmah to do likewise. It was nothing but upsetting and stressful news, but the only person in the world that could comfort him and clear his mind was most likely dead by now, and like many a time before he found himself wishing that he could find some relief through sex or food like so many others.

"Why do they wish to harm themselves? Why do they not want to be happy?" mused Mulat as he stared mournfully out of his simple home on the grounds of the Integra Pol. He gave to them all a bounty, and with it they created famine. Why did the world want to be like it was? Why would you beat your own wife? Kick your dog? Starve your children? He did not understand why people neglected the things that they claimed to love and nurture, but worst of all it was sheer stupidity.

He had hoped that forcing the Quadras to exchange their charges would provide them all with better perspective, but the recent news that they had mostly closed their doors to each other darkened his heart. The arguments he put forth, when instead he could have merely laid down the law, the proof of results presented and attempts to treat them as equals, were now being thrown away. All for fear, fear of not being able to be themselves in the face of having to live with people who were not like them.

Was wishing and hoping to give others the power to create or destroy what they saw fit such a fool's errand? At least there was some solace in Erus Ictus, he had never been ungrateful or wishing to harm another. He was also the only other one to cherish any of Mulat's gifts.

All this despair led Mulat to wishing that there was someone else who could tell him how to function or perform so he knew how to get praise or acknowledgment. Having to be ruled by honor or morals, to have to drag those behind him when they could not see the value in what was needed to be achieved, was tiring. Too tiring.

All he wanted was to help people move forward without too much friction, so that every person would not be worn away by each passing day only to die a shell of their former dreams and aspirations. He wanted everyone to be enriched, and happy.

"Perhaps I did not exert my power enough... perhaps too much?" Mulat thought. "But... how did I not make things better? I abolished the Quadra Logicum's legal punishment based on the productivity of a citizen lost, and everyone was so much happier, and it even boosted productivity! The common person can only see their guilt and fear, while the upper class can only see a fear of having less than their peers — I tried so hard to build a bridge between those two understandings. Was abolishing that punishment really the best? It is hard to operate as both arbiter and interpreter of good and bad between two classes of people, whom to neither I belong, yet am bound to."

Mulat tortured himself with thoughts of self-doubt more than anyone would believe — the man felt no fear from anybody, either from their intellect or power. Unchallenged, Mulat's mind craved an opposing force, walls to box him in, so that he could feel the shape of himself. So that something could give him form.

To that end his battles were against the most powerful opponent he could ever face — himself.

Ж Ж Ж Ж Ж Ж Ж Ж Ж Ж Ж Ж Ж Ж Ж

"Seconsulo? Did I have a meeting you did not tell me about?" asked Criso.

Ever by her side, Seconsulo replied, "No, my Erus. This would appear to be unscheduled."

She smiled lightly at the two now standing before her. "Erus Cogitans, Epula. To what honor do I deserve this audience? All my attempts in gaining one with either of you have been met with some resistance, so this is somewhat a surprise."

Erus Cogitans said, "We are here to discuss the future of the Integrum."

Erus Criso had been dreading this day and believed that they would have waited until after the Ardeo Trial to confront her, which would have allowed her ample time to formulate a plan of her own. This however was too soon. "What do you mean?" she asked innocently.

"The Integra Pol lays empty and the public need a figurehead. You have noticed the increased tension in the populace and we must re-establish order," replied Cogitans bluntly.

"What if Mulat does not approve of your course of action?"

"By all accounts the man is dead, and even if he did not approve he is not in any position to provide his actual opinion. As the Quadra Erus' we must do what we feel is best for this city — Erus Epula and I have reached an accord that we feel is best suited for all, and thankfully avoids any possible altercations between us."

"I assume you are the one who wishes to replace Mulat then?"

"My Quadra will occupy the Integra Pol and repurpose its resources to the pursuit of knowledge. There is nothing evil in my intent."

Criso coldly said, "I've been told that Adsum said something along those same lines before his exile."

Cogitans was not one to get emotional. "Yes, he did. In my findings his failure was in being caught by someone who was capable of punishing him, but the knowledge he garnered from his experiments has been invaluable. We have all benefited from it, and I aim to see the Logicum benefit all once more."

"And what of my charges? Am I to just lie down and let you do as you wish with what I have spent years building?"

"I have no interest in the pursuits that this Quadra chooses, I only desire knowledge. Pass on to me any knowledge you might find and allow my observers full access, and there will be no friction between us. Your current modus operandi has proven results better than those of Ardeo, so you should have no fear in being replaced. I do have some minor alterations to suggest —"

"No!" barked Criso, dropping all pretense and standing up, raising herself to full defiance. "If you wish for no friction then this condition will be met: You can observe only when I allow it, but the ONLY changes to my Quadra are mine, and mine alone to make. If you wish to contest me on this it will come down to sex fighting logic, and over the years, my dear Cogitans, I have found many a 'brain' befuddled by their 'genitals'. We shall see who the people would rather keep: Those who make them feel stupid, or those who make them feel happy!"

Erus Epula chimed in with, "Actually, no, you would be against me AND Erus Cogitans."

Criso slowly sat back down. "And so the pig slides easily into the greasiest trough, Epula."

Epula moved forward with raised hand to smack her for the insult but was interrupted by a sharp jab in his exposed ribs by Seconsulo. "Please do not strike Erus Criso," he said calmly. Epula shot him a death glance, who would dare harm an Erus! Seconsulo however seemed uninterested in his title and gave off a dangerous aura. No doubt this was a pointless battle and Epula retreated to Cogitans' side.

Cogitans sighed. "Criso, you cannot hope to beat us both. In the spirit of goodwill I will retract my suggestions, but in the future I recommend you listen to them. If this city is to survive then the Quadras must be able to cooperate — the easiest way to ensure cooperation, is force, but I do not wish to be wasting energy by having to maintain said cooperation through force."

"... Fine. There will be no qualms from me, provided that Erus Ictus is agreeable."

"A reason as to why we have come here is to collect you so we can speak with him."

"What... now?"

"A united front would allow for decreased desire for hostility and an ease of acceptance."

"I'm in the middle of the Ardeo Trial!"

"Which requires no effort on your part save for reading reports at the end of the day. This, however, is a problem that needs a speedy resolution."

Criso exchanged looks with Seconsulo and they had an unspoken conversation conveying a placement of trust in the affairs in her absence, and to take precautions against her not returning. "Very well. My charges will entertain you if you so wish for the time being, I must make myself presentable for Erus Ictus."

"We will be waiting," said Cogitans. With that both Epula and Cogitans stood, bowed, then left.

"Like a dog following the scrap bucket," said Criso softly to herself as the door closed behind them.

Seconsulo was worried, something that he was not in the habit of being. "Is this course of action wise Erus Criso? We still have the public's hope on our side for the Ardeo Lovers."

"Don't be foolish Seconsulo. They will fail like all others — the Erus' know this and are doing little more than skipping a step. I wish I had more time but I can be patient. I know when to submit in order to find the best time to kick them where it hurts."

"Very well, Erus Criso."

Criso sighed heavily, being confronted so quickly was not on her agenda but she'd had little choice in the matter. "Dress me Seconsulo, and make it imposing. At the very least perhaps I can save darling little Ictus from any changes. The man is not unkind and does not deserve having to conform to Cogitans' so-called wishes, and only *futuo* knows if Ictus won't just attack him on sight."

Ж Ж Ж Ж Ж Ж Ж

Unlike the other Quadras, who had assimilated the Integra Pol guards into their own ranks, the Quadra Musicum was devoid of any kind of armed force. The Erus' were surprised at the lack of resistance as they made their way into the main hall and found that everything seemed to be business as usual. Many of the Musicum's charges were surprised to find the Erus' making a collective appearance but none attempted to block their path as they made their way to Erus Ictus' chambers. They found him sitting behind his desk staring out of his window at the Integra Pol. Erus Epula had expected his usual overly emotional response and arguments about the beauty of music, Erus Cogitans expected compliance, and Erus Criso expected to save a man and his Quadra — like she had wished for her own.

"Are you here to ask me which stick I wish to be beaten with?" said Erus Ictus distantly.

The Erus' shared a collective exchange of confused expressions, unsure of how to proceed from that statement. "We are here to heal the city," said Erus Criso, hoping to grease the path for an amicable outcome.

Ictus spoke without turning to look at any of them. "No, you are here to take what is not yours — that which you do not love and crush it, reduce it to dirty limericks and heartless warblings. I stayed true to the heart of my Quadra — unlike you Cogitans, Epula." The only person to not show any discomfort at the situation was Cogitans, who instead had an expression of intense thought as he was calculating the changing variables of the situation. Ictus finally turned with a face exuding pure clarity of mind and said, "This is my Quadra. Leave, or I will take yours from you."

"To leave now would be counterproductive and ultimately lead to more bloodshed. Given the announcement of a threat in response to us being amicable, I am afraid that I will have to escalate this quickly for a swift resolution. Stability must be achieved, Erus Ictus, and for that: you are to be removed," said Cogitans. Beneath his drab robes, Criso and Epula could see a glowing pattern and began to feel the familiar sensation of vesma being called upon. Everything around the pattern vaporized to reveal an ornate tattoo that pulsated under his flesh. Scars formed on his body as the tattoo began to sink into his skin while black smoke rose as the sensation of power filled the room. *"The crazy bastard has tried to strengthen himself by tattooing vesma directly onto his body!"* thought Epula.

Bracing for the bloody mess that was about to happen, Criso could do nothing but fear what the future was going to be like under Cogitans. The whole room filled with an intense pressure, and Ictus merely remained smiling in the face of certain destruction. Criso had thought the pressure to be emanating from Cogitans but she soon recognized it had a rhythm, it was almost like a kind of drum playing in the background.

Ictus flourished a conductor's baton from beneath his waistcoat and waved it idly before matching its tempo to the accompanying beat. He then thrust the baton at Cogitans and a loud note resounded throughout the room as if a cosmic gong had been struck. Cogitans dropped where he stood, his mouth open wide in silence from shock and pain. The vesma in his tattoos, having nowhere to go, burned violently — searing intricately patterned scars into his flesh.

Ictus watched Cogitans' twitching body and said, "He should be fine, not that he wished upon me any kindness." The other Erus' stood stunned at this turn of events, trying to comprehend that the strange, wiry little man had just bested Cogitans. A violin and flute soon joined in with the drum beats, carrying an eerie sound around the room that made everything feel heavy. Two discordant notes were played harshly and both Criso and Epula found themselves slammed against the ground, unable to move.

Ictus lazily made his way to Cogitans with a glazed expression and looked down at him. "Such a beautiful piece isn't it? I wish you had at least tried to listen to the gifts of song I sent you over the years, instead of simply returning them with notes denouncing them as 'pattern inconsistent'. Syncopation and discordance ARE methods we use to MAKE patterns, why could you not see that? There is... too much beauty in this place for you to destroy." Ictus' eyes finally focused and he cast his gaze over all three of them whilst the music played on.

"You all squabble and fight, but in music there is no need to fight — instruments and singers may compete for parts, yet the music itself does not compete nor demand your attention. Sex, food and knowledge — these things are what people kill for day in and day out, but people DIE and are REBORN through music." Ictus gave the impression of a madman who had broken himself, only so he could be reformed into something different. "And you came to kill the music. My music. I, who created only to please and raise people up. I, who above all reach the soul without greed or malice — you would choose to destroy." He leaned down close to Cogitans. "To the dead I give my thanks of Mulat, the man that gave me the gift of power. Unlike you, I did not squander what he provided — I improved upon it. I shall no longer fear the death of music — you, however, will learn to fear the might of it." Standing up slowly and addressing everyone, he said, "Come, it is time for you to see the rebirth of Orbis. The priorities of the old days will not return, and you can all witness my requiem for the greatest city known."

Ictus whistled a sharp note, and from the shadows emerged a strange group of musicians with eyes and hair milky white, most clutching an instrument as lovers would each other. With another gesture they all filed out of the room while several guards came in and gathered the Erus'.

Following in Ictus' wake, as if tethered to the man and his baton, they spilled out into the streets around the Quadras and played strangely beautiful pieces. The horror that fell upon Criso's eyes was that of her once innocuous and harmless little Ictus, leading a squad of musicians capable of quashing the second most powerful person she knew.

The broken Erus Cogitans was soon paraded around his own Quadra with Ictus leading the procession, ensuring that his performance showed to all that he now wielded the power. The guards posted outside were initially perplexed by the music and display, but when they saw Cogitans' haggard state and the looks of fear on Criso and Epula's face they had a need to act. Helplessly Criso had to watch their faces turn to horror as they were massacred by a strange little man with a baton, that with each wave orchestrated death and destruction.

With each Quadra there was minor resistance quelled and an uneasy acceptance of this new situation — whilst the charge rarely cared who the Quadra Erus was at any given time, they felt uneasy about an Erus from a different Quadra claiming rights.

Eventually the First Ring became thick with people, as a crowd soon formed to watch this bizarre spectacle of a scrawny little man with a faraway look in his eyes conduct his symphonic dominance.

Ж Ж Ж Ж Ж Ж Ж Ж Ж Ж Ж Ж Ж Ж Ж

Erus Ictus and his orchestra of death routinely paraded the street, enforcing whatever rule or law he saw fit. Erus Cogitans was carried high up on a chair for display, while the other Erus' were chained to each other on a row of chairs and carried behind the procession. If there was ever a proof that Mulat was to never return in their mind, it was that this horror continued unabated as the days rolled by.

After a week of Ictus' insanity, Orbis was pervaded with an odd mixture of efficiency and fear. The sounds of the city were no longer those of life and commerce, only a strangled silence that was periodically pierced by strange music.

Criso however had, after that one week, reached her breaking point. "There will be constant riots soon if we do nothing," she said to Epula. Fears of being overheard were pushed to one side, as

Ictus always seemed far more focused on the music and enforcing his law than anything anyone had to say.

"The destruction of the Integra Pol, creba running rampant, and the interruption of the Ardeo Trial? Don't be silly, of course people will remain calm," replied Epula, with sarcasm so thick that Criso wanted to produce a spoon then and there to jam it back down his throat.

"Are you really so keen on being unhelpful, or would you rather help me come up with a way of getting us out of this mess?"

"Oh, so now we can come up with something that we didn't before? Besides, is this really such a mess? We both know it was not going to be you or I sitting in the Integra Pol."

Criso despised Epula's casual attitude. "How is that even relevant?! The man is insane!"

"No, the man is just doing what he feels is right. Besides, I don't have the strength to fight him."

"You used to be a man of ambition," said Criso coldly.

"I used to be a man that could enjoy the flavors and wonders of every thing that touched my mouth, until that bastard Mulat poisoned my mouth with his *gift* of bread and water. An Erus of the Quadra Culinum that can't taste ANYTHING — the only use my tongue could have to my Quadra now would be if I blanched it, prepped it, and lightly fried it in oil to be served at dinner." Epula sighed. "So, what am I supposed to be ambitious about when my passion is dead?"

"Then get angry and help me!" Criso pleaded.

Epula once more took a tone of infuriating indifference. "I haven't been a true Erus for a long, long time Criso. All I've been doing is waiting for death all these years. Now that it's come, I don't feel the need to fight for a life I don't want anymore."

Criso abandoned the pointless conversation and squirmed in her chair. She wished her bonds would allow her to try and rouse Cogitans, but a part of her knew that even if she could reach him the man was too far gone inside his own mind. Growing weak from the constant need to hope, Criso tried to retain a strong face.

For many in Orbis it was the first time they had felt true fear, as with every death, senseless and cruel, melodies rang out along the Quadras, until it became common for people to be wary of anything musical. Ictus had become, in their minds, mad and deluded — music and power corrupted what was once a funny, passionate, wiry little man who had such love for life. The public had come to call his musicians the 'death orchestra', while in his own mind he was winning their favor through the beauty of his compositions.

Ictus constantly sent out invitations for all, free entertainment, enlightenment, and food!

Nobody attended.

In his mind it was simply that word had yet to circulate and so kept at it.

Another week passed.

The few that did turn up did so only out of fear, but even then it was a meager handful.

Ictus took this as a blatant sign of disrespect and so his rage at the uneducated masses increased, but he kept on in the hopes that they would see the beauty that he did. After each near-empty gathering he would return to the streets, angrier than ever, ranting and raving and bringing his death orchestra to full force.

Through those displays Criso noticed that the drums threw a force like a hammer, and that the strings and wind instruments would slice like a knife — but they paled in comparison to the singer with the ornate crystalline collar. The singer seemed to be the funnel of power for all the other instruments, with each note, high and low, storing its power inside the song. As the power of the song would grow a glow would emit from the collar until a force would blast into a direction conducted by Ictus' silly little baton. Gathering all this information she hoped to find a weakness somewhere, but did not know where any weakness lay. The little she did know was that there was no vesma in Ictus' baton — he merely was a general in an army, not a weapon. If anything were a weapon it would have been that singer's crystalline collar, beautiful and intricate though it was.

It did not take long, but there soon came a day when the music played harder and louder than ever before. It got her heart racing and her mind worrying, and she almost wept when at its peak she could hear Ictus scream, "IF YOU CHOOSE TO BE IGNORANT, THEN I WILL BURY YOU IN YOUR IGNORANCE!" The man was lost.

With renewed fervor, Ictus began to conduct his orchestra once more. A crescendo built and once again Criso could feel the power and force crush the air around them — he was going to start destroying homes! She braced herself for the tears to come as her heart could not take any more bloodshed. A shrill note pierced the building rhythm that injected itself into the music and put the entire orchestra off-beat. Ictus turned to where he saw the note come from and almost dropped his baton in fear.

"Hello, Erus Ictus," said Mulat, standing tall in his proud white robes and flourishing a small wooden flute. "I see you have taken my devotarecalis and learned well from her, but of all my gifts to you why must this be the one I see you use most?"

The initial shock of the situation caught Ictus off-guard, but knowing that he had gone too far now he re-doubled his efforts and launched an attack on Mulat — Criso and Epula took their chances and exhausted some of their own vesma to break their chains and flee the streets for safety. A soft rhythm began to rise in the streets, and the music played gave the sense that a great battle was about to take place with a force powerful enough to level cities.

Under Ictus' conduction the music quickly reached full melodic resonance — but each time a crescendo reached its peak Mulat would play a perfectly timed note, each one injecting itself into the music and draining all the power from the song. There was never any fear or concern on Mulat's face — he merely stood calmly in the street, armed with nothing more than a flute.

After playing a few more distracting notes, Mulat began to walk towards Ictus and his orchestra of death. "I have always appreciated music," he flourished his flute, "And the instruments that make it." He then sighed. "Erus Ictus, you have done great by your Quadra and written and performed many beautiful pieces — all of which you are deeply thanked for. I had hoped to wait out and see who attacked me in my Integra Pol, but you forced my hand, and that is... exciting, but now you are being so easily thwarted." The singer in Ictus' orchestra of destruction sang out and a powerful wave of force speared directly towards Mulat, hitting him square in the chest and making him drop to his knees. Ictus was reinvigorated by seeing his creation deal a palpable blow to the most powerful man in Kasmah as he watched Mulat splutter up blood.

Mulat began to laugh uncontrollably, "Ha... haha... hahahaha!" and looked directly at Ictus. "So... this is what it is like to feel someone to be your match? Uncertain? It's amazing! I don't understand what just happened... can this truly be it?" Ictus had no idea how to respond to the manic expression on Mulat's face.

Mulat reached out his arms and beckoned to Ictus with both hands. "Please! AGAIN!" he said with a grin, blood trickling down his chin. He had fantasized about having fear, the fear of death, many times over. Never before had he faced even the remotest possibility of it, and now he was drunk on the feeling. For the first time, he felt like he had access to an easy way out, that he didn't have to carry all the weight of the world because he was the strongest. There was someone more than him.

Ictus panicked and conducted the song to a fever pitch and again sent a force designed to render Mulat to a bloody smear on the pavement. The force struck out, but it was a nearby roof that suffered the blast as Mulat played another note. He began a slow pace to Ictus — like a specter of death, with every step delivering fear to everyone watching, with a flute in his hand. "No! NO! You are supposed to be powerful! DESTROY ME!" he screamed. "I AM RISING TO YOU! RISE IN TURN!"

A spiral note flew towards Mulat and he made no effort to defend himself and it tore into his shoulder, almost ripping it clean from his body and spilling a lot of his blood onto the street. He did not stop his approach as more blood pooled beneath him and his clothes began to cling to his body. "Yes... yes..." Mulat said with a faraway look as he staggered forward.

"So... close," whispered Mulat to himself as he began to slump.

Ictus thought, *"Why isn't he fighting back?!"* The sentiment was shared amongst all watching. The man had diffused him so simply with a flute, why the suicidal march? Why did he seem to be taking joy in walking towards his own demise? With the possibility of victory in his sights and the fear of what would happen if he lost now. Ictus began to weave an intricate melody, a finale to ensure his own survival.

From seemingly out of nowhere, Criso saw Clarus gracefully land directly between Erus Ictus and Mulat, naked, and with her chest burning so ferociously bright that it looked like her skin was on fire. Her expression showed nothing but an intensity that did not recognize the pain, only the situation she was in. She dashed towards Mulat, biting the skin on her thumb hard, and pressed her own bloody thumb into the pool of his blood. The pool reacted quickly and violently, shooting up and encasing them both — protecting them from the outside world. Blood from Clarus' thumb flowed to power it and the barrier absorbed all of Ictus' attacks, but her blood could not last forever.

Clarus turned to Mulat, a man battered and broken, reached out her hand, and caressed his face. "I am home," she whispered lovingly.

"... Juvo?" Mulat murmured and pathetically tried to hand her something. "I saved... your flute... for you...."

She used her free hand to brush his gift aside and guided him to her breast. "You cannot seek death, for I found you first — but you made it hard this time. Do not hide from me again Mulat, please."

"I had to... hide... from everyone, you were... gone for... so long..." he said in despair.

"Yes, and look what kind of mess you got yourself into."

There was comfort in her. There was always comfort. Blissful silence to a mind so used to a thousand thoughts at once. "I am too unique Juvo, I do not belong and only bring disaster. Death should claim me... I do not fear it."

"Nor do I, my dear Mulat. There is an unbroken pattern which links what made us, and all patterns repeat. Death and life will claim us both yet again, but the time for that cycle is not now."

"I... dead... missed you..." said Mulat weakly. Juvo bit her lip hard, leaned in and kissed Mulat deeply — through that act life flowed into him. Everything came surging back and his depression was quashed as relief flowed through him. He lifted his head up and pressed his lips into hers, but soon she had to push him away lest he over indulge.

He saw her now, weak and pale. Her blood was running low — her death was not something he could allow. As if reciting some internal doctrine he said, "We are all but patterns in eternity, and I will keep our patterns flowing," and kissed her on the forehead. He then carefully lifted up her thumb and she gave no resistance, and moved her behind him. "Welcome home," he said without turning his head.

Mulat placed his hand on the blood-barrier and it crumbled like wet tissue and fell to the ground clumped. Stepping out from his sanctuary he spied Ictus ready to launch another attack, but with his mind refreshed Mulat knew it was time to end all this. Bringing Juvo's flute to his lips he blew a few notes, and began walking forward.

Ictus began launching everything he could in desperation — looking on in fear as Mulat swiftly dissolved any attack he threw at him. With a measured and startling speed, Ictus soon found Mulat's large hand wrapped around his face and lifting him off the ground. Without their conductor the musicians instantly fell silent, and a look of fire and vengeance exuded from Mulat.

In tones that carried far more than mere information, and with the expectation that reality could not disobey, Mulat said, "**Da capo al fine.**"

Ж Ж Ж Ж Ж Ж Ж Ж Ж Ж Ж Ж Ж Ж

It had been almost three days since Clarus had left the room without so much as an 'excuse me', leaving Laris very bored and quite confused. His boredom however was interrupted, to his surprise, by Erus Criso and her humorless advisor. As soon as she entered the lavish room in her beautiful dress, Laris tried to capitalize on something he had been thinking about for quite some time. "Hey! Your Taker left so... so that means I win right!?"

In full commanding tones Criso said, "Excuse me? Is that any way to talk to the Erus of this Quadra?"

Suitably chastised, Laris backed down. "... Um... sorry. Pardon me, Erus Criso."

"Now... the rules have been broken but... there are extenuating circumstances. Clarus cannot return, so you are free to do as you wish — but you still cannot leave this room. If you would like some other company please just ask."

Not wanting to argue Laris simply asked the other thing that had been bugging him. "OK, but why did Clarus leave?"

"She had important business, that is all you need to know."

A charge appeared in the doorway and whispered something to Seconsulo, who then relayed it hurriedly into her ear. Criso's face did an expert job of not showing any signs of surprise given what she had just been told. Speaking again to Laris she said, "So, would you stay for the remainder of the month? I am aware it is only a couple more weeks, but we will endeavor to make your stay as comfortable as possible."

"Um... sure, I guess. I hope she's okay, she was a nice girl."

"She is more than okay, I assure you," smiled Erus Criso, and left the room in a sweeping motion.

Halfway down the hall she turned to Seconsulo and screamed, "Tari's GONE?! Where the bloody fuck did she go?! HOW did she even break her conducutis?!"

Seconsulo responded plainly, "I believe she went to seek the object of her obsession."

"Fucking *PLAGA!* I knew Mulat surfacing would trigger her again, but how did she even find out?"

"Tari has quite the ability to get information out of the charges assigned to service the room."

"This is..." Criso quickly composed herself — she had no time to waste on emotions right now. "Those that let slip the information are to be punished. Severely. And FIND Tari."

"What do we do about Ilia?"

"Tell her the same thing I told Laris, that only their Taker has left and they must wait until the end of the month."

"And what then?"

Criso's composure broke. "For fuck's sake man, I have MORE important things on my mind! Get to it!"

FINAL CHAPTER

When in a position of power, you can either abuse or nurture.
If ever you feel at a loss as to what to do:
Listen to the people first;
the law second;
yourself last.

-Teachings of the Integra Pol

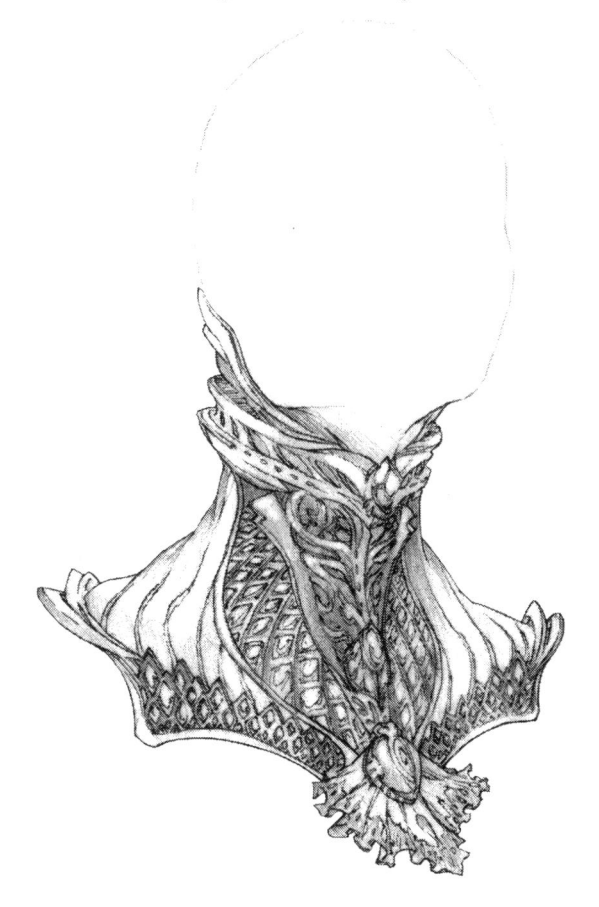

FINAL CHAPTER

Adsum hadn't expected Kahli to burn away all of his vesma tattoos, leaving his chest looking like it'd been drawn on intricately with fire, but it only added to his fascination. Having to fight the constant feeling of flesh and muscle burning though made it difficult to concentrate. Vesma depletion alone should have both killed her and left him in a coma, but for some unknown reason they were still capable of traveling — he could only conclude Kahli to be the answer.

The young woman however kept slipping in and out of a trance-like state, and all attempts to communicate directly were fruitless. The only times she would talk to him were to ask how much farther it would be. While to her the distance and time were a nuisance, for Adsum it was an opportunity to observe her meticulously. An effort made difficult by having to both tend to his wounds and deal with her stupor.

"Subject experiences intense emotional fluctuations, no visible evidence of vesma depletion. Appears to have conversations with either herself or some unknown entity, unable to decipher content — source of her power unknown, possible correlation? Attempts to induce sleep through sedative laced food yields no results, subject has also not slept since the Habiak camp."

"Addendum: Existing Integra Pol plans placed on hold due to loss of Habiak resources — will attempt to utilize subject as replacement. Last report from the city indicated child Habiak distribution network of the cremo faba successful. Need to identify and isolate possible kill switch for subject."

The pair's long journey to the Vios Ocean was littered with sparse encounters of creature and people alike, but they all met the same fate: a gruesome and swift demise. The occurrence had become so commonplace that Adsum merely found an optimal observation spot and watched Kahli either rip them to shreds or burn them alive.

"The strikes that render the most destruction appear to use her physical body the least. Body must be a conduit rather than actual source — vesma being drawn from where if not her blood? Emotional state prior to attacking is one of joy, after the threat dissipates she breaks down into tears. Attempts to engage her in conversation still yield nothing."

Kahli's hostility towards everything resulted in Adsum having to make a lot of good faith gestures to stop her from destroying everything. The journey to the Vios was easy enough, made easier by Kahli's power, but his true problem was in how he would keep her docile enough, long enough, for her to not burn their ship while they were on the Vios itself. He spent a lot of time crafting plans and counter-measures, and worrying.

When they reached the ocean though, Kahli changed. Each step closer brought to her face a calming effect, until eventually she was at its shore and just listlessly gazed out over the waters. He allowed her to remain undisturbed for a while, until it became apparent that she wasn't actually going to move anywhere. Aside from the minimal effort of finding food and feeding herself, and even then she was not picky as to what she ate, she was content to just sit or stand and look out at the ocean. She had become so placid that Adsum even considered performing a few experiments, but decided that it was not worth the risk.

Taking her to the nearest trading port city wasn't an option before, but now that he wanted to he wasn't able to. After considering all the options the only viable one was asking a favor of the Nauta family, who virtually controlled all safe passage across the Vios. Using his old family name was not something he wanted to have to do, but it was a price worth paying.

Taking stock of the situation Adsum concluded that she was in little danger of being disturbed, or even moving, and took the risk of traveling to the nearest port to send his message. Several days later he returned to the site on the ship gifted to him, and found Kahli standing in the middle of a long series of tracks and footsteps around her. *"Well, she has at least been moving since I've been gone."*

With their safe passage ensured on a mighty Nauta vessel, they crossed the tremulous Vios without incident. Kahli never went below deck or paid attention to anyone. In her mind too much was going on for the real world to matter. This was HER choice, and she was determined to be strong, no matter the cost.

"*Is this still what you want?*" Kahli's other voice asked herself.

Kahli replied, "*This is what they deserve.*"

"*And who are you to decide that?*"

"*Who were they to decide for me?! If they have the power to choose, then so do I — I will no longer be kept under someone's thumb! I WILL be who I choose to be!*"

"*Then why choose this path?*" The calmness of the other voice grated on Kahli.

"*They would not let me be me! I just wanted to cook! To clean! To take care of everyone and make sure there was a smile everywhere! Why must I be punished for wanting to love? To care? Why wouldn't anyone let me BE!?*"

"*You aren't letting anyone do those things now.*"

"*Because they chose to sacrifice me, when all I wanted was to do good!*"

"*And what of those who wanted to save you?*"

The memory of the woman who had called herself Kahli's mother flashed in her mind. "*They didn't want to save me, only themselves. So, I will not save them from me.*"

"*I thought you wanted to save yourself.*"

Kahli broke inside. "*I SHOULDN'T HAVE TO! THE WORLD SHOULD NOT BE SO CRUEL!*"

Adsum kept a close eye on her for the entire journey, and in seeing her peaceful state he wondered if her power had run its course. An assumption that was proved wrong when he tried to test her, only to be given a warning shot, and then proved further wrong when they reached the western shore of the Vios.

When they disembarked into the western Maharaan lands and walked far enough to lose sight of the shore, Kahli returned to her emotionally erratic state and he felt her amp up once more. This however was not the curse-ravaged lands of the Jara, these were the lands of the Harat people — those who had no need for battle.

For them there was no honor in fighting, no glory in death, no joy to be found in creating fear.

Through all the different villages, clans, nomadic families, Kahli weaved a steady stream and trail of destruction as she and Adsum traveled south to the Integrum. The intensity of her outbursts had now become so violent that Adsum wondered if she was merely recharging while they had traveled, because whenever he looked behind them he saw the ground itself charred black in their wake. Distant and distrusting of all, Kahli gave no quarter to anything that happened to cross her path. None were spared from the beast she had become.

As they journeyed, Adsum's mind again had to recalculate the risk and reward of trying to earn her trust. What would happen when she finally saw Mulat? Would she even try to talk, or could he leave them to battle it out? Even before all that how was he going to deal with her? Either way, more observation was necessary.

"Tentative conclusion regarding the Orati is that the Jara have found a way to artificially induce a form of cadare, bound to an emotional stimulus. Findings of Kahli's pregnancy lead me to conclude that gestation is being held in stasis and propagated to those who share her blood — possible blood-vesma harmonics? Still unable to find a credible reason for her intense power, even if I allow for the possibility that she is the Mulier."

His leading hypothesis regarding her power made him uncomfortable as it was half-formed at best. He believed that the Orati process was condensing and amplifying all the vesma in her body to her brain which would explain the direct link between her emotions and powers. But what was stopping the vesma from consuming her mind and corrupting her body? He had no way of testing and no direct proof, and with only pure conjecture when a test subject was so close at hand, he grew aggravated himself.

Beyond that, the real puzzle for Adsum was the simple question of *who did this to her*. Mulat was the first suspect as he was the most powerful man in Kasmah, but the man had barely ever left the Integra Pol, and even then only to the confines of the Quadras.

All conclusions led him to only one other name — one that both excited and terrified him. If this deduction was accurate however, then he wouldn't need to do much at all for his dream to be realized.

Indeed, Kahli would be a perfect example of something that one such as Malef would do.

Adsum then did the worst thing he knew a rational man could do.

He hoped.

Ж Ж Ж Ж Ж Ж Ж Ж Ж Ж Ж Ж Ж Ж Ж Ж

Since his exile, Ictus had taken up residence in Lanx Lancis — city of Industry and Commerce, second in grandeur only to Orbis itself. Situated between the Vios and the Calu-Jedde, it acted as the main hub that merged the resource gathering Maharaan and Calu-Jedde, with the artisans and craftspeople of the Integrum.

In his exile, Ictus wondered why Mulat did not destroy him that day, and also why he had been allowed to keep his orchestra — even though it was under special and strict instructions. Mulat had told him, "They belong to you, you raised them and trained them. Without you they are nothing, and while they cannot tell right from wrong, all that defines a person is purpose — and you are the only one capable of giving them purpose. I trust that you will continue to do so." Was he truly so pathetic a man, so little a threat, that Mulat could not even see him as dangerous?

Ictus had come to accept that power had driven him, if not mad, then, just a little off course. It was a source of shame for a time, but now he was in Lanx Lancis! A fresh start! With this second chance he could build something beautiful, and ensure the safety of that beauty with his orchestra. Maybe here he could teach people the wonder of music where he had failed so miserably in his own Quadra. He had become complacent there, he could see that now.

Lanx Lancis was welcoming enough to him — what place in Kasmah wouldn't want the guidance of an Erus? Even an exiled one. Ictus made himself a home east of the main city with minimal effort and set to work. He began to build up trust with the locals, whom he came to love, and shared with them everything he knew about music. The stress of his Quadra and the fear of losing his passion drained away in the light of this new life, and within himself there was new-found tranquility. In that peace he began to write beautiful music in an effort to show people different emotions — hoping to spread the love that music brings.

The days and weeks that passed brought him more comfort than he thought possible. Here he could protect both his passion and the people. He finally felt at home, instead of in an enormous house filled with strangers who would bicker and fight over what and how to play. Along with all of those bloated and unappreciative clients — they did not understand how an artist suffered! But they would throw money and gifts at them as if that somehow proved something.

Here though, based out of this smaller town on the outskirts of Lanx Lancis, there was none of the pomp and rivalry. The musicians that he had trained and nurtured, and misguidedly perverted out of fear to protect his old Quadra, soon became something he could be proud of. He started off small, patrolling with his orchestra to keep the peace in his own little region, and soon was welcomed by the Lords and Ladies of Lanx Lancis to patrol the city itself.

It did not take long for Ictus' patrols to dramatically decrease Lanx Lancis' normally high crime rate, a result aided by the rumors from Orbis of the death orchestra that had brought to it such ruin. Ictus however did learn to temper his music to the hearts that were listening — to calm those that were scared, and create tension in those that would do harm.

For the first time in his life, he was conducting the hearts of the people. Ictus' own heart swelled. He had finally helped his orchestra become what all musicians wish to be: appreciated.

One day during a patrol there was an unusual harmonic in the air, and as one the orchestra stopped playing, and looked north in silence.

His devotarecalis had never expressed anything before, save for when singing, but the look on her face now made him worry.

Sadly, Ictus' peaceful days would not last much longer.

ЖЖЖЖЖЖЖЖЖЖЖЖЖЖЖЖ

Adsum stopped and pointed to the southern horizon. "That is Lanx Lancis, the city that is the melting pot of the western Maharaan, Integrum, and Calu-Jedde. That is our first port of call before we head on to the city of Orbis, where the man who can give you answers resides."

Kahli however did not stop and had kept walking.

Adsum had thought that seeing a fully-fledged city would trigger some form of calm like when she had reached the Vios, then again he had also thought that the mass destruction she had inflicted so far would have quelled her blood-lust. *"No matter,"* thought Adsum. *"Even if she lays waste to Lanx Lancis it may still work in my favor. Still, some caution is warranted."*

Adsum gently guided Kahli to where he could test her reaction: The outer rural limits of the city. The small huts and fields of crops littering the area signaled that they were close to farmland for a village that would be serving Lanx Lancis' needs. As they journeyed further some of the farmers went to greet them, but quickly changed their minds after seeing an old man in tattered clothes, with strange scars underneath, and a young woman covered in dried blood with a faraway look in her eyes. Random spouts of flame would erupt from Kahli, and soon they retreated to their village.

Kahli seemed to be behaving, but with each twitch and spooked expression, every person that walked quickly away or shuffled to one side, she became increasingly distraught and withdrawn. It was a tense walk for Adsum, but the test had to be done. They eventually reached the center of the nearby village, where a fountain in the shape of an ox had been erected as a sign of their prosperity. Lanx Lancis only gifted statues to supplying villages that were vital, so this place was sure to attract some attention.

Kahli sat on the edge of the fountain and turned to Adsum. She gave him a look that made him feel that her eyes were having trouble focusing on what was real.

"Food," she commanded.

Feeling unsure of what would happen if he did not provide, Adsum quickly went about gathering food from the nearest house. He saw no need to care about the occupants, who cowered as soon as he walked through the door, and while he rummaged they fled. Upon returning to Kahli he presented an assortment of goods, and without ceremony she then proceeded to consume them with gusto. This was strange, she hadn't cared so much about food before. Why now?

Adsum had also now noted that there was nobody to be seen, all had fled quite fast — had news of Kahli already reached this far south. Leaving Kahli to herself, he scouted the area and found the entire place to be abandoned. *"Unknown situation: Residents abandoned area. Possible causes: Fear from seeing her emit flames in the fields — Nauta family informed Mulat for personal gain — some of the fleeing Harat have reached Lanx Lancis and rumors of Kahli's power have spread. No audible or visible signs of alerting law enforcement, they must have gone to summon them directly. New time constraint a concern."*

He returned to Kahli and watched her eat with all the mechanical precision the body could provide, but with none of the instinct to eat. Sitting against a nearby wall, he formulated his next course of action. His thoughts were interrupted by a strange melody that caught his attention. Looking to see if Kahli had noticed or reacted, he saw that she still just sat there chewing through the random pieces of nutrition that he had scrounged.

As he listened to the tune a familiar sensation came over him. His skin began to prickle and he found himself having to address a new variable. *"Since when did Lanx Lancis employ this much vesma harmonics in their defenses?"* he thought, and directed his attention to survival. *"This conflagration between two powers should suffice. A shame, Kahli would have made for more interesting investigation."*

Adsum was quite a distance away already before he heard a beautiful singing voice and accompanying drums. *"Why the music? Some sort of attempt to intimidate the enemy? Has someone developed a direct vesma harmonic dispersion technique?"* he wondered, and debated on whether to return just to observe.

But when he did turn, and saw the scale at which the destruction was being performed, he decided to keep to his original plan.

ЖЖЖЖЖЖЖЖЖЖЖЖЖЖЖ

The guilt of Ani's past with the Gozuri did not weigh heavy on her shoulders, despite her crimes, but she could see that Toyo's did. The unease he was radiating as they traveled was palpable, and no matter what she tried the boy seemed adamant to feel disheartened.

She felt weaker by the day and knew that she would soon need to rely upon him if her deterioration continued — so she opted for the more direct approach. He had not harassed her about their sudden departure, but she knew it was going to come up sooner or later. Focusing him on it now would at least get his sullenness out of the way. "What is troubling you, Toyo?"

Toyo stood very still for a moment. So far he had only given Ani measured and terse responses, but now he spoke as if a dam had burst inside of him. "Did we really have to leave?! I mean, they must need people to help them hunt! Am I really so useless?"

"Did you really help them?" Ani asked, hoping to direct his questions towards his guilt.

"I didn't mean to do anything bad!"

"Intent is the path, result is the goal."

Flustered, he said, "I don't know what you mean! I just wanted to help!"

Ani had hoped to not have to stand and argue with a child, there was a long journey ahead. "As Tagai once told you: You wanted to feel useful, more than you wanted to be useful." His face fell so far and fast that she did feel some guilt, and feared she may have cut him too deep. Hoping to heal what she had done, she continued, "You can and will — you will learn how to help. Then you can come back, and help them as much as you like."

"But why are we heading this way?"

"Because this direction leads to my home." She had to omit that she had no idea if her home really still existed, but all the relatively normal landscapes that they had passed did give her hope. If only she'd had the resources and strength earlier to venture through and out of the Gadori to see this for herself.

"... There are others?" he asked expectantly.

Ani found his question strange. *"Does he really not know anything about the world?"* she thought, but in that she found the chance to capitalize on his ignorance. Speaking grandly she said, "Oh there are hundreds! Thousands! There is Orbis, the largest city of all, and that alone holds almost two million people!" Speaking of home rekindled Ani's desire to return, and now with a golden prize to present to her Logicum Erus, Adsum, her re-integration would be that much sweeter. She could finally return to not having to worry about a horrific and uncertain death — not having to suspect every damn flower of being something that wanted to burrow into your skin and redecorate your insides.

Toyo asked, "What else?"

"What do you mean?"

"I mean, what else is there?"

"Well, there's the Vios Ocean and the Calu-Jedde Mountain range — those are called the spines of Kasmah."

"Spines?"

"Yes. They are called that because they both split the three regions of the Maharaan, Integrum, and Gadori from north to south. The Vios Ocean, called the center of Kasmah, is on one side of Kasmah, while the Calu-Jedde on another."

That didn't make sense to Toyo. "Wait, why is the Vios called the center?"

"I suspect because nobody has crossed the Calu-Jedde successfully and that there is no real passage over, through, or under it."

"So... from the Vios, there's an east and west Gadori, Maharaan, Integrum?"

"Correct."

"... And, where are we?"

"Western Kasmah."

"And these other places, do they have the same problems like the Gozuri? The kusabana?"

"Well no, the Ogagi and all things associated with it are endemic to the Gadori forests."

"What does endemic mean?"

"It means it only exists in a specific place."

"Oh...." Toyo's mind wandered, exploring the possibility of what the future might hold. "What about between here and the Integrum? Are there any cities?"

"Mostly small villages. There used to be more before a kusabana broke out of the Gadori forest and spread throughout the Integrum lands — it affected both the east and west. I suspect there would be some trading outposts, farming villages, and nomads that would have survived."

Toyo looked down at his hands and again wondered about being accepted in a new place. He began walking again and Ani sighed in relief. That was until he asked another question. "Will someone know what is wrong with me?"

"Are you feeling sick?"

Toyo waved at her and said, "No, I mean my hands."

Not wanting to crush his hopes, Ani said, "I'm sure there are people in Orbis that would know. All sorts of geniuses live there, we can find out anything you could want to know."

Toyo felt slightly lost. He'd never had a place to call home or somewhere he felt like he belonged. When everything felt alien it was hard to know anything, and Toyo felt like nothing would ever know him, even when he just wanted to help. "How do we get there?"

Ani stopped in her tracks and pointed at the horizon. "When the day is ending and the sun kisses the ground, turn right. If you ever feel lost you just wait until another night kiss."

"Night kiss?"

Ani shook her head. "Old habit. The Gozuri called the sunset and sunrise the night and day kiss of the sun — one kiss when it leaves the ground to travel the sky, and one kiss to welcome it home. It was —" Her flow was interrupted by a sharp pain in her chest and she clutched it, hard.

"Are you okay?" asked Toyo with a look of concern.

"Yes... yes I'll be fine. Just a call of nature, give me a moment won't you?" said Ani, excusing herself to a nearby bush.

In private she pulled the top of her garments aside and inspected the scar on her chest like she had done a hundred times before, and cursed Hoba like she had one hundred more. She had spent days trying to find out what he had done, but she had been a Logicum charge, then Yohju, and her affliction required an answer that only those blasted Gozuri or Natura could give her. Hah, as if asking any of them had been an option — all she knew was that when she drank that foul white paste the pain went away.

Thankfully she had been sneaking small amounts from Hoba even before their fortuitous escape, but it still wasn't enough to ration for the journey home and seek care from the Integra Pol. Her attempts to make it last by taking smaller and smaller doses didn't feel like it was working, but something was better than nothing at this point.

Ani emerged from the bush to Toyo's look of concern. "Is something wrong?" he asked. "You look really pale."

She waved his concern aside. "Yes, yes I am fine Toyo. We just need to keep —" Ani felt a lump of mush slowly rise up in her throat and slide out of her mouth. As it fell to the ground, Toyo looked at her in disgust and confusion.

"*What the futuo did Hoba do to me?!*" Ani panicked inside her head. "Don't worry Toyo, that was... just me bringing up something unnecessary." She coughed and sputtered before dismissing his attempts to aid her and said, "We need to keep moving, the journey will take us many months."

The event preyed on her mind, all the while having to reassure Toyo that she was, in fact, just fine.

Something which she knew wasn't going to last.

☀☀☀☀☀☀☀

As the old lady and young boy journeyed, the days and weeks passing with little of interest, Ani's body started to wither. To distract herself she would talk about what Toyo could look forward to, but over the last few days she had been unable to find the strength to hide her failing body. She could feel her mind slipping, and her pride stopped her from asking for help. As much as she knew she was changing for the worse, she couldn't help but notice that Toyo too was changing ever so subtly, finally fending for himself and providing for her. It seemed to help him stop fidgeting and doubting all the time — less prone to snap decisions and emotions. It was like he was beginning to learn to take his time. It was an observation that made her feel somewhat proud of him.

Toyo had also been taking notice of her, and today was the day where he could not avoid what he had feared. Trailing behind Ani for some time now had been a thin trail of reddish-pink mush. Before he was able to dismiss it as other things, but now.... He didn't know what was wrong, but he knew that it wasn't right. Walking slowly to match her pace, and with many stops and starts from uncertainty, he tried to face the truth they had both been hiding from.

"You are dying... aren't you?" asked Toyo.

Ani kept her sluggish pace and weakly replied, "... I... believe so."

The steps in silence felt heavy. "Why did you lie to me?"

"I did not want you to worry." Her colorless face smiled weakly.

"You know, I once thought that there was nobody else in the world but me, then I met the Gozuri and you took me away from them. So far I've only seen burned buildings and razed land!" He stopped her with his hands and yelled, "AND NOW YOU'RE GOING TO DIE AND LEAVE ME HERE! Why?!"

"Didn't... plan to."

He threw his hands to the sky. "Where are these Integrum cities you spoke of?!"

"I did not think the... destruction," Ani wheezed.

Guilty for screaming at a dying old woman, Toyo asked, "I'm sorry, I didn't mean to.... Are you okay?" Ani stopped in her tracks and pulled the top of her garments aside, revealing her chest scar. "What is that?"

"I... don't know. Don't... worry about... it." She looked north with sorrow "Orbis could... could never...." Ani's words trailed off as she recalled the creatures of horror that she had witnessed over the years. As much as the thought frightened her she knew that it was very possible one of them could have taken root and spread north, infecting and killing everything. The Gozuri'd had years to learn in a confined area how to deal with these creatures, while the Integrum had no way to prepare for what she had seen.

The momentum of walking had been carrying her forward, but now that Toyo had stopped her she found that her legs could not stand. She sat down heavily, and realized that she was sitting on something moist, but couldn't find the strength to make herself more comfortable. Too weak to move she could hear a little *slush slush* and felt a stabbing pain, like there was a tiny man with a tiny spoon mixing up her insides.

"That... bastard..." were Ani's final thoughts, and then she fell to the ground. Dead.

The strength of her pride alone had made Toyo think her indestructible, but the look in her eyes told him that pride could only take someone so far. He bent down, tears in his eyes, and tried to revive her. It was a long time before he accepted that he was doing nothing but prodding and talking to a corpse.

He took a seat up next to her, and felt sad and angry — sad that yet again he could not save someone, and angry that the old lady had taken him on a journey to a land that held fewer people than before. As his emotions raged inside him, he began to hear a *slush slush* sound and looked at Ani, where he saw more of the mush slowly dripping out of her mouth.

"*What the futuo?*" he thought, curiosity getting the better of him. He placed his ear against her body, and the sounds he heard made him feel slightly queasy. *"So... that's what dying sounds like on the inside,"* he thought to himself. He sighed heavily and looked around the landscape. *"I should... what should I do?"*

To the south there were no familiar signs of the forests he had known, and to the north there were no signs of Ani's promises. He was lost, unsure, and in shock. Without the power to make a decision within his grasp, his body made one for him — sitting seemed as good a plan as any right now.

His mind was not so kind. It could only think that now there really was nobody he could talk to — Anma had apparently sent him away, and the old lady now lay dead beside him.

"So, you're the only person that can keep me company now." he thought to himself.

"I suppose so, Toyo," he replied out loud.

"So what do you want to do?"

"Well I don't know Toyo, why not just go the opposite way we were headed?"

"That's an excellent idea, Toyo."

"I know Toyo, glad I thought of it."

"... This is sort of stupid."

"Yes it is... Toyo." He sighed loudly. That wasn't even his real name. Was it? Don't mothers give names? Where was his mother? HIS name?

His mind's demons whirled around and around, but through them all, he heard Ani's stern voice telling him to stop being so stupid and just make a decision. Thoughts are thoughts, actions are actions. With that he concluded that going back empty handed when the Gozuri wanted him to return a man was a stupid idea. He was sent away to prove himself wasn't he? What if he could not get to Anma in time to explain the situation? Would she even listen?

As he battled with both self-loathing and determination, he remembered Tagai's story of giving up your fear so you could save the ones you loved. He wasn't sure if he loved anyone or if it was just guilt, but he knew he had to give up his fear and head north if he wanted to do the right thing. At least then he could return to the Gadori forest.

But, which Ogagi would they would be at? How many of those things were there, or where? He shook his head. Those were problems for later. Focus on the now — Tagai had always said that the 'now' was where everything existed. Focus on the now.

This was his punishment: To only come back when he had value — when he could protect those he said he would. *"Maybe then I can get Anma to come out of that tree stump so we can talk better,"* he thought happily.

Looking down at the old lady he was surprised that he did not care much that she was dead — he attributed that to the fact that she was usually grumpy and didn't treat other people very nicely. Still, someone should shed a tear for her, and she had helped him when he'd needed it most.... If she had taught him anything it was that it was still a long journey ahead, and provisions shouldn't go to waste.

Stripping her for any rations, he stumbled across a strange trinket box in her belongings and remembered how she would fiddle with it often. He thought that it must be something useful or powerful otherwise she would not have kept it — the woman showed little interest in things that served no purpose. Slipping it and all the other rations into their journey bags, he went back to her body and thought, *"Doesn't... seem right to not care. She did talk to me after all."* And with that he decided to stay by her side a little longer. It felt the right thing to do.

While he watched the sun make its journey across the sky, he became aware of a terrible smell and looked over to see that the mush had now turned grey and seemed to be flowing out of every orifice. He almost retched — it was so awful to see her change so quickly and wondered if she'd had some sort of horrendous disease. *"I've spent hours with a dead body that might be infectious, probably a bad idea."* Using that thought as a cue to leave, he happily hefted his traveling gear and, after one final wave to her corpse, began his trek north.

When he was ten steps away a gurgling sound from behind made him turn around, and he saw Ani attempting to stand up. "*Futuo!* You're ALIVE?!" he shouted. Her body had thinned to a grotesque degree, but it was definitely Ani.

The old woman reached her full height and opened her mouth. The only things that came out of it were a gurgle, and more gray mush. She began lumbering towards Toyo, moving like she was propped up from the inside with sticks.

"Ani?" Toyo asked cautiously.

The body moved forward uncertainly but with each step seemed to be getting more control over its limbs, until finally it sprinted at Toyo. Caught off-guard by the sudden change of speed he panicked and threw an overarm swing, which slammed her head into the ground with such force that her skull split open.

Breathing heavily and scared that he may have killed her for good, he was once more confused when he did not see anything resembling blood or bone. More like a tree root had inflated inside her head. The once-Ani quickly recovered and lunged from its ground position to latch onto Toyo's legs. Startled he grabbed Ani's arms and lifted her off him with ease, now holding her at arm's length from him.

What confronted him was a face with skin sagging, and underneath the torn flesh looked to be some sort of living plant. Finally being able to see it as an enemy, Toyo's instincts kicked in and he tore out both the creature's arms from their sockets and watched the thing thrash on the ground, screeching in pain. Its clothes slunk off and revealed a body that was halfway between the woman he once knew and a plant. The sight filled him with mixed feelings, but self-preservation kept him from lowering his guard.

Toyo jerked backwards when both of the arms he had torn out grabbed onto him with surprising strength. He squeezed his hands tight, crushing the hands on the creature's arms, and threw them away while the body of Ani attacked him head on. Without reservation he punched it squarely in the face as hard as he could and sent the creature flying backwards.

Unfazed by what should have been a fatal blow, the creature scrambled over to where its arms had landed and somehow reattached them. The creature then began using both its arms and legs with equal dexterity, its unnatural movement bringing sounds of crackling bone and cartilage. Throwing itself at Toyo once again with the same ferocity as before did nothing to stop him from tearing the creature apart again. He did it again, and again, and again, and just as often, the creature would quickly reassemble itself.

Each blow that Toyo threw seemed to do little, and all attempts to crush the creature in his hands did nothing more than give him a chance to watch it piece itself back together and attack. After so many futile attempts his eyes landed on where the strange small scar that Ani had shown him was. The flesh and roots there looked different to the rest, and so he decided on a change of tactics.

He plunged his hand into the chest scar, grabbed onto everything his fingers could, and pulled. What came out was a strange root-like plant, that looked uncannily like a human child in some twisted way. It had roots still attached to the chest cavity, so he pulled harder, and ripped it free.

As the roots snapped away he watched Ani's body drop lifeless to the ground.

He looked at the creature on the ground, then at the thing in his hand, and wondered what the *valde* was going on.

"*Futuo! Is this what happens when we die? Do I have one of these things in me?*" he thought as he inspected the strange thing. "*Is... is this Ani? Is it like her heart? Like, her soul, or something? Should I keep it?*"

Unsure of what to do he poked and prodded the small thing to make sure it wasn't going to do anything. It responded by resolutely allowing itself to be poked and prodded, which was strangely comforting.

Concluding that it might be important he noticed that it was small enough to fit inside Ani's trinket box. Fetching it from his bag he replaced the necklace inside with the creature-plant and closed it shut. He held his eyes closed and tried to remember Tagai's words about battle. *"Find the calm, do not let the rush consume you. If it is over, seek the next task at hand."* It was strangely comforting, and he couldn't help but feel that Ani would say something remarkably similar. If she could.

Opening his eyes he breathed out slowly and decided to inspect the stone on the necklace in his hand. It was perhaps the most beautiful thing he had ever seen — maybe Ani was more than just a crotchety old bag, he wondered. As he twiddled it in his fingers he tried to remember her fondly. She wasn't a bad woman, and keeping a memento of the only person he'd ever talked to seemed appropriate. Doing the right thing had kept him centered so far, so he saw no reason to stop doing it now.

Slipping the necklace over his head, he then lifted its centerpiece up to his face, and said, "I can see why she would want to keep this. It is a really pretty blood-red stone."

ЖЖЖЖЖЖЖ

Toyo had long since left Ani's body behind, but now felt that he was walking towards... nothing. There was nothing for miles around, and every day brought more nothing. That was until he saw a herd of horses, cows and sheep — creatures that he had no idea of. Frightened and excited he observed them from afar and saw that they were milling around in a wooden-fenced field. They must have been dangerous, otherwise they would not have been caged as such. What danger did they pose? And what power was keeping them confined?

After two days of stalking and observing them from a safe distance, he realized that they were no threat, and actually were rather dull. They did not appear to show much interest in anything, save for grazing on the grass. Despite all this, it was the strangest thing he'd ever seen, and led him to think to himself that perhaps Integrum animals weren't as dangerous as the Gadori ones.

Pressing onwards he kept to Ani's directions of following the sun's night kiss, but his sense of direction had been developed in the forest. The open air for miles was slightly disorientating, and without tracks or plants to recognize he never felt like he was going the right direction. At least the strange creatures kept appearing more often in their strange wooden-fenced fields, and it gave him a sense of comfort. The long and boring journey of day and night however did make him feel that as docile as these strange creatures were — that showed no aggression, or even acknowledged his existence — it would be a nice change of pace if one decided to attack him.

His routine finally encountered something new once more when one day, while waiting for the sun's night kiss to show him the way again, he caught wind of a distant noise. Straining to hear more, Toyo began to feel something inside himself as a pattern emerged from the noises — beautiful sounds that reached out and touched him in a way he had never been touched before. Toyo was, in fact, for the first time, hearing music being played.

Intoxicated by the sounds he rushed towards them, each step bringing more and more of the creatures into view, and, to his heart's delight, buildings. They matched Ani's descriptions perfectly! He sprinted excitedly, sped on by the hope of finding someone — giddy at the thought that Ani may have been telling the truth all along. Buoyed onwards by the music, his euphoria was met with wonderment when he saw one of the strange creatures from the fields made of stone atop a pedestal, with water flowing out of its mouth.

For a moment he wondered what power could have done such a thing, but then the music gripped him once more. Looking towards the source of the music, he saw a funny little man being followed by oddly pale people in weird clothing, each one clutching strange objects. He was immediately entranced when he pieced together that they were making those wonderful sounds! They filled his world with something he had never experienced before, and it moved him deeply.

Sounds flung out and he saw them do powerful things! They reduced the stone animal to rubble, spraying water everywhere, only for the notes to dance away and bounce off surrounding objects. His heart had felt the power, and now he had seen it. Hearing the music and seeing the devastation after each note made him feel conflicted at how something so beautiful could be causing such destruction. The only thing he could say was, "Amazing...."

However, something seemed... off. The people playing all seemed intent on something, and moved with a hunter's purpose. Wanting to see who or what they were playing to, he followed their gaze and spied a young woman on the ground. His heart darkened. Something was very, very wrong. He dashed forward to get a closer look and broke into a full run when he saw the young woman wounded and trying to defend herself.

As he ran and witnessed the audible beauty being directed towards the crying woman, he saw that she had long, jet black hair. A memory surged through him of Nume, the girl whose death was on his hands.

From Toyo's very soul a longing came, and took over. In that moment he knew that he had to protect her, and that was all that mattered.

ЖЖЖЖЖЖЖЖЖЖЖЖЖЖЖЖ

"If you were interested in doing the right thing, you would have done so before being threatened," said Mulat to the standing Erus', assembled in front of the ruins of the Integra Pol. Accompanying him was a bloody and battered Clarus, now revealed to all as Juvorya, standing to one side of him, while Mulat himself was seated on the first step of the Integra Pol. The pair looked worse for wear but their faces showed no discomfort, only streaks of blood.

Cogitans confidently replied, "I did do the right thing. Had I known the variable of Ictus then my actions would have been different. How was I to know about someone you tried to help being turned into a weapon of destruction?"

"What 'variable' has the power to change what one considers to be right?"

"My conclusion stands as the correct one, given the information I had at the time." As with all Logicum Erus' it was easy to mistake Cogitans' certainty for stubbornness.

"In this instance 'Correct' and 'Right' are words where the connotations differ. You would not have served the Integrum as it needs to be served were you to succeed."

"If your contention is that I have to justify my position that power is the best way to rule, then you are a hypocrite."

Mulat sighed. He was tired, more so than he thought he had ever been. "With power comes choice, and those choices are either to abuse or nurture. Like many before you, abuse was your choice. I do not deny I consider the Integrum to be mine, but unlike you, I protect and nurture that which I lay claim to. You have threatened that — how should I respond, Erus Cogitans?"

As innocent and devoid of emotion Mulat had intended the question to be, Cogitans went on the defensive. "You have no right to—!"

Mulat, uncharacteristically, interrupted him. "No right to what? I thought you said that power was the best way to rule. By your logic, what I choose to do with you will be the 'right' thing."

"You can't just isolate and utilize the interpretations as you see fit!"

He lazily gestured with his palm upwards at Cogitans. "You did. Should I not believe myself to be an equal to you and behave in kind?"

"I...." Cogitans felt his own logic being toyed with. Mulat had a way with words that just made everything he opposed as wrong and himself right. He stood stunned in silence.

Mulat raised an eyebrow. "Have your thoughts abandoned you? Ah, sorry — in your terms, are you experiencing a cognitive lapse?" Cogitans just stared mutely at him. "I will take your response as an affirmation. The point here Erus Cogitans is that I am not your equal, even though I spent my youth attempting to be equal to everyone. I believed everyone was smarter than me because I could not understand why I wasn't accepted, I believed everyone to be more powerful and capable — I had no idea of who I was, because I kept trying to be something that I wasn't."

Mulat gently stood up, and his presence made those gathered

wither slightly. "A problem compounded by one simple fact: WHO exists that could tell me what I actually was? In the face of such loneliness I spent many a year coming to understand myself, by myself. In the years I spent in each Quadra, learning about the powers that govern people — there were no teachings for the love of the people. Surprisingly, I found that within."

Cogitans said defiantly, "We are the Quadra Erus'! Our charge, from YOUR Integra Pol, is to help and guide the people with our own teachings. How can you claim US to be wrong?"

Mulat smiled. "I find 'us' fascinating, don't you? Adsum would agree, but perhaps for completely different reasons — yet he would still be 'correct'. We can range from street sweeper, to Erus of a Quadra, to someone like myself, but we all share the same flesh, thoughts, and feelings. Every Erus of the Quadra Logicum, that I know of, has, in the past, had to be forcefully removed from their post. That is a cycle I intend to stop here and now."

Mulat walked to stand in front of Cogitans and placed a hand gently on the man's shoulder. "There will be no punishment for your errors, Erus Cogitans. You will remain at your post, but I will take a personal role in overseeing and guiding your Quadra, until such a time I deem fit that you fully understand your place."

A moment's silence passed before Mulat dismissed him. The man, defeated and dejected, walked as if the executioner's axe had yet to drop, and left with the feeling that he would be waiting a very long time before it fell.

Erus Criso was the first to break the silence. "Is it really so wise to let him go unattended, Mulat? The man —"

"Erus Criso, I have little patience for our game of words today. I have kept myself well informed even without my Integra Pol, and Juvorya has filled me in on some other things." He smiled at her. "I am glad that she entertained you so well." He gestured towards Juvo. "Take her back and let the Ardeo Trial continue, with my apologies for its interruption."

"I... uh... as you wish, Mulat," replied Criso.

Juvorya made her way to Criso's side and smiled at her once more with that strangely innocent smile.

ЖЖЖЖЖЖЖ

After reaching the main Lustrum doors, Criso was consumed with curiosity. It made it almost impossible for her to not stare at Juvorya. It was unsettling though — every time she did, the woman returned her look with the face of someone far more intelligent than the vapid girl she had once pretended to be. It was like discovering that what she had thought she had been reading perfectly, had been reading her instead all along.

As they walked, Juvorya said, "Your questions are best asked now before I am locked away again."

"HOW ARE YOU EVEN WALKING?!" Criso blurted out, unable to hold in her curiosity any longer. Several charges got out of her way — Criso's temper was no secret, and even the whiff of it was enough to warn people to stay away.

Juvorya calmly replied, "As Mulat would say: With my legs."

"But the conducutis!"

"I think a more interesting question for you is: How did Tari do it?"

Criso shook her head in disbelief that her curiosity could be compounded. "How did SHE do it?"

"Oh, I suspect in a fashion similar to my own. Mulat told me that she had been collecting his blood so might have been able to mimic something." Juvorya held out her arms palms up for Criso's inspection, and she saw that her forearms were bright red. "I cannot stop the pain, but moving it somewhere where I can function with minimal distraction was a suitable option. I do apologize for forcing a loss for your Ardeo Trial, but Mulat needed me."

Criso was unable to get over the fact that Juvorya, or Tari, was able to do anything with a conducutis. Every Erus' had one branded on them on their naming day, and they were far more loosely worded than most — to allow for free interpretation of their law. Regardless, the promises etched into their skin weighed heavily on an Erus' mind at all times. Criso looked at her and said, "But that would take immense power to do even that!"

"So?" Juvorya's reply hung in the air, and Criso's words failed her. The companion to Mulat would certainly have access to power, but how would Tari have it?

This was getting her nowhere, and besides, the charges in their path had been giving her strange looks. She was not about to be seen rattled by someone else in her own Quadra! Centering herself as a woman in a position of power once more, she asked, "So, do I call you Clarus, or Juvorya?"

"I came under your care as Clarus, so to you I am Clarus. When I am no longer in your care, I will return to Mulat, and Juvorya is who I will be."

"But he obviously needs you now."

"I am still here for him if he needs me, as I have always been, and will always be."

"But he's hurt, he has a tower to rebuild! Why leave his side so easily?"

"I did not leave him, I did as he asked." Clarus' words felt both unsettling and heartwarming.

Normally Criso would leave what she felt were the words of a stupid woman be, but from Juvorya's mouth they held a different quality. "You do everything he asks of you?"

"Yes."

"Don't you feel —"

"Like a used doll?" interrupted Clarus.

"I didn't mean it quite like —"

"You are not the first to wonder, nor will you be the last. I lost interest in that question long ago, so please excuse my disinterested tone. I did not submit because he is powerful, I submitted because he cared. Before him I starved my soul, I fought, and hated — I was not happy or fulfilled. My power before him was in my beauty and musical talent, but with power you can abuse or nurture, and with mine I abused it to get what I wanted out of stupid people. I hated the world for being so easy, and myself for being so bored. I would let myself be abused because I thought I needed to be punished — I would allow myself to be raped and beaten, and I always thought I deserved it. All because of a body I was born with and did nothing to earn."

As they reached the hallway to the Taker's rooms, Clarus turned to Criso and a lighter tone came to her voice. "Mulat was the first I met that asked for nothing, and he offered me myself. Every time I listened to myself or my demons, I was unhappy — every time I listened to him, I was happy. Each time it happened I became a better me. I may follow blindly, but it is only because I cannot see what he sees, and every time I look behind me, I only see a beautiful path walked."

With nobody around to hear them, Criso allowed herself to wonder once more. "But... he could have anyone. Why did he pick you? He has no interest in sex, and if beauty is all you had to offer...."

"At first he rejected me because I pursued him with my body — when I found out why my pursuit was in vain, all he did was ask everything of me, and in return I would receive myself. I was not the first he offered it to — I was just the first to accept his offer."

"Had... but I would have happily taken —"

"Most people who accepted failed, and regretted failing — some fell very far indeed. Mulat still has yet to find a way to make amends for the one person he truly feels he wronged, even though it was an accident."

"... Who's that?"

Clarus leaned and gave an exaggerated wink. "The person who has been following us since the Integra Pol."

Criso whipped her head around, and scanned the area with paranoia, but there was nobody. Simply the doors to the Taker's rooms.

Raising her voice just slightly, Clarus addressed the hallway in general. "Tari, please return to your role as Taker as I am doing. Do this, and at the end we will have that talk you have been waiting many years to have."

꽤꽤꽤꽤꽤꽤꽤

With all the other Erus' dismissed, it was only Erus Epula that now kept Mulat company. While Mulat's face had dried blood on it, Epula's own began to sweat profusely.

"Is fear the only response you have?" asked Mulat.

Epula felt that the surrounding ruins of the Integra Pol were too apocalyptic a foreboding for his own future, and it showed on his face. "Well? What are you going to do to me?"

Mulat looked at him puzzled. "Have you done something that requires me to do anything?"

Epula felt that if he was going to be toyed with before dying then there was no need to hold his feelings back. "Of course not! But how else could I feel?! You took from me my sense of taste all those years ago! You have the power to destroy the senses, and you say that you do not beat or punish unjustly — you did not kill me, but you killed what made me!"

"Is that how you feel?"

There was no turning back now. Epula was not going to back down from his reality. "It is the truth!"

"Are you aware that since that time you have done little more than help people get fat. I had hoped you to learn perspective."

"From cursed water and bread?! From never knowing flavor again!?"

"From humility. Your Quadra is to serve the people in how to live with food — how to farm and cultivate, how to cook and clean. Before that 'cursed bread and water' you only indulged, gorged yourself, raised yourself above everyone else — after it, you focused on the public. I succeeded in shifting your focus, but I had hoped for a better result."

"You could have just asked!"

"You were so arrogant back then, like you are now. What would you have listened to?"

Epula unceremoniously slumped to the ground. He was tired of Mulat's questions and wanted everything to be over with. "Just... kill me already. I know where this is going, I failed again, and again, and again. I don't care anymore, just do what you will."

"If you know where this is going, then your lack of resistance will make this easy for me. Thank you, Erus Epula."

Epula kept staring at Mulat's blood-streaked face, devoid of expression, and sighed deep in relief. Finally, the time had come — his charade of a life could end. Mulat walked out of view, but Epula's eyes did not follow. Resolute he stared where Mulat had once been standing as he heard Mulat's footsteps, followed by some noise that sounded like he was rummaging for something in the rubble. After a few minutes Mulat returned to stand once more before him. He held an apple that was slightly worse for wear.

Reaching out his arm, Mulat said, "This is from my own little garden."

"A poisoned apple... how appropriate." Epula said to himself softly, before reaching out and taking it. He held it in front of him and looked at it like a man faced with a hard choice, and then loudly spoke, "I am man enough to accept my fate." He looked back up at Mulat with a look of defiance, took a large bite of the apple, and chewed.

Mulat kept his eyes on him, smiled, and waited.

It was not until the third bite was swallowed that Epula's tears began to flow, and his whole face broke as he devoured the rest of the apple with the desperation of a man that had not eaten for years. The sweetness of the apple and the salt of his tears mixed in his mouth, and, as he chewed, his mind and heart did not know what to do. His tongue however, remembered for him. The joy and sorrow in his tears, the bruises and crunchiness of the apple — his tongue welcomed them all.

Mulat reached out and placed his hand on the man's head. "Serve well, Erus Epula."

All Epula could do was weep.

Ж Ж Ж Ж Ж Ж Ж Ж Ж Ж Ж Ж Ж Ж Ж Ж

Oblivious to the haunting music that was encroaching, Kahli could only think of how she had been betrayed as she watched Adsum's retreat. Filled with rage she slowly stood and began to follow him, intent on hunting him down, but the music began to make her feel strange and caught her attention.

The vocals reached a fever pitch, and Kahli looked over to see a weird looking spindly little old man, waving a stick, and being followed by a group of musicians. She could sense power, but was unsure of where it was coming from. In her haze she tried to identify if there was any threat to deal with. All she noticed was that all the musicians were circled around one singer wearing a strangely ornate crystalline collar — it seemed to pulse brighter with each note either played or sung. By that singer's side were two more singers that somehow felt smaller, quieter.

They played on, and as they played her soul began to fill with emotions that were neither anger nor rage. Her heart would not allow for any more intruders, any more influence other than herself, and it began to hate instead.

In unison and harmony all the instruments and vocals merged, and with them the crystalline collar glowed a brilliant blue, brighter and brighter, until a loud sound shot out towards her. Kahli watched the ground be torn asunder as the wave of power traveled towards her — her other voice screamed out for her to defend herself, but all she could do was put her arms up.

She felt the blow strike her, and soon after she heard the sound of a brick wall having a hole punched through it. The sounds then distorted and screeched, and sounded like they'd flown off into another direction. What just happened? Was she just attacked with music?

With a new threat to face all thoughts of chasing down Adsum were forgotten.

The little man with his stick seemed to be in a world of his own as he waved it about, but now each instrument began their own song that resonated with the collared singer. With each crescendo there came an increase in power, until with each note came the punch of the drums, the slicing of strings, the strikes of the vocals.

Kahli tried her best to defend herself, but the barrage was constant, and she still was unsure of what it was she was facing. Savage and unrelenting they came and she weakened — her arms soon fell to her sides, weary from exertion.

When she became too weak to focus, something inside her bloomed and soon her body was encased in a shield of flame. With each forceful blow that got within reach, her shield dulled, distorted and redirected, every destructive note sent her way. All without her thought, as if her power was operating her, instead of her it. Half-conscious, she watched as the man waved his stick back and forth while the musicians and music responded. But after a while, anger came over his face, and he ceased waving his stick.

A lull came to the music. Kahli could see that the musicians were tired, but the little man did not allow them to rest for long before whipping them up into a frenzy once more. The musicians forced themselves to push through, sending each one of them into an eerie independent chorus of their own. Kahli felt the power rise yet again as the singers joined the crystal-collared woman in unison, but this time was ready for it.

A single blast of sheer force erupted from the collared woman, but it was stronger than Kahli'd expected and she was knocked to one side. With their energy spent, the voices quietened, but the singer's silence was quickly filled with instrumentalists playing a ferocious melody.

Kahli got to her feet as her fire-shield instinctively blasted each note out of mid-air, whipping around in a frenzied attempt to match the destructive chords. The distorted tones from the battle filled the small village and could be heard even by Adsum, now a long way away. The strings slashed, the drums thudded, and around her the buildings began to show the signs of the might exerted upon them.

In the midst of it all a small part of Kahli felt tired, and the inkling of fear trickled back into her heart. She rebelled against it, she would not let herself be a prisoner again! She had not come so far only to be stopped now. Abandoning all notion of thought, she charged forward with eyes ablaze. An avatar of fire stalked towards Ictus' orchestra of death as fire whipped around her like a cloak of destruction.

Ictus however was not about to let this aberration bring any more death — he was protector of these lands! There may not be much he could lay claim to, but he did lay claim to the care of these people! Even though he knew his orchestra was tired and weary in the face of such a dangerous enemy, this was a threat that warranted everything they had to give.

Kahli kept moving forward, ignoring everything thrown at her, but Ictus' then brought forth a crescendo of the entire orchestra working in unison that blew her back slightly. Defiantly she still stood, but Ictus was not done. Wave after powerful wave hit her dead on, and she struggled as best she could, until one final blow knocked her down hard onto her back. She lay there, still, uncertain.

Ictus marched his orchestra pensively towards her, keeping the melody low so the musicians could recuperate, but ready in case she were to rise again. The distance was not that great, but caution made it seem like a mile.

Lying dazed and confused, Kahli felt the power drain from her. The toll on her body was so great that no matter how hard she tried to will herself to sit up, she found that she had reached a limit. It was too much, too tiring. The music was quieter now, soothing almost. It was... comforting, gripping her chest as she felt the sombre tones wash over her. She was powerless. Again.

"*I... deserve this,*" she thought to herself as the fear of death let her demons out of their cages. She had destroyed so many people, so many clans... laid waste to her mother, the Habiak, and even the Harat people. All of the western Maharaan lands were charred because of her!

Tilting her head to one side she saw the destruction brought to the buildings around her, and knew that she did not belong. Her whole life she had either been beaten, or a killer... she would never be loved or cared for — that was her reality. Her mind began to fold in on itself, and she finally let the music seep into her soul. Death was coming, and it sounded so sweet. She could not have hoped for a better way for her to go.

She titled her head towards her fate, and was surprised when a young boy with iron hands ran between her and it, ready to fight. *"W...hat ar...e you doing? Run..."* she thought weakly. Thoughts of the wija she had failed tugged at her mind — it had sacrificed itself for her, and now some stupid boy was going to do the same. Death by her own hands she had learned to accept, but she could not accept another diving into death for her — she did not deserve such honor.

The music picked up once more and she saw the boy walk slowly towards them, showing no signs of backing down.

"Please...."

ЖЖЖЖЖЖЖ

"NO!" screamed Toyo, standing firm between the prone girl and the strangely dressed hunched little man. Now that he stood between them he was ever sure of what he had to do. He had seen the destruction around him, caught glimpses of the chaos that this group seemed capable of, yet his brain ignored all warnings of self-preservation. He wanted little more than to protect this bleeding girl in tattered clothes, even in the face of this uncertain threat. This was no place for fear, this was a place for protecting those that needed it.

His righteousness was fueled by all the deaths of others by his hands — a fire that burned all the brighter in the light of his mistakes and sins. It was here where his very soul could be washed clean of guilt, by protecting the beautiful girl with the long black hair. At least this way he knew he was protecting something, even if it was from someone else. Here and now, he could do good. The scrawny old man with wild white hair standing in front of him looked confused and angered by this intrusion.

There was no time to allow for distractions, and Ictus did not know if or how long the girl would remain dormant — he needed to deal with this boy quickly, he might even be as powerful as she!

He whipped out his baton and began to conduct once more, and as he waved it, Toyo felt the music and power build. Without grace or compassion, Ictus let loose the full force of his orchestra.

Knowing what to expect, Toyo merely extended his hands, and Ictus watched in surprise as the notes bounced off his hands. Others he literally grabbed out of the air and threw to one side — as if parrying a sword or punch — and then he started walking forwards. Ictus increased the pace to a fever pitch, his hand flailing deliberately and wildly, and began to feel desperation creep in.

Toyo could feel the panic in the notes, but he deftly dealt with every note thrown at him, and kept moving forward with a steady gait — an unstoppable juggernaut. Blow after blow he advanced, dodging and deflecting everything thrown at him — breaking each musical note as he batted them away like flies.

When he was only a few steps from the group he saw that they were all gaining and drawing power from each other, and that it all seemed to be coming from the woman wearing a crystal collar. That must be the source of all this danger and destruction. That was his goal.

Closer and closer he came, until finally he was within arm's reach. The music screeched and rang, and some of the players trembled. Seeing the panic in her eyes, Toyo felt no love lost for what he was about to do, and he was deaf to the singer's warblings of despair.

Toyo then merely reached out his hand, clasped it around her neck, and the swan song of the singer rang out — not with force, but, with a certainty that those for miles around, would hear her note of sweet sorrow.

Then, with a face as calm as a still pond, Toyo merely closed his hand, and crushed her throat.

A singer lay silent, along with the players that played.

For them all, as one, their music died that day.

ЖЖЖЖЖЖЖЖЖЖЖЖЖЖ

Mulat did his best to content himself with his work for the next few weeks. There was enough to keep busy, what with the restoration of the Integra Pol, refilling the ranks of the Natura and Humanus, along with having to ensure the guidance of the Quadra Logicum.

Sadly, the bigger problems still needed tending to — the Deaspora, and the cremo faba. The Deaspora was a problem that had to wait — his Integra Pol and city needed to be rebuilt first, for the Vir and Mulier could not be located, or identified, with so little at his disposal.

The cremo faba problem however was at least interesting, given the details in the reports made by the Integra Pol guards during their time with the Quadras.

Mulat spent days poring over the reports when he had the spare time. They all indicated that the distribution of the cremo faba was perpetrated by a young Maharaan female with the seeming ability to be everywhere at once. The confusing part was that several reports stated that the guards had killed her on sight, multiple times. It made him think there was some elaborate ruse being perpetrated on his city, but that would require resources unheard of.

"Disguises... clones? *The Jara clan was having some difficulty years ago with a 'Dream Plague' that was making all newborns appear the same — but they would be toddlers still, and Rasak Jara assured me long ago that it was something they had resolved. Regardless, this would take a significant amount of resources to pull off.*"

A drug from the Gadori, distributed by a Maharaan female that appeared to be everywhere at once, that had been manufactured in a fashion that only someone of the Integra Pol, or Quadra Logicum, could perform.

When it finally clicked, Mulat's normally expressionless face broke into a manic grin as he let out a laugh filled with mirth — he now knew who had tried to kill him, and he wondered if that person knew how close they had come. He finally had a nemesis after waiting for so long — someone to make him feel challenged!

The rest of that day was filled with a song in his heart and high hopes for the future, even though the Deaspora had once again been set back. Mulat had never understood why it needed to be kept such a secret, but in some ways he felt that some traditions and habits are more powerful than reason.

With the mystery having an answer, Mulat once again dispatched the Integra Pol guards to the Quadras, and told them to remain there to protect them and the city. There was no need for them to defend a tower that would now only house a man and few others. He then sent out messengers to recall those of the Integra Pol abroad and began to salvage everything he could in order to restore the Integra Humanus and Natura.

There came a day though where his evening work was interrupted by the eruption of an explosive note so loud and sorrowful, that everyone in Orbis looked at themselves in surprise when they found that they, and everything around them, were still in one piece.

Mulat merely smiled as he looked out of his chamber's window at the night-sparks dancing across the dusky evening, and softly said to himself—

And Kasmah Will Grow...

Regional Glossary

"Why do you want to trek over the Calu-Jedde Mountains, or cross the Vios Ocean?"
"Do I 'need' a reason?"
"So you want to circle Kasmah, for NO reason."
"My lack of 'reason' has given me a far more fulfilling life than yours."

-Exere, explorer of Kasmah, conversing with a passing Integrum local

World of Kasmah

Cadare [Ka-da-reh] – The process that occurs when someone dies. The brain attracts vesma, but blood circulation maintains the flow so prevents clumping. When that stops, the vesma that is naturally within their blood begins to clump on the portions that are most used in the brain. Important memories, fears, loves, hates; creating an indivisible and permutative afterlife based on one's own experiences.

Gadori [Ga-door-ee] – The southern region of Kasmah; best known for the immense forest that covers it in entirety from east to west, including over the Calu-Jedde spine but not the Vios Ocean. Its flora and fauna are heavily varied. Farther south is an icy wasteland, where the south edge of Kasmah is located. Its inhabitants have primarily milky-dark skin, are slender with dark hair, and have sharp facial features.

Integrum [In-teh-grum] – The central band of Kasmah where the majority of humans live, due to its mild weather, good farming lands, and scarcity of dangerous creatures. Its native inhabitants are predominantly pale-skinned and are uncommon to see anywhere else, but the region contains and allows for all of Kasmah.

Kasmah [Kaz-mah] – The world's name that is divided into three distinct regions; The Maharaan Expanse, Integrum, and The Land of the Gadori. The two most pervasive geological features of Kasmah are what are called its 'spines'; the Calu-Jedde Mountains, and the Vios Ocean, both of which stretch opposite sides of the world but span from north to south.

Maharaan [Ma-ha-raan] – The northern region of Kasmah; best known for its harsh, hot, and dry environs. To the east are the Jara clan, made up primarily of hunters and warriors; to the west the Harat clan, mostly nomadic traders and scholars. From dry brush, to savannah, to desert; there are also a number of exotic plants and animals. Farther north beyond the Maharaan is a scorched wasteland, where the north edge of Kasmah is located. Inhabitants are dark-skinned with strong facial features.

Night-sparks – Kasmah-wide sky phenomenon that manifests as bright, sometimes colorful, sparks at night. Their frequency and intensity can vary from month to month, and even year to year.

Veneficium Kasmah/Vesma [Ven-eh-fiss-e-em/Vez-mah] – The pervasive source of power within Kasmah. Its most common form is crystalline, however it is also found in all living things; plants and people alike.

Calu-Jedde Mountains [Ka-loo Jeh-deh] – One of the 'spines' of Kasmah; a wide mountain range that spans the entirety of Kasmah from north to south. It is on the opposite side of the world of the Vios Ocean, and like the Vios Ocean, begins and ends beyond the edges of Kasmah. On the surface it is a dangerous and largely unexplored area with few people living, but many have made a life and cities carving out and burrowing down into the mountains themselves. None have yet to successfully cross over it.

Vios Ocean [Vee-os] – One of the 'spines' of Kasmah; the only ocean within Kasmah, and spans the entirety of north to south. It is on the opposite side of the world of the Calu-Jedde mountain range, and like the Calu-Jedde, begins and ends beyond the edges of Kasmah. Given its immense size, the chaotic weather, and creatures that dwell within, most attempts to cross it are fatal. Relatively safe passage can be found through the Nauta family; who have a monopoly on all trade up, down, and across the Vios. Used as the primary geographical feature to distinguish east and west Kasmah.

The Maharaan Expanse

Adacio/Dabuk [A-dah-see-oh/Da-book] – Adsum's assistant, gifted to him by Rasak. Original name Dabuk, renamed by Adsum to Adacio.

Chamu [Cha-moo] – Small, worm-like creatures that inhabit the Maharaan. Vicious and voracious, this creature travels in swarms under, and through, the sand. Constantly seeks moisture for breeding and feeding.

Fetu [Feh-tu] – Youngest female of the Integra Natura cadre exploring the Maharaan. Has short blonde hair, blue eyes, and a cheerful disposition.

Gola [Go-la] – Elderly female leader of the Heca clan.

Habiak [Ha-bee-ahk] – Members of the Jara clan that broke off to escape the curse.

Heca [Heh-ka] – The inhabitants of the village of Toka-Rutaa.

Hidati [He-da-tee] – The drink one must take in order to become, and undergo, Orati.

Isti [Iss-tee] – Honorific title given to the current ruler of the Jara.

Jagu [Ja-goo] – Honorific title given to the partner of the current Isti of the Jara.

Jak and Jall/The Jackals – Younger twin siblings of Kahli.

Jara [Ja-rah] – Ruling clan of the eastern Maharaan Expanse.

Jatah [Ja-tah] – A young, chubby twelve year old girl of the Jara clan. Has a tendency to giggle a lot.

Kahli [Kah-lee] – A seventeen year old female from the Maharaan. Skinny, has long black hair.

Ladak [La-dahk] – A long, medium-sized, lizard-like scavenging creature with powerful muscles. Despite its ability to hunt and kill, it prefers to scavenge.

Makatu [Ma-ka-tu] – A toad known and prized for its stone-foam defense mechanism; serving as both defense against predators and nutrition that can be harvested.

Nujah [Nu-jah] – A man from Maharaan fables who turned into a deity upon his creation of the Vios Ocean. Now serves as keeper of the sky-river, bringer of life water.

Orati [Oh-rah-tee] – The title given to both the ritual and result of a punishment reserved for the most heinous of acts. Designed to rob those punished of their memories and mind until they are empty husks capable of following only the most basic of orders before fading away to nothing.

Pala [Pah-lah] – Oldest female of the Integra Natura cadre exploring the Maharaan. Wise, but quick to irritate.

Phrenesis Clavus [Fre-nee-sis Kla-vus] – A delivery system devised by Adsum in use for his experiments. Created from vesma and certain Maharaan tinctures in order to make a spike one can stab into the intended subject and inject them.

Rasak [Rah-sahk] – Isti of the Jara. Strong-willed, rough face and hands, with dark brown hair, short and tussled.

Ruzu [Ruh-zuh] – An average looking female who had left to form the Habiak clan, but was recaptured by the Jara.

Sasara [Sa-sa-ra] – Large battle-worn male exiled from the Calu-Jedde, now a mercenary for the Jara clan and Jatah's companion.

Sercu [Sir-koo] – Middle-aged female, between Pala and Fetu, and sternest of the Integra Natura cadre exploring the Maharaan. Short black hair, strong face, humorless.

Suta Jara [Soo-ta] – First of the clan Jara, finder of the Tabu.

Tabu [Ta-boo] – A stone of myth, one that proves the Jara bloodline and confers rulership.

Toka-Rutaa [Toh-ka Ru-taa] – The village closest to the Maharaan edge of Kasmah, east of the Vios Ocean, home to the Heca clan.

Wija [Wee-jah] – A desert dwelling animal with a large head, stands a head taller than an average person, with a bulbous nose and tiny dark eyes nestled in a bushy layer of fine off-white fuzz on their face. Their bodies are essentially barrels on legs like small tree trunks, each with large stubby toes, and a thick hide of what started from birth as pure white but became marred over time. Virtually no natural predators, and well known for their compassion for all living things. Tendency to avoid humans.

Land of the Gadori

Anicula Amo/Ani [An-ick-u-la Ah-mo] – An elderly female, once a charge of the Quadra Logicum, who lives with the Gozuri tribe in the Gadori region.

Ara'tai [A-ra-tai] – A common plant-creature with the appearance of humanoid tree roots.

Atmos [At-mos] – The name of an ice giant from a Gozuri tale; Tiyaou's brother.

Brother-in-love – A term used by the Gozuri to refer to your wife's other chosen husband and the one you accept to be bound in love to.

Gozuri [Goh-zu-ree] – The largest known tribe native to the Gadori region.

Odang [Oh-dahng] – A common hachu, consisting of smaller seed-like creatures that find flesh to form their community in. They use the host both for hunting and reproductive purposes.

Hachu [Hah-chu] – The Gozuri term for the chaotic and random creatures that spawn from the kusabana.

Hanraza [Han-ra-za] – The Gozuri's belief that everything must adhere to a balance, with neither good nor evil to be strived for.

Hoba [Ho-ba] – An inducted hunter of the Gozuri. Brother-in-love to Tagai. Short and fat.

Iro'Kamun [Ee-roh Ka-muh-n] – A large swamp; an off-shoot from the Vios Ocean within the Gadori. Known as the southernmost, large body of water within the Gadori forest, and a holy place for the Zobukiri.

Isetu [Ee-seh-tu] – Tagai and Hoba's wife.

Kusabana [Kuu-sa-ba-na] – 'The Flowering Chaos'. The name given to the event when an Ogagi becomes too swollen and explodes; showering the local flora and fauna with sap that reacts wildly with plants and animals, turning them into hachu.

Medishi [Me-dee-shee] – The name given to the Integra Natura that have been adopted as healers of the Gozuri tribe.

Mihame [Mee-Ha-meh] – A small, volatile bean. Reacts explosively when outside of its pod; when ingested imbues the consumer with extremely enhanced physical speed and strength. Overheating is a significant danger.

Mogutougi [Mo-gu-toh-gee] – A sacred Gozuri relic that is housed within the Ogaden.

Monma juice [Mon-ma] – A concoction derived from the monma flower. Used to relax the stomach. Large quantities can lead to temporary paralysis of the stomach.

Mother-Tree – One of the six Ogagis that the Gozuri tend to. An enormous tree that from above the forest canopy can be seen from miles around.

Nume [Nu-me] – Eighteen year old sickly Gozuri female with long black hair.

Ogaden [O-ga-den] – 'Tree home'. Residence of the Ogahigi, crafted from an Ogagi sapling and each looks unique to the Ogagi it came from. Acts as the conduit between the living world and the Ogahigi.

Ogagi [O-ga-gee] – 'Great Tree'. The term given to the great trees that the Gozuri revere, and are tasked with caring for. All Ogagis' sap is laden with vesma; the sap is in a constant state of being made within the tree. If not relieved properly via a ritual called sabana, then a kusabana occurs.

Ogahigi [O-ga-hee-gee] – 'Little Ogagi'. A Gozuri member bonded to an Ogaden. Knowledge of its purpose has been lost.

Sabana [Sa-ba-na] – Cleansing ritual performed by the Gozuri on the Ogagi in order to prevent a kusabana.

Seibutsu-mihame [Say-boo-tsu Mee-ha-meh] – The consumable form of mihame crafted by the Gozuri in order to enhance hunting ability. Carries a high risk of fatality through overheating, can also induce madness in those who have not been inducted as a Gozuri hunter.

Tagai [Ta-gai] – An inducted hunter of the Gozuri. Brother-in-love to Hoba. Tall and svelte.

Tiyaou [Tee-yaow] – The name of a fire giant from a Gozuri tale; Atmos' brother.

Toyo [Toh-yoh] – A young fifteen year old boy that awoke near the Gadori edge. Skinny, pale, short black hair, brown eyes.

Withered Crone – One of the six Ogagis that the Gozuri tend to. Twisted trunk and branches; appears sickly, but sturdy.

Yohju [Yoh-joo] – Honorific title for those of the Gozuri tribe chosen to lead and advise.

Zobukiri [Zoh-bu-ki-ri] – Strange, wandering tribe that straddle their lives between the Gadori forest and the icy wasteland beyond.

Integrum

Abrotonus [A-bro-tow-nus] – The small, southern-most village in the Integrum. Serves as the trading post that bridges the Integrum and Gadori forest.

Adsum [Ad-sum] – An exiled Quadra Logicum Erus, succeeded by Cogitans. An exacting and measured man; has the slightest hint of graying hair and piercing blue eyes.

Androcium [An-dro-see-um] – A small room constructed in secret by Erus Ardeo between the Ardeo Trial's Taker's rooms.

Ardeo [Ar-day-o] – The Erus of the Quadra Lustrum that was succeeded by Criso. Slick hair, cut jaw, stereotypically handsome.

Ardeo Trial [Ar-day-o] – A competition started by Erus Ardeo to test 'young love'. For one month a young couple is sequestered to separate rooms, each accompanied by a charge of the Quadra Lustrum called a 'Taker'. If at the end of the month both young lovers identify that they still honestly love their partner and wish to be with them, without guilt or anger, they are awarded a significant sum of money and lifetime access to all Quadra resources and teachings.

Cadacus [Ka-da-kus] – A tool developed to measure certain traits of someone's vesma. Only able to be used post-mortem.

Captivus Accurro [Kap-tee-vus A-kyu-ro] – An experiment devised by Adsum to see if he could force ingenuity through hardship and imprisonment.

Charge – The term used to refer to a member of either the Integra Pol or a Quadra.

Clarus Prae [Kla-rus Pray] – A female prodigy charge of the Quadra Musicum.

Cogitans [Koh-gee-tan-s] – Current Erus of the Quadra Logicum. A dull man.

Conducutis [Kon-duh-kyu-tis] – Vesma branded into the skin in order to bind someone to a 'promise', can be temporary or permanent until certain criteria are met for its removal. Reserved for very extreme cases and enforces compliance through extreme pain, madness, and, in some cases, death.

Cremo Faba/Creba [Kree-mo Fah-bah/Kre-bah] – An illegal narcotic whose name translates to 'fire bean'. Euphoric highs and extreme behavioral, and sometimes physical, changes affect the user.

Criso [Kree-so] – Current Erus of the Quadra Lustrum. Has bright red hair, deep green eyes, and is a workaholic.

Culinum [Kul-e-num] – The Quadra dedicated to the researching, refinement, and provision of food.

Cupla Mola [Khup-la Mo-la] – A piece of vesma diluted and fashioned into a precious gem; usually worn as jewelery. It is capable of uniquely linking to an individual chromatically, rendering its colors unique to each person. Popular for lovers many years ago, but was banned due to reports of side-effects.

Deprimo Os [Dee-pri-mo Os] – A gelatinous mask used by the Integra Pol to apprehend those that are too powerful to detain by conventional means. Deprives detainee of access to their own vesma and senses.

Devotarecalis [Dee-vo-ta-reh-ka-lis] – The name Mulat gave to the singer who he fused vesma to at their request in order to improve their range.

Deaspora [Dee-ah-spor-ah] – The event where the Mulier and Vir disperse the excess vesma, halting any catastrophes that arises from vesma's pervasive qualities randomly discharging and warping people and places.

Epula [Ep-yu-la] – Current Erus of the Quadra Culinum. Notable features: Strong jowls, stocky, greasy hair.

Erus [Eh-rus] – Honorific title given to those who preside over a Quadra.

Futuo [Fu-too-oh] – A profanity used in conjunction with someone being exposed to a situation or circumstance that they find objectionable. The word was derived from Erus Futuo, First Erus of the Quadra Lustrum, for being well known as someone that nobody wanted to be around.

Ictus [Ik-tus] – Current Erus of the Quadra Musicum. Unkempt white hair, slightly hunched, quite skinny and a bit bony.

Ilia [Ill-ee-ya] – A young girl and one of this year's Lovers of the Ardeo Trial.

Integra Divinitas [In-teg-rah Div-in-ee-tas] – Erus of the Integra Pol, dedicated to serving the people of Kasmah, and serves as final arbiter for all who seek his council on legal matters.

Integra Humanus [In-teg-rah Hue-man-us] – A sect of Integra Pol charges that dedicate their lives to the dealings of humans.

Integra Natura [In-teg-rah Na-tu-rah] – A sect of Integra Pol charges that dedicate their lives to the dealings of nature.

Integra Pol [In-teg-rah Poll] – A large white flat animal tooth-like structure that houses the Integra Humanus and Natura. It is also the seat of power for the Integra Divinitas.

Juvorya [Yu-vor-ee-ya] – Mulat's most trusted companion; affectionately referred to as Juvo. Tall, blonde, and beautiful.

Lanx Lancis [Lan-ks Lan-sis] – A huge city of Commerce and Industry which acts as the main hub of trade between the Integrum and Maharaan.

Laris [Lar-is] – A young man and one of this year's Lovers of the Ardeo Trial.

Logicum [Lo-gee-kum] – The Quadra dedicated to researching, refinement, and provision of logic and reason in all forms.

Lovers – The term given to the couple entering the Ardeo Trial.

Lustrum [Luss-trum] – The Quadra dedicated to the researching, refinement, and provision of sex, love, and reproduction.

Maenyr [May-near] – The term given to the hyper-sexual charges of the Quadra Lustrum. All are sequestered to a special room and their services are granted sparingly given their insatiable nature. One of the oldest rooms in the Lustrum, and the one with the most deaths related to over-exertion during copulation.

Mulat [Moo-lat] – Current Integra Divinitas. Tall, bald, neuter. Has a tendency to get bored very easily. Extremely powerful.

Mulier [Moo-lee-air] – An individual that is a critical component for the Deaspora.

Musicum [Mu-ze-kum] – The Quadra dedicated to the researching, refinement, and provision of the creation and appreciation of music.

Orbis [Or-bis] – A city located on the west of the Vios Ocean, it is the largest and grandest of all cities in Kasmah; main exports are its knowledge and teachings to the rest of the Integrum. Home to the Quadras of Kasmah and the Integra Pol.

Plaga [Pla-ga] – The worst profanity in the vox tongue. Used when expressing an extremely detrimental person, situation, or feeling.

Quadra [Kwad-rah] – One of the four large buildings that encircle the Integra Pol; each dedicated to a specific pursuit set out by the first Integra Divinitas.

Seconsulo [Se-kon-syu-lo] – Criso's advisor. Expressionless and impossible to anger.

Simulacrum Umbrosus [Sim-yu-la-krum Um-broh-sus] – 'Shadow's shadow'. The work of art that was commissioned by Mulat that adorns the hallway to his chambers.

Stagnos [Stag-nos] – Precursor Integra Divinitas to Mulat. Remembered for his apathy that led the eastern Integrum and Gadori lands to fend for themselves from the Gadori incursion; destroyed relations with the lands in the eastern Integrum.

Takers – The Quadra Lustrum charges tasked with testing the Lovers of the Ardeo Trial.

Taker's rooms – The special rooms reserved for the Ardeo Trial.

Tari Scor [Ta-ree Skor] – Daughter of Criso, the spitting image of her mother save for the fact that she dresses far more shamelessly and prefers her own hair short.

Valde [Val-d] – A light profanity used to express general uncertainty.

Vir [Veer] – An individual that is a critical component for the Deaspora.

Vox [Voks] – Kasmah's predominant language. Originated within the Integrum and adopted widely due to its necessity for trade. In recent generations it has usurped the Maharaan region's native tongue.

LEGAL

Copyright © 2015 S. Vagus
All characters in this publication are fictitious and any resemblance to real people, living or dead, is purely coincidental.

This publication may only be reproduced, stored, or transmitted, in any form, or by any means, with prior permission in writing of the publisher.

CREDITS

Illustrators
Yasen Stoilov
John Natividad
Daniel Takamura
Lucian Stanculescu

Editors
Erica Cole
Maria Ronald
Roka Goldberg-Friedler

Special Thanks
Athena Daly
Dawn Danka

ISBN

Audiobook -- 978-0-9875389-4-9
Hardback -- 978-0-9875389-0-1
Paperback -- 978-0-9875389-1-8
Kindle -- 978-0-9875389-3-2
eBook -- 978-0-9875389-2-5

Website
www.kasmah.co.uk
www.svagus.co.uk

Made in the USA
Lexington, KY
13 July 2015